'A hilarious and brilliantly written story from one of our favourite writers'
Bella

'This is the feminist rom-com of the summer'
Holly Bourne

'A cult hit'
Grazia

'Real escapism with warmth, a lightness of touch and vivid characters you really root for'
Ella Dove

Laura Jane Williams (she/her) is the author of international smash hit *Our Stop*, a story the *Observer* said was, 'Smart, sisterly storytelling ... you can practically feel modern romance evolving as you're reading it'. Laura is also the author of non-fiction books *Becoming*, *Ice Cream for Breakfast* and *The Life Diet*, and has been translated into 12 languages in 18 countries. She has previously had columns for both *Grazia* and *Red*, and her essays and articles have appeared everywhere from the *Guardian* to *Buzzfeed*, *Stylist*, *Closer*, the *Metro* and the *Telegraph*, with Dolly Alderton once saying that 'Laura Jane Williams' writing combines sharp, relatable wit and bold, joyful sincerity'.

The
LUCKY
ESCAPE

LAURA JANE WILLIAMS

avon.

Published by AVON
A division of HarperCollins*Publishers*
1 London Bridge Street
London SE1 9GF

www.harpercollins.co.uk

HarperCollins*Publishers*
1st Floor, Watermarque Building, Ringsend Road
Dublin 4, Ireland

A Paperback Original 2021
1
First published in Great Britain by HarperCollins*Publishers* 2021

ISBN: 978-0-00-836545-5 (PB)
ISBN: 978-0-00-839411-0 (TPB)

This novel is entirely a work of fiction. The names, characters and
incidents portrayed in it are either the products of the author's imagination
or used in a fictitious manner. Any resemblance to actual persons,
living or dead, events or localities is entirely coincidental.

Typeset in Minion by Palimpsest Book Production Limited,
Falkirk, Stirlingshire
Printed and bound in UK by CPI Group (UK) Ltd, Croydon CR0 4YY

MIX
Paper from
responsible sources
FSC™ C007454

This book is produced from independently certified FSC™ paper
to ensure responsible forest management.

For more information visit: www.harpercollins.co.uk/green

For Katie Loughnane
Thank you for everything you continue to teach me
(and the patience with which you do it!)

1

I was having the best morning of my life.

'Annie-Doo, you look like a . . . model. No. Wait. Better than that. A *supermodel*,' my little sister Freddie declared, as my BFF Adzo – a name that she once told me means 'on Monday born' in Ghana – put the finishing touches to my lip liner. Freddie had called me 'Annie-Doo' since she was old enough to talk, which, my mother never tired of reminding us all, was basically straight out of the womb – unlike me, her disappointment of a daughter, who sat brooding and silent for three years, almost giving her an anxiety disorder. She never tired of reminding us all of that, either.

Freddie tilted her head to one side, assessing Adzo's work. It was pretty handy having a best friend who yes, was a theoretical physicist, but who also knew her way around a contour stick. Not that I was highly strung or anything, but no way would I have trusted anybody else.

'You look amazing,' continued Freddie. 'What's the word when you're, like, the boss? The one in charge of everything?'

'Regal?' supplied Adzo.

'Yeah! Especially with the flower crown!'

She gives the best compliments, my sis.

'Come here, you,' I mumbled with a grin, pulling her tiny thirteen-year-old wrist towards me. We'd spent the night in the suite of a fancy hotel in Mayfair, paid for by my soon-to-be in-laws as a girly treat. The three of us – me, Freddie and Adzo – had arrived yesterday and settled in for gossiping and giggling and doing silly dance routines for social media in our matching dressing gowns to celebrate my last night as a single woman. It had been perfect – and I had only cried twice. I was excited to get married, but I can truly say that if I accidentally fell into a sinkhole before I got to the church then I would die having had the most beautiful twenty-four hours ever. Everything had been magical.

Adzo fussed about with the tousled brunette waves curling down my back – another thing I entrusted to nobody but her – and I lowered my voice to tell Freddie: 'You can still stay over as much as you want. This doesn't change anything.' I nuzzled into her neck and looked at our reflection in the giant mirror before us. 'Alexander loves you.'

'Even on Saturday nights?' she asked.

'Bear, I don't think you're going to want to hang out with your fusty old sister on Saturday nights for much longer.'

'I will.'

I scrunched up my nose, making her giggle. 'We'll see about that.'

Adzo stepped back, gave me the once-over, and downed the last of her mimosa – a visible sign that she was satisfied with her morning's work. She was gorgeous, her Black cheekbones heightened even more than they naturally sat because of how she'd used the highlighter cream, forcing the light to bounce off her face as though she was somehow lit from within. Her dark eyes were lined like a cat's and her braids piled in thick coils on her head. Thank heavens she wasn't walking down the aisle with me, for surely all eyes would have been on her.

She'd actually refused to be a bridesmaid before I'd even had chance to ask. 'I don't go in for all that,' she'd stated, after I first showed her the ring. 'Don't even ask me, okay?' I'd chuckled and agreed. Typical Adzo. She doesn't do what everybody else does. A lot like Freddie, actually, she marches to the beat of her own drum.

'Are you year eight, or year nine, Freddie-Frou?'

Adzo had quickly caught on that nobody called each other by their proper given name in our world. Everyone was Doo this or Frou that, a bear or a bug or a piggy-poo. Freddie responded to say that she was just starting year nine.

'She's thirteen going on twenty-five,' I teased. Freddie was actually called Frederica, but when she learned about the gender pay gap had decided she wanted a name 'where you can't tell if I am a girl or a boy on my CV, so they can't discriminate'. She's smart. Smarter than me.

Freddie relaxed into my lap and I inhaled the scent of her; Watermelon body lotion and hairspray lightly dancing through her loose ombré mane. I paid good money to get my roots a darker brown and my tips a lighter colour, but hers annoyingly went that way naturally.

'Thank you for being my flawless bridesmaid,' I whispered. 'You're my best girl.'

'You're *my* best girl,' she whispered back. Then she had a thought, twisting up her nose in distaste. 'But have you got a Tic-Tac? Your breath smells.'

I squealed, reaching to blow a raspberry on the back of her neck a beat too late – she'd already wriggled from my grasp in glee.

'Not the lip gloss!' Adzo howled, lunging over to separate us. 'I've never made somebody look so good!' Freddie bounded over to the other side of the room and, mindful of my dress, I moved comically in slow motion to chase after her. To her luck we were interrupted by the arrival of my dad as he let himself into the room with the key card we'd left at reception. We froze, collectively aware that playtime was over and wedding days were probably supposed to be a more serious affair than we were currently demonstrating.

'Daddy!' Freddie padded towards him. 'We've had the best night. We had afternoon tea! And pizza in bed!'

He was wearing his favourite navy-blue suit and a fat red tie with a matching patterned handkerchief in his top pocket, his long Norwegian limbs looking longer than ever in his tailoring. He already had a tiny flute lily in his buttonhole, made to match my bouquet. Putting his arm around Freddie he took a breath and beamed at me.

'So this is you on your wedding day, Froogle,' he said as way of greeting, taking me in as I stood before him.

I grinned back. Seeing his eyes glisten made me tear up too, rendering me mute. Bloody weddings. You think you'll be all nonchalant and not like all those other brides, and then bam: it hits you. You're just as sappy and emotional as the next chick in white.

'You look beautiful,' he said. 'Truly beautiful.'

Freddie tugged on his arm, slipping her hand into his. 'I said she looked *regal*.'

'Queen of the world.' Dad smiled, and Adzo waved a tissue in front of my face in anticipation of what was to come.

'Dab, don't wipe,' she instructed sternly. 'Gently dab or you'll smudge it all.'

I took a deep breath. My wedding day.

The dress was designer, Dad was walking me down the aisle, and I was taking Alexander's last name in less than an hour.

Before I started wedding planning, if you'd have asked me how traditional I'd be on a scale of one to ten I'd have said a two or a three. Adzo and I had talked endlessly about how to be a Strong Independent Woman Who Just Happened To Be Committing Her Life To Someone. So much of what was expected of the bride was rooted in the notion that she was somebody's property (i.e. being 'given away') and valuable because she was pure and untouched (hence, the virginal white dress). In our lunch break one day Adzo had wondered if Alexander would double-barrel our surnames, or even take mine, and I considered asking him. But, when it came down to it, I actually found huge comfort in the age-old traditions of a conventional wedding day and gave in to almost all of them without much of a fight. I wanted the ritual of it all, the history and the expectation.

My only outward feminist declaration was that I was going to give a speech at dinner before anyone else. At my friend Jo's wedding she'd tapped the microphone and said, 'Good evening. Thanks for coming today. My magnificent father and wonderful best man and handsome new husband are going to give their speeches in a minute—' at which point everyone roared and cheered. 'But I'll be giving one first, because over my dead body am I letting a bunch of men speak for me—' at which point everyone roared and cheered even louder.

I'd thought she was hilarious.

5

Mum thought it was crass for the bride to speak, but I wanted to do the same.

'Right then, Mrs Mackenzie, are you ready?' Dad said, his face suddenly falling. 'Crikey. *Mrs Mackenzie.* You're not going to be a Wiig anymore.'

He turned to Freddie and, in a mock-serious voice, insisted: 'Don't you ever get married, okay? You're the next-generation Wiig. We need you to carry on the family name.'

Freddie playfully rolled her eyes. 'Daaaaaad.'

'I know, Fred, but you won't understand how it feels until you have your own kids who grow up and stun you with the people they've become. It's very affecting.' His hand went up to his heart, as if he could massage his feelings away from the outside.

'I'm still a Wiig right now,' I soothed him, reaching out to his shoulder. 'And even when I'm not, I'll always be your daughter.'

'With the added bonus of giving me a son-in-law.'

He smiled as he said it, but I had purposely never asked Dad if he liked Alexander because ever since the first time I'd brought him home for the weekend, I'd been on the edge of a suspicion that I wouldn't like his answer. Now wasn't the time to get into that, though. I loved Dad, but I was sure of my future. *Don't stick your hand down the rabbit hole,* my grandmother used to say before she passed. *You'll only get bitten.*

'Exactly,' I said, placating in tone. 'You're not losing anything – you're gaining.'

Dad bent his arm at the elbow, inviting me to take it.

'Let's get a vodka shot on the way out,' he suggested. 'I need to steady my nerves. They should have some sort of special guide for dads on their daughter's wedding day. I feel all . . . jangled up. Nervous.'

'Come on,' I said, feeling the heat building in my cheeks and knowing it was a warning sign that I was about to sob if I didn't change the subject. 'Let's do this!'

Adzo gathered up the last of the things she'd need to keep me looking fresh and bridal for the rest of the day, and Freddie did a final twirl in the mirror and picked up her bridesmaid flowers. Mum had already gone ahead to the church to play hostess. She loves an audience, and being the centre of attention, so chose to do that over staying with us in the hotel last night. She said she'd only get in the way, and she'd be better on the day if she slept in her own bed the night before. I was a bit relieved when she'd said that, to be honest. Our relationship is . . . complicated. I try not to dwell on it. Everyone has friction with their mother to some extent, don't they?

I looked from my dad, to my sister, to my best friend. The people I loved most in the world were there for me, ecstatic for me. I was loved by Alexander – of course I was – but since we got engaged everyone had rallied around and fussed over my plans and ideas and it had been a slushy, cosy cocoon of magnificent romance and well-wishes. Thinking about it, and how when I returned to the suite later I'd be Mrs Mackenzie – *married! Me! Finally!* – made my breath catch in my throat. I couldn't imagine anything making today any more special. It was like all my insides had been supercharged with electricity and even simply existing was amplified. Colours were brighter, emotions stronger.

Everything was just so *right*.

2

When Jo, my university friend who'd given the funny speech, got engaged, it had really made me question what Alexander and I had. I'd seen it written somewhere before that funerals aren't about the dead, they're about the living, and I think weddings often aren't about the couple at the front of the aisle so much as the congregation. Has anyone ever been to a wedding and thought about anyone but themselves? I haven't. I mean, obviously when Jo got married I was over the moon for her. She'd met Kwame on an app, swiping right on him one lonely Sunday evening, meeting him for the first time two days later, and within a month was calling him her boyfriend. It had surprised me, if only because the last person she was with was her girlfriend, and I just assumed she'd never date a man again for all she slagged them off. Humans exist to surprise us, I suppose, and who am I to write off a mate's sexuality into a box just so that I can feel better about where they sit on the spectrum? It was wrong of me to assume anything. (*Assuming makes an ass out of u-and-me,* was another thing my grandmother used to say.)

Anyway.

Three months in Jo and Kwame were saying 'I Love You', and after six months they got a house together. I wanted to be a good friend, as did Bri and Kezza – the two others who, alongside Jo, make up our Core Four friendship group – and so tentatively we approached the idea that it was all moving quite quickly. What was the rush? Jo didn't freak out or get mad when we raised it; she just smiled. I remember it really clearly. We were at Bridges in Stoke Newington one Saturday afternoon, eating quinoa and sausages, right as spring was starting. She'd shrugged and we'd all known it was the real deal when she dreamily said, 'This one just feels different. We want the same things.'

We want the same things.

That stuck with me, because by that point I'd been with Alexander for nine years and we still had separate flats and separate social lives, and even though we had fun together on date nights or the weekends he wasn't playing rugby, we couldn't quite seem to align what we were working towards. I didn't want to be a nag or That Girl. Everyone knows That Girl. The one issuing ultimatums about getting engaged or breaking up. *I want all of you, or none of you!* That sort of thing. I wanted to be cooler than that. And I was. For the whole of our twenties I was the cool girl, but then as my university friends got engaged, and then married, and then pregnant, bam-bam-bam, I went from being twenty-nine and happily ambling along to the other side of thirty, with everyone moving on without me.

In that time Bri had met her boyfriend, too, and because of immigration stuff got married for the paperwork and only told us afterwards. Kezza had already been approved to adopt as a single woman and was actively family-finding, having used us all as references in her committed support network. She refused to settle for a mediocre man to do the most important job of her life with, she said, declaring that she was happy to go it alone and meet somebody later because motherhood was more important to her than marriage. So that left me, then, out of the four of us, not really doing anything besides treading water. The Core Four broke off into different parts like a star hitting the earth's atmosphere and cracking into pieces. It made me panic about my place in the world.

It's a lie what they say about friends being the family you choose. Friends pair off and go on to make their own families, and it did make me wobble, standing beside Alexander in the church as one of my favourite people committed her life to somebody she'd known just over a year. That's when I finally brought it up with him – that we needed to think about our own future. I think the wedding had moved him too, because the next week he brought over all these bits of paper for houses in Islington that his parents wanted to give him a deposit for. He wanted me to live with him, and I was thrilled – and relieved.

There's no rush like it, when somebody says out loud that you're the person they want to build something with. I think the most uncertain bit of my life was turning thirty and feeling like everyone else had plans and I wasn't quite an adult yet. Moving in with Alexander made me a grown-up, on the same track as everyone else. I made him dinners and organized our furniture, and got curiously into doing stuff I swore I never would – being the one to buy his mum's birthday card, or suggesting dinner parties so I could meet the partners of his work colleagues and rugby pals. I enjoyed it. Revelled in it. We finally wanted the same things, too.

When I arrived at the church with Dad, Freddie and Adzo, it was a surprise to see the wedding planner outside, looking corporate and businesslike in a black suit with cropped pants and flat ballet pumps, her silky dark hair in a low ponytail. She'd told me the night before, in her lilting Sri Lankan tones, to take all the time I needed to get out of the car, to fuss with last-minute touch-ups and pruning and to take a big breath. *Everybody waits for the bride,* she'd repeated, over and over. *You can take your time, okay?* She was supposed to be waiting for me at the church doors, having made sure everyone was seated. Seeing her, I frowned.

'Who's that?' asked Freddie, clocking my furrowed brow.

'Happy,' I muttered, my palms immediately clamming up. My body knew before my mind could catch up that things were about to go wrong. My spidey-senses were doing somersaults. 'Something's not right. She should be at the church doors.'

Dad peered out of the window. 'I'm sure everything is fine,' he intoned, cautiously. 'I can't imagine why it wouldn't be.'

We let what he'd said hang in the air.

Happy approached the car as we pulled up, looking tired and wan   categorically *not* how you want your wedding planner to look. Instantly I thought that the minister had taken sick and we'd have to get married by somebody we'd never met before. That was the first thing that popped into my head. The second thing was that maybe something was up with the cake or we didn't have enough ice for the champagne buckets. But catering stuff was at the reception, a problem for later, not for now.

Maybe she's come to tell me how emotional Alexander seems.

Maybe he's sent a message for me.

Maybe she's come to tell me how much he loves me, how he wants me to get into the church as fast as I can.

But that's not what she said.

'What do you mean he's not coming?'

'Urm . . .' Happy stalled, uncomfortably. 'He messaged me. And it seems he's had . . . a change of heart.'

All I could do was parrot back what she'd said to me. I couldn't form my own words.

'A change of heart.'

Her eyes were wide but got wider still, willing me to understand. But I didn't.

'I did try to call . . .' she pressed.

She gave an apologetic smile to my dad and sister and Adzo, whose whole body had frozen, like if she moved an inch the world would come crashing down. Only her eyes moved, switching between me and the wedding planner. I'm not even sure she was breathing.

Alexander wasn't coming.

It was my wedding day, and the sky was blue and my dad was by my side and the wedding planner, who had a smear of pinky lipstick on her front tooth that made me instinctively run my tongue against my own in case I did too, had just told me my fiancé had texted (*texted!*) to say the wedding was off.

'Sorry. I'm just trying to . . . get a handle on all . . . this.' I gestured to the air in front of me. 'Just to confirm – did you try to call me, or did he?'

My eyes were itchy, my thoughts pulled through treacle. I

blinked quickly. Happy didn't blink at all as she measured out her words.

'Me,' she said. 'I called him to begin with, but when he didn't pick up I called you. Of course, you didn't answer either.' She paused, deliberating over what to say. 'I'm so sorry, Annie.'

'Can I see your phone?' I requested, my words clipped. I needed proof. 'The message?' My voice sounded far away. I was moving my mouth, but everything was happening at the opposite end of a very long tunnel.

I sensed Dad move to say something, but he thought better of it. Instead, he put his arm around Freddie. She stared at me, her bright eyes darting between us adults, reaching up to take Adzo's hand. The look on Adzo's face made me feel sick.

'Please,' I added. My voice was squeaky and high. Strained. I took a breath and forced a smile at Freddie, trying to tell her not to panic. She scowled. She knew what today meant, and had been so excited that I was excited.

Happy smiled back painfully, her face a portrait of compassion. She must have got it all wrong though, I reasoned. She must have got confused, must have misread his message. Alexander wouldn't simply *not turn up* on our wedding day. That would be an awful thing to do. Unforgivable. Of course he was coming. We were engaged. People were waiting. I'd not eaten a full meal in six months, was fake-tanned to within an inch of my life, and had already ordered the 'Mr and Mrs Mackenzie' thank-you cards.

The moment we'd got engaged flashed into my mind. He'd asked on Christmas morning, right when we woke up, the box having appeared on my bedside table at some point in the night.

'What do you reckon?' he'd asked, smirking, his lean naked torso stretched out as he lay on his side. All I'd done in reply was scream, slipping the ring immediately onto my finger, forgetting that was something he was supposed to do for me. I'd never thought it was possible to want to faint from happiness until that point, but wearing it made me more delighted, more ecstatic, more *everything* than I'd ever been in my life. That ring cemented my future.

'I'm guessing that's a yes?' he'd said, and I promptly burst into tears, nodding and making so much noise that his mum had knocked on the bedroom door of the shared holiday cottage we were in to see if everything was all right.

Happy unlocked her iPhone and pulled up a text thread. My hand was shaking as I took it, my mouth as dry as gin. I focused.

Happy, you've been amazing in sorting out today but I'm not coming. I can't do it. Please tell Annie I'm sorry. I'll be sure to settle your invoice in full by the end of next week. Thanks for everything. I trust you can handle the guests. Alexander.

People insist that they feel like they've been slapped when they find out something shocking and it's such an overused, clichéd saying. But as I read the text again, and a third time, a fourth – desperate to find the hidden meaning in it, the bit Happy had misinterpreted or got wrong – I was clammy and bilious. I thought of Alexander's grinning, handsome features. How could he do this to me? What the hell had happened since I'd seen him yesterday afternoon? Was there somebody else? Was it a joke? My brain couldn't do the complicated maths to understand it. The text was so brief. I read it again: I was an afterthought, my name appearing in between a compliment and a fiscal promise to a woman we'd known eight months.

Alexander had known me since uni. None of this made any sense.

My eyes filled and a tear fell to my hand. Just one. Not a steady stream of them, no big wailing or crying or sobbing. I absent-mindedly passed my flowers to Freddie and then, swallowing hard, handed the phone back to Happy. With both trembling hands free I could press my fingertips under my eyes, forcing myself to think.

How do I fix this?

I didn't have my own phone with me, what with planning to spend the day with every single person I knew who could possibly call me anyway. I couldn't call him using my own phone, or see if he'd called me.

He'd better have bloody called me.

I needed to hear his voice. *He* could fix this. He could explain, and then laugh at this terrible misunderstanding, and Adzo could touch up my face and we'd joke that I'd ever got my new and blue knickers in such a twist.

Right?

RIGHT?

'Dad, can you ring him? This can't be happening.'

'It can't be, love,' he agreed, setting his mouth into a thin straight line. 'Let's talk to him.'

'You'll be all right,' Adzo said, softly. 'I promise.'

Dad fished about in his jacket pocket to retrieve his mobile, then scrolled to Alexander's name and hit the call button. I could hear the voicemail prompt playing immediately – there wasn't even a dialling tone. His phone must have been switched off.

Hi there, you've reached Alexander Mackenzie. If I've not picked up I'm either in the lab or training for rugby. Either way, leave a message and I'll get back to you. Cheers.

15

He sounded so normal. So ordinary. I'd heard his outgoing voicemail so many times that I knew it by heart. How could a man who had left his bride waiting be somebody who could also sound normal and ordinary? Where the hell was he?

'I'll kill him,' Dad said, finally. 'This is unbelievable. I'm going to absolutely throttle him.'

In a wobbly voice and with her brown eyes wide Freddie said, 'Annie?'

And then that was it. I could be strong if everyone else was being strong. I could hold it together for as long as everyone else acted as if this could all be resolved. But the anger in Dad's voice and the fear in Freddie's made it real: Alexander wasn't coming, and everybody knew it.

'Right,' Adzo prompted. 'Everyone back in the car. Come on. Quickly. Quickly!'

'I'll let everyone inside know,' the wedding planner whispered to Dad. And then to me: 'I really am sorry, Annie.'

I pushed into the back of the car – thank goodness it was still there, and that the driver hadn't headed off for a smoke break around the corner or kept the engine running by circling the block. Dad waited behind me on the kerb and then helpfully lifted up the trail of my dress so it wouldn't drag or get dirty. As if that even mattered now.

'What will you say?' I croaked from inside the car. Freddie clung to my arm tightly. This was the worst thing to ever happen to me.

Happy gave a gloomy grimace. 'Don't worry. I've had to do this before. Unfortunately.'

She closed the car door and Dad wound down the window.

'Thank you,' he said to her, woefully.

'Look after yourself,' she directed at me.

16

I let Freddie sneak in under the crook of my arm and stared out the window. Adzo tapped her foot but didn't speak. Even she didn't know what to say. The car inched away from the kerb, and within seconds the church was a speck in the rear-view mirror.

We drove in silence. Things kept coming into my mind – questions, mostly – leaving as quickly as they arrived because then a barrage of other thoughts elbowed their way in, and then some more for good measure.

Was this really happening?

Had he ever wanted to marry me?

Was it because I was too fat?

Because my teeth weren't straight enough?

Had he had an affair, and got somebody else pregnant, and only just found out and thought choosing her over me would be the more moral choice?

Was he gay?

Had I hallucinated him ever wanting to get married in the first place? Did I imagine the ring, the way he had thoughts and opinions about the invitations and the seating plan, how overjoyed he'd been to discover the band from his cousin's wedding had had a cancellation and so could play at ours, now?

What if he'd changed his mind again, then got to the church after I'd already left?

What if he was waiting there, sorry and ashamed, praying my driver would turn around the car and as we circled back around to the church he'd be waiting, running up to us, crying, overcome with his own foolishness and practically dragging me inside before either of us could screw it up again?

What would Mum say?

It looked as though Freddie wanted to cry and was trying really hard not to.

I hated this. I hated this. I hated this.

'Stop,' I said to the driver. 'Stop the car.'

'Are you sure?' he replied, slowing down and glancing over his shoulder. 'Are you okay?'

I made for the door, grabbing at the handle before we'd fully stopped, forcing the driver to slam on the brakes. Somewhere near Kings Cross, I elbowed my way out of the car, tourists and buses and black cabs and shoppers lingering to watch me throw up all over my gown.

'She looks like she's having a bad day,' I heard somebody say.

3

The immediate aftermath of being stood up on my wedding day was exactly as crap as anyone would imagine.

I couldn't bear to go back to the hotel suite to get my things, so Adzo went for me. I'd asked the driver to take us to the house – but when we arrived it turned out I didn't have a key, what with it BEING MY WEDDING DAY, and so Dad had to go across the road to the neighbours', Dash and Lenny, who kept our spare set.

The church was small and we only knew them a bit, so we hadn't invited them to the ceremony, but they'd been expected at the evening reception, along with their twin toddlers. The evening do was going to be a live band and a dance floor and a hog roast out in the gardens behind the venue.

I'd gone to bed dreaming of that evening reception for months. There's something about all the formalities being over, when folks no longer have to be on their best behaviour. The evening part is always the best bit of a wedding, so I'd really focused a lot of my meetings with Happy on making sure there were going to be flip-flops in a basket by the dance floor for when everyone's dress shoes started to rub, and there was going to be two children's entertainers so parents could relax too. We'd ordered thousands of lights for the trees and hundreds of candles for the outdoor tables so that the last of the summer could be enjoyed when the music got too much. I'd even made sure the smokers' corner was comfortable since everyone would inevitably end up out there anyway – even if, like Alexander, they'd given up their smoking years ago.

I stood and watched Dad knock on Dash and Lenny's door, and the ensuing conversation. Dash shook his head as Dad spoke, as if he couldn't digest what was being said, and then Lenny joined him in the doorframe, looping his arm around his husband's shoulders casually, the perfect illustration of exactly what I'd lost. All three men turned in my direction, catching me staring, so I lifted a hand to confirm that yes, the balding sixty-something in the wedding suit was my father, and yes, we were indeed locked out of the house.

Lenny slowly, uncertainly, raised a hand back, and wasn't as subtle as he thought he was as he looked my dress up and down with pity. Dash dipped his head to say something to him, and then Lenny retreated back inside. They both lingered at the front door after he reappeared with the key and watched, slack-jawed, as Dad trekked across to me. It was as if they were eating popcorn and watching a heist movie with a plot twist, not bearing witness to my disintegrating life.

I assumed they didn't need it explaining that there would be no party for them to go to tonight.

As Dad came back and unlocked the door he said, 'Honey, let me get a bin liner for the dress.' I looked at him, confused and hurt, until he explained, 'The vomit, you see – you don't want that in the house, do you? Fred-Fred, can you go and get a T-shirt and some bottoms for your sister from her bedroom?'

Freddie paused on the stairs to look back at me as I waited in the doorway. Once I took the dress off that really would be it.

'You still have me,' she said tenderly, her face innocent and hopeful. I blinked. It was all impossible to compute. She ran up the stairs and Dad returned with the bin bag. He looked a hundred years old with concern.

'Put your dress in here.' He handed it to me. 'I'll sort it out.'

Freddie re-emerged, a pair of pyjama bottoms and an oversized rugby shirt of Alexander's over her arm. I looked at it and she realized, only now I'd wordlessly pointed it out, that giving me a piece of his clothing to wear wasn't exactly a mastermind idea.

'It was in your drawer,' she apologized, sounding trite. 'Sorry. I thought it was yours.'

'I'll wait in the kitchen,' Dad said. 'I'll make tea.'

Freddie patiently undid the fifty-three buttons laced down my back, and then I arched myself forwards so she could stand in front of me and inch the sleeves off my arms. Black globs of mascara fell on the silk that was already speckled with sick. I could smell vodka from the shot we'd had less than an hour ago, but the hotel bar was another life. I was half-naked and weeping as my mother banged on the door, her silhouette a murky outline of bright cerise contrasted with even brighter turquoise.

'What in the name of Des O'Connor is going on?' she trilled, high-pitched. Only her family and certain dog breeds could hear her, I was sure. 'Annie. Where's Alexander? What's happening? There's a church full of people!' She rattled on the glass with the palm of her hand. I knew she was doing it to avoid ruining the jewels in her rings. 'Annie!'

I stepped out of the way so Freddie could let her in, holding an arm across my naked chest and letting the sunlight and Mum's disapproval leak through into the hall. She considered me, jaw dropped. Two dog walkers ambled past, briefly glancing in at the scene: me in a flower crown and pyjama bottoms, Freddie holding a crumpled wedding dress, my mother cooking up a fury that added at least half a foot to her height, which was funny because she was still only barely as tall as Freddie. We'd both inherited Dad's lanky Norwegian genes over her stumpy Yorkshire ones.

'Oh, bloody hell,' she said. 'What have you done?'

Freddie scowled and stomped her foot. 'Don't be mean to her,' she implored, her soprano voice quivering right alongside her bottom lip. 'It was HIM!' She trembled, her little body unable to hold room for all of her feelings. I hated what Alexander had done to me, but I hated that Freddie had to do the complicated mental gymnastics of grown-up emotions even more. 'He's a . . . he's a BASTARD!'

She dared to look our mother in the eye, to see if her outburst was going to get her into trouble. For a moment I wasn't sure which way it would go, either. Nobody swears in front of Judy Wiig.

My mother stepped inside decisively and closed the door behind her.

'I see,' she settled on. Freddie and I held our breath as we waited on what she would say next. She rearranged her facial features into something approximating comfort. She wasn't pleased.

'Right. That's very unfortunate. I assume your father has already put the kettle on?'

4

'I spoke to Fernanda. Finally,' Mum said as I crept towards the breakfast bar, a blanket from the sofa pulled around my head like an elaborate trailing veil. The irony of it.

She was pushing teabags around the pot and warming cups and commenting that I should switch to one per cent milk because you can't tell the difference between that and semi-skimmed. This was exactly how it had been for the past three days: me, unwashed, sad, largely unable to communicate in full sentences, and my parents, staying even though I hadn't asked them to, trying to keep busy, organizing things, shouting at people in lieu of being able to shout at the person they most wanted to: Alexander. In another world it might have been a sitcom setting that I'd offer up to Kezza's production company. It could even be reality TV: *Zero Days a Bride*.

'She's as baffled as anyone, Annie – and mortified. I can understand that, really, because honest to God if the shoe was on the other foot and you'd skipped out with everyone there, I don't think I could show my face again. I'd be devastated, owning a child who'd be so reckless.'

Freddie peered over at us from the sofa, muting the TV so she could listen in. What a boring, sad way for her to spend the last days of the summer holidays. I wandered over and ruffled her hair. She stood up, balancing on the cushions so we were eye to eye, and opened her arms.

'I love you, Froogle,' she said, and I kissed her smooth, soft cheek. As she pulled away to look at me – assess me, really – I stuck out the tip of my tongue. I was trying to be funny, but the way she cocked her head made me realize she felt sorry for me. My tiny baby sister pitied me.

Mum handed over a cup of tea that was too milky, but I didn't say anything. I'd have preferred a coffee.

'You two are in role reversal,' she commented. 'You act as though Frederica's the thirty-something and you're the child, Annie.'

'Hey!' Freddie objected. 'I'm not a child. I'm a *teenager*, thank you! And my name is FREDDIE.'

Mum gave a vague dismissive *hmmmm* sound as she returned to the kitchen island for her own mug.

'Not to sound cold-hearted,' Mum continued – which meant that she knew she was being a cow, but cutting commentary on somebody else's shortcomings was her personal passion and she wasn't about to let up on Judgement Day now – 'but I'm truly relieved you're the one left standing and not the one doing a runner. At least you've got sympathy on your side. The Mackenzies are going to have to bow out of public life for at least a year. At *least*!'

'Mum.' I sighed deeply, the migraine I thought had gone suddenly knocking on my temples with a sledgehammer. I pulled the blanket into a fist at my chin. 'Alexander's not some naughty member of the royal family who cast shame on the Queen. He's not getting a slapped wrist and a low profile as his punishment. He's just a man. The world will keep on turning for him. Nobody is going to have to *bow out* of public life.'

'More's the pity,' she tutted, wiping down the work surfaces with a soggy cloth from the sink. 'Flash, darling?' she added, waving the kitchen spray at me. 'Try the Dettol next time – it smells better. And anyway, Fernanda was appropriately distraught but still couldn't fill in any of the blanks. Nobody knows where Alexander is or why he did what he did – only that he's still off-grid and that his phone goes straight to voicemail.'

The sledgehammer pounded harder.

'Hmmmm,' I responded, because what could I say?

'Or, at least, nobody is admitting to knowing anything. I think that's the thing when you have a son – you don't get to know them like a daughter. All the clues were probably there, she just didn't know how to read them.'

I stood and looked out at the garden. It was only August bank holiday, but autumn was setting in, the leaves starting to change into rusts and ambers. *Summer is over,* I thought, with an abstract idea of seasons and cycles and the nature of things that probably related to my life, but I couldn't see how. When Adzo had dropped off my stuff I'd frantically searched out my phone to see what Alexander had had to say for himself, but there wasn't anything. I'd had no direct communication from him. In shock (humiliation? Disgust? Outrage?) I'd turned it off and left it in a drawer since. The bedsheets on his side still smelt of him. His post was on the counter, notes in his handwriting stuck to the fridge under a magnet. I'd hated Freddie giving me his jersey, but I hadn't taken it off. I wanted him nowhere near me, and I wanted him all around me – here, back with me, everything normal again. I'd forgive him if he did come back. I'd let him in, tell everyone else to go home. I didn't want any of this to be happening.

'Annie? Hello? It's polite to respond to questions.'

Freddie had gone back to watching TV, with Carol snoozing on her lap. Technically Carol had been a gift to me – a tiny King Charles spaniel from a rescue shelter – but Alexander had named her. His sexual awakening was prompted by watching *Countdown* after school and developing a crush on Carol Vorderman, and he said he'd always promised himself that one day he'd have a dog named after her.

'Huh?' I mumbled.

'His clothes. I've ordered some boxes that should arrive tomorrow. We can pack up his things.'

'But this is his house,' I countered. 'Shouldn't it be my things we box up?'

Mum didn't say anything. The plan had been that after the wedding I'd go on the mortgage paperwork. After the wedding, I would have my security. For two years I'd paid Alexander for half of everything, but legally we hadn't added my name yet. I'd basically been his lodger. But I'd had no reason to think that was a risk. I had a ring on my finger! I could never have imagined I'd end up in this situation! Mum's silence spoke volumes. Her silence said: how could you have been so stupid, Annie?

It might have been getting cooler outside but it was warm in the kitchen. I pulled the blanket off my back and let it fall to the floor. The pain in my head was constant. Where was I going to live? Moving would have been like trying to collect fireflies in a jar with no lid right now – impossible. Surely Alexander would let me stay for a while, until I knew what to do next. Surely he wouldn't be so cruel as to kick me out onto the street. I wanted somebody else to tell me what to do. But I also I wished I could be home alone. I wished Mum and Dad knew to take Freddie back to their house, ready to start back at school, so I could be miserable and lonely and uncertain in peace.

'I *like* the smell of the Flash,' I said, finally. 'Don't criticize my cleaning products.'

She looked up, throwing her hands up in the air. 'I give up,' she moaned, to no one. 'I truly do. It's like I'm a ghost nobody can hear. Honestly!'

The sound of the front door caused Freddie and Carol to lift their heads, simultaneously curious. The scent of Indian food wafted down the hall, and they both leapt up when they realized dinner had arrived.

'Grub's up!' Dad trilled. Freddie made a noise, exciting the dog, and Dad blew a kiss over at her as he lifted the food onto the kitchen island. 'Can't mend a broken heart without some sustenance,' he whispered to me, setting several bags down and leaning over to kiss my forehead. I forced a grin to communicate that I was grateful for him breaking up the tension. 'Judy,' he carried on. 'Did you warm the plates?'

'Thanks, Dad,' I croaked, but I wouldn't eat any of it. I could barely keep down water, or tea. Even the smell was making me queasy.

'Give me half a second, Peter,' Mum said, right as Dad accused me of not having brushed my teeth today.

'I just got up,' I said, wearily.

'It's already 5 p.m. . . .'

'What's your point?' I asked.

I could see Mum furiously shaking her head from the other side of the kitchen, warning Dad not to push me too far. The way she did it made it obvious I was supposed to see, her way of acknowledging I was 'in a mood'.

'No, no point,' Dad said, changing tack. 'I was just saying, it's 5 p.m.! Where does the time go!'

My mother nodded in approval at his seamless change of diplomacy.

'The plates, Peter,' she said to him, setting them down next to the forks she'd left out.

'Did you get pickles?' Freddie asked, pulling things out of the brown paper bags and discarding them on the counter. 'I can't find them.'

Dad busied himself in the search for Freddie's poppadum accompaniments as Mum started to repeat to him what she'd just said to me, almost word for word.

'I spoke to Fernanda, *finally*,' she started, and Freddie drolly rolled her eyes in my direction.

Everyone tucked into their food.

'She's as baffled as anyone, Peter – and mortified. I said to Annie, I can understand that, really, because honest to God if the shoe was on the other foot and Annie had skipped out with everyone there, I don't think I could show my face again. I'd be devastated, owning a child who'd be so reckless . . .'

Freddie stacked the dishwasher once we'd eaten – or rather, once they'd eaten. I'd pushed some saffron rice around my plate and barely nibbled on the corner of a Peshwari naan.

'I'm going to take a nap,' I said. 'Will you tell Adzo to come straight up when she gets here?'

I couldn't stop thinking about where I was supposed to live. I'd never known adult life without Alexander. Why was this happening? What was I going to do? The grief came in great crashing waves, threatening to pull me under.

I closed my eyes to gather myself.

'Oh, darling,' Mum said, her voice full of something alarmingly close to sympathy. 'Shall I chill some spoons for you? It's supposed to help with eye puffiness.'

Like I gave a rat's arse about my eyes. Every bone ached. Being awake for more than an hour was a Herculean effort. I'd failed at the one thing that was supposed to make me an adult – marriage.

'Sure,' I replied, ducking out of a fight. 'Chilled spoons sound great. Thanks Mum.'

She sighed. 'I'm just trying to help, Annie. I don't know what else to do.'

'I know, Mum,' I whispered over my shoulder, shuffling back up to bed. 'Nobody does.'

5

I'd heard rumours about Alexander before I'd ever laid eyes on him. By second year he was known for being a bit of a charmer. Not the type who slept around and got notches on his bedpost, but somehow every girl on campus had a story about him. He'd had a high school girlfriend who'd gone to another uni, and they'd kept it going throughout first year. But when he had returned to York the next October as a single man, the news spread amongst the student union bar like wildfire.

Learning who he was from titbits of gossip and second-hand information was like tuning an old FM radio, the hum of white noise getting sharper and sharper until we were queuing one Tuesday night for prawn crackers and old-skool R'n'B at The Willow, and there he was. He stopped to talk to the people in front of us – I was there with the Core Four, who'd been my immediate pals since Freshers' Week – and we caught one another's eye. Alexander spent the next five minutes looking over the shoulder of who he was chatting with to do it again, and again. Staring. I remember the girls nudging me, getting silly on my behalf.

It took a year for anything to happen. I'd been half-heartedly seeing a guy I'd met on holiday, and although it was hardly fireworks with him once we got home – holiday romance has the word 'holiday' in it precisely because it doesn't work when you're back – I would never have cheated.

I couldn't believe Alexander was interested in me anyway. I'm pretty enough, I suppose, but I'm more of a best friend pretty than a leading lady knockout, and I'm clever, but not a genius. I'm like a good wallpaper: happily part of the background but when you notice it you might point and say, 'Oh! That's nice.' It's okay. Being exceptional would mean being visible, being seen. But if you're seen, you're talked about, and I'd had enough dissection of my body and personality and intellect at home, with the beady eyes and rolling commentary of Mum. I preferred flying under the radar. And, if Alexander could have his pick of anyone, why would he have wanted me? I was a seven-out-of-ten kind of a girl, and all the full scores lusted after him. He was eleven out of ten himself, with big brown eyes and a square jaw that was defined enough to make his broken, crooked nose look as though it was part of the design, not a flaw. He'd been to private school and had a confidence about him. The world had never told him no, so disappointment was a foreign theory. It was a law of attraction: he only expected the very best for himself, and so the very best is what happened.

We studied together sometimes, which was a convenient way to spend time with him up close without admitting I fancied him. It was a thrill to sit next to him in the library. He'd sometimes come from rugby practice with his hair still wet from the shower, all floppy over his forehead as he rounded over his stack of books. He'd bring me an iced bun from the cafeteria or steal two plastic cups from the water fountain and split his Red Bull without even asking. I could see other girls eyeing us suspiciously, and got a thrill from being the one in his spotlight. I liked the sense of being chosen, of being special. We both did summer internships in London that year and would meet up in Soho Square or go to the cinema at the weekend, and by final year we were a couple. We were in my room one night – he was sat on my bed watching me finish my make-up as the rest of the Core Four started a drinking game in the kitchen.

'You don't have to wait with me,' I'd said. 'I'll be done in a minute.'

'The party doesn't start until you get there anyway,' he'd replied, and my stomach had done a loop-the-loop over the fact that he wanted to be with me, that I was the prize to him. I'd turned around from where I stood at the sink unit in the corner of my room, and he didn't get up as he said, 'So is this a thing now or what?'

That's how he'd said it: 'Is this a thing now or what?'

We'd been together ever since.

Well – until we weren't.

'Annie?'

There was a light tap at the door. Adzo. I was lying in bed, turned away from the door on my side to face the wall. I'd closed the curtains but accidentally left a gap between them, and a slither of fading light shone through just before the sun disappeared from the sky. It's where I focused my gaze, a meditation point between half-closed eyes, neither fully sleeping nor fully awake. I rolled over, feebly smiling.

'This is a shitshow, isn't it,' I simpered, and she smirked, cautious of encouraging me to make jokes about my pain but obviously pleased I was still willing to. Everything was ridiculous. Who gets jilted? It was absurd, really – and devastating. Mostly though, if it happened to somebody else, I'd barely dare believe it *could* happen. Maybe it was all a bizarre hallucination, or a breakdown episode. Maybe I'd wake up and think *urgh, what a horrible dream.*

'I'll say.'

She lingered, taking in the scene, wandering over to tenderly stroke my hair. I let my eyes drift closed again. I'd been pals with Adzo since my first day working with her. The Core Four were wonderful, but they were also all very settled. Meeting Adzo had reminded me what it was like to feel motivated by the possibility in the everyday. She was good for me. Took me out of my own head.

'Not being funny, doll,' she said, in precisely the way somebody says 'I'm not being funny' when they are about to be exactly that, 'but do you mind if we let some air in? It's a bit ripe in here.' She gave a little cough to illustrate her point.

I made eye contact and pursed my lips, then gave a small nod of agreement. She slipped off her shoes and navigated her way through the throw pillows strewn across the floor, picking them up and piling them beside the wardrobe. Then she flicked on the dressing table lamp and eventually reached the window, opening it and pushing back the curtains to make the gap wider.

'I brought you a Lucozade, by the way.' She stuck her hand into her vintage Chloé handbag and pulled out two orange bottles.

Lucozade was our private joke. At work, if I came in with a Lucozade, Adzo knew without me even needing to say it that I was hungover. It didn't happen often, but that's probably what made it worse. I was unpractised at having hangovers. Drinking made me lose control and rule number one when I was growing up is that I was *never* to lose control because it was unladylike. Adzo was well-practised when it came to hangovers. She was a machine, out at a party seemingly every night, always with a tale to tell the next morning about seeing Jude Law's son here or one of the old *X-Factor* contestants there. And yet she was better at her job than all of us, able to navigate the top boss with ease and command a team naturally and with a sense of humour.

That's what had drawn me to her too. She was one of those people who the gods had blessed. Even the hard stuff didn't seem like a struggle to her; she just smiled and dealt with whatever life threw up – which was, admittedly, quite a lot of hilarious dating stories and men falling at her feet, desperate to buy her things. Once she had the whole La Mer skincare line sent to her desk followed by one hundred red roses, and last Valentine's Day two blokes had got in a fight in the downstairs lobby when they both turned up to take her out. As they were interviewed by the police for public disturbance, a third guy had pulled up on his motorbike, but Adzo had decided she'd rather go out for a drink with me, anyway. Alexander had been away on business that night and she knew I wouldn't be rushing home. The less she cared about men, the more they chased her.

'I thought you could do with the sugars. And I know this sounds peculiar, but,' she added, coming to sit beside me on the bed again, 'I just learned about this. Add this to it.' She showed me a tiny sachet.

'Salt?'

'It's what the tennis pros do when they're dehydrated, apparently. I figured with all the crying . . . just trust me. It will help.'

I drank. She studied me.

'You're cultivating quite the look, by the way.'

'Am I a mess?'

'A beautiful one,' she replied, kindly. 'But if you go and take a shower I'll change your sheets, okay?'

I shook my head. 'But they smell of him,' I protested. I knew how pathetic I sounded.

'They smell of sweat and heartache, Annie,' she pressed. 'You deserve nice sheets, darling.'

I thought about it.

'Okay?' she pushed.

'Fine.' I decided that, in the list of things worth fighting about, that didn't make the cut. 'Fresh sheets. But at least let me sleep in another one of his T-shirts. I know it's stupid, but I don't care. It helps.'

She'd already started peeling the pillowcases off. 'Deal. But throw that one through the door once it's off,' she instructed, gesturing to the rugby shirt that clung to my sticky limbs. 'I think we're going to have to burn it. I wouldn't be surprised if it could walk itself to the fire pit.'

'Ha-ha,' I replied, pulling it up from the tops of my thighs and tugging it over my head. 'Very funny.' I did notice my body odour as I lifted up my arms, though, so she wasn't totally without a point.

I stayed in the shower a long time, the water so hot that my chest burned bright pink. When I finally climbed out, I needed to sit on the edge of the bath to catch my breath. But once the room stopped spinning, I was noticeably better in myself. Cleansed. It made a difference to brush my teeth. I even used mouthwash, revelling in the sensation of the cool mint in my mouth, a blast of cold air hitting my whole face, eyeballs included.

I could hear Adzo talking to Freddie and, wrapping a towel around me, I opened the door of the en suite to a bedroom transformed. Between them they'd changed the bed linen and lit a couple of scented candles. There were flowers on the dresser, music softly playing, and a clean T-shirt displayed on the bed for my consideration.

I grabbed the shirt, turning my back to them to drop my towel and put it on. I tried not to hide my body from Freddie – I didn't want to add to any kind of cultural narrative that we have to be embarrassed about our bodies, or be ashamed of our nakedness. I didn't want to make a big show of *not* making a show though.

'Your spine looks funny. It's trying to escape your skin,' Freddie commented.

Self-consciously, I whisked a hand behind me. I could feel the hard bone. I'd been dieting leading up to the wedding anyway, to the point where the dressmaker at my final fitting threatened violence if I lost any more weight and ruined the fit of the gown. I had a faraway thought that I couldn't allow myself to start physically wasting away just because emotionally, I was. If I wanted to disappear, not eating was one way to go about it, but it was a senseless one. I honestly hadn't had an appetite though.

'Finish your Lucozade,' Adzo insisted. 'Get your energy up.'

I pulled on a pair of cotton knickers from the drawer, hoping nobody had clocked what was meant to be my wedding night surprise for Alexander – I'd had my pubes waxed into the shape of a love heart as a bit of a prank. That seemed totally ludicrous, now. When I crawled back under the covers Adzo took my hand and dolloped lotion into my palm, massaging the bit below my thumb, rubbing her hands over mine with tenderness.

'I know some Shiatsu,' she said, nonchalantly, when I told her it was like she knew what she was doing. 'I had a few dates with the guy who runs the Harrods spa.'

Normally I'd be begging for details, but the thought of men and women and dating and learning massage techniques from each other were dots I couldn't connect. That was the outside world. In this world, in between the safe four walls of this bedroom, the only thing that existed was shame and self-loathing.

You're so disgusting you couldn't make him stay.

He never loved you.

You tricked him into being with you and he finally found you out.

My inner voice was loud and clear about who I was and what I was worth.

'Frou, don't cry,' Freddie said, and I wished I could stop. 'You're the adult I want to be when I'm grown up,' she declared, her tiny body a thin sheet of insulation against my side. My eyes were a silent Niagara Falls. 'You're the best, best, best.'

'You're the best, best, best,' I said, strangled by the tears.

Adzo said, 'Actually guys, I think I'm the best, best, best?'

I let out a snotty laugh.

'You're nine and three-quarters best,' Freddie avowed. 'But my big sister wins because those are the rules.'

Adzo considered it. 'I think those are the rules, yes,' she mused. 'I've never settled before in my life, but I can settle for nine and three-quarters best.'

We sat together, hugging.

'I don't understand how anything will feel normal again,' I said. 'I'm so embarrassed. I can't believe he did this to me.'

'He did it to all of us,' Adzo said. 'We all believed in him. In the pair of you. He was part of your life, of your family.'

Freddie loosened her grip. 'But not anymore,' she said. 'I hate him.'

'You don't have to hate him, Frou. That's okay.'

'I do,' she insisted.

'I do too,' Adzo agreed.

I hated him as well. I hated him, yet still loved him more than I'd ever loved anybody. Where was he? What the hell had happened to him?

'I talked to Chen this morning about you coming back to work,' Adzo said. 'Just so you know . . .'

I didn't say anything. I'd have to walk back into that building with every single person knowing what happened to me. It was going to be horrific.

'There's a letter in my bag for you. I think Chen might be worried that you're going to go nuts and burn your life to the ground and leave the company to live in a tent in the fields of Myanmar. She said that's what she'd do if she was you, but she can't afford to lose you.'

I still didn't say anything. Burning my life to the ground sounded seductive, actually – especially if it meant never having to be the subject of gossip and speculation in the staff kitchen, people wondering out loud why I couldn't keep a man. Where exactly was Myanmar?

'I told her to add up all the overtime you've done – all the early starts, the weekends, the vacation days you've never taken and lost – and she's basically agreed to compassionate leave, letting you stay off until you'd planned to take holiday days anyway. For the honeymoon. The letter is quite formal, but she told me to tell you: screw him, and do what it takes to feel stronger. You've earned it, Annie. Chen really wants you to look after yourself. We all do.'

I did the quick maths – I'd had three weeks booked off

for a honeymoon and, with the extra time Chen was offering, that would be six weeks off in total. What the hell would I do if I wasn't working for six weeks? I was already going increasingly mad. Once Mum and Dad left, work – and the dog, for her morning poo – would be the only reasons to force myself out of the house at all. And God, the honeymoon. What a waste. Alexander's parents had spent so much time planning it. What a shame it would go unused. What would I do instead? House-hunt, I supposed. I could use the time to figure out my next steps. But I didn't need six weeks for that.

'I'll look at the letter,' I said. 'I don't think I'll need it though. I'll pull myself together. I've got no choice. I'll be okay. I have to be. I'll probably be back to work as soon as I can, to be honest. It will be a good distraction. Thank you, though. I appreciate the thought.'

'Consider it properly, won't you?' Freddie agreed, adding: 'What's so good about work anyway?'

She had a point.

6

During the day I wanted to hide out in bed, where somehow it was easier to doze into bouts of fitful sleep that lasted an hour or two before I got woken up by Mum shouting something about taking in Freddie's new school skirt or popping out for some mince, since that charming butcher across the street was so lovely, or else the dog barking because Dad had shown her the lead before he'd put on his tennis shoes and she knew she was about to go for a walk. Nights were harder. It was too quiet. Too still. It unnerved me. I lay awake most nights from midnight until the sun came up, tossing and turning and catastrophizing, and after almost a week I couldn't bear it anymore. I was going crazy in my own skin – if I could have torn it off and worn somebody else's I would have, just for a break from being me.

I'd been exercising six times a week in the lead-up to the wedding, but the first time I slipped out from under Mum and Dad's continued loving scrutiny I hadn't meant for it to be for a run. I just couldn't be in the house anymore, and at 5 a.m. I knew it would be at least another two hours before anyone else got up, so I could steal out undetected – not least because Carol had been sleeping on Freddie's camp bed in Alexander's office, so I didn't even need to navigate her yapping to get out of the door. At 5 a.m. there was no chance of bumping into anyone I knew out there on the streets, or having to explain myself; 5 a.m. was freedom.

I was sick of trying to put words to it all. I'd only intended to walk, but walking wasn't enough. I'd got faster and faster until I was easily doing less than a nine-minute mile. The faster I went, the better I felt, and over the course of the next couple of days I started to leave a house key under the plant pot by the door, going from Newington Green to Highbury Fields, looping down to Old Street sometimes too, every single morning, no music, nothing weighing me down, just the sound of my feet hitting the tarmac.

One morning I passed by a Barry's Bootcamp. I must have passed it several times, actually, but that morning was the first time I'd noticed it. Barry's was high impact and almost killed you – or so Kezza had once told me. She used to go to one near her office. In a big, red-lit studio, she'd said, you basically take turns running full pelt on one of the lined-up treadmills and then doing burpees and lunges and squats and arm lifts with a series of weights. I thought about it for the rest of the day, deliberating slowing down in front of it to peek my head in the door the next morning. I think it was expectation of loud music and darkness that drew me in. I didn't want to lose any more weight, not like I had done for the wedding – if anything, I could probably have done with putting some on. Even my running gear was a bit loose, and I'd sized down for that when I got it. But bootcamp could be about something else. Strength, maybe. Endurance. Resilience. Power. The idea of it spoke to me.

If I was mentally at my worst, there was something that wouldn't leave me alone about physically being stronger. The thought of lifting weights and doing squats was exciting. Being all knees and elbows (thanks, Dad), losing weight came easily, but I knew my core strength was non-existent, and that I could barely use my spindly arms to push up off the sofa, let alone do a push-up properly.

This is a thing I can control, I thought, and so I spent another twenty-four hours trying to build up my courage to go in and sign up for a taster class. *I can't control anything else, but I can control getting stronger,* I reasoned. *I can control that.*

Kezza was right – it did almost kill me. After my taster session I signed up for ten more, heady off the dopamine and serotonin a good sweat session can foster. It was like being high. I'd not been very good, but it had been so dark and loud, and everyone else had been so focused on themselves, that I'd returned the next morning. I'd ached, but felt oddly determined. Maybe it was being somewhere new, doing something that Alexander would have no idea about. The Annie he knew didn't go to bootcamp, but he'd given up any right he'd once had to know anything about me. I'd progressed from shock to outright anger. I told myself I didn't even care where he was. *Screw him,* was my mantra. I wasn't sad now. I was furious.

Barry's teemed with incredibly fit people, literally and figuratively. I'd never seen so many toned and tanned bodies in one place – I suppose everyone must have been away in the summer and had the bronzed skin to show for it. I mostly kept my head down and ducked in and out as quickly as I could, but on the way into my third class I sensed the eyes of a man on me, and when I looked up his face was inquisitive. I scowled at him, just in case. I didn't want to speak or be spoken to. In fact, I hadn't talked to anyone except my family and Adzo. I couldn't face it. My phone was still off, and I was working up to seeing the Core Four, even. It was the anonymity at Barry's that I enjoyed; screaming and sprinting and lifting with fifty other people doing the same, and then swiftly getting back home again. It helped.

The man in the lobby looked away quickly, his face screwed up like he was trying to work out what two plus two was. I paused before going in to the studio, scanning the space to make sure I wasn't anywhere near his treadmill as I mounted my own. I needed men to give me a wide berth. I needed men to not exist – which was the next best thing if I, myself, couldn't cease to exist. I was quite happy with my shrunken world and didn't need anybody else elbowing their way into it before I was ready.

I was totally soaked afterwards. I didn't know it was possible to sweat as much as I had done in class. I looked around the changing room, assessing how long it would be before everyone was gone and I could have some space to catch my breath, but reasoned that by that point the next class would be starting and a whole new bunch of boot-campers would be traipsing through. *Sod it,* I thought. *I'll head back home sweaty.* I grabbed my backpack from the locker and wove through half-naked bodies to get to the entrance.

I'd worn a Lycra pull-over jumper on my way in, but it was proving impossible to pull back on now my body was slick with sweat. Standing off to the side so I wasn't in anyone's way I tried to inch my arm in, using my other hand to yank the fabric up and then switching to do the same on the other side. It stuck on me, like a needy child clinging to their mummy.

'Annie?'

I yanked my jumper over my head just as I heard my name, turning in the direction the voice came from but seeing nothing because I was . . . stuck. I couldn't see anything but my Lycra-polyester blend.

'Oh, sorry,' the voice said – a male voice. A deep, brooding male voice. 'I didn't mean to startle you. I thought I knew you.' There was a pause. '*Do* I know you?'

I wriggled around, my hands searching for the neck of my pullover so I could part it and find my way out. Trust me to be stuck in a bloody jumper, and with an audience, too.

'I can't see you to confirm or deny,' I said, muffled by the fabric. The more I moved the more jammed I seemed to get. I hadn't realized how hard I'd pushed my arms in class until I tried lifting them to get dressed. Everything was sore already. It was a good sore, but also a limiting one. I knew my muscles would get tighter and tighter as the day wore on. Would I even be able to reach up a hand to signal for the bus?

'I'm Annie, yes,' I continued, because I could still feel somebody stood near me, but I said it as less of a statement and more of a question, still muted by a mouthful of Lululemon. 'If that helps.' The warmth of human touch approached my stomach, and with a firm yank at my waist by wide, manly hands, suddenly my head popped out through the jumper neck and I could see again.

'Sorry to manhandle you,' the guy in front of me apologized. 'I just didn't want to start my day by watching you perish through jumper asphyxiation.' He tilted his head to the side, like Carol does when I talk to her and she's trying to understand. 'Especially if I wasn't sure if I knew you or not.'

44

My eyes adjusted, taking in the face of a stranger. How did he know my name? I had no idea who the crooked smile and Roman nose and twinkling eyes in front of me belonged to.

Oh, except: hold on. He was the man from earlier who'd been looking at me, the one I'd given daggers for daring to notice my presence. Had he been trying to get my attention because we knew each other? He was about my height – my generous tallness, despite everything else about me being overwhelmingly average, meant that our eyes were level – and he was smiling, wide and bright. He had shorts pulled over Lycra leggings and a grey marbled T-shirt that clung to his body to reveal not exactly a Brad Pitt physique, but definitely a healthy dad bod.

Alexander always made me feel a bit inferior because I didn't have defined abs and a peachy bum. Although heck, it was nice to rub a hand over that stomach of his. When he walked around in his boxers sometimes I'd catch a glimpse of him and think, *Holy hell, there's my man.* But then he'd eat a boiled egg for breakfast and I'd slurp at my cereal and I wondered if he ever looked at me and thought, *Holy hell, there's my woman.* I mean, obviously he didn't, otherwise he might have stayed.

The man in front of me was friendly-looking and approachable. An everyman. You might not turn back to look at him on the street, but you wouldn't be mad if you got sat next to him at dinner. He wasn't intimidating to look at, but he was cute. I didn't mean to compare him to Alexander. God. Would I always compare every fella who crossed my path to him? Urgh. That made me so mad. For all I knew Alexander was in Timbuktu with a harem of attractive women who did CrossFit and took turns blowing him on the hour, every hour. 'Annie Who?' he probably said as yet another grape was delivered to his perfect mouth by a woman with an arse pert enough to park a bike in and tits that bounced like basketballs.

I refocused. The man in front of me, with his wavy dark blond hair and thoughtful eyes, was looking at me intently.

'You've got no idea who I am, do you?' He smirked. He had a levity to him, like he wasn't laughing at me, but that we were in on a joke together. It made me want to catch up and be light, too.

But I wasn't light. Instead, I was suddenly panicked. Maybe he was a friend of Alexander's. Had he been in the church, at the wedding that never happened? I steeled myself for an outpouring of sympathy. This was exactly what I hadn't wanted to happen, and exactly why I was loath to leave the house.

'Drama camp. Summer of 2002 . . . Maybe 2003?' He offered.

I shook my head, the penny dropping. 'You went to Yak Yak Theatre Program?' I said, slowly.

'Yes, ma'am.' He nodded. 'I did set design for *Bugsy Malone*, and I think you . . .'

Colour climbed up my neck and to my cheeks. If he was there for *that* . . .

'Oh my gosh! I was a showgirl! And the understudy for Tallulah. I got to do one show when that girl – oh crap, I can't remember her name – she broke her leg on the very last day and I got to perform!'

'Standing ovation, as I recall. The whole place went wild. I was there. It was electric. I mean, I was a teenager so that's a loose definition of the word electric, but I remember it. I remember your face. You don't look any different.'

I marvelled at the memory. Yak Yak was my favourite place in the world when I was just into my teens. Actually, when I was about Freddie's age. For the whole of August, kids from all over the country got shipped off to the New Forest by their parents, living in a big holiday home, like American summer camp. We played silly games and did trust exercises and painted sets and ran lines and performed monologues. It was incredible. Totally incredible. And for some reason I just stopped going. The summer I was fifteen I didn't want to go back, and so it turned out my last stint on stage was exactly the moment this guy whose name I didn't know remembered.

'Patrick,' he said, as if he could hear my thoughts. 'I'm Patrick Hummingbird. You might remember me as Paddy?'

As soon as he said it, it was like his face did one of those reverse 'Evolution Of' videos that they do on people.com of celebrities through the ages. They start with a photo of George Clooney when he was in *ER*, and then it morphs into a photo of him in his first feature film, and then becomes a photo of him as Batman, and so on until it's a photo of him walking into Prince Harry's wedding with Amal on his arm. In my head I had to shrink the biceps in front of me and add in a bit more hair and un-straighten his teeth and make him shorter but then, suddenly, I could see him by a light rig working out where to put a spotlight and talking to a senior drama teacher and helping people memorize lines and laughing. That's it. I remembered him as always laughing. He'd been the group clown, the boy always guaranteed to put a smile on your face.

'Paddy Hummingbird! Yes! Shit! Out of all the bootcamps in all the world . . .'

'I squat-lunged into this one,' he supplied, getting my

Casablanca reference immediately. He added: 'And it's Patrick, now. I'm trying to do the grown-up thing.'

'Patrick,' I echoed.

'Can I give you a hug?' he questioned, taking a step towards me.

'Oh, urm, yes, sure! I'm so sweaty but hi!' I opened out my arms and tried to keep my armpits from having contact with his clothes. I could feel my own dampness even through my jumper – *that* is how hard I'd worked out. I was still pouring sweat fifteen minutes after finishing. 'It's so nice to run into you!'

I got a whiff of him as we dipped in, and then pulled away. He didn't smell old or fusty. He smelled manly. Potent. Paddy Hummingbird. What were the chances?

'How have you been?' he asked. 'I thought I saw you here the other day. I'm so pleased it's you! Are you new here?' His face was indisputably kind. Some people just have those faces you want to tell everything to, and Paddy – *Patrick* – Hummingbird's was one of them. 'I mean, you look great, I have to say.' He loosely gestured to my athleisure wear with his thick fingers, the veins on his forearms popping.

I shook my head. 'Noooo,' I said, self-consciously touching my face. I didn't have a lick of make-up on and could feel the sweat on my brow had already turned to a salty crust. 'I'm a mess. You don't have to say that.'

'I know I don't,' he countered. 'But I am. Look at you . . .' He trailed off, catching himself and changing tack. 'Are you married? Kids? Getting a good rate on a self-investing pension plan?'

It was such an innocuous question. If you hadn't seen somebody in almost twenty years that's the question you'd ask, isn't it? And I should have just smiled and waved a hand.

I should have said something sweeping and general, and I started to, kind of. I started to say, 'Oh pfffft. No news on my end!' But I couldn't even get the whole sentence out. Up until what had happened, I adored being asked about Alexander because I got to show off my ring and whip out a photo of us on holiday in Cornwall, demonstrating how much I had my life together, how loveable I was after all. But now, urgh. I was sobbing out my guts before I could stop myself. It was all very undignified.

'Are you okay? I'm sorry, I didn't mean—' Patrick was lunging at me in sympathy. He was a blur, though, because of the tears in my eyes. Jeez, that had escalated so quickly I'd not even noticed it was happening.

I waved my hands in front of my face. 'This is mortifying,' I insisted, batting at the air to cool my eyes and stop them leaking. 'I'm so sorry.'

I suppose everyone else in my life knew what my situation was. Meeting this stranger – this old friend – was the first time I'd had to search for the words that now summarized my new relationship status. I'd not said it in years. *It's just me. I'm single.*

I'm single. Isn't that code for: *I'm not good enough?*

'Come and sit down,' he insisted, pulling on the sleeve of my jumper and picking up my backpack for me. 'Just for a minute. I'm so sorry if I've upset you. I honestly didn't mean to.'

He steered me to a waiting area by the main desk. Two guys with thighs the size of hams and branded sleeveless T-shirts were making smoothies and throwing their heads back laughing and flirting. Patrick saw me notice.

'Awful when other people are happy, isn't it?' he observed.

I let out a splutter of agreement and he handed me a

tissue from his gym bag. We sat, watching the love scene in front of us unfold. I tried to slow my breathing and, credit to him, Patrick didn't look at his watch once. He just waited with me, and let me do what I needed to do.

'I've calmed down,' I stated after a while. 'If you think I'm unhinged, I understand. It's okay. I think I am. I'm just having a bit of a time of it.'

He waved a hand. 'Memories of Yak Yak are enough to bring anyone to tears,' he joked, and it was a thoughtful thing to say. He was giving me an out – making sure I knew I didn't have to reveal anything to him if I didn't want to. It was only seven in the morning, after all. And on a Monday, too! He probably just wanted to get off to work. It was much too early for confession.

'It was the time of my life, that camp,' I croaked. 'Best summers ever.'

'Me too.' He nodded. 'I don't think I've ever laughed as consistently and freely as I did then. Or worked as hard. I remember constantly smelling of B.O. because I hadn't figured out deodorant yet. I was furious once I realized where the smell was coming from – that it was me. Why did nobody tell me I stank?'

I chuckled again. Thank goodness it was this man I had crumbled in front of – this man who was being such a gentleman about it.

'What do you do now, Pongy Paddy? What became of the great lighting maestro?'

He dropped his jaw in pretend outrage. 'Is that what people called me?' he asked. 'Pongy Paddy?' He was smiling with one half of his mouth, exactly like he used to do when we were twelve. 'I knew it. I knew people had to have noticed!'

'Noooooo.' I shook my head. 'I'm messing with you.'

'Liar.'

I shrugged. 'If it's any consolation I've got no qualms telling you that you smell now.'

He tipped back his head to reveal a row of pearly white teeth as he hooted. His laugh made me smile. His laugh made me feel charming.

'Annie Wiig, so do you. That's what an hour with D'Shawn will do to a person.'

I snickered and lowered my voice like a gossiping old woman in a bingo hall.

'Did you see him before class, going from a handstand into a press-up that way?'

Patrick kept a straight face. 'It was me who taught him that actually,' he clowned.

I smiled again. I really did feel better now. We sat for a moment, testing my resolve at keeping a brave face. The two men near us had graduated to pulling out their phones, swapping numbers. I looked at the clock on the wall.

'I should go,' I said, standing.

Patrick stood up too, and held out a hand. 'Maybe we'll bump into each other again.'

'Maybe we will,' I agreed, and he walked ahead to hold the door open for me, letting me go through first. 'I have a ten-class pass, so . . .'

'So I've got nine more chances of supervising you getting dressed,' he supplied, cheekily.

I gave him a spirited look.

'Six, actually. I've got six classes left.'

'Noted.'

He walked me to the side of the road.

'See you then,' he said, as I pressed the button for the

51

pedestrian crossing. We both looked at the little red man, waiting for him to change.

'Thanks for being so kind to me,' I stuttered, embarrassed all over again to even have anything to express gratitude about. 'That was very good of you.'

'I'm a good kind of guy,' he said, that lopsided grin making another appearance, his eyes sparkling with the mischief I recalled.

'I remember,' I said.

The green man sounded, alerting me to the fact that it was safe to cross over.

'See you,' I said, and he lifted a hand to wave goodbye, watching me with a smile that I caught only as I turned back to glimpse him one more time over my shoulder, smiling too.

7

'I thought I'd seek you out in case there were any more jumper-related emergencies today.'

I hadn't seen Patrick in the bootcamp class. I'd arrived late and it was already dark in the studio, the overhead lights dimmed and the red and blue lights around the edges blaring to get us riled up. I'd rushed straight to my spot as the instructor, in her tiny crop top and shorts, chanted, 'Push to your limits! How do you know what's possible if you don't understand that the only limitation is mental? Go beyond what you ever thought you were capable of!' If we'd thought D'Shawn knew how to push us past crying point, Sinead knew how to make us cry and also thank her for it.

I was waiting for a green juice by the reception area instead of going straight home – I'd quickly learned, after five classes in six days, that trying to keep moving at full pelt after cooldown was impossible. I needed twenty minutes to just sit and recover, and a green juice was the best excuse for it.

'Hey! Patrick!' I exclaimed. 'I wondered when I'd see you again!' I'd kept an eye out for him, wondering if he'd be around to reminisce about Yak Yak. I'd liked that. I'd surprised myself with how much I'd liked talking with somebody who thought I was as carefree and funny as I had been at twelve years old. The future was so uncertain but the past never changed, and that was a comfort. I looked towards the barista. 'I'm just getting my spirulina fix for the day.'

'Because what's a day without an unpronounceable smoothie add-on?' Patrick chuckled.

I grinned back, my body pumped full of endorphins after the exercise and feeling . . . not happy, exactly, but certainly flushed with something other than doom, at least temporarily. Bootcamp had been the only anchor to my day since I'd started. I'd get up, go straight there, and for one glorious hour think of nothing. Back at home I'd stare at the TV paying no attention to what I was watching, the dog in my lap and Mum and Dad, who continued to stay despite me suggesting they didn't have to, pretending not to be worried. 'Exactly. I actually had to point at the board just to order and then I asked Google how to say it afterwards. I only told you about it so I could practise.'

He leaned against the counter and tilted his chin up at the guy serving.

'All right, mate, I'll take a Coco Loco, please – and I'll pay for the lady's.'

He pulled a card from inside his body warmer and slid it away from him towards the server.

'You're kind,' I said. 'But I object to being called a lady.'

'Annie Wiig ain't a lady?' His sandy waves were slick with sweat, swept off his face by a thin elastic headband like footballers wear, and he hadn't shaved yet, a dance of dark blond stubble gathered across his chin. I wasn't sure if it was a trick of the light, but there might have been the tiniest bit of red

54

in there too. His green eyes glimmered brightly. I think it must have been the Norwegian in me that was at home with his height and his fairness, his breadth.

'Oppressive word,' I said. 'Lady. So full of expectations. I'm in a season of liberation as it happens.' I looked to my hands in front of me as I said it, betraying the jocular tone of my voice by tapping my fingers nervously. I was prepared to tell him about the break-up this time, if he asked. I still felt like shit, obviously, but I wanted to. I just knew he'd say the right things.

'Ahhhh,' he said, light-heartedly. 'There she is. That's the Annie Wiig I remember. Always making her own rules.'

I let out a small guffaw. 'God, I wish,' I asserted. 'I'm about as close to the party line as a person can be. I'm going to beat myself up for the rest of the day that you treated me to a smoothie and I still gave you attitude.'

'Really?' he countered, seemingly genuinely surprised. 'I'd get that seen to immediately – I'd hate for your Past Self to inadvertently get caught up in the plot of a time travel movie and come visit Present You on your way home, only to be disappointed that she follows the rules.'

I picked up my drink and took a huge slurp.

'Thank you,' I said. 'And thank you again, for being so sympathetic to me the other day. Your kindness really meant something.'

'I know heartache too,' he replied. 'So don't go thinking you're alone in feeling alone, whatever made that particular morning a bad one.' I wanted to ask him more about what made him feel alone, but he carried on speaking. 'Which is to say: you're welcome.'

Patrick grabbed his drink and we wandered over to the same bench where I'd cried on him two days ago.

'I *was* pretty spunky at drama camp, wasn't I?' I mused. 'I forgot about that. Do you remember staging that big midnight feast in the dining hall when we all got busted by the counsellors?'

'Hadn't that whole thing been your idea?'

I considered it. 'I wanted us all to get together and sign a petition to get ice cream served after lunch as well as dinner,' I recollected.

'See, that's what I remember about Annie Wiig. She knew what she wanted and how to get it done.'

'Yeah!' I exclaimed. 'Wow. I just . . . totally forgot. You're right. And it worked, didn't it?'

'You were literally all anyone talked about that whole summer. Even after you stopped coming people told stories about you as this urban myth of a student. I'll bet you're still spoken about now.'

He was right – I had been pretty precocious growing up. I saw a lot of myself in Freddie and how she behaved. I suppose I was so protective over her because I didn't want her to lose her edge, like I had done. Huh. That was a horrible thought to have. I'd lost my edge? When had that happened? I immediately changed the subject.

'What about you?' I said, tipping the straw of my cup in Patrick's direction. 'What kind of man did Patrick Hummingbird grow up to be?'

He considered it. He sat with his chunky, muscled legs sprawled apart and his elbows on his knees, easy in his own body and happy to take up space. 'I grew up to be . . . a bit lost, I think.'

'Lost?'

'I think that's the word. But I don't mean it in a bad way. I just don't have a plan. And that's unusual for a lot of people.

Makes them anxious. But I'm cool just . . . ambling.' He swirled the straw around his cup pensively. 'Does that make sense?' he asked, looking at me. 'That I actually find a lot of comfort in not having a plan?'

I thought about the last ten days. I thought about the last fifteen years. 'I think it takes strength of character not to plan,' I decided. 'I feel so much pressure – and I don't even really know where it comes from. Myself, probably. Society? The patriarchy? My mother?'

'You're afraid of disappointing people,' he said.

Was that a statement or a question? For some reason it landed like an accusation. Afraid of disappointing people? I think that was my default setting. Mum, Dad, Freddie, work, Alexander, the Core Four, Adzo   I didn't for a second want to do anything that displeased them or made them think less of me. If everyone around me was okay, then I was okay. On the list of priorities in my life, I came at the bottom, because that's what good, selfless women did, wasn't it? They looked after everyone else to prove their goodness. Nice women found their worth in that, and I wanted to be nice. I wanted to be considered good.

I sighed. 'Yeah,' I agreed. 'Something like that.'

'There's this writer called Glennon Doyle who says that it's not worth disappointing yourself to please somebody else. She says life is the opposite, in fact. That you have to make a game out of disappointing other people for as long as it takes to *never* disappoint yourself.'

The notion of that was outrageous to me.

'That sounds . . . selfish,' I said, a tiny voice in the very back of my head contradicting me as it roared: *That sounds AMAZING, actually!*

'I don't know,' he mused. 'Think about it: if we are all

disappointing ourselves over and over in order to never upset anybody else, aren't we putting the same pressure on them? If we all put ourselves first, wouldn't that give permission for other people to put *themselves* first? Wouldn't we all be happier?'

I thought about what he was saying, but it sounded suspicious to me.

'Is that how you live? Honestly?'

He shrugged. 'The way I see it, we're all looking to each other for permission to be free, so I'm happy to go first and give it. Nobody knows how much time they have left, so there's no point wasting it trying to be good when it's so much more fun to keep having fun.'

'Your life sounds nice.'

He hit his shoulder against mine good-humouredly.

'Your life isn't?'

I glugged at the last of my smoothie, the sound of the last bit of liquid going up my straw making a loud and very unladylike noise.

'Sorry,' I said, and he shook his head.

'What for?'

I'd meant my bad table manners, but it was obvious he didn't give a damn. He hadn't even noticed.

'You could teach me a few things,' I disclosed. 'I am having a very physical reaction to everything you are saying right now.'

'You're flirting with me!' he said, making his voice high-pitched and silly.

'Nooooo,' I said, embarrassed at the accusation. 'I didn't mean it that way.'

His face flickered roguishly. 'How disappointing.'

I must have been light-headed because of the class, or because I hadn't eaten properly yet, because suddenly I was

58

dry in the throat and a little bit woozy. I went from watching his understanding, playful mouth talking, to the room closing in on me, *bam,* just like that.

'Offft,' I said, closing my eyes and leaning my head back against the wall behind us. 'I think I might have pushed too hard in there. Wow.'

I inhaled and exhaled deeply for a few breaths.

'Y'okay?' he asked. 'Can I do anything?'

I shook my head, trying to focus.

When I opened my eyes again I said: 'Breakfast time, I think. That smoothie didn't even touch the sides.'

I stood up gingerly, depositing my cup in the recycling and pausing to take one more deep breath. I looked at Patrick. He was handsome, I realized. The faint creases on his strong face softened him, his huge height was commanding and assured. He wore a combination of blues and greens that complemented his glistening eyes. His lips were full. Kissable, even. But I honestly hadn't been flirting. The thought of it made me feel sick. I'd never take a risk again, I was sure of it. Who would want me anyway? My fate was to die an old maid. I knew that much.

'Until next time, I suppose,' he said.

I couldn't place what I thought about the notion of there being a next time. But I still replied, my smile bashful and heart skipping the tiniest of beats: 'Yes. I'll be here.'

On the bus home I didn't even need music to drown out my thoughts. I just watched the world go by, an almost imperceptible smile on my face. *I want to be friends with that man,* I thought. I was jealous of him, in a funny way. He seemed so relaxed with himself, so content. Had I really once been like that too? Because hanging around him, I could almost believe it.

* * *

59

I was still in my towel after my shower as I stood on the small IKEA stepladder to reach around in the top of the wardrobe. I could just about see the turquoise box, standing on my tiptoes to grasp at the nothingness in front of it before I could lean far enough to hook my finger under the lid and drag it to the edge of the shelf. My memory box.

I sat on the bed and flicked it open. I hadn't added anything to it for years. From the age of nine I was obsessive about recording my own history, collecting fragments of memories like a magpie: cinema ticket stubs, photos taken with my pink Polaroid camera – the one that everyone at school had. I hadn't looked through it in ages and in an instant, I was reminded why. Sometimes it was just too painful. There was an innocence to who I was when I was younger, a hopeful way of seeing the world that made me sad about how I saw the world now.

After my last summer at Yak Yak everything changed. I came home from drama camp as full of life and energy as I ever had been, but it was that school year that shifted who I thought I was allowed to be in the world, and I never went back. I started playing by the rules, started self-monitoring how I showed up in my life so as not to ruffle any feathers. I found a photo of us all stood on the stage of *Bugsy Malone*, about one hundred kids, me in the front row proudly sporting a leotard and feather boa, delighted as I've ever been. I scanned the faces for Patrick and found him at the back, not looking to camera. In fact, in a way, it almost looked as though he was staring in my direction.

I smoothed the photo out on the bedroom floor, letting myself remember, and decided to prop it in the corner of the mirror on the vanity, next to a picture of Freddie and me in a photo booth at our cousin's thirtieth, both in big glasses and moustaches. Why couldn't I be that carefree all the time? The photos on the mirror reflected the woman I wanted to be more than my actual reflection.

I was pulled out of my thoughts by Mum appearing at the doorway.

'Jesus,' I said, jumping out of my skin. 'Mum. You scared me.' I had a faraway thought about asking Adzo to suggest they think about leaving. This was too much, now. I was going to be okay. I was. They could go.

'It's Fernanda,' she said, holding out her mobile. 'I think you should take this, Annie. Come on.'

I gave her a quizzical look and took the phone from her wordlessly. Alexander's mum was on the phone? As Mum left she closed my bedroom door behind her. She hadn't given me privacy in my whole life. It made me nervous.

I took a breath and told Fernanda I was pleased to hear from her.

'Annie,' she intoned, her Brazilian Portuguese vowels crashing into each other. 'Listen. My son is a foul and ungrateful little *desgraçado* and I'm going to kill him when I see him. I raised him better than this! No! Don't say anything! I did. But in the meantime, I've got an idea. Now you must let me finish before you say anything, okay?'

'Okay,' I agreed, and I had to admit that despite the shock of her calling, my blood began to pump a little more as she told me what she had in mind.

8

'So basically,' I said, gesticulating with my freshly delivered espresso martini and forcing the foamy top off the edge and onto my wrist, 'Fernanda practically begged me to take the honeymoon. On my own. Isn't that just the oddest thing?'

That morning my parents and Freddie had finally left the house to go back to theirs. I'd thought I couldn't wait to be home alone and have the house to myself; to have my place be *my place*, with no busybodies swarming around. But then ten minutes after I'd waved them off with promises to stay in touch daily and Freddie whispering in my ear, *I love you Annie-Doo*, the silence was deafening. Being in the house alone now was different to being there and waiting for Alexander to get back from rugby training or the pub, or hearing the sound of him through the wall in the kitchen, or upstairs plodding about. Being in the house alone was sad. It was a museum to what I was grieving, and an email to the Core Four (I *still* hadn't switched my phone back on, I just couldn't face it) was responded to as an emergency. They booked a table at a restaurant around the corner, and we were already two cocktails deep half an hour after meeting. They'd been a bit flummoxed I hadn't reached out sooner, but had also admitted that they knew I'd shout when I was ready. They'd been in contact with Mum by text, and she'd kept them in the loop with how I was, they'd said.

'Nooooo!' marvelled Jo, using a nacho as a shovel for some guacamole. She was wearing her afro hair in its natural curly state, and her only make-up was a sweep of bright red lipstick. She looked flawless – especially compared to me. I'd tried to do my make-up, but I knew it hid little of how I was really feeling. I still looked grey and sallow, despite the endorphin rushes of my daily workouts. 'Are you going to do it?' A blob of avocado fell to her pregnant belly, big enough to be a month away from taking maternity leave from her job as a history professor at UCL, and five weeks from her due date. She looked down to where her bump had caught it and sniggered. 'Ooooops.'

Bri – petite, blonde and blue-eyed, a marketing director for a start-up run by one of the original employees of Google and the smartest person in any room, hands down – passed Jo a napkin, the corner of which she'd dipped in her water glass. 'I'd totally do it,' she said in her Lancastrian lilt, and took a glug from her gin fizz. She has mild cerebral palsy and so her muscles shake a bit, and I could see her deciding the cocktail was too full to lift without spilling, so she'd leaned forward to use the straw instead. Kezza hit her arm.

'Don't you dare offer to be her plus-one. If one of us is up for that it is I, the only other member of The Single Girls Support Club.' She beamed at me and fluttered her long eyelashes as she made her case, impersonating an angel with an Essex twang, which is funny because Kezza is as tough as nails and angelic isn't in even the top one hundred words I'd use to describe her.

Kezza has a theory that no matter how well-meaning a friend might be, there always exists a chasm between coupled-up friends and their single counterparts – whether they are single on purpose or not. She says only another woman who leaves a coffee date or meal out to go back to an empty bed truly understands certain things, and that sometimes, even knowing her friends are going home to another person leaves a heavy, peculiar sensation in her stomach. She'd had this theory since university. Even, she said, if a woman starts to loosely date a man after previously being in The Single Girls Support Club, she automatically leaves the club because she's going home to the *idea* of someone, and that separates her from her single friend in a way too.

I'm in the club again, I thought, *Urgh.*

I glugged down the last three gob-fuls of my drink as a way to quiet intrusive and unhelpful thoughts. The girls waited for me to carry on.

'It's all bought and paid for. Apparently Alexander's parents won't get their money back if they cancel,' I continued, and out of the corner of my eye I saw Kezza motion to the waiter to bring us another round. I pushed my empty glass to the edge of the table, shameless in my thirst. It was the Core Four who used to tease me about being too much of a 'good girl' to get involved in the £1 shots at The Gallery club where we spent most of our nights at uni, but even by their standards I was necking the booze ferociously tonight.

'Try tasting the next one,' Kezza winked. I suppressed an eye-roll. If I couldn't get wasted now, when could I?

'They spent so much time planning it,' I explained,

ignoring her sass, 'that they want me to have it. Mum told them I've been offered to stay off work for a while—'

'What?' interrupted Jo, pulling a face.

'No, no, no,' I said, trying to abate her obvious and immediate concern. 'Not signed off or anything like that. I had three weeks booked off anyway, for the honeymoon, and Chen, my boss, sent a letter saying to take these weeks in between as paid leave too. She called it a sort of discretionary compassionate leave. It's really nice of her, but I wasn't going to accept ...'

'A *paid* six weeks off work,' Jo interrupted again. '*And* you're being offered an all-expenses-paid trip to Australia from the nicest in-laws in the world to boot? Whoa.'

'And that's the whole thing,' I agreed. 'The flight leaves after the weekend, and it turns out Fernanda and Mum are in cahoots that I should do it.'

Our waiter appeared with our next drinks – more cocktails for us and a non-alcoholic beer for Jo.

'Do you want me to take a sip out of that for you, so it's not as full?' Kezza asked Bri.

'Bugger off,' yelped Bri. 'Don't use *me* as an excuse to steal extra drink!'

Kezza pouted as she played with her fire engine red hair, pulling it back into a ponytail and wrapping it around itself until it held in a bun for a second and then slowly uncurled itself again.

'Crazier things have happened than being offered a free honeymoon,' observed Bri, which is true. She'd met her own husband, Angus, in Las Vegas, and came home from a week-long hen trip for a friend at work with a husband of her own. It had surprised us zero per cent, though – it was a very Bri move to pull. She's cheeky and fun, but more than that she's romantic enough to take a chance on love. There is a bravery to it, I'd always thought. A bravery to believing.

'How are *you* feeling, Annie? Because I for one still can't believe all this.' Jo pushed her empty plate away from her, having made light work of the nachos that we were supposed to be sharing. I knew enough from her first pregnancy cravings not to get in between her and the melted cheese, though. When she was waiting to give birth to Bertie she'd once eaten four Mars bar ice creams dipped in parmesan breadcrumbs – all in a row – whilst crying and telling me that it was 'the hormones'.

'I feel. Just . . .' I didn't know what word to finish the sentence with, so I didn't bother. I didn't know where to begin.

'Yeah,' she said back, nodding in sympathy. 'I would be too.'

Bri coughed lightly, about to make an announcement. I narrowed my eyes at her. 'I've tried calling him,' she admitted sheepishly. 'Over and over. It mostly goes to voicemail but . . . Look. I'm not trying to cause trouble, but I did get an international dialling tone once. Do you think it's possible he's gone abroad?'

It made sense to me if he had. I kept asking myself where the hell he was. Where does somebody who has jilted their bride go and hang out? Do they carry on as usual? Go to work and hope nobody notices that they never get around to wearing a wedding ring, because the wedding never happened?

'Work!' I said. 'I didn't think of that before but his office was always on about him going out to the Singapore HQ for a bit. I kept wondering if he'd maybe taken a vacation or something but that would make total sense if he was out there.

He was supposed to go back to work like I was, and I can't see how he'd be able to simply take off without reporting in.'

If I knew for sure where he was, maybe it would settle my mind a little more. Maybe if I had some more concrete details I'd be able to put some mental pegs in the ground – have some cold, hard facts to tether myself to. I didn't realize until Bri said he might be out of the country just how desperately it would help me to know for sure. I wasn't sure if he was going to show up at the house any second, or pass me in the park on the way to bootcamp, or waltz through the door of the restaurant we were sat in, right now, talking with his old school friends and stopping off to shake someone's hand, because he was the little brother of somebody or other – Alexander always bumped into somebody he knew. I couldn't even be sure he'd stop to say hello if he did end up in the restaurant at the same time as us – that's how little I'd obviously meant to him, which was unfathomable. I'd been willing to marry him, for crying out loud! And he didn't care about me at all!

'It's like a form of psychosis or something,' I confessed. 'As though I imagined the whole relationship, the whole of the past ten years. It's hard to reassess everything. *Everything*. How could he do this to me?'

'Oh God, Annie,' Bri said, reaching a hand across the table to grab mine as it played with the napkin Jo had discarded. 'I wasn't sure if I should say – I didn't meant to make you cry. I'm sorry.'

I tried to roll my eyes to demonstrate how much I hated that I couldn't control my reaction. Shaking my head to try and free myself of the emotion clutching at my throat I squawked, 'If I'd left my bride I'd flee the country too. I'd be too ashamed to show my face.'

'Jesus,' muttered Kezza. 'That little shit.'

I wondered when he'd bought his plane ticket and how long before he refused to show up that he'd known he was going to do a runner. What if he'd known when we were organizing the Spotify playlist that was going to play during the wedding breakfast, or when we went for the final menu tasting? If I'd given in and agreed to the mini Yorkshire puddings with sliced roast beef would I be sat here a married woman? Did my insistence on having the chilli crab blinis cost me my future? I didn't even really like seafood that much! I had only wanted to make the unusual choice!

'I can't believe he gets to screw up your whole life, and then go on a jolly. That's not right. That's really not right.' Kezza was raging, and I could tell by how hard she was trying not to let on. She'd kept her voice level but I'd known her since we were eighteen: she was hopping mad.

'There must be a reason for it all,' Jo mused. 'Right? I know he could be an arse, but he wasn't totally heartless. Something *must* have prompted it . . .'

I narrowed my eyes and looked at her.

'Do you know something?' I asked. She was talking as if she was leading to revealing some big piece of information. I wondered if he'd been seeing somebody else. Men don't jump ship from relationships unless there's a lifeboat in the distance. They just *don't.* Half of me was frozen in fear that I was finally about to get the piece of the puzzle I'd been obsessing over and the other half immediately prayed to the heavens that she knew nothing. I didn't want to know, yet I wanted every last detail. I wanted to be seen, and to hide. Freed by information and safe from reality.

She shook her head quickly. 'No, honey, I'm sorry. If I did, I'd tell you. I promise.'

'You guys are hiding something from me,' I started, looking from Jo's face, to Bri's, to Kezza's. 'If you do know something . . .'

Kezza reached out a hand too. 'Honestly, we're as clueless as you are. I promise.'

I exhaled loudly. 'Okay. Phew.'

'But,' started Bri, and my eyes flickered up to her, my chest tight as a protester's fist.

'Yes?'

'Obviously we know you loved him.'

I balked. 'I mean, yes. That's why we were getting married . . .'

'I think all Bri is trying to say,' Jo offered, softly, 'is that . . . he was lucky to have you.'

Bri smiled, but it was a forced one. 'And look, whatever makes you happy – that's all we want for you . . .'

Jo cleared her throat. 'He was just a bit of an idiot sometimes, wasn't he?'

My jaw went slack. 'I beg your pardon?'

She slurped from her bottle, buying time so as not to answer me right away. 'It's only that we think you're amazing.'

'And sometimes it was like he didn't realize that,' finished Bri.

What they were saying was a knife to the heart. A betrayal. How long had they wanted to say all this? Were they telling me I'd been an idiot to think he'd ever make it to the church at all?

'You didn't like him.'

'No!' said Jo. 'It's not that we didn't like him.'

Bri shrugged. 'I didn't,' she said, plainly. 'I don't.'

The others gasped.

'We said we'd try the gentle approach?' Jo whispered, lighting a fire in my belly.

'Is this some sort of mediation?' I asked. 'Are you kidding me? I've just been shat on from the greatest possible height and you're all gathered here today to tell me . . . what? That you're pleased about it?'

'Hey,' Bri said, her tone sharp. 'We're your girls. We suffer when you suffer, okay? So you don't get to do that. You don't get to act as if we're the ones who hurt you. We didn't. Your boy Alexander did, and we're beyond mad about it.'

'Furious,' said Jo.

'I'd cut his dick off,' muttered Kezza. 'The little prick.'

Jo changed tack. 'But maybe this is a chance to see that you're worth so much more than he gave you. If you're at the place where you can hear us.'

I glanced up at her from under my eyelashes. 'Go on,' I said, sulkily. My heart beat in double time and my cheeks flushed. I knew what she was going to say before she said it, but I knew I had to hear it, too.

'There was definitely a star of the show in your relationship,' she said. 'And it wasn't you. I can't speak for everyone else, but that made me sad for you! It was so obvious that he was your world, but it wasn't as obvious that you were his . . .'

'He's very dreamy, but he's not the sun – you are,' Bri added, citing one of our favourite quotes from *Grey's Anatomy*.

I swallowed hard.

'Goddamn it,' I said. My eyes welled up. 'I don't know what to do. I don't know what happens after this. I thought this was my life sorted out. I can't go back to having nothing. I'm too old to start all over again . . .'

I dropped my head into my hands and let it wash over

me. Did I have to be strong? How long could I let myself feel weak? Was there a formula for moving forward? A secret 'Jilted Brides' handbook I could buy with next-day delivery?

The three of them let me take a moment to find the courage to admit I knew they were right. Alexander always came first in our relationship. That was true. But I just wanted him to be happy. I wanted him to get the promotion, and go out with the boys to let off steam when work was hard, and to relax at home because home should be a place where a person can do that. I never nagged him, because I didn't want to play that role. It was worse to ask him to repeatedly do something – unload the dishwasher, or put together the new drawers for the spare room, or take the laundry out of the machine – than it was to just do it myself. Anything to avoid an argument.

He told me he loved me and said I was the best thing to ever happen to him, but I couldn't lie to myself anymore: for a decade I'd pushed away the thought that I'd prefer him to show it rather than say it. I never told him that, though, because it sounded too much like an emotional burden. I didn't want to be an emotional burden to my partner. I wanted to be his respite, not his problem. I thought that was what everyone did for their person. I thought that was how you showed love to someone.

'It must feel horrible right now,' Bri said, kindly. 'I said to Angus: if the secret to happiness is having someone to love, something to do, and something to hope for, he's just robbed you of two of those things.'

'No,' said Kezza. 'We love you and you love us. The only thing he's taken is the hope. But that will come back. You can hope for other things, eventually.'

'How?' I said. 'I feel so humiliated. I can't ever imagine

smiling, or laughing, or dating – oh God. Do I have to start dating?'

Kezza growled, 'If he tries to kick you out the house, by the way, I will go after him, I swear.'

'I'll have to leave eventually,' I said. 'It's his, after all.'

'Yes,' agreed Bri. 'But you can make that move in your own time. No hurry. We'll make sure he doesn't rush you. If he's abroad . . .'

'Do you really think he is?'

'Maybe. I don't know.'

'You should paint a big black mark on my back so everyone knows I'm damaged goods,' I said. 'A warning to everyone that, at any moment, I might snap.'

'We've got you, okay? But, honey, I need you to listen really closely when I say this,' said Kezza.

'I'm listening,' I replied.

'You have to tell us what you need. We're not mind-readers. We're good, but we're not psychic, okay? It's time to learn to ask for help.'

Ask for help? The thought sent shivers down my spine.

'I can do that,' I said nodding. 'I can't do the honeymoon, though. That's too much. I'm still too raw.'

'And that's absolutely fine,' Bri soothed. 'Whatever you want to do, we're here. I swear – this is not going to be your undoing. It's going to be your becoming. We'll make sure of it. None of us is screwing up like we think we are.'

I took the iPad to bed with me when I got home and used the browser to log into Instagram. I don't know why I did it. Addiction, I think. Isn't there some research that says the average person scrolls about three miles a day? That Silicon Valley design their technology to be so dangerously addictive that most of them won't even let their kids have phones because it fries the brain? I knew looking online would upset me, but I did it anyway.

I hadn't uploaded anything since the night before the wedding – a photo of me with Adzo and Freddie, all of us in hotel dressing gowns pulling funny faces. Underneath I'd written: *Last night as a single woman, hanging with my best girls.* Rereading it made my stomach do a double flip.

I went to the homepage, trembling as I typed in Alexander's username, but he hadn't posted since August 2016. I just wanted to make sure his new life, without me, hadn't yet begun, I suppose. Then I scrolled my feed. Dinners, restaurant trips, date nights out with couples in their outfits and the caption: *Dinner with this one,* followed by a heart-eyes emoji. I wondered if everyone was as happy as they made it seem. Had I been happy, before now? I once posted a picture of Alexander and I at a fancy pizza restaurant whilst sleeping alone in our spare room. We'd argued over dinner, after the photo had been taken – I think about how to spend the Easter break. The thing is, arguments are never about the thing you're arguing about, are they, and the fight continued after the bill had come and then all the way home.

Thinking about it now, I'd tried to hint that it would be nice if we could spend some more time together. Sometimes I was on the list after work, and rugby, and his time in the gym, and then his alone time, his 'chilling out' time. Only then did I get his full attention. Anyway. I still posted the photo of us, telling the world we'd been out for dinner and ordered extra burrata, even though I barely remembered the food. There was no mention of our fight in the caption, or me thinking I was never enough no matter how many shapes I contorted myself into. In fact, the more shapes I contorted

73

myself into the more he withheld what I needed. No. Instead, I'd typed exactly what everyone did: *Dinner with this one #datenight #extracheese.*

Sighing, I was about to exit the app, but found myself typing 'Patrick Hummingbird' into the search bar before I realized I was doing so. Nothing came up. I tried Paddy Hummingbird. Nothing came up then, either. It was senseless that I'd even tried. Why had Patrick even crossed my mind?

I idly pushed at buttons, logging in and out of apps without thinking. The news, Pinterest, the health app. When I did that, an alert popped up.

You haven't logged a period this month. Do you want to do that now? it asked.

Oh God. I hadn't had a period? I looked at the chart on screen and realized that was true. I should have come on last week. It was probably the stress. Even lying in bed my jaw was so tight it was practically up at my eyebrows.

I tapped through to email and put Alexander's work address in the 'to' box. I left the subject line blank. In the body of the note I typed, deleted, and retyped: *Where are you?* I lingered over the send button and held my breath as I pressed it. I needed to know.

I got his Out of Office immediately:

Hi there. I am currently working from the Singapore office, so you may experience a delay in my response due to the time difference.

I knew it. Singapore. That can't have been a last-minute decision, surely. Urgh! He threw a hand grenade into my life and then got on a plane. I was beyond outraged, but strangely, being able to pinpoint down geographically where he was made me breathe deeper. I hated him and everything he'd done, but at least I now had a direction to send my hate in.

9

It was as if Patrick and I had pre-arranged to meet by the smoothie bar after class, because there we both were, and it seemed to be even less of a surprise to him than it was to me.

'I've got something for you,' he said, smiling from a distance so that we had to hold eye contact as he approached. I was loitering in reception, having spotted him halfway through the class when we were switching between the treadmills and the weights. He'd winked at me, and I'd spent the rest of the session trying not to look over in his direction. I couldn't say why. I think because he was my new-old friend. I just liked talking to him. I suppose that was the silent agreement that we'd catch up afterwards.

'Is it a puppy?' I asked.

'No,' he said.

'A gold bar worth a million pounds?'

'Nope.'

'Have you got me . . . a pastrami sandwich?'

'I don't even know what pastrami is,' he said, and I didn't

admit that neither did I. I just saw somebody order it in a movie once.

He took his backpack off his shoulder and rifled through it until he found what he was looking for: a small manila envelope.

'Ta-da!' he said, as he opened it to reveal a photograph of me at Yak Yak, dressed up as Tallulah, wearing a leotard and fishnet tights, a feather pushing up proudly from a bun pinned at the nape of my neck. I had a drawn-on beauty spot and was looking off-camera to the person taking the photo.

'You're laughing at me in this,' he said, pointing, as I studied it closely. 'I'd told you a joke so you'd smile, and when you did it was as if I'd been awarded an Oscar for services to drama camps. I'd been trying to make you laugh all summer. I think I had a crush on you.'

I batted him away. 'You did not,' I said, self-consciously. 'You had a crush on my friend Jasmine. And I laughed at you all the time. I remember you being the funniest person there.'

I went to hand the photo back, but he told me I could keep it. I stared at it again.

'Thanks,' I said. 'Good memories. I'll put it somewhere I can see it, as a reminder.'

'Not to sound too forward . . .' he began, and I knew what he was going to say before he'd said it, and also knew in that exact moment that I wanted him to ask. Bad things didn't happen when I was talking with Patrick. The future didn't exist, only the past, and it was a relief. 'If you ever want to hang out *not* in this lobby, to reminisce, we should do that. We could find a draughty bus station, or a crowded sandwich shop . . .' He creased up his brow, taking in my reaction. 'Or . . . not . . .' he faltered, knitting his forehead together in disappointment at my lack of enthusiasm.

'I want to,' I said, quickly, reaching out to touch his arm. 'I do. I just hope it doesn't sound presumptuous to say that . . . my situation . . .'

'Just say it,' he prompted, kindly. 'It's okay.'

I swallowed. 'Embarrassingly,' I began, and the mention of embarrassment made his lip quiver, just the tiniest bit, in amusement. 'I've just been dumped.' I didn't want to give him my *whole* life story, but I'd been promising myself I'd tell him what had happened. 'So I'm not dating. If that's . . . I don't know if that's what you meant. But I wanted to check.'

I felt so awkward. Patrick's lip quiver turned into a smirk, and then he said, casually, good-humouredly: 'What a fool he must feel now,' he said. 'Or she. Whoever *they* were.'

'He,' I replied. 'It's crazy, seeing somebody from the past, I think. You knew me when I was . . .' I was going to say 'happy' but stopped myself. 'When things were simple. Adulthood, man. It's rough!'

'I'm glad you told me,' he said. 'I mean, I'm sorry that happened. Being dumped is brutal. Losing somebody you love is very hard.'

'I'm a mess,' I admitted.

'I know that feeling.' I stole a glance at him. He made it so straightforward to be honest. He was funny when something was funny, but he didn't use humour as a way to distract from the gritty stuff, or deflect true emotion. I didn't know a lot of men capable of that.

'If you do know this feeling, then I'm sorry.'

He studied the floor, and for a second I thought he was about to give me the details. He sort of opened his mouth to speak but then clamped it shut forcefully, as if the devil on his shoulder had silenced him.

'I should let you get on with your day,' I said, driving the conversation to a halt. 'But, same time, same place another day?' It came out wrong. I meant to say a *different* time, a *different* place, as in: yes, let's go out and reminisce. I was an idiot. What was I doing? My tongue was looped in knots. Why did I feel nervous? I was allowed to have a drink with a friend, for crying out loud.

'I'm here every morning,' he said, getting ready to leave. I'd bruised his ego. I could tell he was trying not to show it, but I had.

'Every morning?' I asked. I'd only caught him occasionally, but we must have been working out at the same time all week.

'Most, yeah. Helps keep the demons at bay.'

'Good for you. I've certainly got demons who could do with a healthy bollocking, that's for sure.'

He cocked his head, exactly like he had done the day we first talked – the way the dog does it.

'What?' I asked.

'It's just, you really haven't changed since camp. It's so strange. The way your face moves – how your eyebrows jump up and down your face, all expressive. It's mad.'

I giggled. 'My eyebrows?' I wiggled them suggestively.

'Like I said.' He grinned. 'It's mad. Let me know about a non-date, anyway. It'd be cool to hang out, but no pressure.'

I wanted to find the words to accept it, there and then, but I didn't feel brave enough. The conversation had taken a turn. I wanted to spend the whole day with him and have him tell me more stories about my eyebrows at camp, and remind me of the late-night rehearsals and talk about the time he came with Jasmine and me, and another boy, too, whose name I couldn't remember, out on the lake for a midnight swim, the water deep and cool, the moon lighting up our faces like we were the stars of our own private show.

I couldn't stop thinking about Yak Yak, and *Bugsy Malone*, and because of all that, Patrick. When I saw him at boot-camp and he made a beeline to talk to me, I planned to ask him outright if he wanted to go out for a drink, or dinner, just to reminisce. When it came down to it, it took bumping into him twice more before I actually did it.

'I just really want to catch up,' I explained, feeling ridiculous. 'Theatre camp, midnight adventures. All of it.'

He replied: 'Whatever the reason you want me at the same place at the same time as you, on purpose, I'll be there. It'll be fun.'

'Okay,' I said. 'Excellent. Tomorrow? Oh no. Wait. It's Saturday tomorrow. You probably already have weekend plans.'

'Nope,' he said, breezily. 'I'm yours.'

'Great. Tomorrow afternoon. One platonic old-friend-non-date it is!' I don't know what made me say that. I just wanted to be clear. Dating was absolutely not on the agenda. I was dead inside. It just occurred to me that maybe I'd somehow made it sound romantic or loaded with intention. I hadn't been single in a decade – at university any time spent with a boy would have been considered a potential hook-up. That was all I was going off.

'One platonic old-friend-non-date indeed,' he said. 'Let me give you my phone number?'

'I don't have my phone on me, actually.' I thought of it sitting in the drawer of my bedside table.

'Give me yours. I'll text you.'

'Do you think we could email? My phone is my enemy at the moment.'

'Email,' he considered. 'Absolutely. How very 2002. Very fitting.'

'I think it's great,' Adzo said as we walked back from Pret on her lunch break. I'd met her outside the office, not quite graduating to going in. The house was too empty, too much of a reminder of my aloneness, so I'd grabbed Carol and we'd trekked into town in the September sun, desperate to tell someone about what was happening. 'It's the perfect balance of him being somebody who has no idea what's happened these past few weeks – or the past twenty years – without being a total stranger. He's a man, so you can remind yourself not all men are trash, but it's platonic, so you don't have to wear an uncomfortable bra just to make the old girls look good.'

'This is an interestingly specific assessment of me simply meeting up with an old friend.'

Adzo took a bite of her falafel wrap. 'Would we even call him that? An old friend? You didn't even recognize him when you saw him.'

We loitered outside our work building, but then I worried I'd bump into Chen and so guided us around the corner to a bench.

'I can't explain it, but—'

'You enjoy how he remembers you, and you want to remember that version of yourself too. Yes. I know.'

'Sorry if I'm repeating myself.'

'Only be sorry if you're repeating yourself as a way to excuse wanting to hang out with him. You're heartbroken and have been trampled on, and you're still allowed to feel this . . .'

'Pull,' I supplied. 'It's a pull towards him. He's funny, and light-hearted, and—'

'And he makes you feel funny and light-hearted too. Yup. It's all there in the log book for judge and jury to see. All the evidence is accounted for.'

I threw my crusts to the ground for Carol and wiped my fingers on the hem of my dress. 'You're a horrible friend.'

'I am. I've made a note of that in the evidence system too. Now gimme a crisp, will you. I should have got a packet myself.'

'Why do I feel nervous?' I asked her. She looked at me, and I thought she was going to say something cutting and witty again, but instead she smiled and said, 'Annie. Chill your beans. He sounds like a good friend to have. Just enjoy it. If Old Annie was all about planning everything down to the very last detail, I definitely think New Annie can afford to be in the moment a bit more, consequences be damned.'

New Annie. I turned the notion of her over in my thoughts, examining the catch. I couldn't find one. I did want to be new. Different. All of this had to be *for* something, didn't it? Isn't that how people survived things – they gave them meaning?

'Okay then,' I agreed. 'I'll seize the day.'

I deliberately showed up in my glasses, with my hair unwashed, to avoid any accidental inference about my intentions. I needn't have worried, because he showed up in a paint-splattered T-shirt after painting and decorating all morning and, I have to say, meeting for an afternoon pint was very much like something friends would do. We'd settled in to a booth in the corner of the pub, him on one side of the table and me on the other, the street and everyone passing us by on the other side of the glass. The chat had been easy and entertaining, exactly as I'd hoped.

'Were you there the year we did, urm – oh gosh. The one with the grandparents in bed . . .'

I dropped my jaw in faux-shock that he couldn't remember the name of it. '*Charlie and the Chocolate Factory*!' I giggled. 'How can you not know the name of *Charlie and the Chocolate Factory*?'

'I'm an old man now,' he said, shrugging. 'The names of shows escape me. I can still remember every lyric to every song in *Aladdin* though.'

We'd been reliving old memories and filling in the gaps of each other's blanks for two hours and three drinks' worth of time.

'That's good going,' I said, and then, changing the subject slightly: 'It's sad, really. But I've not done any theatre since Yak Yak. I suppose I left the summer before I did my GCSE year and then once I'd finished school I figured I was too old for that sort of stuff.' I drained my glass, totally lost in the back-and-forth between us. 'What did you do then?' I asked. 'After school?'

'Inter-railed Europe, got my heart broken by a French girl, wrote some bad songs about it,' he admitted, his face making it very clear that he knew how to laugh at his eighteen-year-old self.

'That sounds suspiciously similar to the plot of *Before Sunrise*,' I countered.

'Are you calling me a cliché?'

'That depends,' I teased. 'Did you grow out your facial hair into a patchy moustache and spend the next four years wearing a smelly old vintage leather jacket that you'd tell anyone who'd listen you got when you travelled Europe?'

'Wow, were you my twenty-something stalker?'

'You have to say it in the voice, too. You can't just say, "Oh! I got it when I travelled Europe!" you have to be all gruff and mysterious.' I dropped my pitch by a few tones and grumbled, '"I got it when I travelled Europe." As if you were sent to the Battle of the Somme, not drinking 50p beer in the Czech Republic.'

'Okay, okay,' he said, holding up his hands in surrender. 'Get out of my head now please. I cannot withstand this character assassination, for I am but a humble, sensitive insurance salesman now. And anyway – who were you after you left school? Ms Goody-Goody?'

'That's too easy,' I retorted. 'Because I've already told you I was. And that I still am.'

'I'm not buying it,' he declared. 'There's gotta be a wild one in there waiting to get out.'

He held my eye as he said it, provoking me. The sun hit him in a way that lit him up, making him golden and youthful. His wide frame occupied a pleasing width of the booth, and it had been hard not to notice how big his hands were. I could barely hold my pint glass with one hand when it was full, despite my limbs being like Stretch Armstrong, but his hands – he could have wrapped his palm around a whole barrel.

'Changing the subject . . .' I said, refusing to get drawn in. I didn't even want to flirt for sport.

'Humour me!' he insisted, getting up for another round. I was going to protest before I realized I didn't want to. I wanted to keep drinking, and to keep talking. It was exactly how I had hoped it would be. It was exactly what I'd been craving. Being with him was an escape.

The afternoon bled into early evening, and the conversation took a turn with it. Somehow we were trying to distinguish the difference between sex and intimacy.

'I have a vested interest in *intimacy*,' Patrick explained. I had no idea how we ended up there. We'd talked about everything and anything and nothing and the world. And we were tipsy by now, too. 'Because it involves showing your true self to each other.'

I shook my head, but I was grinning. 'A vested interest in intimacy? That sounds suspiciously like another way to say, "my hobby is getting people to sleep with me", pal.'

Patrick feigned outrage. 'Well, well, well – that's incredibly presumptive.' He took a swing from his pint glass. 'It's good to know where your thoughts lie, Annie Wiig.'

I raised my glass to him in a mock cheers. 'I just call 'em as I see 'em.' I'd grown sillier and sillier as we'd talked. He made it easy to be that way.

'On a scale of one to ten, how good are you at admitting when you're wrong?'

'Couldn't tell you.' I smiled. 'It's never happened.'

He set his drink down and leaned back. 'Real talk,' he declared. 'I honestly think sex and intimacy are two totally different things. You can have sex without being truly intimate, and you can feel closer to somebody than anyone else in the world without having touched one another.'

I narrowed my eyes, trying to get a hold on how serious he was.

'Go on,' I said, lending him enough rope to hang himself. 'Intimacy isn't champagne and candles and foot rubs. It can be part of it – but it's not all of it.' He continued. 'Modern life – all the "having to be at places at certain times, the bills, the responsibilities", we're over-burdened. We complicate things and make ourselves busy, and we think that gives life meaning.'

I thought about all the times I worked late, or Alexander worked late, or the weekends we sat in the same room but on our laptops, eventually ordering a takeaway and leaving the dishes for the cleaner.

'On top of all that,' he continued, 'we all live apart from our families, often apart from our oldest friends, too, and we put all this responsibility on our relationship to fulfil what we need financially, emotionally, not to mention the sex. We ask a lot of our romantic partners, and I wonder at what cost.'

A waiter appeared at our table, order pad in hand and drinks tray under her arm. We'd been in the pub so long that they'd switched from afternoon bar bites and empty tables to full-blown restaurant-style menus and table service. I was glad he hadn't said he had somewhere to be. He hadn't even looked at his watch.

'Two more?' the waiter asked, pointing a pen at our table. Patrick looked at me. I looked at the waiter. The waiter looked between us as if to say, *I can't decide for you, can I?*

'Go on then,' I capitulated, passing over the empties. 'Shall we eat, too?'

Patrick nodded.

'Do you have pizza?' I asked the waiter. 'Or burgers?'

'Both,' she replied.

'Pizza,' Patrick said. 'Good old-fashioned margherita pizza?'

'Biggest you've got,' I agreed. 'And can you bring a bucket of mayonnaise out with it? Thank you.'

Patrick looked at me and uttered, 'Mayonnaise?' as if he was disgusted by the very thought of it.

'I'm not defending my condiment choice to you,' I stated. 'And, please, continue with what you were saying . . . I'm interested in where this is going, because it still sounds to me like you're one big player.'

'Where was I?' he mused.

'We expect too much of each other,' I supplied, feeling guilty all over again about how much that resonated.

'Oh, we do,' he warned. 'But we're all having bloody iAffairs, too. There's three people in every relationship! You, them, and bloody technology. We're glued to our phones and wonder why our partner doesn't feel glued to us.'

'You didn't even put your phone on the table,' I said. 'Do you even have one with you?'

Patrick patted his coat on the bench beside him. 'In there somewhere,' he said. 'You deserve my full attention, after all.'

He really was a charmer, but I let him get away with it because he was also totally charm*ing*.

'So we're all addicted to tech,' I repeated. 'We're not having sex because we don't feel connected . . . You're really painting a rosy picture of modern life here. I'm full of the joys and hopes of living.'

'My point is: intimacy is about connection. And I took this course on it because I wanted to feel more connected to . . .'

I thought he might tell me about his ex, or exes – I thought I was about to get a morsel of real and concrete information from him about his romantic history. It was strange to know so little about how he'd spent his time in the twenty-ish years since we'd seen each other last. I knew about how he'd got Delhi belly when he'd done yoga teacher training near the Nepalese mountains, and that he'd had a bunch of jobs but hadn't really stuck at anything because work was just that to him: work, not a career he had to excel at. First it was recruitment, and now he sold insurance. He was so . . . I don't know. In the moment? I'd zoned out as he'd told me why he'd taken the course. Damn.

'We did a lot of study around intimacy being about trust, and teamwork. I mean, think of your best platonic relationship – the person you trust most in the world.'

'Oh, easy,' I interrupted. 'That's my sister, Freddie. Or my best friend Adzo.'

'And have you had sex with either of them?'

'I presume my silence can be your answer.'

'So you get my point. Those relationships are intimate because of the trust, and being a team. Being present. Demonstrating your care for them and sharing parts of yourself. Your thoughts, your hopes, your dreams, your fears.'

'Who do you share that stuff with?'

He thought about it. 'All kinds of people,' he settled on. 'I mean, we're sharing now, aren't we?'

I didn't know what to say. Suddenly it was like a date, but this wasn't a *date*. That would be crazy. A date, right now? No. I picked up the candle holder that had appeared in the middle of the table and passed it between my hands. I was never dating again – that's what I'd said. And anyway, it obviously wasn't a date for him because he'd barely made the sartorial effort. I'd even noticed a little paint in his hair, and across his clothes. I could have been having this conversation with anybody. Couldn't I?

'It's cool we get to hang out,' I said, avoiding his gaze. 'All those memories. I was so *free* back then. I loved it. I really did.'

'But you never came back . . .'

'And you stayed right until the last year of school? I think I'm jealous.'

'It obviously wasn't as much fun without you there.'

I laughed. 'That's the correct answer,' I said, and we laughed some more.

'Whoa,' Patrick marvelled later, dipping his crust into the mayonnaise I'd ordered, fully on board with it being a non-negotiable part of pizza eating now. 'When you said you'd been dumped, I never for a second thought . . .'

We were officially into the evening, and our chat had been saved from becoming too slurred by the food we'd stuffed ourselves with. As we'd eaten, I'd spilled the beans on exactly why I was now single. He'd asked outright, emboldened by the beer and easy banter, and I hadn't wanted to lie. I'd told him everything.

'That I got dumped whilst wearing a big white dress? I know. It's probably the most dramatic thing that has ever happened to me.'

'It's probably the most dramatic thing that's happened to anybody, ever. I am so, so sorry.'

I wiped my hands on a napkin and pushed my plate away from me. I hadn't realized how starving I was. We paid the bill and meandered down to a converted warehouse Patrick knew about where we could play mini golf and eat candyfloss. It was good to stretch my legs – we'd been sat in that booth for almost six hours.

'And they really want you to take the honeymoon as a holiday?'

'It's such a hard conversation to have. I just feel so . . . awkward. They're so apologetic about what Alexander did, but it's wasted. They're not the ones who did something wrong.'

'It's sweet they'd try.'

We took our putters and our balls and waited in line to start the course.

'Do I sound awful if I say it feels selfish of them? They want me to tell them I'm okay, but I'm not. And possibly that makes them feel ashamed of their son, or that maybe they could have stopped all this from happening. But that can't be my problem, can it? I make everything my responsibility but just lately, since all this . . .'

'The sod-it function has kicked in?'

I smiled. 'Exactly. I've done everything like I was supposed to, my whole life. I've been a good girl, and studied hard, and done all the right extra-curricular stuff. I've kept in shape, I went to a good university, I see my friends and try to cook and read and watch all the TV I'm supposed to watch. I've moulded myself to be as nice and non-confrontational as possible, and for what? I've ended up a fool. I just don't have it in me to do anything other than live in self-protection mode now. I'm exhausted. I don't want to manage anybody else's emotions. Only *mine*.'

I was talking and talking and talking because I could. Because Patrick listened to every word I was saying and didn't interrupt or look away. He was interested. Interested, and also drunk. His eyelids were drooping just a teeny-tiny amount. It was nice, though, being tipsy and just moving on from one topic to the next, delighting in the way the other person thought or framed something.

He lined up a shot with his ball, holding his club lightly and getting a hole in one.

'All power to you,' he said, satisfied by his point. He leaned towards me and executed a very poor stage whisper. 'I've got to tell you though: you're in luck.'

'Why?'

'Because life has handed you lemons, and you can make a honeymoon out of it.'

I sighed audibly and took my turn. 'A honeymoon without a husband is just a lonely singleton nightmare, I'm afraid.' I shocked myself by getting a hole in one too. I think my inhibitions had been lowered, and so it loosened up my swing or something. Maybe it was beginner's luck. We walked to the next part of the course.

'Don't go alone then.'

'Alexander is in Singapore, Patrick. He's gone. It's over. I'm sure the last thing he wants is to fly to Australia with the woman he jilted. And that's fine, really, because I don't think I ever want to see his stupid face again.'

'I reckon *we'd* have a great honeymoon together,' Patrick supposed, and then stuck his tongue firmly in his cheek as he went for his next turn.

I scrunched up my face. I was sort of seeing double. I needed water.

'Sure,' I said, calling his bluff, and I realized I was slurring a bit too. 'You and me on the other side of the world. Absolutely. Let's do it.'

Another hole in one for him, but this time I missed.

'Oh, you joke,' he said. I moved to hit the ball again, landing it on the second try. 'But I'm damned serious. I'll take a free trip to the other side of the world. You said they're loaded, right? And want to spend money on easing their guilt? If you need a partner in crime to do that with, it could actually be a hell of a lot of fun. I'll pay my own way if I can use the spare ticket.'

We moved along to the next hole.

'You want to come to Australia with me?'

He took a shot and missed, but got it the next time he tried.

'Why not. YOLO.'

I got a hole in one again. I gave a pointed look of victory.

'We don't even know each other.'

'We do.'

His turn again, a point pinging up on the small handheld screen we'd been given.

'Okay then, yeah, sure, let's go on my honeymoon together.' Sarcasm dripped from my every word. 'You can carry the suitcases and I'll get drunk on the plane and leave you to explore on your own.'

My turn. I got it in one. By the next hole, the tone of our conversation had shifted from a joke to a legitimate pros and cons list. Patrick was waiting for me to say something else, so I told him: 'You just focus on shooting your shot, please. Look, we're holding the people behind us up.'

He swaggered over the golf ball and made a show of adjusting his jeans to allow for maximum movement, wiggling his bum at me.

'Just play!' I squawked.

He hit the ball and it went straight into the hole. 'He shoots, he scores, he flies to Australia!' he cried, waving his hands in the air.

'It's a terrible idea,' I said. 'Stop teasing me with it.'

'Au contraire,' he countered, as I putted my ball. 'It's a brilliant idea. You said yourself you're desperate to say sod it to the rules. What could make the point better than running off into the sunset with your old pal Pongy Paddy?' The use of his old nickname made me suck in my cheeks to stop myself grinning.

We headed over to the last hole of the course. We were

neck and neck on the scorecard, and suddenly I wanted to win more than anything.

'Ladies first,' he said. 'If you score, it can be your brief moment of winning before I come right up behind you. So to speak.'

I put the ball on the ground and did my own peacocking. It made him laugh. I liked the sound of it – carefree and genuine. He made me feel funny, instead of performing a role for him. I didn't have to act like a girlfriend or fiancée or wife or good girl. I was just being me.

'How did you get to be this way?' I asked. 'This YOLO spirit?'

I hit the ball gently and we both watched as it glided over the fake grass into the next hole.

'Nice work,' he said, and I acted like it was no big deal. It all came down to the next shot: if he missed this one, I won. If he got it, we'd have to go to a tie.

'Okay, here's the deal. If this goes in,' he suggested, 'I get to decide if I'm coming with you.' I raised my eyebrows as if to say, *is that so?* 'And if it doesn't, you get to decide if I'm coming with you. But either way, you're going.' He used his club to point at me. 'Almost three weeks in Australia? Who'd turn that down?'

I didn't say anything.

'And the YOLO,' he continued, 'comes from exactly what you were saying. That there are no prizes for playing it safe. Life is short, and precious, and we only get *one*. It could end tomorrow. I won't be the guy who has it end on his way back from the office, thinking about all the could-have-beens. I decided a long time ago to be a today man. Anything else is just too sad.'

He lined up his shot, closed one eye, and hit the putter

against the ball. I could tell immediately that he'd given it too much force and it was going to make him overshoot the mark.

I was right.

The ball sailed past the hole, making me the winner. And the decision-maker.

He looked at me. He'd totally done it on purpose. I could tell by the lopsided smirk that he was revelling in pushing me to be more spontaneous. More carefree. But I'd told him that's what I wanted, hadn't I? He was nudging me in the direction that I willingly wanted to go. Maybe he'd be good for me, then, being a nudger. Maybe it wasn't wrong to take the trip, to take the money, to take a plane and see what my problems looked like from half a world away. That's what Alexander had done, wasn't it? Put thousands of miles between him and his problems?

'I can't believe I'm saying this,' I began, and Patrick walked towards me, eyebrows raised and his gaze penetrating. 'Potentially, this will be the worst hangover I'll ever have. But . . . Patrick . . .'

He batted his eyes at me like a cartoon character.

'Would you consider coming on honeymoon to Australia with me?'

He put a hand under my chin and tilted my face up, just slightly. For a terrified second I thought he was going to kiss me. He didn't. Instead he looked deep into my eyes and adopted a pretty convincing Australian accent to say, 'Babe. I thought you'd never ask.'

10

I love airports. I love airports, and I am good at them. It's a learned skill, and actually one that Alexander taught me. You need time in an airport, and also an airport budget. Airports are the black hole of money. You can go into Boots for a bottle of water and come out eighty quid down, *poof*, on last-minute wet wipes and deodorant and adapters.

Adapters!

It was a good job I'd remembered. I'd never been to Australia before, so there hadn't been any Australia-specific plugs in the travel drawer at home. I couldn't forget to pick one up. Or two. That way Patrick would have one as well.

The Core Four were *not* convinced by the whole Patrick shebang, I think mostly because they worried that they'd never heard of him before now – I mean, why would I ever have mentioned a boy I knew twenty years ago, who I've never seen since? – and that somehow he'd taken advantage of me. I saw them for brunch the morning after our old-friend-non-date at mini golf, and they'd seen my face when his email had come through on my phone. I'd felt good enough earlier that morning that I'd finally turned it on, deleting every text that came through about the wedding without even reading them. I didn't care. I wasn't thinking about the bloody wedding for a second longer. I had a future, and only I could decide how to shape it. In the subject box of what Patrick had sent it said: *DOWN UNDER* ;)

In good faith, he'd written, *I hereby offer you a get-out clause. I had plied you with multiple beers and the heady sense of mini golf victory last night . . .*

I'd explain to the Core Four that I'd rolled over in bed with excitement bubbling for the first time in ages that day – albeit quite hungover. As I'd stared at the space in bed where Alexander should have been it hit me: *why not?* What was the worst that could happen if Patrick was the buddy Fernanda and Charles had suggested I find? Sun, sea, wine tasting, the good company of somebody who made me laugh? I actually didn't have a single doubt. A switch had been flicked in my head – in my soul, even – where I understood how I could choose how to frame my life. And I was choosing the honeymoon with Patrick – a man who remembered me as I wanted to be.

'Aren't you worried, though?' probed Jo. 'Okay fine, you knew him twenty years ago when you were kids, and he's made you laugh in the handful of times you've seen him at bootcamp, but . . . going on holiday with him?'

'HONEYMOON,' interjected Kezza. 'It's her honeymoon . . . but he isn't her husband!' she squealed. 'This is just too good. I love it. I mean, obviously you should have picked me, but whatever. Work is super busy right now anyway, and I'm saving cash for my impending motherhood. I would have come if pushed, but this Patrick fella sounds good enough. Can we see a photo of him?'

'I did not see this coming,' mused Bri. 'This is *quite* left-field.' She said 'quite' with an emphasis that I knew meant 'two hundred per cent left field' but I let it wash over me.

'What are you going to do if you need a poo and you're sharing a hotel room?' asked Jo.

Kezza enquired: 'What are you going to do if you have to share a bed?'

'We're not sharing a bed,' I said. 'That would be . . . no.'

I hadn't actually thought about the sleeping arrangements. The only thing I'd thought about was having somebody else to watch my luggage at the airport when I needed the loo, and another person in the car speeding from beach to beach, radio playing, wind in my hair. Now I knew it was happening, the pull of vacation was overwhelming. I'd been going through the motions of my old life to try and get through a day but now, with all this to look forward to, I was reinvigorated. Like Adzo had said – New Annie was peeking out of the shadows of the old one. I didn't have to go through the motions: I could craft my own story, and in that story I could be wearing a sunhat and a kaftan.

After a brunch of eggs royale with a side order of defending myself, I'd emailed him back:

Yeah, you're right. I accept the get-out clause. Thank you.

He'd replied: *But we can mini golf again, can't we? I had fun!*

I grinned whenever his name appeared on my screen. His words pumped me full of helium so I could float above the doubt I had about myself. *We can,* I'd sent back. *Let's put mini golf on the itinerary FOR AUSTRALIA, BABY! Of course I haven't changed my mind!!!*

Adzo thought the whole set-up was the best thing she'd ever heard, but then she often contradicted whatever the Core

Four said – I think as my Work Best Friend she shouldered a responsibility to offset their more conservative predilections. Adzo definitely thought they were all a little bit square because they were all so traditional in their life paths of jobs and husbands and children, but then she hadn't turned thirty yet. Something happens in your brain when you do, I swear. I don't know if it's society or culture or the biological clock or witchcraft or what. But it's real. And I don't think blokes have it.

'It's a perfect plan,' she'd extolled. 'Totally perfect! We keep making this distinction between the Old Annie you were, and this New Annie you're going to be, and I've got to say, I for one am very encouraging of this. People are supposed to evolve and change. Look at the nice blonde woman who they made a movie about – she travelled the world and discovered herself and got to go to bed with Javier Bardem, and then in real life evolved again to go decide that actually she wanted to be married not to him, but to her best female friend. And I don't say that because I want you to secretly fall in love with *this* best female friend.' She pointed at herself as she said that. 'I tried the old vajayjay in a threesome with one of the guys from Blue and his PR and it wasn't for me, but my point is: you deserve to do this YOLO thing. I love this for you! I really, really do.'

She actually didn't let me get a word in edgeways she was so enthusiastic.

And my parents? They didn't technically know. I didn't outright lie to them because I didn't *ever* say: *I am going to Australia on my own.* But I also never told them I was going with Patrick. Freddie knew, though, because I don't wilfully omit information from my baby sister if I can help it – and I'd used it as a bartering system with Carol.

'If you do most of the dog-walking and dog-feeding and dog-cuddling so that Mum and Dad don't have to,' I'd wagered as I'd dropped her off, 'I'll tell you a secret.'

I would have told her anyway, but I needed to ensure she'd help with the dog-sitting as much as possible so that I wouldn't lose any dog-sitting privileges in the future. There'd be repercussions once Mum and Dad found out I was honeymooning with another man. I could hear Mum's voice already, rising to a frustrated high pitch as she wondered about the optics of going away with a man who wasn't Alexander so soon after he'd left me. I knew how her brain worked: she'd worry that people would think I'd been having an affair, and so it was my fault Alexander did a runner. I refused to manage those mental gymnastics on her behalf by quietly slipping away and letting forgiveness set the agenda instead of permission. I was a fully-grown woman, after all. So fully-grown that I was terrified of what would happen on my return, but still.

I was also a bit afraid of what would happen at the airport. I'd told myself that even if Patrick didn't show up, I'd still get on that plane – come hell or high water.

I hoped he did show up, though.

Heathrow teemed with people. Our flight was at just after 1 p.m., getting into Perth at 1 p.m. the following day, but I couldn't figure out if that was 1 p.m. tomorrow UK time, or Australian time. Dad always used to say on holiday: 'Is it today, tomorrow, or yesterday?' If the flight was nineteen hours and Perth was eight hours ahead . . . then that must mean . . .

'G'day, mate!'

Patrick appeared before me. He was wearing a hat with corks dangling all around off the brim, and carrying a stuffed kangaroo.

'Sheila, hold this so I can throw another shrimp on the barbie.'

I took the kangaroo from him. People were staring as they passed – tanned limbs walking to the exit on their way back from vacation, and paler ones headed towards check-in. My mouth was agape. Did I love that he'd showed up this way, or was I mortified? He'd certainly fully embraced the theme. He must have been able to tell that I was taking a beat to process his demonstrable enthusiasm because his face fell a tiny bit.

'Is the accent too much?' he said, using his normal voice. I allowed myself to soften – he was cute when he was checking where the line was.

'I'm afraid so,' I replied, solemnly but with flickering eyes. 'I'm pretty sure that you doing the pretend *Home and Away* accent is as annoying as people doing the posh English accent and saying things about five o'clock afternoon tea with the Queen. Sorry.'

He kept a straight face and volleyed back: 'I normally take my tea with Lizzie at four thirty, actually.'

I jutted my chin at the monstrosity on his head. 'Did you buy the hat especially?'

'Will you think less of me if I did?'

I kept po-faced in response, the pair of us in a comedic stand-off of who would break first. I did actually want him to take it off, but I had to admit it was nice that he was so keen, and also apparently oblivious to the reactions of everyone around us. He only wanted to make me smile, and didn't mind being a plonker to do it. I pulled the hat off his head and tugged it onto my own, adopting a grin and giving him a wave of jazz hands.

'Strewth! You look a million bucks!' he exclaimed, the accent returning.

'The hat can stay,' I replied, wagging a finger at him. 'But the accent has to go.'

'Right you are, ma'am,' he replied in his normal voice, understanding that I meant it. He clapped his hands together and looked around the hall. 'Okay then. So. We're going to Australia.'

'Apparently. But if you want to chicken out . . .'

'Yeah, good prompt actually. Thanks for the exit opportunity.' He pretended to walk away, leaving his suitcase by my side but swishing his arms like a Swiss marching guard.

'Don't make me drink my airport beer alone!' I shrieked after him, and he turned on his heel and yelled, imitating a sergeant major:

'Make it an airport gin and tonic, and I'm sold.'

'You're paying,' I cackled, as he came to retrieve his luggage. 'So you can have whatever you want.'

He took the tickets from me.

'May I?'

I stepped back. I vaguely knew which direction we had to head in but I hadn't figured out which check-in desk yet because I'd been so busy watching everyone and thinking about Boots.

'I need to buy travel plugs,' I said. 'Once we're through.'

'I have four,' he responded, not looking up. 'We can share.' Then he creased the tops of his eyebrows together, looking perplexed. 'Annie, these are business-class seats. Did you know that?'

I took the paper from him and looked. 'How have you reached that conclusion?'

He pointed at the bit that said: BUSINESS CLASS.

'That was my first clue,' he noted.

Business class? I mean. It was nineteen hours to the other

side of the world, so if that was right I wasn't going to be upset by it, but did Alexander's parents really pay for business class? They weren't exactly on the bread line, but business class to Australia must have cost thousands of pounds.

'That feels like a lot,' I observed, and he watched me chew the information over. 'Why don't we go and see what they say at the desk? I'm not saying you're wrong, but also, I am going to owe Fernanda and Charles an *incredibly* large Toblerone if it turns out you're right . . .'

'This way then,' he instructed me. 'Down to twenty-two to twenty-six D.' He pointed a finger at the departure board and I quickly tried to locate what he was alluding to. *Qantas*, the board flashed, *check-in desk 22–26 D*. It turned out my travel buddy was good at airports too.

'After you,' I said, my tummy inexplicably somersaulting as he took my suitcase alongside his own. It was nice that he was a gentleman that way. He was looking after me, and I wasn't too proud to admit to myself that I liked it. I made a mental note of that detail to report back to Mum on the other side. *He looked after me, Mum! He was kind! Stop making me out to be somehow unethical!*

I needed to stop worrying about my bloody mum. Fernanda had loved it when I'd called her and asked if I could use Alexander's ticket for Patrick. I wasn't sure how she'd react, but she wouldn't even let him pay for the name change – she'd been overwhelmingly delighted for me, and didn't even ask how I knew him or if she'd met him before. I tried to squash down the guilt at her generosity, because it made her happy to do this for me, she'd reasoned. Her bigheartedness was humbling.

Patrick trotted ahead, cargo shorts that I'd normally think no man should be seen dead in sitting low on his hips, his collared polo shirt lazily half-tucked in at one side, the muscles in the backs of his arms twitching as he moved.

Over his shoulder he said, 'Stop staring at my bum and hop to it, you.'

'I thought you had tissue under your heel,' I said, too quickly, and he stopped to lift his shoe and check.

'You don't,' I continued. 'Trick of the eye.'

He frowned at me.

'Hop to it,' I repeated, letting myself lead the way.

11

Patrick had been right: we were in business class. At check-in we were ushered into a designated VIP lane so we didn't have to queue with everyone else, and then we got whisked through a different lane at security.

'I normally hate airports,' Patrick had said as he took his shoes off to go through the X-ray machine. 'But this makes it all so easy.'

'I guess money can't buy you happiness, but it can buy you convenience,' I quipped.

'Heck if that isn't right,' he'd agreed.

As we navigated through to the lounge he gasped: 'Aye caramba.' A smiling woman in a uniform of sleek beige skirt and fitted white shirt explained the set-up to us.

'Sit wherever you feel most comfortable,' she told us, waving a manicured hand towards the views of the runway. 'You can take a look at the spa menu and book in for up to two treatments whilst you wait – a back massage and a mini facial, say. Help yourself to the newspapers and magazines, there's a salad bar and treat bar over there, and at the end of the hallway you'll find the locker rooms where you can freshen up.' The whole place was a sumptuous palace of cream hues and suited-up businesspeople. 'Food menus are on each table,' she continued, 'and in each pod. We'll be happy to help with anything else you might need – just flag one of us down.' Patrick and I bobbed our heads in understanding. 'Mr and Mrs Mackenzie,' she said, 'Have a most comfortable morning with us, and a beautiful honeymoon.'

My eyebrows shot up so high on my head that they were practically on the ceiling.

'Oh, we're not—'

I was mortified she'd basically called Patrick my husband, and used Alexander's surname to do it.

Patrick immediately put his hand out to my arm and smiled at me gently as if to say *it's okay. No offence taken.* I just didn't want him to think I *enjoyed* being mistaken for his wife, that's all. I wanted absolutely no suggestion that I was pathetic and wounded enough to think of him as a surrogate spouse. This was my honeymoon, but it didn't feel sad or loser-ish to be there. I hoped that was clear to him. I was feeling pretty strong. Pretty resilient. Barry's Bootcamp had done what I'd needed it to: I was strong. Able. New Annie was engaging her big girl bravery, leaving Alexander's memory behind at the airport, with nothing but new experiences awaiting her on the other side. I was determined to be a phoenix rising from the ashes, leaving thoughts of not being a Mackenzie in the departure lounge.

We settled on a corner booth with views of a fleet of Qantas aircraft sat shining and proud in the autumn sun. I snapped a photo on my phone for Freddie and she instantly replied:

Whoa. Everything looks so fancy! I wish I was coming with you.

I texted back: *I'll bring you back the best presents bug xxxx*

She sent a selfie of herself with the dog and underneath put: *And one for me, too! Love, Carol x*

'I'll never get over how a big metal box can take us anywhere in the world, thousands of metres above the clouds,' Patrick admired. 'It's incredible, isn't it?'

'Yeah,' I agreed. 'It is. I hadn't ever really thought about it, but you're right.'

He shrugged. 'It's incredible how we're here – you and me, sat in the business-class lounge of an international travel company, reunited after all these years.'

'Do your friends think you're crazy for being here?'

'Yes. Don't you think it would be weird if they didn't?'

I shrugged back. 'I don't know what's real, what's incredible, what's crazy or what's normal anymore, to be honest.' I picked up a menu and ran my finger over the edge of the page. 'My friends have asked that I text daily. Just to make sure I'm alive.'

'Oh, that's very thoughtful of them,' Patrick replied, signalling to a waiter. 'They're happy for you to go away with a potential axe murderer but need you to confirm if he's finished you off or not every twenty-four hours. Got it.'

I giggled. 'So they know the exact date and time of my demise I suppose.'

'Would it help if I sent them a text once the job was done?' He addressed the waiter. 'Gin and tonic for me, please,' he said to her. 'Annie?'

'Same,' I said, before changing my mind. 'Oh, actually. Something fizzy? Champagne?'

'Good shout,' Patrick declared. 'Me too. Thanks.'

'Back on point – about the murder and then the text. They'd appreciate that,' I tittered. 'Keeps everyone in the loop that way.'

He grinned, but then got sombre and said: 'Seriously though, do you want some ground rules? Not to sound serious, but it might help for us to set out expectations, or guidelines or whatever.'

It made sense.

'Like what?' I asked.

He considered it. 'For example,' he began, 'I presume these places will only have one bed. As your guest, and as a gentleman, I will obviously take the sofa or the floor wherever that's the case.'

The waiter returned with two flutes of bubbles and set them down.

'Oh, that's kind but . . .'

Patrick held up a hand. 'No,' he insisted. 'That's what makes *me* feel most comfortable. We can always ask for twin beds whenever we check in somewhere, but if that isn't an option then you take the bed and I'll kip elsewhere. It's only right. Keeps things proper, doesn't it.'

'Okay,' I said. 'That's a generous thing to say, and probably sensible too. Can you imagine if you woke up to me spooning you because I thought you were . . .' His name caught in my throat. I didn't want to say it out loud to Patrick. Obviously he knew all about Alexander but I didn't want to sully the trip by there being the shadow of a third wheel present. Plus I wanted the practice of nipping any thought of him in the bud, too. That's another truism my grandmother had always said: *Only water the thoughts you want to grow.* I wanted thoughts of Alexander to wither away to nothing. 'Anyway,' I continued. 'Good ground rule. For both our sakes.'

'Is there anything you want to add? Oh, and cheers by the way.' He held up his glass and tapped the rim of it against my own.

'Cheers,' I echoed. 'Here's to . . .' I thought for a moment. What did I want to cheers to? To being there. To saying yes. To taking a chance. That's what I wanted to celebrate.

'Cheers to the "why not?",' I settled on.

'Cheers to the "why not?"!'

We took tentative sips and the bubbles hit my tongue and fizzed in my mouth. It tasted like freedom.

'We should have a code word,' I said. 'In case we irritate each other.'

'Do you think we will?'

'That's just it, isn't it? Who even knows? We don't actually know each other much at all, so we could . . .'

'True, okay, so . . . what? If we need some space or a time out we say . . .?'

A music video played on the TV just beyond Patrick's head, and as my eye drifted in an attempt to retrieve a clue from the world I immediately found one.

'Mona Lisa,' I stated, pointing. 'Look at her. That's a woman who needs a break. She's not even impressed by Jay-Z and Beyoncé.'

'Excellent code word,' he said and laughed. 'Yes! I can't stand the way you chew your bread so I'm going to go and Mona Lisa.'

'Your inability to check out at the supermarket without talking to the cashier for twenty minutes is really grinding my gears. Let's have a Mona Lisa afternoon.'

'The hacking up of your morning phlegm as my wake-up call is too much. I need breakfast à la Mona Lisa.'

'I do actually do that,' I admitted, sheepishly. Alexander

had always hated it. 'The morning phlegm thing – I'm a very mucous-y person. I blow my nose a lot. I have used tissues in the pocket of every item of clothing I own.'

'I'll remember that when I try to borrow your bikini.'

'I can treat you to a new swimsuit,' I jokingly offered. 'Your hips are narrower than mine. We can get you one of those thong ones with the string.'

'Ooooh!' he trilled. 'Where one little tug of the fabric and poof! Off it comes!'

A thought suddenly hit me. 'I mean, what if that happens?' I asked.

'What?'

'What if you meet somebody, and you want to go and—'

'Take my bikini off with them?'

'The situation could arise. Cute Englishman and all that, getting hit on left and right because of your accent.'

He shook his head. 'No, Annie. I'd be a pretty bad friend if I ditched you on your honeymoon for a shag. I'm not in the market for that. I don't really do relationships. It's a non-issue. These next three weeks are about you, me and the open road, okay?'

I don't do relationships, he'd said. I'd have to follow up on who hurt him. I wanted to know. Who would let a kind, funny gem of a man like Patrick go? I'd bet she still stalked him online or through friends, kicking herself for being so careless. Whoever it was, she'd obviously done a number on him. Any time he'd even come close to mentioning his ex his face clouded over in a sudden storm and his entire body seemed to slump into itself, however momentarily. It happened quickly, but without a doubt it always did.

'Can I pull the jilted bride card and make you steal some

magazines for me?' I asked, trying to keep the mood upbeat. I finished my glass and waved at the waiter for two more.

'They're free, so it doesn't feel I'm being too subversive in undertaking that task,' he replied, standing. 'Any requests?'

'Nothing with a happy couple on the front,' I said. 'And nothing political. Just single girl fluff, please,' I concluded, and as he headed over to the rack it hit me once again: single girl.

Patrick did a mischievous hip wiggle as he headed over to the reading rack, turning to make sure I'd seen him and then winking coquettishly when he concluded that I had. I caught the waiter laughing at him as she delivered our next round, and when she realized I'd seen she commented, 'Laughter is key, isn't it? My boyfriend is just the same.'

She'd disappeared before I could find the words to explain.

12

On the plane, which quite frankly came too soon considering we didn't even have time for one of the spa treatments we'd been told were available in the lounge, Patrick sat opposite me, the yang chair to my yin. As I was sipping on another glass of champagne, he was playing with the buttons that adjusted his chair, sliding it down so that it lay flat with his feet up on the footrest, and then moving it back up into a big cocoon. He pulled his TV out of the armrest.

'This is bigger than my laptop screen,' he announced. And then, 'Annie! They have all the Marvel universe on here!'

A couple across the aisle looked at him with amusement. They had the refined and weary air of people for whom this obviously wasn't a novelty, all polished blazers and loafers and expensive skincare with phenomenal results. But I had to admit, I was in as much awe as he was. I'd never turned left on a plane. For my thirtieth, Alexander upgraded us to Economy Plus when we went to New York, but being at the front with seats that reclined all the way back so we might actually sleep, and nice cabin staff waving about more champagne and hot towels to freshen up, was really, really special. I couldn't believe Fernanda and Charles would be this lavish. I also couldn't believe I almost wasn't going to accept. This was truly already the most memorable trip of my life. What an adventure! My tummy bubbled elatedly. God, it felt good to feel good.

I pulled out my tiny toiletry bag from my hand luggage and produced a wet wipe.

'Taking no chances I see,' Patrick noted, rifling through the reading materials in front of him.

'Even fancy people have germs,' I replied, handing him one.

His eyes widened. 'Annie, it's a seven-course meal they serve up here,' he muttered, absent-mindedly taking the wipe but not looking up. 'And it also says there's a business-class bar?' He moved to look around the cabin. The older man of the couple who had been staring at us piped up, 'It's up there, son. Open after take-off.'

His partner – the younger, blonder man – said, 'Just remember the golden rule: every one drink in the air is worth three on the ground.'

The older man chuckled. 'Martin learned that the hard way, didn't you, darling?'

Martin grinned sheepishly, and we all laughed in understanding.

A bar! In the air! The notion of it was heady. I was going to take all my make-up off and apply my lotions and potions so that my skin could keep hydrated, but if there was a bar . . .

I finished wiping down my seat area and right as I did a cabin crew member offered a gloved hand and said, 'I'll take that for you, ma'am.'

Patrick mouthed at me, 'Ma'am!' and pulled an impressed face that reflected exactly how I felt, too.

The reminder to turn our electronics to flight mode echoed on the announcement speakers above our heads, and I rifled through my bag to find my phone. Jo had texted me, and before I switched it off I opened her message.

Friend, I am totally with you on this if you're happy but I just need to do due diligence and ask: are you sure this is a good idea?

There was a follow-up text.

Unless you're already on the plane together, in which case: have a great holiday!

I smiled. I knew she'd sent her text outside of the group chat. I knew she'd gently check I didn't want to back out.

I have no clue if it's a good idea, I wrote back. *But I think that's kind of the point. I'm sick of doing a risk assessment for every decision in my life. If this is a bad idea, I'm confident I will survive it on account of the fact that I am currently surviving worse!!!*

I chased it with three crying-laughing emojis to make sure she understood I was being happy-go-lucky and not bitchy. She cared, that was all. But I'd explained myself at brunch and wasn't going to waste any more energy trying to get her – or anyone – on board. Not least when the seatbelt sign had just pinged on. I was excited! Excitement was awesome!

I trust your judgement, she wrote back. *Just make sure you send lots of photos! To the group chat, but to me privately too. I'll miss you! Also please forward me Patrick's number in case of emergency. SORRY TO BE A MUM ABOUT IT.*

I'll miss you too, I said, doing as she asked and sending his

details through. She had a point. *I'll bring you back a koala*
xxxxx

It was when we were in the air, somewhere over the southern tip of India, the cabin in darkness and everyone snoozing after yet another meal served up by the crew, that I pulled out my notebook. Patrick and I had been and checked out the bar then, back at our seats, had laughed and chatted until we realized we were probably being quite annoying to everyone around us. We'd synchronized watching a movie together and done a lot of staring at the clouds, too. I couldn't not think about my life when I did that. I couldn't not let the swell of pride rise up in my chest that not only had I survived the past two weeks, but by being on that plane and enjoying it I was actually close to thriving.

I could allow myself that, couldn't I? I could let myself do whatever it took to heal? It helped having somebody with me. I really would have boarded alone if Patrick hadn't shown up, but I was so glad he had. I just felt safe with him. My gut told me we'd travel well together. How long had it been since I'd actually trusted myself? Listened to my gut? It was time to reclaim that. Less head, more heart. More feeling, less over-analysing with thinking.

I flicked through to the first empty page of the notebook and wrote: *Vows to myself.* My pen lingered over the paper and I thought about what I wanted to say. I looked at Patrick, sleeping, his face lit up by an episode of the TV show he'd closed his eyes in front of. I might not have been able to rely on Alexander, but I sure as hell would make certain that I could always rely on myself from now on. Me, myself, and I – that's who I could trust. That was the pledge I'd make, no more second-guessing.

From this day forward, I wrote, smiling, *I will stop trying to be perfect.*

Yes. That was it. Trying to be perfect was impossible, because nobody is ever perfect. No wonder I always fell short.

For better, for worse, I continued, *I will throw caution to the wind.*

Patrick did that, didn't he? Because life was too brief, too quick. He was right. It was.

For richer, for poorer . . . I will say yes to every opportunity that comes my way.

Like Australia. And whatever happened in Australia I'd say yes to as well.

To have and to hold, from this day forth, I commit to my own happiness.

This is my solemn vow.

Forever and ever, Amen.

I drew a box around it, making it all stand out on the page. Yes. I wanted to please myself and try new things and make some mistakes. I'd been holding my breath, seeking approval to exist, taking up as little space as possible and being who everyone else told me I was instead of who I am. And I was over it.

I looked at Patrick again, leaning over to switch off his monitor. We both fell into darkness.

I closed my eyes and slept heavily, dreamlessly, contentedly, only waking up in time for breakfast before landing.

13

In arrivals, a pretty, tuxedoed woman in a driver's hat stood with a huge sign that said ANNIE + GUEST on it.

'Oh,' I said to Patrick as we both clocked her. 'I wasn't expecting anyone to be picking us up. I assumed we'd just hop in a cab . . .'

Patrick yawned lazily. 'I'm very quickly learning to put aside any and all expectations to be honest. You really undersold this honeymoon, you know.'

I knew what he meant.

Fixing my face into a smile I waved at my name. 'I'm Annie,' I said, trying to sound less exhausted than I was. Even in business class, flying to the other side of the world was no mean feat. 'Annie Wiig. Are you for me? Did the hotel send you?'

'They did indeed,' she replied, surprising me with a Cockney accent. 'I'm Bianca. I'll be taking you the three hours down the road to Margaret River.' She stepped in front of Patrick to take the luggage trolley from him. 'This way,' she instructed, chirpily. 'Follow me.'

Patrick whispered: 'You were going to get a cab to take us three hours?'

Thank the Lord the hotel had sent a car.

We had to break into a jog in order to weave behind Bianca through the crowd, her neat ponytail lacing down her back. It was almost 2 p.m. local time and surprisingly mild – I didn't need the cardigan I wore to guard against the aeroplane's chilly air conditioning, and wondered if she was warm in her suit jacket. We stepped outside into blue skies with only the odd cloud and, as I went to move around the back of a stretch limousine to cross the road, Bianca called to me, 'Annie, love? This is us.'

She popped the boot and started to load our bags in.

'Please,' she insisted, waving a hand. 'You get inside and get comfortable.'

'Christ,' Patrick uttered in delight as we shut the door behind us. The whole inside was cream leather, and there was wine and water and snacks, although the thought of any of it made my tummy lurch. I was disorientated and unsure, and mostly just really wanted a shower. The screen dividing the back from the driver's area at the front came down.

'You ready?' asked Bianca.

'Born ready,' said Patrick, and I grinned. I'd never been in a limo before.

'Excellent,' she said. 'Make sure you pick up that envelope and give it a read, won't you? It's got your itinerary in it. Honeymooners, right?'

'No, actually,' I countered.

'The lady here is treating me because of a big award at work,' Patrick supplied.

'Oh really?' Bianca asked, pulling away from the kerb.

'I work for MI6 though, so I can't talk about it I'm afraid. I've already said too much.'

Bianca signalled to get onto the highway. 'I don't believe you for a second,' she hooted. 'If you're James Bond, I'm the guitarist for The Rolling Stones.'

'Oooooh,' said Patrick. 'Can you get us tickets for the next tour?'

She talked our ear off as we settled in, heading south to Margaret River – I think Patrick's chitchat had won her over. The road ran parallel to the coast, so as Bianca babbled away through the speaker system to us we watched endless sea meet endless sky out of the window. She told us she was born in Hackney to a Mexican mother and Aussie father who'd died the week before she'd been born, and that Bianca loved rhubarb gin before it was even a 'thing'.

'Of course,' she continued, 'it's all about the wine out here. At least for the tourists, anyway.'

She told us, apropos of nothing, how she 'takes no BS, but I'm sensitive. Just because I have a big gob, people forget that.' I had an inkling she'd been betrayed by somebody recently, and was trying to reason with herself that it wasn't her fault. She didn't seem to care that we'd stopped much responding beyond a polite 'Oh, really?' or 'Mmmmmm!' sound. I was sleepy and relaxed – it was wonderful stepping off a plane and being whisked to our destination. My brain shut down synapse by synapse, letting everyone else's organization lead the way.

'Anyway, it was my dad who grew up out here,' she yapped, and I watched a seagull surf the air, bobbing down smoothly and then shooting back up. 'And when I turned thirty-three last year I just had this pull to come out and see what he saw when he was a kid. I can't explain, but this feels more like home than anywhere else in the world to me. Some things just feel right, don't they?'

'Not a bad place to feel at home in,' Patrick observed. It really was beautiful. I hadn't even had time to pick up a guide book for the trip, and my knowledge of Australia was limited, pitifully, to having watched *Neighbours* after school growing up. It was greener than I'd assumed, with huge leafy trees swaying contentedly in the breeze, and grassy banks and gardens and parks so luscious and verdant it was like looking through a filter.

'So what's the trip really for?' Bianca asked, when she caught Patrick and I smile at each other through the rear-view mirror. 'You're booked into the best villa in the hotel. It's *really* good. Stunning.'

I didn't even need to look at Patrick to know what his face said. I knew he'd be looking delighted and jiggle his features at the mention of the fanciest villa. He was so excitable. So enthused by every piece of good news – and the good news really was endless, it seemed.

'We're here to celebrate the very essence of being alive,' Patrick said to her, his voice sing-song and happy.

He made Bianca laugh almost as much as he did me. 'Aren't you just full of the happiness of spring?' she giggled. She looked between us in the rear-view again. 'It's nice to see people so content.'

'Only way to be,' Patrick replied. 'Isn't that right, Annie?'

I shook my head at him teasingly and went back to looking out of the window. Australia. Half a world and a universe away.

'I'll get the truth out of you sooner or later,' Bianca warned. 'MI6 my arse. You two have got a story. I just know you have.'

* * *

I couldn't believe the hotel. Bianca had gently woken us as we rounded off up the private lane, and twilight set in making everything a dusty pink. I looked at the car's clock up front: because we'd stopped off halfway to stretch our legs, it was now just after six. The clouds lit up from behind and reflected in the lakes either side of the road perfectly so that it was as if we were gliding through the sky itself. Up ahead was a grand lodge made of lightly coloured stone, surrounded by lavish gardens with plants that looked like they'd had their saturation turned up: purples and oranges and blues and pinks in their full brightness, an exotic fair for the senses. The lodge had a huge wrap-around porch where sets of guests sat out with their drinks and snacks, and a firepit burned just behind it, where more couples sat on reclining wooden chairs, blankets splayed across their knees. Two perfect white helicopters waited in the distance, and I was sure I saw a peacock dragging its feathers behind her over in the field, too. It was astounding. As we got out of the limo and took it all in, I couldn't believe I was there. We'd pulled up in paradise.

'It's not bad, is it?' Bianca said. 'You just wait until you see your villa.'

14

'Okay, listen to this,' Patrick said, reading from the pamphlet. We'd been shown to our cottage out towards the edge of the compound, driven there on a little golf cart to save our legs from the tiny pedestrianized pathways that snaked through the grounds. The first thing Patrick had said when we'd opened the door was that if I was getting Fernanda and Charles a giant Toblerone, he was going to gift them a kidney. I made a mental note to call them as soon as it was morning back home – although words wouldn't be enough to express my thanks.

'Postcard-perfect shorelines,' he read. 'White sand beaches. Towering forests. As far as God-given beauty goes, Western Australia's Margaret River region hits the jackpot . . .'

'Oh my God,' I murmured under my breath. 'All of this is for us, Patrick. Wow.'

Everything inside was glass and birch wood, meaning the whole place filled with the last of the light and the inside merged with the outside, as if there was no distinction between the two. A huge central seating area with plush, biscuity sofas was sunken into the middle on three sides, and when I went over to the balcony door I saw that you could slide it all the way across so that the whole back was entirely open. Birds sang and some sort of exotic-sounding creature issued a soft cooing sound, and I crept through the rest of the place with my jaw slack.

It had three bedrooms, which was a relief. Unexpected for a honeymoon but great for a holiday with a guy I used to go to drama camp with. I figured it was normally used for whole families. We checked in solely under my name at reception, and I remembered that Bianca's sign had only my name on it too. Alexander's parents must have given strict instructions for that, and I was so grateful. They hadn't given any feedback when I'd given them Patrick's details, other than Fernanda saying, 'I'm so glad you changed your mind, darling. I think this will be really, really good for you.' After the faux pas in the departure lounge I really wanted to make sure we avoided any further Mr and Mrs mishaps – and so far, so good.

'Did you know about all this?' Patrick asked as I went back through to where he was lying on his stomach across the big sofa. 'We're right in the middle of the food and drink scene here, and Bianca was right – it's where literally *world-class* wine is made.'

'Oh, actually, that does sound familiar,' I acknowledged. I had vague recollections of talking to Alexander's mum about the honeymoon ages ago, but mostly they'd kept the details of it as a surprise for us. Fernanda had said that as Alexander and I had planned everything else down to a 'T', we'd be grateful somebody else organized the honeymoon once we were on it, and that all I needed to do was trust her. This wasn't how I'd imagined experiencing it, but I had to hand it to them – this was dreamlike in every sense of the word.

'There's art galleries and every Saturday there's the

Margaret River Farmers' Market. Oh. I guess we missed that this week, but will we still be here for it next week?'

I considered it. 'I think so? We're here six nights before we go to Sydney.'

'What day is it today?'

'It's definitely one ending in "y",' I joked. I was knackered, and I literally didn't have a clue.

He beamed at me, amused. 'I feel the same. Are you tired? Could you eat?'

'I can *always* eat. But I can also feel a thin layer of sweat across my whole body and I know that if I don't take care of it immediately, it will definitely result in some sort of rash. Which sounds gross, but is nonetheless true.'

'Room service? My treat? It's basically night-time now anyway, so we could order food, shower as we wait for it to come, get a good night's sleep with full bellies and then be Margaret River ready tomorrow?'

I sighed, happy that our vibe was so similar. 'Yes,' I said. 'THAT is a perfect plan. There are three rooms, by the way. So that's good.'

'Cool. You get first pick. I'll unpack in a minute. This itinerary they've sorted out is blowing my mind.'

I woke up brand-new. Patrick was awake before I was and he'd already spoken to Bianca, who'd said she thought that for our first day she should drive us out to the beach. Apparently she was our designated driver for the week we were on the west coast, before we flew over east to Sydney. I'd texted the Core Four: *We have a limo driver!* and received a slew of jealous emoji responses in reply.

'Ready, ready, chicken jelly?' Patrick shouted from his bedroom.

Ready, ready chicken jelly?

'I beg your pardon?' I yelled back. 'What . . . are you even saying?'

He appeared at the doorway in a pair of pressed navy shorts, Birkenstocks and a rumpled Oxford shirt in a blue check. His hair was ruffled and unkempt, twenty-four hours' worth of stubble lending him a dishevelled aura that suited him, like he was officially in off-duty mode. In one hand he had a beach towel, in the other a tote bag weighed down with what I could tell, from the hard corner poking through the fabric, was a book.

'My mum – Mama Jess, to my friends – used to say it when we were kids.' He shrugged. 'I don't think I have ever said it as an adult, except for randomly just now.'

'What's your dad's name?'

'Mark.'

'Jess and Mark. What a son they've raised.'

He looked at me, then, for the first time. He sort of blinked in rapid succession and I swear I could see him recalibrating his brain, a computer that needed a moment to open a new tab because it already had so many other tabs on the go. I wondered if we were destined to keep dipping in and out of formality for the whole trip, losing ourselves and then pulling back as we realized there was actually still so much we didn't know about the other. I couldn't tell which camp he was currently in. I wanted to skip this part the getting comfortable with each other bit – and just be cool. I supposed that's the problem with bringing a virtual stranger on holiday with you – there was so much unknown ground. I wanted to fast-forward into the comfort of friendship.

'You look pretty,' he told me. I flared my nostrils and made myself go cross-eyed.

123

'Fanks,' I slurred, self-consciously. There was something about how his pupils had dilated that made an innocent compliment feel more loaded than it was. It made my skin tingle.

There was a beat where we looked at each other awkwardly and he said, 'Do you have sun cream? I forgot mine.'

'I do,' I replied, trying to switch up the mood. 'To the beach! Yee-haw!'

'To the beach!' he echoed, but I was timid walking ahead of him. I hoped I looked okay. He'd called me pretty and I wanted, puzzlingly, to do that compliment justice, even if I'd been terrible at accepting it. I'd put on a bit of waterproof mascara but that was it, because there's no point getting dolled up for the beach. I figured he'd seen me looking worse at bootcamp, and even though I'd lingered over my make-up bag in the bathroom and had briefly considered making more of an effort, ultimately I wasn't trying to impress anyone. Not that I only wear lipstick to impress men, obviously. Mum would think I was lazy for being so low-key, but it wasn't a beauty pageant. And anyway, make-up or not, Patrick had seemed to mean it when he said I looked nice.

I pulled at the strap of my bikini and smoothed out the fabric of my jean shorts. When I half-turned to hold the door for him, I caught him looking in the hallway mirror and patting down his hair with his free hand, like a little boy on picture day. It was a tiny gesture of self-doubt at odds with his outward confidence.

'After you,' I said, deliberately smiling widely like a good, friendly mate. The door clicked closed behind us.

The beach had mammoth grassy banks and winding narrow roads that led to miles and miles of curved picture-perfect white sand. The water was the colour you choose when finger painting as a child: light blue with crisp white breaks where the waves crash in, although it was calm further out. Trees and sand dunes lined the banks behind us as we walked down to the shore, deciding where to set ourselves up. Bianca honked her horn as she drove off. Being hand-delivered to the beach by a limo was the most glamorous thing I'd ever do in my life.

'Here?' I said, wanting to throw down a blanket and rush out to put my feet in the water. Patrick placed the picnic hamper the hotel had packed for us on the sand, sighed cheerfully, and closed his eyes.

'What's that song about sand dunes and salty air? I've got it playing in my head.'

'Oh yeah,' I said, unloading sunscreen and my book from my bag. 'I know the one.' I inhaled deeply and closed my eyes too. All I could hear was the waves, and all I could feel was the warmth of the sun on my face. Glorious. Needed. Perfect.

'Do you mind?'

I opened my eyes and Patrick was waving the bottle of sun cream at me.

'My shoulders, you see. They burn.'

I took it from him. 'Come here then,' I said.

I squeezed some into my hand and he watched me before I signalled with my head for him to turn around. I rubbed the lotion between my hands so it wasn't too cold on his skin, and then placed my palms on the top of his shoulders. They were firm, rippling beneath my touch as I went from the tops of his arms to the base of his neck in slow, long sweeps. He was firm and toned – all those bootcamp classes had made sure of it. It got easier to glide over his skin as the lotion spread, soaking in to make it shimmer.

'Should I . . .?' I patted further down his back.

'Please,' he replied. 'Go for it. Everywhere you dare.'

He was so smooth to the touch, and everything tensed as he bent over slightly so the cream didn't drip off his skin. I rubbed, oiling him, not sure how close to I should get to the top of the patterned swim shorts sat low on his hips, perching just above the slight arch to his arse. As I got to the base of his back and smoothed the cream out towards his front, circling around to his belly button to get the excess off my hands, he suddenly coughed, embarrassed, and said, 'Right-o, think you're done there, thank you. I'm going in now.' He didn't turn around before abruptly walking the short distance to the shore and stopping to stand at the water's edge. He shook his leg a bit, as if he was expelling a bad feeling.

I watched him wade into the water until it came up to his knees. I could tell it wasn't exactly warm, but he wasn't putting up a fight. I spread cream over all the parts of my own body I could reach and decided to let it soak in before I went down to the water myself, enjoying watching Patrick's head bob out in the distance instead. It was so wonderful just to sit and see the sand blow with the breeze. Big open water feels so relaxing. I could have stared at the horizon forever, until I was in a trance. In fact, whether it was delayed jet lag or the undeniable pull of sun and lotion and sand, eventually I lay back and closed my eyes, not thinking of very much at all.

15

'Hey,' I said, my sleep disturbed who knew how much longer later. 'Something's happening.'

Through sluggish eyes I'd noticed a group of people gathering down by the dock. The beach was so lazy and languid when we arrived – Bianca had said this was the part with the fewest people, which is how we'd decided on it – so now the sudden activity was jarring.

'Patrick?'

He was asleep beside me on his front, snoring heavily. He looked so peaceful and, for a second, just like the teenager I used to know – but I was worried something bad was happening so persevered with waking him.

'Mmmmm?'

I pointed. 'I think there's a shark or something. I don't know. Look.'

Patrick rolled over and propped himself up on an elbow, his gaze dreamily following where my finger was pointing and scanning what was happening.

'Stingrays,' he concluded. 'See the black thing in the water?

They come here.' He rubbed his eyes with one hand and searched for his sunglasses. 'I read about it. Come on, let's go and look.'

As we approached I could see a shadow floating on the sea's surface.

'Aren't they dangerous?' I asked.

'Stingrays? Nah.'

'Didn't Steve Irwin die from a stingray . . .?'

A woman with a blue mohawk and septum ring overheard me.

'He was pierced through the chest by a stingray barb. Freak accident. These fellas won't hurt you, though. We're lucky to catch them.'

'That's dreadful. Wow.'

The man next to her, also with a matching blue mohawk, only slightly longer and brighter, volunteered: 'These lads are here to feed and look good, ain't that right, guys?'

The thin black ripple in the water must have been as long as me, and half as wide. It was so strange to look at, like a black bin bag floating just below the surface, gleaming and glassy. It was slow, in complete control of itself whilst also seemingly at the whim of the current. It was so serene. I was enthralled.

'What do they eat?' I asked the woman, and then I felt silly for assuming she was some sort of stingray expert. The man spoke for her.

'Crustaceans, mostly. The stingray senses the electrical current in their prey's muscles and nerves, and then the prey is sucked into the mouth and crushed. The flesh is swallowed and the shell fragments get expelled back into the sea through the slits in their gills. As long as we don't disturb them, we're fine. You make sure to keep your distance, all right?'

'Paul,' the woman said to him, rolling her eyes teasingly.

'You just told her that as if I wasn't the one who explained it all to you.'

'Thank you both for sharing your collective knowledge,' said Patrick, charismatically. 'It's kind of beautiful to look at, isn't it?'

'You tourists?' the woman asked.

I nodded. 'Here for the week.'

'It's unusual to see these so soon. The water is clear enough in the summer but we're still early, really.'

Patrick draped his arm over my shoulder as we huddled in close to watch the strange beast head into deeper water. I could feel the warmth of him spreading across me, his fingers gently curling around the top of my arm. The weight of a person's touch, of a man's touch, was something I hadn't experienced in weeks. I didn't dare move once I'd realized Patrick was there. I didn't want any sudden movements to scare him off, or worse, to hurt me. He was my human stingray, and I was his observer. It was heady, being so close to someone.

'Isn't it extraordinary?' He sighed. 'I'm so glad we got to see this.'

He dropped his arm as I looked at him to smile, and for a moment I thought I'd ruined it, that I'd spoiled the moment. But then the tips of his fingers brushed against the tips of mine and he purred, 'Come on, let's see what's in that hamper the lodge sent us with.'

As he held on to my wrist and led the way back up to our spot, the oddest thought popped into my mind. I thought: *Am I imagining this?*

The thing was, I couldn't quite articulate what 'this' was.

Around five o'clock in the afternoon is my favourite time on a beach. It's when you're warm to the touch and salty and everything moves slowly, like a Jack Johnson song about sepia-toned photographs. It's just heaven. We were lying side by side on the hotel beach blanket, a discarded beer can at each of our feet, some kids playing frisbee within earshot, screeching with glee before being hushed by their father. I woke up from another peaceful doze to their sound right as Patrick did.

'Hey,' he said, sleepily.

'Hey,' I replied.

We were half a foot apart as we woke up, our eyes locking. I was aware of the rise and fall of my chest, his proximity, as the sun lowered in the sky.

'Penny for your thoughts.'

I looked away to just over his shoulder, but it was nicer to be looking at him. We were both on our fronts, as if we'd woken up in bed together, not on a beach.

'I'm so relaxed,' I said, and I realized my voice had dropped. I wasn't whispering, but he was so close to me that I didn't need to make an effort to be heard.

'Yeah,' he hummed. There was a pause. 'I like this feeling.'

'The holiday feeling?'

'After a beer, on the sand, the sun going down. There's nowhere else I'd rather be. It's at this time of day, beside the ocean, that time suspends itself doesn't it?'

'Yeah,' I agreed. I closed my eyes again and took a deep, tranquil breath.

'You seem happy. It's nice to see.'

I didn't open my eyes to respond. 'I am,' I said, without thinking, and that forced me to turn properly to look at him. I'd surprised myself. 'Crikey,' I said, with more vim. 'I actually think I am. I'm properly happy for the first time since everything happened.'

He turned over and sat up to open another couple of beers, handing me one before pulling his knees up beside him and coiling his arms around them. I mirrored him and did the same, still close.

Neither of us spoke.

We looked at the water.

I was far away from my actual life, but closer to my real self than I been in ages. I didn't even know where my phone was. No emails, no calls or texts. No need to document what was happening, finding a great angle for a photo to upload later – Patrick had his camera for memories. I hadn't thought about work, and as easily as thoughts of my parents entered my head they left again. I missed Freddie, but I always missed Freddie, even when she was right beside me.

Right now, crucially, I did not miss Alexander. I wouldn't have been doing this with him. He wouldn't have lain out on a blanket beside me, reading and sleeping and chatting. He'd have been off on the water doing extreme sports, leaving me to take videos of him on land. Being with Alexander would have been lonely, but being with Patrick I was part of something. He was there with me – *actually there*. He'd made me a sandwich from the hamper and read me a passage from his book that he'd thought was funny. He'd listened when I talked about the merits of grated cheddar versus sliced in a sandwich, eventually agreeing with me and telling me he'd once heard a very good poem about a cheese and pickle sandwich that we'd have to look up when we got back to the lodge.

I studied his profile. He had this strong, classical nose and a wide smile, his neck a gentle sloping curve into his expansive shoulders. His blond eyelashes were longer than I'd first realized, and he had a way of moving that was graceful but solid, almost like a dancer. It was fact: he was undeniably gorgeous. I hadn't fully seen that, before. Maybe it was getting to know him made him more attractive as time went on.

'You okay?' he asked, without looking at me.

I dragged my eyes back to the horizon.

'Yeah,' I said. 'Of course.'

We drank our beer.

16

When we got back to the lodge there was a tiny smear of copper inside my swimsuit gusset. My period had arrived. Whatever stress my body had been holding on to, she was finally starting to let go.

'Annie? Your phone is ringing!'

I froze from my place on the toilet, and then made an instinctive decision to pull up my bottoms and deal with my period once I'd handled the call. It could only have been somebody from home. I could hear Patrick's footsteps approaching and so flushed the loo and shoved my hands under the tap as a gesture of hygiene.

'Freddie!' I said, after sliding the button across the screen to answer. 'Hey you!'

I could immediately tell something wasn't right. She was wearing her glasses and her face was blotchy and red, her voice wavering.

'I can't find Carol!' she wailed. 'I'm really, really sorry. I let her off the lead at the park and I was on my phone googling Hamelin Bay like you told me to and when I looked up

I couldn't see her, and she didn't come back when I was shouting for her!' She pulled a tissue apart in her hands, shredding it with worry. I walked with the phone to the breakfast bar and propped it up against a glass bottle of water.

'Okay,' I said, grappling to keep my voice neutral. I could cry when she hung up, if I needed to, but right now my sister needed me to be strong. 'Froogle, that's okay.'

She wiped at her eyes with her sleeve.

'Mum said I shouldn't tell you because I'll spoil your holiday but we've been looking and looking and now I don't know what to do and nobody will help me! They just say she'll turn up!'

Patrick hovered off-camera, shirtless and in bare feet. Concern radiated from him. My heart raced and my skin prickled. The dog was gone?

'That's true though, Froogle.' It was taking a lot to sound calmer than I was. 'I know it's scary, but if you've looked everywhere then maybe she's at somebody's house because they found her. She's been chipped, so if she gets taken to a vet they'll be able to read her information and get in touch with me, okay? This isn't your fault.'

'Yes it is!' she said, and this time she really cried. Freddie was confident and clever, but she held herself to the same impossibly high standards that I did – those set by Mum. Seeing her so worked up was heartbreaking, and my own eyes stung with tears.

'It's not, Freddie.'

'I'm really sorry!'

'It could have happened to anyone. It could have happened when she was out with me, even.'

It was awful seeing her upset, and nothing I said seemed

to console her. If anything, me being kind seemed to make it worse – at least if I yelled she could yell back.

Patrick motioned for permission to come and talk. I nodded helplessly.

'Hey,' he said, looping his arm onto the back of my chair so we could both fit in frame. 'I'm Patrick. I'm your sister's friend.'

Freddie waved sadly down the phone.

'Listen. I can tell that you're really upset. It must feel scary to be in charge of something for Annie and then feel like you're letting her down. Is that right?'

Freddie dipped her head up and down. 'Yeah,' she agreed in a small voice. 'And I'm scared for Carol.'

Patrick mirrored her body language. 'A few years ago my dog got lost in the park as well,' he offered.

Freddie eyed him suspiciously. 'Are you just saying that to make me feel better?' she asked.

'No. I don't think lying to you would be a very good first impression to make, would it?'

Freddie softened, shaking her head. 'And what did you do?'

'It was really unlike him. It had never happened before. He was a little white West Highland terrier called Maktub, and all I did was buy an ice cream from the truck parked nearby. It took me thirty seconds, if that. He'd always been really good at trotting off and then coming back. I even kept turning around to make sure he was there. But then suddenly he wasn't. I didn't even get to eat my ice cream because I was so worried. I looked for him everywhere, and asked everyone in the park if they'd seen him.'

Freddie's eyes had grown wide and curious, but she'd stopped crying. 'Did you find him?'

'Not exactly.'

She took a breath, preparing herself to dislike what came next.

'He found me,' Patrick pressed on. 'He was gone for two whole days, and then on the third day I heard a bark at the front door and there he was, just chilling out, on his own. I tried asking him where he'd been, but he was pretty tired.'

Freddie seemed to understand what he was saying.

'We'll find Carol,' I said, sensing that she was able to actually understand me now she'd relaxed. I'd relaxed too – what Patrick had said had soothed me into submission as well.

'I'll go out again now, Annie-Doo. She must be out there somewhere. Dad said he'll come too, once he's had his cup of tea.'

'Perfect.'

'Okay.'

'I love you.'

Patrick waved goodbye. 'Good luck, Freddie!' he said. 'Try to think like a dog!'

She smiled and then caught herself, as if she didn't want to be seen as anything other than devastated.

Once we'd rung off I said, 'That was very level-headed of you. Thank you.'

Patrick smiled. 'Are you okay? Are you worried?'

'I mean, obviously. But there's nothing I can do from here, is there? She's a good dog. I just hope she doesn't try to cross any roads or anything. Surely somebody would see a little thing on her own and look at her dog tag? Or if she didn't have her collar, they really would take her to the vet's?'

'Exactly,' he agreed. And then: 'Hug?'

'Okay.'

Patrick wrapped his thick, strong arms around me and rested his chin on the top of my head as I pressed my cheek

136

into his bare chest. He was warm from the sun, and smelt like coconut. He rubbed my back and I sent a little prayer up to the doggy gods to keep Carol safe, and get her home as soon as possible.

'Carol will come back to you,' he said sympathetically. 'Like Maktub.'

'I've never heard that name before,' I replied. 'Maktub.'

'It's not really a name,' he explained. 'It's a saying. It's Arabic for *it is written*. Sort of a nod to fate. Everything was meant to happen because we were always supposed to be here,' he said. 'It was all designed to lead us up to this precise moment.'

'Maktub,' I repeated again, still pulled into his chest. 'I like that. Do you still have him?'

'Jess and Mark have him, now. They're retired, so he gets better company with them.'

'Oh,' I said.

'Keep the faith, okay?'

I tugged away from the hug, believing that if Patrick said Carol would be all right, she would be. He dipped to kiss my cheek, doing it with such tenderness that I instinctively reached up to touch where his lips had been. I held my hand there, suspended, before letting my fingers drift back down to my side. He'd already turned away from me to grab a piece of fruit from the fruit bowl we'd been gifted, as if what he'd done was nothing.

It is written, I thought, as he bit into an apple, watching the way his hand wrapped around it, how a tiny speck of juice landed on his bottom lip.

It took me ages to get to sleep that night. I lay in the dark replaying the day. I thought about the way Patrick wore his checked shirt with two buttons undone on the way to the beach, but with three buttons undone on the way home, a sliver of toned stomach on show through the gap. I tried to remember how close I'd stood to him when I'd put suntan lotion on his back. Had I been an arm's length away? Or had I been the measure of my own breath, close enough to feel the rise and fall of his body as he inhaled and exhaled?

I'd liked it when he'd told me I looked pretty, but then he'd instantly looked like he regretted saying it, as if he'd already changed his mind at the trick of the light that had made him think so. If I'd have stood on the shore looking at stingrays with Freddie, I might have put my arm around her, but I couldn't think of another person I'd feel that comfortable with. I'd had to lean in close when he'd read me the paragraph from his book. Before we'd gone to bed he'd found me the poem he'd promised he'd look up, and it was as good as he'd said.

I played all of it over and over in my head, eventually grabbing my phone to message the Core Four.

Greetings from Aus! I typed. *Just to say all is good here. Patrick a gentleman, sun unseasonably warm, period has finally come. Carol is missing though, so bit worried about that. Freddie hunting her down. Taking photos analogue so don't use phone a lot – loads to show you though! Xxxx*

I texted Freddie, too, just to say, *I love you, Frou. Try not to worry!*

When I lay back down I thought I'd toss and turn about the dog, but my mind went straight back to Patrick's shoulders as he'd propped himself up on the towel that afternoon, the dusting of sand stuck to the backs of his firm, glistening biceps, sweat pooling at the back of his neck as he'd looked out to sea and said there was nowhere else he'd rather be.

17

'So, apparently the cabernet sauvignons and chardonnays are consistently rated amongst the region's best, and we get a private tasting in Eric's Room, named after the estate founded by Eric Smith.'

I'd woken up to find Patrick sprawled out in his boxers and an open dressing gown on the sofa, sunlight streaming in where he'd unpeeled the patio doors so that the rustle of the breeze in the trees and soft birdsong was our soundtrack. I thought I was good at getting up early, but apparently he was even better.

'Hmmmm,' I said, a plate of creamy eggs and smoked salmon in my lap. I reached for the jug of orange juice. 'Do you think Eric will mind that I'm an ABC girl?'

'ABC?'

'Anything But Chardonnay.'

'Ha! Let's wait to see the look on his face, then. Well. Maybe not *his*. But it does say sommelier-led tastings featuring limited-release wines, so it's going to be somebody who knows what's up.'

I spooned the last of the eggs royale into my mouth.

'I wear a nice dress to a winery, right? That's a thing people do?' I had visions of flouncing through vineyards in something cotton and floral.

'Personally, I couldn't give a hoot what you wear – I do know you're not supposed to wear perfume or cologne for wine tasting though. Something about interfering smells. Oh, and pack your bathing suit because fifteen minutes away is Surfers Point, and this says we can admire the deep-blue might and majesty of the Indian Ocean.' He did a posh voice to say that, like a butler announcing dinner.

'I still can't believe we're here,' I said, for what must have been an annoying millionth time.

'It's beautiful, isn't it? They must have really liked you to make sure you still came all this way.'

I'd texted Fernanda as we'd waited for breakfast, sending a photo of the beach yesterday and telling her 'thank you' didn't seem enough. I almost couldn't think about it too much, that they'd insisted I come, because the kindness of it was overwhelming.

Patrick stood up and stretched dramatically, and my eyes automatically fell to his waistband and the tiny tuft of hair running from his belly button down to . . .

He saw me looking and wrapped his gown around him, hurriedly. I forced my eyes back up to his face as if my gaze had lingered there purely by chance, which . . . it had, hadn't it? He was a man, standing in front of me in his underwear. I'd forgotten myself for a second, that was all.

'Yeah,' I said. 'They did like me. Do? I don't know if I have to talk about them in the past tense because they're no longer my in-laws, or if I get to stay in touch forever, which, obviously I'd like. Especially after all this.'

'You don't have to figure that all out just now,' he soothed. He put the pamphlet he'd been reading on the coffee table and began to head for his room.

'I really liked his mum,' I said, getting up myself. 'People joke about hating their mothers-in-law, don't they, but I liked her. I liked spending time with her. His dad was a bit iffy, but mostly because he was just really old. Eighty-something. Second marriage for him. She dotes on him though, even if she is more of a carer than a wife, I think.'

He stopped and turned. 'I guess that's what you sign up for in marriage.'

''Til death do us part can feel a long time when you're with somebody like that though,' I said, before a hand flew up to my mouth. 'I didn't mean that,' I explained. 'Oh, that was an awful thing to say. Especially after they've been so wonderful! God, please don't think I really think that. I don't know where that came from!'

'It's okay,' Patrick insisted. 'I knew what you meant.' He looked at me, taking in what was surely a look of horror. 'Seriously.'

'It's not. I need to think before I speak.'

He walked over and put a hand on my arm. 'Annie, don't police yourself for me. You shouldn't police yourself for anyone.' His touch was sturdy and earnest. I felt horrible.

I wanted to make a joke about my mother and how I was raised to police myself for her, but stopped myself. When I pushed myself at school, teachers would note in my reports how hard I could be on myself, and on the way back from parents' evening once Mum had said, plainly, 'I wish the results of her being so hard on herself were a little better.' I wasn't supposed to hear. She thought I was too far ahead of her and Dad to eavesdrop, but I wasn't. I heard Dad try to pacify her, saying something about letting me grow in my own time, but I could tell by the sharp hushed tone of her reply that she didn't like that idea. I was raised to constantly monitor myself, so that I could continue striving to be better than I was.

'Let's get ready,' I said, switching up my voice to a Julie Andrews-esque song. 'Leave in say, half an hour?'

'I'll call down to reception to let Bianca know,' he replied. 'And seriously, don't give what you just said another thought. I won't.'

The wine tasting was exactly as the movie in my head had played it: huge, cavernous rooms underground with oak barrels and special rooms where the wine had to lie at a specific angle, at a specific temperature. I'd worn a calf-length floral cotton dress that tied at the waist and puffed out at the sleeves, which were short because Bianca had advised us that wearing long sleeves could get in the way of the tastings. My make-up was natural-looking with tinted pink lips, and I'd pulled my hair back at Bianca's behest, too – she said I'd be thankful of that advice when it came to spitting. I felt cute. It was fun to be dressed up.

Patrick spoke to everyone, asking questions and making friends, and it was true that we must have looked as though we were together as we giggled and made jokes and pointed out cool things to each other, but I didn't care. Out touring the expansive vineyards, Australian spring sun warming my bones, there was only right now, and right now was lovely, as it happened. If Patrick worried that everyone else on the tour thought we were a couple he didn't show it, steering me from tasting station to tasting station with a light hand on the small of my back or making faces across the room to make me grin impishly when we were apart. In the ebb and flow of getting to know each other, today we were flowing.

The vineyard was just as sumptuous as the hotel. I understood, now, why people raved about their honeymoon for years after it happened. Everything was premium, an upgraded version of what you might normally allow yourself. Whatever packages my non-in-laws had signed us up for, the clear truth was that it was the best, or the top, the most superlative version of any one thing. We sat outside on a private terrace, several wooden boards of charcuterie and cheese in front of us, and a row of glasses and bottles as we continued to sample more of what the winery had to offer. Back in the cave they'd taught us how to swirl our glasses, take a sniff, swish and then spit. The trick was, apparently, to use quite a bit of force when spitting so that it didn't dribble down your chin – but now we were alone we didn't bother with that part, and instead tucked in, swallowing in big, unabashed gulps.

'I could ogle this view all day,' I said, as Patrick topped up my glass with an SSB – a sauvignon and semillon blend.

'I *have* been told I'm quite handsome.' He smirked.

'Ha-ha.'

The chairs had been arranged side by side so that we could both look out at the vista: rows of grapes pleasingly uniform as far as the eye could see, set against a backdrop of undulating hills. Taking it all in, I could feel my breathing getting deeper. London continued to fade away in my mind – in less than another twenty-four hours it wouldn't even exist. Alexander wouldn't exist, my aching heart wouldn't exist, my mother's constant criticisms wouldn't exist. There was only the view and the wine, and it was everything I needed.

'My shoulders have dropped about six inches overnight,' I said, taking another mouthful of the wine. I was holding the glass by the stem, like they'd taught us, and had spun the liquid around the glass to help increase the oxygen in it to release the flavours. I hadn't even realized I'd been doing it until Patrick pointed it out – I was practically a sommelier myself after four hours in the caves. 'They were all bunched up around my ears from the stress, but now . . .'

'But now you've had a bottle of wine?'

'I'm not drunk!'

'Liar.'

'I'm not!' I insisted. 'I'm trying to be deep and meaningful here if you don't mind. I know you're Mr "In The Moment" but for some of us this is quite the novelty, *thankyouverymuch*.'

'It is a skill I've worked hard on. I appreciate you noticing.'

I stuck my nose into the rim of my glass and inhaled deeply. 'Do you think I'd get yelled at if I put a cube of ice in this?'

'Ice? You savage.'

We stared at the view some more.

'How *did* you get so capable of being in the moment?' I asked after a while. 'You're so unafraid and enthusiastic. It's nice to be around. I wish I could be more like you, really.'

'Hmmm,' he replied, noncommittally. He sounded uncomfortable at the compliment, which was strange because since we'd been hanging out Patrick never seemed uncomfortable. 'Life's short.'

'But is it?' I mused. 'Or is that one of those things we half believe, when the reality is that life is actually very, very long, and so we need to be responsible and plan things and take it all seriously? Because that's what I was always taught.'

Patrick considered what I'd said.

'Look,' he started, and I hated how my body sensed a big revelation was coming before my mind did. Was I bugging him? Had he already had enough of my neurotic and tightly wound sense of self? I couldn't blame him if he had. He-who-I-was-trying-not-to-name wasn't enamoured by those parts of me either. 'There won't ever be a good time to tell you this, but you should know . . .'

Bugger.

Bugger.

Bugger.

He was going to tell me being here with me was a ghastly mistake and that he wanted to part ways, wasn't he? Officially only Day Two and he was going to call Mona Lisa.

'Annie, I'm a widower.'

His eyes were sorrowful, his face hung in anticipation of how I would respond. My stomach sank for him. Oh poor, poor Patrick. Jesus. It occurred to me that what I said next was really important. I was only going to get one chance to say the right thing, but wow. I'd never known somebody my age whose spouse had died. What *was* the right thing to say? He'd said he'd had his heart broken but I never for one second thought he'd been separated from the woman he loved through *death*.

'Patrick. I am so, so sorry,' I said, finally, shaking myself back into the conversation. 'That's . . . so horrible. I had no idea.'

'I didn't mean to keep it as a secret,' he deliberated. 'But, it's a funny one. When do you tell people? Because once you do, they act differently. They tiptoe around you, or look at you the way you're looking at me right now.'

I scrunched up my nose. 'Sorry.'

'It's okay. Death is a head-screwer. People worry it's catching, I think. That if my wife died, maybe theirs could too.'

I shook my head. 'That's not it,' I said. 'People don't think that.'

Patrick helped himself to more wine, then put the last of the bottle into my glass and played with the toothpicks meant for the olives.

'How much do you want to talk about it?' I asked. 'And do we need to move to something stronger? Straight shots, maybe? Snorting tequila from each other's belly buttons?'

He gave me a half-smile. 'Nothing stronger. The wine is good. Although I am in danger of being slightly tipsy.'

'Go steady,' I said. 'Last time we got drunk we hatched this little plan, and look at you now. Halfway around the world with *me*.'

Patrick looked down at the toothpick he was flipping between his fingers. 'We were married almost three years,' he continued, and I could tell he'd really been building up to telling me. I moved my chair so that instead of facing outward I could be opposite him, resting my elbows on the table and giving him my fullest attention. 'I loved her very much. She died two years ago, and it's the worst thing I've ever lived through. Dreadful. And it was so dreadful I decided that I could either feel miserable for the next seventy years or somehow try to enjoy myself, as a sort of tribute to her. Mala. Her name was Mala. She was twenty-seven when she died, and . . .'

'That's too young,' I sympathized. 'I'm so sorry.'

'She was the most annoying person you've ever met,' he remarked, his eyes contemplative and wistful. 'She was bossy and headstrong and came from this huge Asian family that were always in our business, always having opinions on how everything should be done and the rule was that she could slag them off as much as she wanted but the one time – honestly, *once* – that I said something about them she didn't speak to me for a week. She was so stubborn. She left stubble in the bath after shaving her legs and watched so much reality TV – I'd come downstairs of a morning and the bloody real housewives of wherever would be on and that's how she'd start her day. I hated it. She couldn't cook and was incapable of properly closing a kitchen cabinet and would sing these songs from Bollywood movies constantly. She was always talking, or singing, or watching other people talk or sing. There was nothing ever quiet about her. And I loved it. She drove me absolutely potty, totally round the bend, but she was my favourite person in the whole world and absolutely irreplaceable. And then . . . yeah. She died.'

He took a breath after speaking, as if the words tumbling out one after another had worn him out. He had tears in his eyes. He took another mouthful of his wine. 'I really am drunker than I thought,' he said. 'Sorry.'

'Don't say sorry,' I replied. 'I don't even know how you're functioning. That's such an unfair, crap hand to be dealt.'

'It was a car crash. An old woman who had no business still having a licence crashed into her on a dual carriageway.'

'Thank you for telling me,' I said. 'Thank you for trusting me with this.'

He nodded. 'I wanted to tell you before we flew out here. I wanted to tell you the moment you said you were hurting, because I wanted to let you know you're not alone. But I didn't. I don't know why. I suppose you made out I was so full of life that I didn't want to let you down. It can all be a bit fake-it-until-you-make-it. Anything to get through the day, sometimes.'

I'd had no idea at the amount of pain that lay behind his cheeky-chappy exterior. He did such a good job of deflecting that.

'Patrick, you can talk to me about it whenever you want. Mala sounds like she was an incredible woman, and I cannot imagine how much you miss her.'

'I do miss her,' he agreed. 'I don't think it will ever go away, how much I miss her. I'll never get married again. But I also know my life has to go on. Does that make sense? I need to find a way to miss her, and also feel my own life is worth living.'

His words hit my gut. I needed exactly the same attitude, but I didn't want to say as much because comparing my very-much-alive ex to his wife who had died didn't seem right. But it made sense: if you miss somebody, miss them. If you miss what you had with somebody, that's okay. Nobody had framed it that way to me before: that we can feel more than one thing at once. Sadness and hope. Regret and pride. Shame and longing. Despair, but also a pull to keep on.

'I think I needed to tell you because I know we laughed at my being mistaken for your husband at the departure lounge, but it feels disloyal to Mala somehow. I am her husband. Or was. I actually only stopped wearing my ring a few weeks ago. I put it in my bedside drawer the day before I saw you at bootcamp, as it goes.'

'Going forward we'll make it crystal clear to everyone that you're Mr Hummingbird and I am Ms Wiig,' I pledged. 'I promise, okay?'

'Thanks,' he replied. 'Not that she's coming back of course. But if I can be so woo-woo as to say that energetically, it doesn't feel great?'

I reached out a hand to his. 'Patrick, I am so pleased you recognized me that day at Barry's. I'm so pleased to know you again now. We'll have fun this trip, okay? It'll be good for both of us. No obligations, nobody telling us how to feel or justifying ourselves – just doing what we want to do, when we want to do it, even if that thing is different from what the other person wants to do. Okay?'

'Okay,' he granted.

Our eyes drifted out to the vineyard again, companionable silence coming with it.

'Annie?'

'Mmmmm?'

'That was the perfect reaction. Thank you.'

'Thank you for telling me,' I said. 'Mala must have felt so loved by you.'

'I did my best,' he replied, sorrowfully. 'Most days I still can't believe she's actually gone.'

18

I hated that I wasn't sure how to navigate our conversation after Patrick had told me about Mala, and I hated that he knew it, and so was demonstrably more chipper than he'd ever been, like he was communicating that it was okay for us to continue to have a good time. I played along because I didn't want to give the impression that I saw him differently now, even though I did. Of course I did. His wife had died. I replayed every conversation we'd had, looking for the clues. All that talk of seizing the day, and knowing what loss was like. I thought he'd been dumped!

I knew he was a good guy, but the only conclusion that I could draw was that he was an even stronger, kinder man than I'd first realized. To get up every day missing somebody that way – to be robbed of a life with someone, but still find ways to bring goodness to the world, to make people smile or to be helpful. It was staggering, really. I knew I couldn't make the death of his partner some sort of quirky backstory for him, or a personality trait, but it did make me double down on my admiration. I couldn't help it.

'And how does the type of flask impact the flavour?' Patrick was asking the winemaker, who looked delighted to delve into a detailed and informative answer for him. Patrick nodded, wineglass in hand, his mint green polo shirt contrasting with the deep ruby red in his glass and the golden halo of his hair. He looked as if he was posing for a painting to be done only in the brightest of colours.

'Annie,' he summoned. 'Have you tried this one? I think I'm going to get some bottles to take home.' I rushed to be by his side.

'Don't you two look like a couple of lushes?' Bianca observed as we wandered down the pebbled path of the vineyard entrance to where she waited in the limo. 'Thanks for walking down – there's nowhere to turn this thing around up there.'

'Thank you for picking us up,' I said, my face burning from the wine. I was flushed and smiley, and there was no way to hide it. 'It's really so great to have somebody to navigate us to where we need to be. I'd be rubbish at map-reading and we'd probably only end up seeing the motorway.'

We climbed into the back seat and Bianca rolled down the partition to keep chatting.

'I think you two would have fun even parked in a service station car park,' she quipped, and Patrick smirked at me.

'I think so too,' he said, holding my eye. I stuck my tongue out at him. Any earlier tension had melted, ebbing and then flowing once again.

We took turns to get changed in the back of the car once we got to Surfers Point – a bikini under my wine-tasting dress would have been the height of trashy – and Bianca pointed out where we could walk to get barbecue from. We asked if she wanted to come down with us to the beach, but she insisted there was a man she needed to see about a dog at a nearby bar, so we wandered out alone.

'I need to sober up,' Patrick said. 'I think I did a little too much swallowing and not quite enough spitting.'

'That's what she said,' I quipped. He snickered.

The water was cold but refreshing, waking up every cell in my body as we swam out from the shore.

'I really do love the ocean,' Patrick said. 'I love how small it makes me feel.'

'What else do you love?' I asked. I stopped swimming and turned to float on my back, gently distancing myself from him so I could do a sneaky wee.

'I love Nina Simone,' he said, 'and I love bootcamp. I love volunteering at the literacy charity in Hackney—'

'You volunteer?' I said. 'Patrick! You're too much!'

He turned to float on his back too. 'What do you mean?'

'It's a cool thing to do, is all. Volunteering. Is it adults, or . . .?'

'Kids.'

'And he's good with kids as well, ladies and gentlemen,' I announced to an invisible crowd.

'I don't know why me not being an arsehole continues to be a surprise,' Patrick said. 'I can't be the only person in your life who volunteers.'

'You're not,' I replied. 'Adzo goes into schools sometimes, to speak about Black women in science, and Freddie reads to a pensioner in the old people's home once a week. I used to help run student support services at university, but I suppose once I started working I thought I didn't have time anymore.'

I flipped back over onto my stomach, changing to a slow breaststroke back in the direction of the shore.

'That's fair enough. You are a pretty big deal. I don't think I even knew theoretical scientists were real, let alone that I'd ever meet one.'

He followed me in a front crawl.

'I sort of fell into it, really,' I told him. 'I'd have liked to have done some more acting, or looked at psychology. Being a therapist would have been cool. But when I finished school the arts were becoming saturated and there were loads of science jobs opening up because of EU grants, and then poof! Ten years later and it's my thing. That feels a bit stupid, sometimes. The job is okay, but . . .'

'You don't enjoy it?'

'Do you enjoy what you do?'

'I sell insurance, Annie. I go to work for the paycheque and then it doesn't cross my mind again once I clock out for the day.'

'Hmmmm,' I replied. 'I do a lot of early starts and late finishes to be honest, and the odd weekend from my laptop at home. Stay one step ahead. Be prepared.'

We reached close enough to the shore that our feet could touch the ground. I pulled myself up to sit so that the water came up to my middle. I was cold, but I didn't care. The horizon was starting to turn pink, making the ocean go on forever.

'You could always do something else,' Patrick offered, and I laughed.

'I couldn't,' I said. 'Especially not now. I need one constant in my life.'

Patrick shook his head, spraying water out all over me.

'Hey!' I said, reaching into the sea to splash him, the flirty love interest in a Nineties teen movie.

'There's one thing I think you'd be terrible at if you did switch careers,' he said, splashing me back.

'What's that then?' I asked, genuinely interested in his take.

'Anything that involves keeping a secret or being stealthy.'

'Being stealthy?' I repeated. I didn't get what he meant.

'You're the worst secret pee-er in the world, Annie. I totally knew you were having a wee out there.'

I squealed. 'Argh!' I said, laughing, burying my face into my hands, embarrassed. 'Shut up!'

'Nope,' he replied. 'Because you're very cute when you blush.'

I splashed him again.

'I'm serious though,' he continued, once we'd settled back into conversation. 'I told you about Mala, and I told you about how that taught me to *carpe diem* more, because fuck, I don't know how else to make sense of life otherwise. If you don't love what you do enough that you want to do something else, you should totally look into that.'

'Yeah,' I said. 'Maybe.'

'Maybe?'

'Don't push me!' I laughed. 'The personal growth I am experiencing right now is already quite dramatic. One step at a time, boss!'

He pulled me up and we towelled off before walking the length of the beach to investigate the barbecue food Bianca had recommended. I checked my phone for a Carol update, but there wasn't anything.

'Can we send another joint prayer out into the world for the dog, please?' I asked him.

'Still no news?' he asked.

I shook my head.

'I'm wondering if I should let Alexander know she's missing. She was his dog too . . .'

'Does he know you're here?' Patrick asked, as we passed a

154

couple of teenagers making out on a blanket, so ferociously it was almost obscene.

'Alexander?'

'Uh-huh.'

'No idea,' I said. 'And screw him, anyway. He's lost the right to know my travel plans. So on reflection, no. I won't let him know about Carol. I don't even want to say his name again.'

Patrick slowed to read the menu of a rib shack. 'That's the spirit,' he intoned. And then, 'I'm not actually that hungry, are you?'

I shook my head. 'I ate nearly all of that sliced meat they put out at lunch,' I said. 'I'm good.'

The sun had lowered enough that the temperature had dropped significantly, and I rubbed my hands up and down my arms to try and warm up.

'Oof,' I said. 'It's chilly now, isn't it?'

'Actually yeah. I think Bianca should be ready and waiting for us by now though. Shall we head?'

'Good idea,' I said.

Patrick rifled in his tote bag and pulled out a jumper.

'Guess who had the good sense to come prepared?' he said, holding it out to me.

'Smart arse,' I grinned, accepting it. 'Who packs a jumper for the beach?'

'It was cold on the way home yesterday!' he exclaimed. 'I'm a quick learner!'

I pulled on the smooth navy wool he'd given me.

'How do I look?' I asked, rolling up the sleeves.

'Oddly sexy,' he replied, clutching his hand to his heart like he was outraged by the suggestion.

'Sexy!' I squealed. 'Ewwww!'

155

His face fell serious. 'Yeah,' he said. 'It suits you.'

I picked up my bag and crossed it over my body, awkward at the suggestion of 'sexy'.

'You sure you don't want it?' I said.

'Nah. Car is just up there.'

I could see the limo up in the distance, the headlights on to help guide us. Darkness was falling quickly.

'Here,' Patrick said, as we reached the rickety old steps we'd taken down. 'Let me help you.'

He threaded his hand through mine, leading the way and holding on tightly to make sure I didn't slip. I liked being looked after – to be looked after by him. His grip was firm and reassuring.

'I've got you,' he said. 'It's okay.'

I followed him.

'Thanks,' I said, as we reached the top. He stood, pausing for a moment, backlit by the car headlights so that he had a glow around his messy, sandy hair. He'd let go of my hand because we were already back on solid ground, but he took it again to guide me to the car door, opening it and squeezing lightly.

'Thanks,' I said, squeezing back, and we only let go so that he could climb in behind me.

19

He called Mona Lisa the next morning, over coffee on the balcony.

'It's not that I'm not having the best time ever, because I totally am,' he said. 'I was just thinking it might be good to wander about on my own a bit and then meet you for dinner later? I just don't want you to get sick of me.'

Patrick's whole demeanour had changed. The Patrick I'd said goodnight to was relaxed and insouciant, but overnight he'd become agitated and uncharacteristically standoffish – as if, on reflection, he wasn't as okay as he'd made out.

'Oh,' I said, trying to catch up with this change in temperature. 'Sure! Whatever you want.' My voice was high, my smile too wide. Was this because of what he'd told me yesterday? We'd been fine with each other on the way home from the beach, even after the hand-holding, which now I thought about it was probably just him being extra careful in looking after me because he was a gentleman. I didn't know why I kept thinking about his hand reaching for mine, or how he'd looked at me once we were back in the villa and I'd peeled off his jumper, giving it back to him.

We'd stayed up late talking about favourite foods and sibling stories – I'd told him about Freddie, and more about how awesome she was. We kept dipping back into Yak Yak memories too, and bootcamp. It was easy and fun.

I did have questions about Mala, though, which I hadn't thought appropriate to bring up yet. I wanted to know what happened after he'd found out, what he'd done with her things, if he still saw her family. I wanted to know if he'd dated since, or what he thought about dating in the future. I knew he needed to be the one to bring it up. I didn't want to douse his mood with a bucket of cold water if he didn't want to discuss it. But on the other hand, I'd googled it before I'd gone to bed, reading that when you lose somebody, the best gift is to be asked questions about them. What had Patrick said about people being scared of grief being contagious? I couldn't decide what the best thing to do was: ask about her, or wait for him to bring her up again.

'It's lovely, hanging out with you,' I replied to his suggestion, my ego a tiny bit bruised. 'But I'm totally happy to take my book and go read down by the lake. I probably haven't explored the grounds here enough anyway, and we leave soon, so I should get on that.'

He clapped his hands together as if the decision had been made. 'Excellent,' he affirmed. 'I'll head off to explore, then. Great. Yeah. Cheers.' He got up and left his drink. He couldn't get away from me fast enough.

I didn't want to ask if everything was okay, because clearly not everything was okay, but I knew I'd spend the day worrying I'd screwed up. And if I had screwed up, it would be better to know instead of not knowing and so not fixing it.

'You good?' I asked, as he gathered up his things.

'Me?' he replied. 'Yes. Why wouldn't I be?'

'No. Nothing.'

'We decided on Mona Lisa for a reason, right?'

'Totally,' I said, privately thinking we'd never actually use it. 'Enjoy your day. Go and collect some stories to regale me with over supper.'

'Cool,' he said, already halfway out of the door.

I splayed out on the sofa and watched the trees move in the breeze outside. He had definitely been strange, despite his protestations. Maybe I could bring things down a notch – I had been talking a lot, and potentially been a bit silly by the time we'd drunk all that wine at the tasting. Yes, that was it: I'd pull back, try not to be as 'much'.

I grabbed the iPad from my room, my heart twinging at the wallpaper photo of Carol, right after her last fur trim. *Please be okay,* I wished up to the stars. I connected to the Wi-Fi so I could research how to spend the day. The Core Four had sent texts overnight: Kezza had just signed a new writing duo on a project she was sure she could get greenlit, Jo had suffered Braxton Hicks and was betting the baby would come early, and Bri said that Angus had a new job he'd interviewed six times for, each time getting higher and higher in the food chain with who he had to impress. *I honestly thought he was going to come home and say his final round had been with God herself!* she'd written.

I sent back some snaps of the vineyard, including a photo I'd sneakily taken of Patrick holding a wineglass by its stem, leaning in to smell what was in it. The collar on his polo shirt was up, his blond hair floppy and un-gelled, making him look like a moneyed actor in a still from a movie about a summer romance. They'd said they wanted to know what he looked like, after all.

Mum had messaged too.

Annie. Who was the man on the phone to your sister? I know you didn't meet him there because he didn't have an accent. Freddie says her lips are sealed, but I don't think it is appropriate to have a child keep secrets for you. Mum.

I almost sent her the same photo, just to wind her up, but knew it wasn't worth the hassle.

I texted Freddie to ask if she'd heard anything about the dog, and to see if she was okay. I'd tried not to let my thoughts drift into catastrophizing, but without Patrick around to distract me I suddenly had room in my head for wondering. *Please be okay, Carol. Please.* Nobody had tried to call me, and the vet she was registered to hadn't emailed. I told myself I'd give it twenty-four more hours. If we hadn't heard anything by then, I'd allow myself to have a meltdown of worry.

Finally, I hit the email app to satisfy the blinking '1' that sat in the corner of the logo, letting me know there was something waiting for me. Bile rose to my throat when I saw his name in bold at the top of my inbox, next to an empty subject line. Alexander. I opened the message before I could change my mind.

Annie, it said, and I noticed right away that it was a huge chunk of text – a big paragraph.

I dropped the iPad onto the sofa cushions. I didn't want to know.

I did want to know.

I didn't.

I did.

Annie. I need you to forgive me. Your mum has messaged me, and Jo wrote and said some pretty horrible things in several emails, but we both know I made the choice that was the best for you, and for me. As you probably saw from my out of office I'm in Singapore, working from the HQ here. I'll stay out here until you call the dogs off – we can't talk if everyone is just going to shout at me, and we do need to talk. I think you know we couldn't get married. It would have been a tremendous mistake. We were university sweethearts but not life partners. We got carried away. The way I did everything wasn't great, but I think I was waiting for you to be the one to finally say it, and then it was almost too late . . .

Dad said you went to Australia without me. I hope you find the courage to move on out there, to want something more for yourself. I want more for myself too. I think that's okay to say. This is best for both of us.

A x

Everything that had begun to mend inside me came crashing down, all at once, every word unpicking my self-esteem. My stomach sank, my neck was red hot, I wanted to be sick. Where was his kindness, his softness? *We were university sweethearts but not life partners,* he'd said. What the hell!

I paced around the sunken living area, up and down, processing his words. I wanted to scream. I wanted to cry. I wished Patrick was there to say something silly and witty and oddly insightful.

Patrick. What would he have told me to do?

Patrick would have said we only have one life, and to make the most of it. That if Alexander didn't want me, I could just go on right ahead and enjoy myself without him. He didn't get to elbow his way into my inbox and change the whole mood of my holiday. And Patrick would be right.

I went into the bedroom and pulled on my bikini, wiping away the tears that had gently fallen down my cheeks without

161

me really noticing. Resolutely, I put on my sunglasses, picked up my bag and a bottle of water, and pulled open the door. On the other side was Patrick, and I almost collided with him.

'Jesus!' I screamed.

'Hi! Hello! Sorry, I didn't mean to scare you.' He looked sheepish, and held out a fridge magnet that said, *I love Margaret River.*

'What's this?' I asked, taking it. If I sounded angry, it's because I was. I was angry at Patrick, at the email, at the world.

'I missed you,' he said.

I pouted at him. 'You've been gone less than half an hour.'

'I know. I was being stupid. I don't know why. I don't need a Mona Lisa day. Can you forgive me?'

I took his gift and inspected it in the palm of my hand. Alexander had never apologised to me. He'd never snapped and made it right immediately, or opened the door to reconciliation after a fight. It was always me, my fault, and if I brought it up he told me never to make a fuss. And then here was Patrick, apology gift and all, accepting full responsibility for acting like a weirdo.

'Only because this is an exceptional magnet,' I settled on, softening. 'Yes.'

'Good,' he replied, and he exhaled loudly. I hadn't noticed he'd been holding his breath, bless him. 'I got all caught up in my head, but that's not for now. I want to spend time with you, not in my thoughts. So, wherever you were going – can I come with you?'

I grinned. 'Yes. Of course you can. Come on. Let's explore.'

He held out his arm for me to loop my own through, and together we headed off.

20

We spent the last few days in Margaret River wandering around the grounds of the lodge, which went way further than I'd realized, lying by the pool and playing board games in one of the cabanas. We borrowed hotel bikes to cycle in the local area, and on our last afternoon played tennis with an old married couple we'd gotten talking to, before crashing a water fight for the children of the guests, each commandeering a team and lobbing balloons of water across at each other until we both doubled over laughing so hysterically that we were asked to consider leaving the kids to it. We read at the lake, ate from the barbecue for dinner, and sat out on the back porch with a bottle of Margaret River wine and a lit candle, playing Bananagrams and talking about Carol. I was starting to worry about her more and more, and had emailed the vet about what to do next, but Patrick was hopeful. *Maktub,* he reminded me. It was a wholesome, beautiful time, despite its rocky interlude.

'No!' I squealed, frustrated by how quick Patrick was at

assembling words from the random tiles we'd been assigned. 'You're too good at this! Too fast!'

The aim of the game was to use the twenty-one tiles we'd each been given to make words that all interlinked, sort of like playing Scrabble but without a Scrabble board.

'Bananas!' he cried, letting me know he'd used up all his tiles and was declaring himself the winner.

I still had two more tiles to place, but had ended up with a 'q' that was impossible to do anything with. I looked over at what he'd done.

'FITTIE is not a word.' I giggled. 'You're cheating!'

'It so too is a word. It's a way to describe somebody who is hot.'

I shook my head. 'You call somebody fit, and fit is a word in the dictionary, but no way is *fittie* in there. It's slang.'

'I know for a fact it is, because there's a photo of my face beside it,' he retorted.

I made a gag sound. 'Cheeseball,' I said.

'Who says "cheeseball"?'

'I do. I also sometimes say cornball.'

'You didn't try and play that as a word, did you?'

I squealed. 'So you admit it! You are "trying" to play a word that doesn't count!'

He burst out laughing. 'Urgh. Fine. Whatever.'

'No, not whatever,' I said. 'Not when this is my Bananagrams reputation on the line. I always win. Alexander didn't beat me once, not in all the time we were together!'

Patrick stopped laughing, and suddenly we shifted from larking around to being serious and sombre. I had a feeling I shouldn't have said Alexander's name.

'Shall we go again . . .?' I started, but he shook his head.

'Nah. I'm good. In fact, I'm almost ready for bed.'

I looked at my watch: 10 p.m. It was earlier than I'd go to bed at home, but being in the sun all day, and running around like we had done, meant I was pretty sleepy too.

'Sorry,' I pressed. 'I shouldn't have brought up Alexander. He emailed me the other day. I've been trying not to think of him ever since.'

Patrick nibbled on his bottom lip. 'What did he say?'

'The truth,' I admitted. 'That he called it off in the worst possible way, but that we should never have got engaged.'

'Is that true, though?'

'A week ago I wouldn't have thought so but now I'm here, now I've got a bit more perspective, maybe. Yeah. I think we were just too scared to break up because we'd been together so long, and so instead we just did what was expected.'

'Hmmmm,' he said. 'Okay.'

The thought had been wheedling its way onto my tongue for the past few days. It was like a confession, and in saying it to Patrick I'd released the power of it. Alexander was right. We shouldn't have been getting married. I'd been scared of being left behind. Understanding that made me feel ashamed. It was upsetting to admit – especially to somebody who'd been married and had been very much head over heels about his partner.

'You certainly took a right turn on what was expected by bringing me along on your honeymoon, anyway,' Patrick said. 'And if it's okay, to say thank you, I've organized a surprise for our first day in Sydney. So disregard the itinerary, because it's Paddy's Plan for our first full day on the east coast.'

'A surprise?' I echoed, aware at the back of my mind that he always seemed to drive the conversation away from Alexander. 'What?'

'Just trust me.' He shifted in his seat, looking quite proud of himself for the very fact of having a secret.

'Pretty please?' I requested, fluttering my eyelashes. I wanted to talk about the day after tomorrow. Tomorrow would be even better than today, and the day after even better, because I'd be even stronger. Even happier. I didn't want the trip to pass by quickly, but there was a comfort in knowing that time really did heal.

Patrick moved his weight again, this time so he was leaning over the arm of his chair, closer to me than he'd ever been. I swallowed hard and licked my lips, my throat drying up at what could happen.

'Now, now,' he said, lowering his voice. 'Play fair. With those big eyes you're abusing your power, Annie.'

I exhaled loudly. 'I don't know what you mean,' I whispered. If anyone had been around to accuse me of flirting I would have denied it, but I was potentially on the verge of it. Fooling around, I made my eyes bigger and puckered my lips more, holding eye contact suggestively. 'I'm only asking for a hint . . .'

He gave an internal hum of a laugh. 'You're very used to getting what you want, aren't you?'

'I mean, no. Obviously.'

Was he on the verge of flirting too?

'I'm putty in your hands,' he said.

If he was, was he the one pushing the boundary, or was I?

'If that was true you'd tell me at least what I need to wear for this surprise, Patrick. So I'm prepared.'

He leaned in a tiny bit more, if that were possible, getting so close that his breath tickled underneath my nose. My heart beat in double time, my breathing shallow at his proximity. He definitely did have red in his stubble. I'd thought so once back after class at bootcamp, but now I could see it up close and clear as day. Part of me wanted to reach out and touch it – to feel the masculine contours of him. He had a streak of sunburn alongside one eye where he'd missed his sun cream application, and in the dim light his eyes seemed darker. Instead of being green they looked like pools of chocolate, his lashes bleached by the sun but still long. He looked solemn, wrestling with a decision and totally torn over which way to go. It made me want to tell him it was okay, that whatever he was concerned about was totally fine. I wanted to cure him of whatever was making him seem so confused.

'Look as lovely as you always do,' he said, his voice low and gruff and – it was impossible to ignore – kind of suggestive. He added, testing the limits of a thing I couldn't quite put my finger on: 'You know how it undoes me.'

I let out a guffaw in nervous shock, the sound of my laugh shattering whatever delicate thing we'd just been holding between us. 'Pongy Paddy!'

He pulled away. 'You'll enjoy it,' he said, standing up and cricking his neck. He rubbed at his shoulder, and the awkwardness of it was the least self-assured I'd ever seen him. I wanted to reach for his hand, to tell him I was here, to go back five seconds in time so that I wouldn't ruin the spell he'd been weaving. He gave me something I wanted more of – the nearness of him was intoxicating, the way the air shifted when he was teasing me lulled me into breathing deeper and smiling wider. I'd hated it the other morning, when he'd disappeared and acted odd. Sitting next to him was better than not sitting next to him. I couldn't wait for it to be morning so that we had another full day together, and then another one after that. Saying goodnight was my least favourite part of the day.

'Just trust me,' he said, already back in the living room. 'Sleep tight . . .'

'Sleep tight,' I called after him. 'Remember it's an 8 a.m. pick-up in the morning so we have plenty of time for the flight.'

I sat staring into the darkness long after he'd gone, my heart racing but not quite sure why.

21

The second leg of the trip was the east coast, so Bianca drove us to the airport and we headed from Perth to Sydney on another business-class flight.

'You two are the cutest,' she said as she pulled us into a three-way hug at departures. 'I wish everything for you that you wish for yourself.'

'Thanks, Bianca,' Patrick said. 'You've been the best tour guide.'

She waved a hand like it was nothing. 'Just doing my job,' she said. 'Enjoy the rest of your non-honeymoon.' Patrick had finally revealed the truth about our adventure as a parting gift for her, and she'd had hundreds of follow-up questions about it.

'I'm going to tell this story to everyone I know!' she declared. 'You came on your honeymoon anyway, Annie! That's so badass!'

It took just over four hours in the air, where we slipped into a calmer dynamic – there was less pressure to chat and keep each other entertained, and so we sat side by side in contented silence, occasionally pointing things out in the in-flight magazine, but otherwise amiably quiet. I found myself really enjoying those peaceful moments with him, where we didn't scramble to make sure the other was having a good time. Patrick wasn't always the 'razzle-dazzle' guy I'd first thought he was – he could be muted and thoughtful. I liked discovering that side of him. I liked peeling back the layers the rest of the world didn't get to see, unearthing the depths of him and how he trusted me. Having Patrick's trust was a coup. I was special because of it.

There was a driver waiting for us in Sydney, who wasn't half as friendly as Bianca had been but was only employed for that one trip instead of for the next twelve days. He drove us right to the water in the city, where our hotel had views of the opera house on one side and the harbour on the other. The lobby was cool marble with huge pillars that ran up a triple storey and plush areas for drinks and business meetings in velvet chairs and on battered-but-expensive-looking leather couches.

I'd worn flip-flops and cut-offs to fly in, which had been fine for Margaret River, but fell a little short in the fancy Sydney hotel with its fancy guests. Where we'd spent the past week had been relaxed and informal. Our new hotel was the poshest place I had ever had a room in – I could tell that even from the uniforms the staff wore. Everything was perfectly arranged and polished, and I swore I could smell jasmine and patchouli, as if even the air was fancier there.

'It's a twin room, right?' Patrick asked the clerk at reception.

The clerk looked from Patrick to me and then back again, assessing our dynamic. It must have seemed odd that we were in one of the best suites (God bless Fernanda and Charles, yet again!) but sleeping separately.

'Twin room as in—'

'Yeah, we need two beds please,' Patrick said, and he shot me a nervous smile, almost apologetic.

'You're in the penthouse suite . . .' the clerk replied, prompting Patrick to shoot me a second look that said *of course we are* without him having to do anything other than lift one corner of his mouth. I couldn't help but notice that whilst we were getting closer, there were boundaries about our friendship that he often gaffer-taped on the floor for everyone else to see. But then, I was also allowed access to tiny moments and in-jokes with him, where nobody else existed. Half the time, me and my friend Patrick had our own little language, our own little world for two.

'. . . And the penthouse suite has two king-sized rooms joined by the living quarters. I think you'll be quite comfortable Mrs—'

'Ms,' I interrupted. 'Ms Wiig is fine, thank you.'

'Very well, Ms Wiig. If you'd like to head to the private penthouse lift at the very end of this corridor, one of our porters will follow with your luggage shortly. And if you use this key card—' he slid a small embossed paper envelope across, two shiny black key cards poking out of the top '—the lift will open directly to your quarters. Enjoy your stay, won't you?'

The suite was outrageous, but the novelty of such continued luxury hadn't worn off and so we both spent a good fifteen minutes walking around exclaiming about the size of the beds, the depth of the bath, the TVs in every room, the view – all of it. It was all modern, angled furniture and floor-to-ceiling glass, even in the bathroom. I'd be showering suspended in the Sydney sky, and beyond grateful for it. I didn't think I'd ever go on such an extravagant holiday for the rest of my life. In fact, I knew I wouldn't.

'Would it be acceptable if I took your almost-in-laws out to dinner when we get home, so I can thank them?' Patrick asked. 'Or maybe I could offer to mow their lawn for a year, or kneel on all fours in their living room to be used as a footrest?'

'Oh,' I said, suddenly remembering. 'They say hi, actually. I've been trying to let them know what we've been doing every day, and Fernanda specifically asked if you were having fun. I hope you don't mind, but I sent her the photo of you after you'd lost the water fight.'

'Not my finest hour,' he conceded. 'But of course, send her whatever you want. That's nice, that you're chatting.'

'It's the least I can do – keep her up to date with our activities.'

We were stood at the floor-to-ceiling window overlooking the harbour, late-afternoon sun making the water look like it contained hidden diamonds that sparkled just below the surface. There were the white sails of fifty or so boats scattered about, and high-rise buildings on the other side, which I presumed was the downtown area or the business district. It was everything a person could want from a city all in one eyeline: water, culture, business, the promise of good restaurants and a vibrant nightlife. I knew this part of the trip would be a totally different taste of the country, and I tingled with anticipation of what was in store.

'And yes, to answer your question: definitely offer the footrest thing.' I giggled as I pressed my nose against the glass and looked down. We were *very* high up. 'No talking though. Footrests can't talk.'

'I think I'd struggle with that,' he retorted. 'I don't know if you've noticed but—'

'Oh, I've noticed,' I replied, and instinctively I reached out a hand to his arm. As we touched it was like gripping live electricity wires and I withdrew as quickly as I'd reached out. *What the hell?* That was super strange. I'd only meant to emphasize my point, not set us both on fire.

We were interrupted by FaceTime trilling on my iPad.

'How is that even connected to the Wi-Fi?' I mused aloud, as I dived into my hand luggage for it.

'Freddie, Froogle! Hi!' I said, and at the sound of her name Patrick stood very still over by the L-shaped sofa that occupied most of the joint living space, knowing this would be news about Carol.

'We found her!' Freddie said. 'We found Carol!'

I exhaled and dropped my head, tears pushing at my eyes because only when Carol was safe could I admit I'd been terrified of losing her. I walked over to the sofa too, flopping down in relief.

'Oh thank God,' I said, pulling my feet up underneath me. 'Excellent news, bug. Where was she?'

'You won't believe it,' Freddie said. 'She was next door! In their garden! I heard her barking this morning when I was getting ready for school. They said they found her at the park and brought her home, but that when they tried to call the number on her collar it was an international dial tone so they hung up. Look, here she is now. She missed us!'

Freddie pulled the dog to the camera right as Patrick looked at me and pointed to ask, *Can I say hi?*

'Patrick!' Freddie squealed. 'We found Carol! You were right!'

'I never had any doubt,' said Patrick, settling in beside me in the nook of the 'L'. 'Annie told me how clever you are. I knew you'd figure out a way to track her down.'

Freddie beamed. 'Okay I gotta go to school,' she said. 'What time is it there? It's breakfast time here.'

'It's almost suppertime here,' I said. 'And as somebody who has already experienced the day I can tell you; it's a good one!'

'I just wanted to tell you she was okay,' Freddie continued. 'Mum and Dad said she can sleep with me tonight, like she does when I'm at your house. I never want to let her out of my sight again!'

'All right, Frou. Thank you so much for telling us she's safe. She looks really happy to see you. Snuggle her from me, okay?'

'Yeah,' said Freddie, letting Carol lick her face. 'Okay.'

After we hung up, Patrick turned to me and asked: 'Ready, ready, chicken jelly?'

I rolled my eyes at him playfully. 'Are you still trying to make that happen?'

'We have a whole new city to explore,' he exclaimed, reaching out towards me and putting my cheeks between his hands. 'And now we have an extra reason to celebrate: Carol has been found! We're in Sydney! Let's go eat!'

It was impossible not to get swept up in his enthusiasm.

22

Our first full day in Sydney was what Patrick had spent the previous night calling Paddy's Perfect Surprise Day. After a buffet breakfast in one of the four restaurants in the hotel, I was instructed to pack for the day and be comfortable, but not 'daggy'.

'I just remember them using that word on TV,' Patrick had smiled. 'It means uncool. I mean, at least I think it does.'

I'd chosen cropped baggy blue trousers with my Birkenstocks and a white top that I thought made me look quite glow-y, now I was matching Patrick in the getting-a-tan department. I left my hair loose and un-straightened, and wore one simple gold chain around my neck. With a sweep of bronzer and my sunglasses I was going for modest but stylish. I grabbed the small leather cross-body bag I'd worn wine tasting and headed downstairs, where Patrick had instructed me to meet him out front.

I spotted him immediately. He stood across the road to the hotel, his khaki knee-length shorts revealing the toned calves of a runner. He had Birks on too, and a white linen shirt so that we accidentally matched, like those old married couples who wear his 'n' hers fleeces. His grin was huge, and it made me burst into a smile right back, a joy at seeing him that practically bloomed out of me. We stood there looking at each other, a pair of loons, staring and smiling, light traffic passing by between us. I liked how it was to enjoy somebody so much. He made things better. We'd only been apart fifteen minutes, but I'd yearned for him.

'We're taking a road trip!' he yelled across the street. My eyes adjusted and I saw that he was standing beside a sleek black Audi convertible, and that he was twirling keys around in his hand.

'Wait,' I said, figuring it out. 'You're driving?'

'I thought it might be fun,' he shouted, opening the passenger door and gesturing to me that I should cross the road and get in. 'Wind in our hair, going where the road takes us. Where the sat nav takes us, anyway.'

'I see. Wow. Okay.'

The fawn leather was soft under my thighs, the smell of new car powerful. Patrick told me to mind my fingers and closed the door behind me before climbing in the other side and starting the automatic engine.

'What's the plan, man?'

'The destination is a little town about two hours away to the south, still near the coast, for the music festival there tonight. Figured we'd stop along the way if we can, goggle at the sights, play spot the kangaroo. Bonus points for a koala.'

I took off my bag and put it by my feet, fastening the seatbelt and declaring that I'd best connect my phone to the speaker.

'This is going to need a soundtrack,' I insisted.

'Don't let me down, DJ,' Patrick replied, putting on his sunglasses and starting the engine. 'I'm gonna need some singalong classics, if you please.'

Ten minutes later we were singing 'If It Makes You Happy' by Sheryl Crow at the top of our voices, the trees on one side of the road getting denser and denser, the ocean sprawling out alongside us on the other. Patrick was a good driver, slow and steady: we were in no rush. It was basically one straight road we were on, and I loved how the wind rushed through my hair, the sun bright on my face. When the music stopped and nothing else played, we plunged into the contented silence we'd been practising already.

'If it makes you happy, it can't be that bad,' Patrick said, repeating the lyrics of the song to me. He stole a look quickly, but just as fast turned his eyes back to the road. What was that supposed to mean? I didn't say anything, looking out the passenger window at the landscape whizzing by. It hit me all over again that Carol had been found and I let the relief flood my system. I'd have to get Mum and Dad's neighbours something to say thank you for finding her. Patrick started to tap out a beat on the steering wheel, and I admired his beautiful hands for the twentieth time.

'You could play the piano with those hands,' I observed, and he smiled at me.

'I do,' he replied. 'Grade eight. I'm pretty good, actually.'

For God's sake. Volunteering. Working out. Sorting out distressed little sisters. And now piano. Was there nothing this man couldn't do?

It was green and lush in the town the sat nav delivered us to, littered with small white wooden buildings with pointy roofs, cute and idyllic, and much less built up and urban than the city.

'I'm starving,' I volunteered as we slowed down to get the lay of the land. 'Can we eat?'

'You read my mind,' Patrick agreed. 'Let's park up and see where our noses lead us.'

We climbed out and headed off.

'It's really cool that you do that,' I said. I was shy saying it, but I wanted him to know I'd noticed.

'Do what?'

'That you trust everything's cool. That it will all work out. Even just parking up and saying we should follow our noses. It's spontaneous, but not reckless. I'm learning from you.'

He nudged his shoulder up against mine, something I noticed he did whenever he was trying to connect or reassure me.

'There's not much I can teach you,' he replied. 'And I mean that.'

We approached a little quaint café in a market square, with tables and chairs scattered outside and views of the central town hall. We didn't even say out loud that it was where we would settle – we just instinctively headed towards it and pulled up a chair each.

Patrick closed his eyes and tilted his face up to the sun.

'Heaven,' he said.

'Heaven,' I agreed.

We ordered an early lunch of coffee and tortilla wraps with avocado and cheesy eggs before deciding, after the café owner's suggestion, to head for the back of town towards the estuary of the river. It was wide, with huge grassy banks along the trail. The water was still and perfectly reflected the odd cloud from above, like the water by the lodge had done on the night of our arrival in Margaret River. I wondered, again, what it would have been like to travel here with Alexander. Would he have hired a car and driven us places? Would we have ended up straying from the itinerary and finding a tiny town in the middle of nowhere, an adventure tailor-made for two? I doubted it. He could *maybe* have surprised me with something as romantic and spontaneous, I suppose but . . . no. Alexander and Patrick were polar opposites. Totally.

I liked how Patrick talked with the waitstaff and the owner at the café. I liked how he talked to everyone. Alexander sometimes treated service staff like they were beneath him, but I don't think I ever really let myself notice at the time. It was just Alexander, who he is. When you love someone you accept them for who they are, don't you? You don't ask them to change or alter themselves, because then they wouldn't be who you fell for. But being in such close quarters with another man I was starting to see all the ways Alexander wasn't right. Or, some of the ways, anyway. I couldn't deny that I still missed Alexander, and I couldn't help but wonder what it would be like if he was, indeed, here instead. It was hard to think of him, but I couldn't not, either. He was all I'd known for so long. He made me who I am. But then Patrick did something kind – offering me the first bite of his vanilla slice or surprising me with a road trip – and I'd think, *Is this what I've been missing? Did I settle for scraps and this a full meal?*

Not that it was romantic with Patrick, of course. I was only making that comparison because he was a man. I wouldn't be having those thoughts if Jo was with me, or Kezza or Bri.

Obviously.

'Let's climb out onto the rocks, shall we?' Patrick's voice

cut through my thoughts. 'Whoa, you were miles away there. You okay? You've been quiet since the café.'

'Yeah,' I told him. 'Yeah, I'm fine. To be honest with you I was thinking about Alexander. Again.'

I'd meant to poke fun at myself, but Patrick's face fell and he set his mouth in a firm line.

'Not in a good way,' I offered. 'But, just thinking about what a different trip this would have been with him.'

'Sorry you've got second prize,' Patrick said. His voice was light, but something about his body language wasn't.

'Hey, you.' I tugged at his sleeve. 'Thank you for today. This is amazing.'

He nodded, and took a seat away from me on a massive boulder. After a while he said, 'Do you wish he was here instead of me?'

There was something about the weight of our silence that meant I wasn't surprised he'd picked the conversation back up.

'No,' I said, from where I balanced a few boulders away. 'I don't know what I've done to make you think that, but obviously that's not true.'

'What makes it obvious?'

'Are you kidding?'

'No.'

There was a good stretch of rock between us, so I couldn't reach out and touch him like my instinct was telling me to. I couldn't see his eyes beneath his sunglasses, either, but the edge to his voice was new.

'Patrick,' I said. 'Every time Alexander has crossed my mind I've actually thought how much crappier this trip would have been with him. I can't believe I get to be here with somebody so present. You're twenty times the man he is, and I think I'm having some self-doubt where the blinkers are coming off and I can't believe I ever thought being with him was a good idea. I didn't know there was another way for a relationship to be.'

Patrick started to lift his sunglasses off his head to try and look at me properly, but the sun was so bright off the water he squinted and then decided against it.

'That's a nice thing to say,' he said.

'I mean it,' I replied. 'This is the best honeymoon ever.'

As soon as I'd said it I realized he couldn't say it back, because this was probably the second best honeymoon he'd ever been on. It wasn't that I was jealous about that, but I definitely did feel something. I suppose the trip was unfolding to make me realize so much about my life, in all the best ways, but I worried it wasn't as transformative for him. I was having epiphany after epiphany and he was simply having a lovely time, and probably thinking about his wife whom he loved and missed.

'You must think about your wife a lot,' I said, deciding to test the waters on bringing her up.

He sighed. 'Less, just recently,' he admitted, and it wasn't the answer I thought I'd get. 'And I feel guilty for that. The more time that goes on the further away from her I am . . . And I need to get on with my life but it's a life she's not in. I have all these feelings . . .' He stopped talking and took a breath. Half of me wanted to get up and walk over to him, but the other half of me was glued to the spot, waiting for him to keep talking.

'This has been such a special trip for me,' he continued, still looking out to the water. 'Honestly, I don't know how to thank you for bringing me. I've been more of my old self than I have done in years. I suppose that's a bit scary when I'm so used to . . .' He didn't finish his trail of thought.

'So we're two happy people, happy to be here, happy to be having this adventure, but being cross with each other and sitting practically on opposite sides of the river?' I offered.

He laughed, but it was kind of a sad laugh. 'That's about the measure of it,' he said, and it made me laugh too. 'But I did just want to say to you, I'm the same Patrick I was before I told you about my wife. You get that, don't you?'

'Yeah,' I said. 'But also, you're not. Not in a bad way, but I'm getting to know you, aren't I? If you were an outline before, and I get to colour in parts of you, telling me about Mala was a big bit to add to what I know. You said yourself it has shaped who you are.'

'I suppose so,' he said picking up a stone and throwing it out to the river.

'It hasn't become your overriding personality trait, if that's what you mean. I understand it's a thing that happened, but it doesn't define you.'

'The thing is,' he muttered, so quietly I wasn't sure if I'd heard him right, 'it does define me.' He sighed deeply. 'It's just that sometimes, I really wish it didn't.'

Back in town the marketplace had been transformed. There were streamers and bunting everywhere and a wooden dance floor had been placed off to one side, where the beginnings of a band set-up was happening.

'Looks like this is going to be quite the event,' Patrick commented to an older guy sat on a bench, watching it all unfold beside us. We'd grabbed a couple of ginger beers from a corner shop and slurped at them as we recovered from the walk. It had been much hotter coming back than heading out to the river.

'I'll say,' replied the man. 'We know how to have a good time all right.'

A guy with a ponytail and Eighties Levi's jeans headed across and said to our new friend, 'All right, Bobby.' Bobby tipped his head in response.

'Tourists?' Bobby asked us, eventually.

I nodded.

Patrick said, 'Yes, sir. Just here the week, but we'll be back. Won't we, Annie?'

I smiled and nodded. 'It's been really special,' I said.

'Look at you two,' Bobby observed. 'I remember being in the honeymoon phase with my Rosie. Couldn't take my eyes off her for forty-five years. Just like you.'

I opened my mouth to explain, but Patrick gently rested a hand on my arm. I waited for him to pull away, but he didn't.

'Sounds as though you were very much in love,' Patrick said, and Bobby nodded.

'Best woman you've ever met,' he said. 'She passed ten years ago this Christmas.'

Patrick let that sink in. 'You still talk to her?' he asked, as if it was a totally normal question. That got Bobby's attention.

'In the house I do,' he said. 'She's near me, I know that much. Listening. I hear her voice in my head all the time, reminding me to water her garden, telling me to get my saggy arse out of the house and down to the pub or to call our sons.'

'Yeah,' said Patrick. 'Looking after you. I know what that's like.'

Bobby looked at him crookedly, and then down at Patrick's hand. He shifted and looked at my hand, and I realized he was looking for our wedding bands. I could see the understanding reach his face.

'Still,' said Bobby. 'We had a good run. I never found anyone else, but I tell you now, if I was lucky enough to, I would've jumped at the chance. We're built to be part of two, aren't we? Doesn't mean we love the one who has gone any less.'

Patrick didn't say anything to that, and neither did I. Bobby stood up, wobbling on his feet, and Patrick handed me his ginger beer so he could help.

'Enjoy the music, won't you? Maybe I'll see you later on.' He winked at me. 'Might try and get you for a dance,' he teased, and I smiled.

'Deal,' I told him. 'See you later.'

We both watched him wobble away and, after he turned a corner and issued a wave, I said to Patrick without looking at him, 'You okay?'

'I think so,' came his reply.

I knew not to push it.

23

Bobby was right: the town knew how to put on a show. The square had transformed right before our eyes, filled now with locals who'd come out to listen to band after band as they danced and waved at each other and switched partners easily because everyone knew who everyone else was.

Patrick got properly into it – you'd think he was drunk with the abandon he had on the dance floor. I mean, I hoped he wasn't, since he was my ride home, but I loved seeing it. He reminded me of Yak Yak Patrick, jumping about and getting hot and sweaty and losing himself in the music.

'Isn't this fun?' he shouted to me over a band covering Nineties indie songs as upbeat disco tracks. We were laughing and twirling and my hand was in his as he spun me around, and then my back was pressed up against his chest as he pulled me in close from behind. I looked up at him, and he looked down at me.

And then our lips were touching.

And we were kissing. Kissing, right there in the middle of the dance floor of the market square.

It was chaste, our lips pressed up against each other, slightly parted to leave room for more. Nothing mattered, and then everything did, and my whole body plugged into the mains supply of a thousand volts. Patrick and I were kissing!!!!

But then he smiled, and reactively I smiled, and before it could get deeper we shuffled away from each other and whatever had hooked me up to the mains dissipated as quickly as it had powered me up.

Bobby was beside us with his walking frame, and so we sort of danced around him for a bit, including him in what was happening, and Patrick started to do the robot, and I watched him take so much pleasure in making the old man laugh that my heart burst one thousand times over. And then it clicked that we'd had the chance to take our friendship to the next level and we hadn't. We'd pulled away.

Patrick was my friend. And he was wounded from pain, and I was wounded from pain, and I wasn't blind – I knew that for somebody he'd be an extraordinary partner. But we'd agreed that we weren't that, that it wasn't romantic. We'd got carried away, was all – the kiss hadn't meant anything. I didn't even know if you could call it a kiss. It had barely happened.

I wasn't kissing somebody else on my *honeymoon*.

It had just been the sun, and the stars, and the adventure. That was all.

Patrick was already spinning somebody else around, a twenty-something in a short dress that lifted up enough for me and everyone to see her pants underneath, and I told myself then, in that snapshot of time, that I could have been anybody as we'd danced, and that he could have been anyone too. It was just a thing that happened. We didn't even have to talk about it – adults bump lips sometimes. It would have been childish to linger over it.

'Mona Lisa!' I cried at him, over the din of the music and merriment. I pointed to a shadowy corner near the café we'd eaten at before, and his eye followed my finger as he understood.

It was good to get away from the noise. It was as if the volume had been turned up on the speakers to twice what it was, and what had been spacious and open had shrunk in size. I couldn't get enough oxygen to my lungs and, leaning against the wall, put my back to the cool brick and hands to my hot thighs.

'Do you need to sit down?'

Patrick. He'd followed me.

I shook my head feebly. 'No, no,' I insisted. 'I'm only catching my breath.'

'I could do with that too.'

He rested against the wall alongside me, first at a normal distance and then he shuffled along to be closer.

'You good?' he asked, and I knew the unsaid part of the question was: *with the kiss?*

'Oh for sure,' I said. 'That was a bizarre little moment there wasn't it! Ha-ha.' I wasn't looking at him, we were both fixed on a point in the distance. 'I lost myself for a second. Heady with the thrills of holiday! Let's not even talk about it. Honestly.'

'Oh,' he said. 'If that's—'

'Obviously it is! My old pal Pongy Paddy!'

I sounded deranged, but preferred that than him having to solemnly take my hand and reject me explicitly. No way could I be in that position and survive. Not one bit. I was stronger, but I wasn't that strong. I didn't want it to be a thing, even if for one-tenth of a second I'd almost enjoyed it. That's not what this was. I knew that. I did.

'I don't know about you,' I said after a while. 'But I'm ready to hit up that dance floor again. Shall we?'

'If you're feeling better.'

'I'm feeling great,' I insisted, already trotting off ahead, determinedly holding my head up high. 'I might even put a request in. "Mustang Sally" should do the trick, don't you think? These guys are really very good.'

We were too self-aware after that, and so lasted fifteen more minutes before I caught Patrick looking at his watch, and I told him I was ready to go if he wanted to leave.

'Do *you* want to leave?' he shouted over the music.

'I want to do whatever you want to do,' I yelled, affably.

'It's a yes or no question, Annie!'

His tone took me aback. He'd never snapped at me before.

'Yes!' I cried. 'Sure! I want to go back!'

We found the car and drove in silence. I couldn't get a handle on why Patrick was the one acting like *his* knickers were in a twist, unless he thought I'd overstepped the mark by kissing him.

Had I kissed him?

Or had he kissed me?

I tried to rewind the night and play the moment back in slow motion but it was a blur. We'd been dancing, and then somehow our faces were pressed together, and just as quickly as it had happened it had stopped happening. I hoped he wasn't building up to some big speech about how he would never have come away with me if he'd have known I had ulterior motives. I hadn't asked him for that reason. And plus, he'd basically begged to come!

About an hour into the drive, I reached forward to the dials of the radio so that I didn't have to examine my thoughts, but as soon as I flicked it on, Patrick flicked it off again.

'Before, down by the river . . .' he said, as if we were already halfway through a conversation and hadn't just spent the past sixty miles brooding and confused.

I didn't say anything. I wanted to stop him from doing this. I couldn't bear to have him remind me that I was not the woman that men chose, not least him, a man still in love with the wife he had so tragically buried and who nobody would ever replace. My heart broke for him because of that, but I was devastated for myself, too. I knew nobody wanted me. I didn't want him to remind me of it. And it's not like I was in love with him or anything.

'It's okay,' I said. 'Really. We don't need to do this.'

He hit the steering wheel with his hand. Not hard in a way that scared me, but hard enough that I could tell I was really making him cross.

'For crying out loud, can a man just say what he needs to say? Jesus!'

I shut my mouth.

'It just blows my mind that you can't see what a lucky escape you've had from Alexander. The way you talk about him, how he made you feel . . .'

His voice trailed off, his mouth and brain needing time to catch up to each other. He sighed. 'It's not even about how he left you outside the church that way. He didn't do just one bad thing to you, Annie. He continually made you feel like you aren't enough when all the evidence to the contrary is that you are perfect. It's driving me up the wall that you can't see that. I know you're hurting, but get it in your head. It was all him. All of it.'

'Oh,' I said. Nothing else came out.

We drove. The quiet roads got busier, and the lights of the city guided us up ahead, our lighthouse out at sea.

'I'm hardly perfect, Patrick,' I settled on. 'But I get what you're saying.'

'I don't think you do get it. You *are* perfect. You're bossy and shy and unaware of how absolutely gorgeous you are. You snore—'

'What?'

'On the plane. Sorry to break it to you.'

'That doesn't count. Even in business class your neck is at a funny angle.'

He shook his head. 'You're incapable of taking a compliment, which is why you're changing the subject.'

Hmmmmm. I stared out of the window, folding my arms across my chest.

'What I'm saying is that he was a douchebag, and you are glorious, and if you could just put yourself at the centre of your own world for one second you'd see how much you deserve to be there.'

'Okay,' I countered, the roads up ahead becoming familiar. We were close to the hotel, now. 'Alexander *was* awful to me. But what does it say that I loved him anyway?'

'That you search for the best in people. I don't know. I just really need you to . . .' He stopped talking, cutting himself off.

'Go on.'

'I don't know!'

We pulled up outside the hotel, and I was already unclipping my seatbelt before we'd even parked. Patrick reached out to my knee and gripped it firmly so I couldn't get out before we'd resolved the fight.

'Just say it Patrick,' I told him. 'You're pissed about something, so just say it.'

He sighed and then blurted out: 'Alexander! I'm pissed

about Alexander! I wish you'd stop focusing on him for just one afternoon. One hour!'

'Fine,' I said, noting where his hand was, forcing him to wrench it back. 'I get it. You're bored of me talking about Alexander. Objection noted.'

I was hurt by how mad he was at me, and embarrassed that I'd somehow done something wrong. But, it takes two to tango, doesn't it. Patrick could take some responsibility too.

'Sorry I'm not over it fast enough for you,' I told him, letting myself be mad for maybe the first time ever. I deserved to be! I was allowed to be! 'But I'm doing my best and in my defence, I was very clear this was a honeymoon for a marriage that never happened *because I was jilted.* So if you hadn't connected the dots that maybe – just maybe! – I'd need to talk about my feelings occasionally then that's on you, NOT ME.'

I clambered out of the car and slammed the door shut behind me. I was so humiliated, but empowered by saying how I felt, too. It was freeing! I must have been the most mind-numbing holiday companion in the world, talking about my ex and boring Patrick rigid, but I was right, too – he was on a free holiday, and if me being a bit repetitive sometimes was the price he had to pay, then he couldn't hold that against me.

I went up in the lift alone, and then straight to my bedroom, fuming that Patrick was even the tiniest bit right about Alexander. Alexander *had* chipped at pieces of me. I'd let him. His email basically admitted to me that he'd known he'd been doing it, too. And if I was really, truly honest with myself, I'd stayed because I was scared and wasn't sure how to ask for more. I hadn't even been sure I deserved more.

Mum always taught us that nice girls don't beg, nice girls don't nag. But nice girls could still get angry, couldn't they? I wasn't a bad person for having wants or needs or feelings.

I flopped down on the bed and stared at the ceiling. I heard Patrick come inside, run the kitchenette tap, and then go into his room.

Alexander, I could live without.

Alexander hadn't been the beginning of the end for me – he'd been the end of the beginning. I was ready for the middle bit of my life now. I was only just getting started. Calming down, I could see how I deserved for it to be better than I'd been accepting, out here in Aus with all the perspective that brought. And I could see how meeting Patrick was a change of pace, of direction. Since hanging out with him it had altered the cadence of my days. Yeah I could survive without Alexander – happily! – but I couldn't live without Patrick now he was in my life. I didn't want to. I'd seen what being with somebody kind and thoughtful was like. He was fun, and yeah, also bruised, but still trying. I'd tasted non-judgement, and curiosity, and just general *nice-guy-ness*. I knew what steak was, now, and that didn't make me miss the cheap hamburger of Alexander at all. I didn't want to fight with him.

Oh my God, I realized, sitting bolt upright.

Oh crap.

I think I like Patrick!

24

Sleep was impossible. I searched around for my AirPods and texted Adzo to see if she was free. This was an emergency. I couldn't fancy Patrick. Absolutely not. I couldn't even let myself explore the idea that I fancied Patrick because then I wouldn't know what to do with that and we still had eight days in Sydney to get through together. That would be a *long* time if I was trying to keep a secret from him.

I didn't get a reply from Adzo, which meant I wouldn't get one for probably the next month. She was like that: either immediate, or fourteen working days to care. I needed to talk this through though. I thought about the only other person I knew in The Single Girls Support Club – Kezza had been the most supportive out of the Core Four, but still sided with the majority that coming away with Patrick wasn't the smartest move I'd ever made. I needed her though. She picked up on the second ring. It must have been about lunchtime at home.

'Hey, babe!' she said. 'Are you okay?'

'Listen,' I replied, my voice lowered as much as I possibly could. 'Can you talk?'

She lowered her voice to match mine. 'Why are we whispering?'

'Hold on.' I grabbed a pair of shorts from my laundry pile and then pulled on a cardigan. Still barefoot I slipped out into the lift of the suite and pressed the button for the lobby. I couldn't risk being overheard. 'I need a Single Girls Support Club meeting.'

'Top secret,' she said, gravely. 'I swear. What's going on? Shoot.'

I sighed melodramatically as I found a corner chair in the lobby to settle into. 'It's about Patrick.'

I could hear the line crinkle from the other end and I knew she was smiling.

'Go on . . .'

'Do I have to?'

'You've shagged him?'

'Kezza! No!'

'Oh.'

'But I think I want to.'

She considered the information. 'I see.'

'What do I do?' I was panicked and fraught. I knew the cat was out of the bag and I was desperate to push it back in, despite getting scratched bloody in the process.

'Hmmm,' she said. 'Do you think he wants to shag you?'

Did I? The way he'd told me I was pretty, how he leaned in to my face, my personal space, with increasing frequency, the way he was always broadly flirty that I'd pooh-poohed as just the way he was with everyone – it was possible. Potentially. He certainly hated when I talked about Alexander, and he'd skirted around the edges of wanting to forgive himself for moving on from Mala. I barely dared hope.

'Maybe,' I said. 'I'm out of practice. And it's a bad idea, isn't it?'

'Depends,' she replied. 'How are you doing? In general?'

'I heard from Alexander,' I revealed. 'I didn't put it in the group chat because I didn't want to give him the airtime, or the brain space, but you were right. He's in Singapore.'

'Is that all he said?'

'He said we never should have got engaged.'

'That son of a—'

'He's right though, isn't he? I hate that he is, but . . . I don't know. We'd been together so long. It seemed like the logical next step. He admitted he went about it all the wrong way, but if I push the wedding aside, I can see that he's right. And that you guys were right, too – I deserve more than I had in that relationship.'

'Hmmmmm. And Patrick – it's not love? It's a fling?'

'Okay, this really is top, *top* secret because it's not my story to tell, but he was married.'

'A divorcé, huh? Interesting.'

I shook my head, but obviously she couldn't see that down the phone. 'No,' I corrected. 'She passed away. He's a widower.'

'Jesus. What happened?'

'Car accident. Two years ago.'

'God bless him,' she said. 'How is he?'

'Still loves her, obviously. Misses her. He said something ages ago, right when we first met, about not being a relationship guy . . .'

'So it would definitely be a fling? Are you okay with that? Could he handle that do you think? I can't imagine how it must feel to lose a partner . . .'

'I know. It's unbearable. But then, he's playful. Maybe it's flirting? And he's so hot, Kez . . . I knew he was attractive, but he's so fun, and he's catching the sun really quickly so has got this tan thing happening, and a freckle thing happening, and we're half naked most of the time, which heightens everything . . .'

'As soon as you said he was coming with you, I think it was pretty inevitable you'd end up in bed together.'

'Shut up!' I volleyed back.

'I'm not judging you! Even if you couldn't see it, I think it was evident to everyone else. A delightful man, a hot woman like yourself, three weeks on the other side of the world? It's a recipe for romance.'

'Not romance,' I warned. 'I don't think? Gah!'

'I'd be surprised if he hadn't been expecting something to happen all along. It's written on the wall.'

'I'm having a lot of thoughts about this.'

Kezza tittered. 'I think if you're careful, getting under one man to get over another could be a wonderful, exciting thing. Be gentle with him, though, and be gentle with yourself. If you called for my advice, my advice is to go for it.'

'I think I was calling for permission,' I admitted. 'Maybe I did know this was going to happen. Urgh, I don't know! We kind of kissed. I thought he'd pulled away first, but to be honest maybe I did. We get on so well . . .'

'Plan not to plan, babe. If it happens, enjoy it happening. If it doesn't, you've had something pretty to look at for the duration of the trip.'

'Right. Yes. We've still got a week to go, so . . .'

'So don't waste it on the phone to me! Go get some sleep. It must be late there. I'm here if you need me, but otherwise I've only got one last thing to say.'

'What's that?'

'Make sure it's as much fun for you as it is for him. A gentleman always makes a lady come first.'

'That was very helpful, thank you, Kezza. Thrilled I called.'

She laughed. 'Love you!'

I got up early, hoping to beat Patrick, but he was already at the breakfast table by the windows, his boxers on show through his open dressing gown, set against the backdrop of another beautiful day.

'I owe you one thousand apologies,' I said as I approached. 'I flew off the handle last night.'

'Correct,' he said. I couldn't read his face. I assumed he was going to let me speak and then tell me where to shove it, because he didn't want to be around anyone who couldn't regulate their own mood swings, but I tried to be as girlish and cute as possible. I wasn't being manipulative – but I was definitely trying to appeal to his most forgiving side.

'I'm sorry,' I carried on. 'I was defensive and I shouldn't have stormed off. We'd had that whole almost-kiss thing – I hate to bring it up, because I'm embarrassed, but you were there; you know how it went down – and I just want you to know I so value you, and you being here. Friends don't storm out of cars and go to bed without saying goodnight. You were only trying to be my cheerleader. So in short: I apologize.'

'As it turns out—' he smiled '—I'm quite honoured that you'd lose your rag with me. From what I've gathered, you don't let a lot of people see that side of you . . .'

That much was true. I'd swallowed anger and hurt and squashed down ever needing anything, really, in case I was 'too much'.

'No,' I said. 'I don't.'

'So it's cool.' He shrugged. 'Thank you for saying sorry for storming off, but it's good you've told me how you feel. Thank you. Now come here for a hug.'

His naked chest pressed against the thin cotton of my pyjamas. I loved the smell of him: woody and earthy and warm.

'You ready for another wonderful day in paradise? I thought we could wander the harbour and get lunch and be back here for the 3 p.m. pick-up for the sunset canoeing?'

Sunset canoeing with Patrick. Something in the bottom part of my pelvis throbbed and now, instead of pretending I couldn't feel it, I let myself acknowledge it.

OMG, I texted Kezza, knowing she wouldn't reply because of the time difference but needing to say it anyway. *I'm in so much trouble, girl. Even the touch of his hand on my back is turning me on. I'm screwed!*

Later she texted back: *Hopefully!*

I didn't know how to do it. I had no idea how to non-verbally suggest that we should kiss again, and mean it this time. We had a perfect day mooching about the harbour, but I was self-conscious and a bit awkward. Patrick asked me twice if I was okay, noting that by the time we'd gone back to the suite to change for the afternoon trip, I seemed different. I was different, of course. I had a crush! Crushes make a girl act crazy!

'We should think about leaving,' Patrick said, and I could tell by the extra peppiness in his voice he was trying to make my awkwardness less strange. 'We don't want to be late for the driver.'

'Absolutely,' I said, looking at my watch and seeing that he was right. I'd taken a quick shower and thrown on a short linen playsuit with big buttons running up the front. I'd gained weight over our trip, even in this short time, so it was more snug than I was used to. It made me look good, though. I suited being a bit fuller. Maybe I could buy a few cute dresses when we were out shopping. I could worry about saving money to move house back in the real world. 'Let me just get my bag. It's all very romantic, isn't it? A sunset canoe?'

'You sound as though you're making plans to seduce me.' He chortled. He looked handsome as ever in his pressed shorts and another shirt – baby pink, this time. My grand-mother always said it takes a real man to wear pink.

'What?' I said, colouring up. See! I knew he could tell I was thinking about his lips!

'Annie,' he said. 'I was kidding. No need to look so horrified.' If only he knew.

Everything about Patrick was amplified now I knew that I'd somehow – whilst nobody was looking – developed feel-ings. I couldn't do anything about it, and so I kept my distance physically as we navigated our way to the car. I steered conver-sation to the things we could see as we drove to the drop-off point, about thirty minutes away, so that we didn't dance around anything that could be accused of being flirtatious. That was hard because we did naturally bounce off one another – exactly why it had been so great to see him at bootcamp, and how I'd ended up with the ill-advised crush in the first place – but now it was a minefield where I could embarrass myself at any moment by stepping over the line when it wasn't warranted. I couldn't figure out if the things he was doing were friendly or flirty. He'd open a car door for me and I'd think: *Oh. Friendly.* But then he'd do the thing where he saved a secret smile just for me, and I'd think: *Flirty.* Then he'd smile at our taxi driver or waiter or a random person with a nice dog on the street and I'd change my mind again: *Friendly. He's just friendly.*

We headed upstream in our separate canoes from the launch spot the taxi dropped us at, gliding across the water past limestone cliffs that glistened, illuminated by the late-afternoon sun. The estuary was wide and quiet, lined with leafy vegetation and the low hum of insects.

My canoe was dark green, and the tip of it cut into the deep water like a knife through butter, parting it and pushing through with ease, making me feel like the Amelia Earhart of the backwaters, breaking new ground. For every one loaded, intensified moment I'd had with Patrick so far on the trip, there'd been ten more moments like this – quiet reflections and private re-centrings, flashes of perfection that made me feel like everything really would be okay. I knew London existed as a concept, that home was real and there was loads to figure out on my return, but it didn't matter when the sun was burnt orange, the middle of a Guy Fawkes Night bonfire, nature putting on her best show just for me. How spoiled I was to have that. How lucky I was to be gifted such a radically fancy experience so that I could heal. Fernanda had wanted this for me all along. I was starting to want it for myself. I was whole. I was enough.

By the time we got to a tiny private beach, the sun dropping behind the trees seductively and ice clinking in the glasses waiting for us on the shore, osprey fishing in the water, we'd lulled ourselves into the intimate silence that came with being in total awe of the moment.

'Crikey,' said Patrick, eventually, absorbing the new dusty twinge to the light, the stillness of the water. We were clocking up a lot of sunsets together.

'Yeah,' I agreed. 'I think this might be the most peaceful I've ever been in my life.'

I wiggled my toes in the sand at the bottom of the huge throw we were lounging on. It was colder underneath, where it hadn't been exposed to the sun. My skin was sunbaked, my hair wild around my shoulders, my smile involuntary but undoubtedly there.

'I don't want to go back to my real life as it was,' I said. I don't know where it came from – mostly that I didn't think it was possible to feel this way once we left Australia, and I wanted to feel like this always. Suspended in time and cocooned by nature. I wanted to examine every cloud in the sky and each leaf of the trees so that I could commit it to memory.

'Can I ask you something?' he said.

I made a noise that signified he could.

'Why aren't you happy at home?'

'Just a small question, then,' I joked. 'What's the meaning of life? Are you happy? Why is the sky blue?'

'Love. Yes. Science.'

I shook my head. 'You've got an answer for everything.'

'Only because I spend so much time asking questions.'

His body was close to mine. Was he leaning into it too? Maybe I was imagining it because of his kindness. Maybe I was hoping for something absurd.

No, this is real, a voice from inside me said. *You're safe to feel this.*

'Go on,' he prompted. His voice was lowered, a priest pacifying me into revelation.

'Why aren't I happy at home?'

It was his turn to make murmurs of encouragement.

I continued. 'Honestly? I feel like I'm too much. Or, no, not enough.'

I kept moving my toes in the sand.

My body angled towards him a little more, responding to him doing the same. More and more we inched in the other's direction.

I wanted to believe he might have a crush too.

'I was bullied at school. I didn't come back to drama camp because . . . It was when I got back after that last summer there and went into year ten, suddenly the popular girls didn't like that I'd done something. It was as if they decided to hate me because I was excited about this thing that I loved. And for a whole school year they tormented me, and when the school finally called my parents because they were worried that I'd become withdrawn and stopped participating, Dad was really nice about it but Mum . . . wasn't.

'She made out that if other girls thought I was awful then I must be doing something wrong. She didn't push for me to go back to drama camp and about halfway through that summer I came up with this plan to be the girl everyone said I should be. I know it sounds unreasonable but it had been such a horrible and lonely year when I was myself that I thought being somebody else wasn't a bad little plot. Now I think about it, I realize I'd basically been pretending to be that person right up until the wedding.'

'Annie, that's horrible.'

'Yeah. The thing is, I don't think I ever did stop to think about it. Staying in a dead-end relationship, sticking with a job I'm not crazy about—'

'I've been thinking about this,' he interrupted. 'You're a theoretical physicist. You're basically a genius . . .'

'But it's not my passion.'

'My work isn't my passion,' he countered. 'It's just the way I make money to enjoy my life. I think making your job your personality is a very modern-day thing. I don't understand it. I know I said to leave if you don't enjoy it, but what I missed out is that it's okay not to love what you do.'

'That's fair,' I said. 'But I've been thinking about it too, and I need it. I can't spend thirty-five or forty or sometimes even fifty hours a week doing something I'm not really into. That's a third of my life, and the other third is spent sleeping.'

'Better make that last third count, then,' he said, cheekily. *Friendly or flirty? Friendly . . . or flirty?*

I dropped my eyes to the lower half of his face, to his lips.

'I can see so clearly that you're ready to move on with your life. But then just when I think it's clear you trash-talk yourself, or talk about Alexander and I think, oh no. She's not ready. She doesn't want to move on.'

'I am ready,' I said, quietly. 'I just need to find my courage.'

His voice was quiet, too – almost inaudible. 'And have you found it . . .'

It wasn't a question, what he said. With his voice low and his chin inches from mine and the weight between us, it was almost definitely an invitation.

I swallowed.

Something is happening, I thought, clearly. *Something is definitely happening.*

I could almost hear the cogs of his brain whirring. He inhaled decisively, and right before he could execute the inevitable, our tour guide's canoe hit up against the shore and she said: 'Righto, guys, if I can invite you to hop back into the boats. If we leave it any later it'll be dark, and the mozzies that come out then are so big you'll have to play little spoon.'

Patrick leapt up like he'd been caught doing something he shouldn't. 'Be right there,' he said.

He looked down at me and offered his hand. I reached out for it.

'Thanks,' I said, and under his breath he muttered, 'Sure thing. Yup. Uh-huh.'

As we piled back into the taxi I thought back to the vows I'd made on the plane over. I'd promised myself that I'd stop trying to be perfect. That for better for worse, I'd throw caution to the wind. For richer and for poorer I'd say yes to every opportunity that came my way.

I stole a look at Patrick. His profile had become so familiar to me already that it was a comfort. The way his hair flopped across his forehead made me want to reach across and smooth it away for him. I imagined what it would be like to unclip my seatbelt and slide across to the middle seat, just to feel his thigh against my own. I wondered how it would feel to press my face to his, on purpose this time, slipping my tongue into his mouth.

'You okay?' he asked.

I issued a weak smile. 'Sydney is amazing, isn't it?' I couldn't tell him what I'd really been thinking about.

'It's wicked,' he agreed, and then he did the most bewildering thing. He unclipped his seatbelt and slid across, reaching his arm out and forcing me to duck my head so he could reach across my shoulders and pull me in. My thigh was against his. I froze for half a second, checking I hadn't misunderstood, before giving in to how good it felt. I let my head loll to one side so that it rested against his chest. He let out a small sigh – a gratified one. As I watched out of the window at the sky whizzing by I let my hand drift to his knee. His free hand met me there. We rode home pushed up against each other with every part of our bodies, except our faces, testing this new normal.

As we got out of the car Patrick's hand came to the back of my neck, and I liked it being there. We didn't say anything as we walked up to the private penthouse elevator, the heat of his touch intensifying as we went up floor after floor. I was the one with the key cards and as I stood in front of the buttons, his body came close behind me, so close and yet so far away. I realized I was taking shallow, short breaths. If I had wanted to suspend the moment of being in the taxi together for the rest of all time, now I wanted to get upstairs as quickly as possible, because I knew what was going to happen on the other side.

My hunger for it made every second feel decades long. It could only have taken moments to reach into my bag, to pull out the key, to hit it against the security box and hear the roar of the pulley lifting us towards the thirty-sixth floor, and yet it took hours, days, *millennia*. I set my bag down on the sofa in the central living room and pulled my water bottle out. I chugged it down, but it didn't satisfy my thirst. Wiping my mouth with the back of my hand I knew what I was going to do next.

Patrick watched me. I stood, and let him. I smiled. I refused to look away, or be shy.

I wanted him. I had done for probably longer than I'd realized.

'I'm going to kiss you now,' I said, putting the cap back on the water bottle. 'Is that okay?'

It was three steps.

My heart thudded in my chest.

One step.

Thud.

Two steps.

Thud.

Three steps.

Thud.

I put a hand up to his face. I didn't want to rush. I didn't want to launch at him. I didn't want to take any of this for granted. I wanted to mean it. I wanted to remember it.

I looked into his eyes. He was serious and solemn. I ran my thumb over his lips and then leaned towards him, on purpose this time, lingering for one last moment right before my mouth met his.

25

I couldn't remember the last time I'd made out with someone. Why did that ever stop? Why do we have so much focus on kissing having to give way to getting naked when there's so much joy, and heat, and passion in kissing over and over, speeding up and slowing down, just being together?

'I need to take this slow,' he breathed into my mouth, and I immediately understood: *he hasn't had sex since his wife died.*

'I want to take it slow too,' I reassured him. I hadn't been with anybody but Alexander in a decade so it was all new to me, too. All new proportions and lines and motions. 'I'd like that.'

I could feel him bulging through his shorts. He lifted me up onto the counter of the small kitchenette and my legs were parted so he could stand between them. I pushed my crotch to his because I couldn't help but arch my back to feel him, but everything else stayed strictly PG, even though the pulsing in my underwear was rated 18.

There was a tenderness to the way he kissed me. We were

vulnerable – like we'd agreed, through the way we were touching, to be sensitive with each other because we both knew that was what the other needed. And as his fingers dug in to where he held the tops of my thighs, creeping towards my bum in a cradle, I could feel him losing himself, surrendering to me; it made it safe to surrender to him, too.

I trust him, I thought to myself, and then I stopped thinking at all.

26

We lay on the sofa in the dark. It must have been way past
midnight – I honestly had no idea. His body pressed up
against mine and we drifted from kissing to talking in
hushed whispers, the hushed whispers giving way to more
kissing.

'Is this weird?' I asked, because I couldn't help it. 'Do you
feel weird about this happening?'

He shook his head, and he was so close to me that it
forced his nose to knock against mine in an Eskimo kiss.

'It's the opposite of weird,' he told me. 'It's weird how not
weird it is. I've wanted you. I've been consumed with guilt
about it, and I tried not to, but I have done since the day I
helped you put your jumper on.'

His fingertips gently tickled my thigh so that they disappeared up my shorts and back again. I moaned, lightly, a
signal that he made me feel good.

'You understand how much I want you, don't you?' he
asked. 'Taking it slow, it's not . . .'

He didn't finish the sentence.

'There's no formula we have to follow,' I replied softly. 'Sex is overrated anyway.'

He pulled away and tipped his head. 'Bullshit,' he roared.

'Yeah,' I replied, laughing too. 'Come on, get off me. It's bedtime, and I need a cold shower. And . . .' I pointedly looked down at his crotch, illuminated by the moonlight. '. . . I think you do too.'

He grinned, totally unashamed at the tent he appeared to be pitching in his trousers.

'I'm just a man,' he said, rolling off me. 'I told you I'm putty in your hands.'

'Goodnight, Patrick Hummingbird.'

From the sofa he watched me go and replied, 'Goodnight, Annie Wiig.'

I turned back and flashed a smile at him. Alone in my room I replayed exactly what had just happened. How hard my heart had beat before I said I was going to kiss him, where the tips of his fingers had caressed as he'd kissed my mouth, my neck, my chest, how giving in to what I'd been feeling was a victory and surrender, all at once. I drifted to sleep committing every detail of it to memory.

27

I woke up beaming inanely, and desperate to tell Kezza what had happened. I couldn't believe Patrick and I had kissed. Not even kissed – *made out*. I was a grown woman who did not need to run back to her group of girls to unpack what that all meant, like a teenager trying to figure out if her crush was going to ask her to the end-of-term dance. Except . . .

Kezza, I typed into my phone. *I wish the time difference meant you weren't always asleep when I'm awake, and that I wasn't always awake when you're asleep. I have things to say!!*

I started typing out the ins and outs since she'd coached me on the phone, but it was hard to know where the story actually started and what my point was. I thought about it. The point was, Patrick and I made out, and now I was lying in bed the morning after the night before trying to decide how to play it when I came out of the bedroom. He would, inevitably, be sat eating breakfast in his underwear, just as he was every morning.

Underwear that contained quite the excitable beast, too, if last night was anything to go by.

I deleted everything I'd typed in the text box to Kezza and replaced it with: *Patrick and I kissed. I am freaking out because . . . I liked it??? But also: omfg??? I wish I could talk to you!!*

I added: *Nothing further happened, we just kissed. He kisses like you hope to be kissed. I'm obsessed. I had to . . . you know . . . relieve myself (!!!) once we'd said goodnight!*

'Annie?'

Patrick's voice came through from the lounge area, but it sounded like he was approaching my room.

I pulled the bedsheets around me for protection – from what, I don't know. I cleared my throat and tried to sound as neutral as possible as I replied, 'Yes?'

There was a soft tap on the door.

'Can I come in?'

Patrick pushed open the bedroom door and, true to form, was in his underwear and an open dressing gown.

'Morning,' I said, distracted by how good he looked. His hair was stuck up on end, and his eyes were still sleepy and small. I wanted to reach out and pull him into bed with me. 'You okay?'

He nodded sagely. Making eye contact made my stomach lurch.

'I have something to say, and I could have waited until you were up but . . .'

Oh God. Was he going to tell me it was all a mistake? That we were about to spend the next six days in the most self-conscious, awkward, embarrassed way possible? I wished I could recall my text to Kezza. The only thing worse than explaining that we'd made out would be explaining that afterwards I got rejected because *NEWSFLASH!* no man wants me! It's hilarious I ever thought they could! I'm not the woman men ever fancy!

I waited for the blow to come.

'I just wanted to see your face,' he continued, 'when I told you that . . .'

I wished he'd bloody hurry up and spit it out.

'You sent your text to me instead of one of your friends. You freaked out at me instead of Kezza.'

I instantly leapt across the bed to pick up my phone and open it to the screen I'd just been writing on. At the top of the thread it didn't say Kezza. It said Patrick. I'd been thinking about Patrick and so I'd texted Patrick.

'Gah!' I squealed, pulling the covers up to my face to hide myself from a level of mortification that might actually kill me. I could hear his laughter through the sheets.

'No!' I insisted. 'Noooooo!'

His laughter came closer and his weight sank into the bottom of the bed.

'Permission to enter?' he said, and his face peeked under the sheet from the other side of the bed.

'I can't believe I texted you and not Kezza. That's so humiliating. Forget everything it said, *please.*'

'Hey,' he said. 'Come on. Now you've got me in your bed, so at least some good came of it . . . Or did you need some more special alone time?'

Why had I told Kezza I'd masturbated? PATRICK NOW KNEW I'D HAD A WANK OVER THE THOUGHT OF US SNOGGING.

'Are you okay?' he asked. He'd stopped laughing now, but was still smirking.

'My ego needs another ten minutes,' I winced.

'Did you really think today would be weird?'

I shrugged and looked at him through my fingers. 'Maybe. I don't know.'

'You told me you'd wanted it to happen for ages.'

'You did too!' I said, like the whiny teenager I was trying to avoid being, which made us both laugh again.

'Look,' he said. 'First and foremost we're friends, right? But I'm just going to be very, very honest here: if the kissing happens again, I wouldn't be sorry about it.'

I finally looked at him properly.

'That got your attention,' he joked.

I smiled. 'Okay. This was still horribly embarrassing and I still need you to leave. But, cool. Deal. We're friends first.'

'And . . .?' he prompted.

'And if the kissing happens again, I wouldn't be sorry about it either.'

'Good talk,' he said, and I thought that was the last of it. Then he turned and winked as he told me: 'I can't lie. I had to alleviate a bit of the tension last night too, by the way.'

I squealed and threw a pillow at him, but he moved too quickly and closed the door, forcing it to hit the wall with a thud before landing on the carpet.

28

We spent the next few days ticking off all the tourist spots Sydney had to offer – we saw a musical version of *American Psycho* at the opera house, as well as a proper opera about Elizabeth the First having to choose between her heart and her country. The food scene in Sydney was remarkable. There were tons of places with amazing Asian dishes, and we got stuck in to Sydney rock oysters one lunchtime in the harbour, washed down with a bottle of wine, and I'd tried Vegemite for the first time (it was a thumbs down from me, but Patrick purchased six jars to take home with him because he loved it so much). I had a newfound obsession with Tim Tams, and the concierge at the hotel told us to order our burgers with beetroot on, because apparently that was the thing to do.

We clocked up a morning cooking class, a walking tour, the Museum of Sydney, a harbour boat tour, afternoon tea at the Queen Victoria Building, and took the ferry out to Manly to explore the promenade. No two people in the history of people had ever Sydney-ed as hard as Patrick and I Sydney-ed. In fact, for five days we Sydney-ed so hard that from eight in the morning until ten at night we barely had time to directly talk to one another except to point something out on the skyline or to ask the other to pull out their phone to look at the maps function. And in between it all, the kissing kept happening.

I was never not aware of him. At dinner we started to choose seats next to each other at the bar rather than opting for a table where we'd sit opposite each other, ordering a drink and almost immediately necking. Patrick instinctively moved chairs in outdoor cafés so we'd sit side by side and look at the view, feet finding each other and knees knocking. On the ferry to Manly Beach it had been busy enough that we'd had to take seats a few rows apart, and I caught him staring at me. I'd looked out at the water and smiled into the breeze, appreciating the way my forearms had deepened in colour and enjoying the looseness in my shoulders and, thoughts of Patrick aside, the emptiness in my own brain. Sure, we spent a lot of time discussing travel itineraries and planning where to eat, but that was cool, day-to-day stuff. On that boat I couldn't even remember what else there might be to worry about, only that worries existed somewhere, somehow – just not here, with me. It was then I'd sensed his eyes on me, and when I looked across he just grinned, stared, and then lifted a hand to wave.

I miss you, he mouthed, making me laugh even more. When we disembarked, he laced his fingers through mine and held on to me like he would never let go.

Darling Annie, Fernanda texted me, as we stopped for elevenses. *I hope Sydney is a dream. Do let us know how you're getting on when you get chance! You haven't texted in a while. We'd love to see some more photos!*

Fernanda messaged more often than my own family. Freddie had obviously returned to school with gusto, forgetting about her big sister – out of sight, out of mind. Mum and Dad didn't stay in touch, but Fernanda continued to check in every few days, I think out of an anxiousness that she hadn't sent me on a fool's errand and that I really was enjoying myself. Shame flushed through me – I couldn't exactly let her know just how much I was enjoying myself, could I? That, to be totally honest, yeah, Sydney was amazing, but my absolute favourite part of Sydney was probably Patrick's mouth.

It had been so touching that she'd continued to check in and take an interest in the trip, but now things with Patrick were murkier I felt dishonest with her. I told her it was wonderful and sent snaps of the hotel, reiterating how much I loved her, and appreciated her.

You didn't plan it, Kezza reminded me when I begged her for perspective. I held on to that truth. I hadn't, after all. So why did I feel so bad whenever Fernanda pinged on my phone?

'You okay?' Patrick asked, noticing that I was lost in my messages.

'Yes,' I said, quickly. 'Yes, of course. It's Fernanda again. She's so lovely.'

We spent a night out in the Blue Mountains, on a luxury coach tour that only took a couple of hours' drive. I'd never heard of the Blue Mountains, and it was a million hectares of tall forest, sandstone cliffs, canyons and waterfalls, all with a blue horizon of eucalyptus trees that seemed to just go on and on. We trekked deep into the middle of it to admire the native bushland, gaping at the rock formations and exploring the underground caves. We got to listen to Dreaming stories told by Aboriginal guides and admire the work of resident artists too, picking up a few packable pieces to take home. We loved it so much that we arranged to go back a second time, trekking part of the Six Foot Track to look out over Wentworth Falls, Kings Tableland and Mount Solitary, before being driven to a nearby resort for some much-needed R and R after absorbing such majestic nature and clocking thirty thousand steps a day.

And the kissing. Little pecks. Deep, passionate kisses. Two make-out sessions before bed, each one more intense than the last.

One afternoon by the pool we kissed again, and I wasn't sure how much longer I could keep locking lips without jumping his bones. I tried to revel in the novelty of going slowly, of getting to know somebody's life and personality before I discovered their body, but I craved him. We were charged magnets.

Urm, but . . . I thought this was a lust situation, not a love one, Adzo texted. She'd finally replied to me and I'd been able to fill her in on what had happened the night of the sunset canoe trip. She'd basically said what Kezza had – that apparently everyone except Patrick and I knew we were going to hook up even before we actually had, or even before either of us had thought about it. Part of that really bugged me because there was a low-level accusation that men and women couldn't just be friends, but then, this woman and that man hadn't just been friends, had they?

218

29

'It isn't that I'm not grateful for all we've done as we've been here,' I said. 'But wow. A whole afternoon at a spa resort? That definitely hits the spot for me.'

'I'm with you on that,' Patrick replied. 'My calves – I'm not used to so much walking. They should put "walk fifty thousand steps" on the Barry's Bootcamp workouts. Not even D'Shawn's class makes my legs feel this heavy.'

He pulled out the leaflet of where we were headed from his backpack and opened it up.

'You're the information king,' I said. 'I've literally never met anyone as obsessed with reading up before, during and after an event as you. Where do you even put all that information?'

Our waiter delivered two toasties to our table, where we'd found our daily café – a place we ended up coming to at least once a day, to the point where the barista knew our order before we even had to say it.

Patrick took a big bite and, with his mouth full, said, 'To be fair it pretty much goes in one eye and out the other. That's why I have to reread everything.'

I was glad I hadn't already taken a bite, because a shooting 'Ha!' left my throat in amusement before I could stop it.

'It's true!' he said. 'I think I might be dyslexic actually, but it hasn't ever been diagnosed. I don't know. Not that it matters but yeah, sometimes I do feel like my brain doesn't work like everyone else's.'

'Oh,' I said, taken aback by his vulnerability. 'That's the first time you've said anything.'

He kept chewing. 'You're so smart, and I'm . . .'

I held up a hand. 'Don't even say it. Don't you dare.'

'What! It's true! You're a scientist. And use words so long that half the time I think I only just catch the drift of what you mean. All I can say is, it's a good job your face is so expressive. That helps.'

'I won't stand for this,' I said. 'If you are dyslexic, it obviously hasn't held you back. You've developed other skills to compensate. You challenge me to think differently. It's one of the things I . . .'

Crap. I almost said *love*. Not that I was *in love* with Patrick. I was only using it as a turn of phrase.

'. . . *Enjoy* about you most. You're not like a lot of other people I know. I don't know if that's why, or what. But, you're amazing. Obviously you could stand to better your sense of direction a little more . . .'

It was his turn to issue a 'Ha!'

'Don't even start, Annie. It was you who got us lost on the way to afternoon tea that day, not me. Don't even try it. That really will be a Mona Lisa moment.'

'Hey,' I said. 'When you had your Mona Lisa morning, in Margaret River – when you left but then came back?'

'Yeah,' he said.

'What was that?'

He pulled a face. 'Me being ridiculous.'

'I was worried I'd annoyed you.'

'You could never annoy me,' he replied. He carried on: 'I was just freaked out, that's all. After I told you about Mala, I was glad I had and it was the right thing to do, but I think I knew I was starting to catch feelings for you. That's why I told you. I didn't want anything to happen without you knowing about her. I don't tell a lot of women, but . . . you're not just any woman, are you?'

'Aren't I?' I teased, and he rolled his eyes.

'Finish your food and let's get to this spa,' he said. 'I want to be kneaded like a sourdough starter.'

'Holy hell,' Patrick said as we walked through the doors. 'Is this Narnia?'

We stood side by side and took in the majestic sight of the marbled entryway of the spa, with a huge glass panelled back that looked out onto acres of opulent green gardens, the occasional robed human meandering peacefully by.

'Welcome to Serenity Gardens. You must be Annie Wiig? We've been expecting you.'

I opened my mouth to speak but the person behind the desk continued talking.

'My name is Storm, and my pronouns are they and them. If you need anything today, please ask any member of staff, and do request me personally if you feel called to. You're booked in for the couples retreat, so here are your robes and you're in bathhouse ten today. Follow this corridor outside and then you'll see the signs there.'

Storm did *not* pause for breath.

'We're nudist here everywhere except the main swimming

221

pool, which I'll mark on the map here—' They pulled out a laminated map from behind the counter and circled where they meant in red pen. 'So please do adhere to that. It's just more sanitary that way.'

Patrick interjected, 'It's more sanitary to be nude?'

'It's better for your body, yes. Enjoy your stay!'

Slowly we took the map from Storm and headed in the direction we'd been pointed. Neither of us spoke as we navigated the grand corridors furnished with lots of natural light and huge stone pots littered with green plants and exotic-looking flowers.

The inside gave way to outside and it became apparent that the bathhouses were private shacks with changing spaces and a terrace, and would be where our couples massage took place. At the back of the property was an outdoor, open-plan bathing area with a massive jacuzzi and open-air shower.

'Hello and welcome to Serenity Gardens. My name is Leslie and my pronouns are she and her.' A young Asian woman with her hair artfully styled into a low bun stood at the door to the cabana, a tall man with what looked like Māori tattoos beside her.

'My name is John, and my pronouns are he and him. We'll be your massage therapists today. Are we okay to begin in fifteen minutes?'

I looked at Patrick.

'Absolutely,' he said. 'Do we just wear . . .?'

'It will be a private space,' said Leslie. 'So each take a table and lay the towels on top of you. You don't need to wear underwear.'

'Righto,' I said. 'No underwear.'

'There's champagne waiting for you, but we do suggest

that you start with a big glass of water to stay hydrated, and save the bubbles for afterwards.'

'That's a great tip,' Patrick said. 'Thank you.'

The inside of the bathhouse was light and airy, and it became apparent immediately that the only scaled-off part of the space was the small toilet by the back. We both clocked it at the same time, and Patrick said, 'I'll go in there and let you get settled in here. I'll come out when you're ready – preserve our modesty?'

He disappeared and I practically ripped off my clothes before diving under the towel laid out, terrified he might catch me half-on half-off the bed in some horribly compromising position.

'Ready!' I said, when I was covered and settled, and Leslie took that as her cue to come in from the front door right as Patrick took it as his cue to leave the bathroom, stark bollock naked.

'Oh!' Leslie cried. 'My apologies! I thought you were—'

She spun around fast, crashing into John as he entered the front door after her, meaning she stepped on John's toe and then leapt back herself in surprise, stumbling back and heading right for me. Patrick reached out to catch her, releasing his hands from where they'd been cupped at his penis to reveal the full size of the thing directly at face-height from where I was on the massage table. His penis came towards me, his hands outstretched to help support Leslie, John hopping up and down in agony, and in grave panic I rolled over and off onto the floor, crouching down, naked as the day I was born.

Patrick caught Leslie, who excused herself so that she could give us a moment to regroup, and then he threw me a towel and wrapped another one around his waist.

'Are you okay?' he said, concerned. 'Did you fall?'

'Your . . . thingy, your . . . it was LUNGING at me,' I exclaimed.

'My thingy?' he raised an eyebrow. He was a lot calmer than I was. I was traumatized.

'Your willy! I've seen your willy!'

He grinned.

'I've seen your boobs,' he said, like a dirty old man. His smile reached from ear to ear.

We burst out laughing.

'I guess that's broken the naked-spa-day ice then,' I commented. 'The hard part is over with?'

Patrick looked down at himself and quipped, 'I can't guarantee the hard part won't come back to be honest.'

'Patrick!'

He held out a hand for me. 'Come on, up you get. We've definitely earned those massages now. I think we're going to have to leave them a very big tip, by the way. When Fernanda and Charles paid for all this I doubt they budgeted for willy-gate.'

He helped me up and I straightened out the massage table.

'Turn around as I get on this,' I instructed. 'That's enough boob-gate for now, too.'

He turned and faced the wall as I got settled, lying back down on my front and covering my bum with the towel.

Still facing the wall, Patrick said, 'Annie?'

'Yes?' I replied.

'Just to be clear – they're bloody great boobs.'

There's nowhere much you can go once you've seen the junk of the man you're on your non-honeymoon with. The massages went on for ninety minutes and we both made noises as humiliating as each other, and once Leslie and John had gone we drank another glass of water and then popped open the bottle of champagne and took it out to the hot tub in our swimwear. We weren't ready for the communal naked areas.

'I don't know if I can face a naked sauna,' Patrick said as he lowered himself into the tub. 'I know I'm supposed to be a sort of male manic pixie dream girl, all carefree and daring, but I'm afraid we've just found out where my boundaries are.'

'Manic pixie dream girl?' I said, stepping down to join him in the tub.

He held out a hand for me to grab in case I slipped. 'Manic pixie dream girl,' he repeated.

I stared at him blankly.

'How do I explain it? Urm, in a movie, the manic pixie dream girl is the eccentric, crazy love interest designed to spark a renewed desire for living. Like Kate Winslet in that film about erasing memories – *Eternal Sunshine of the Spotless Mind.*'

'Patrick – oh my God. That is so true! That's so you!'

'Thank you, thank you,' he replied, taking a pretend bow.

'That's how you were at drama camp. You've always been that way.'

'Maybe,' he said. 'Maybe not.'

'What do you mean?' I asked, exhaling in satisfaction. 'There's no maybe about it.'

I sipped at my flute full of bubbles then lay my head back to enjoy the sensation of being a tiny bit tipsy and also so tranquil I was basically horizontal anyway.

'I was pretty messed up after Mala died,' he said. 'I went off the rails a bit. Definitely wasn't much fun to be around then . . .'

'I like hearing about her,' I said. 'You know you can talk about her as much as you want, don't you?'

He nodded. 'She'd have loved it here,' he offered. 'I don't know why I got so mad when you talked about Alexander, because Mala has been on my mind like crazy. I'm starting to wonder if that's just part of moving on.'

I stayed quiet, careful to let his train of thought keep going.

'I suppose you have to kind of look back to where you've come from to understand how to get where you're going or something,' he continued. 'I can feel myself moving on and it's like I'm cheating on her. And that makes me so sad. How can I feel so happy and so sad, both at the same time?'

I considered it. 'There's something my grandma used to say – my dad's mum. I've not thought about this in ages actually, and I'm probably going to get this all muddled up but . . . she said that life's highs and life's lows are so entwined, the happiness and sorrow is so interconnected, that it's impossible to ever just be totally happy or totally sad. It's good and bad, light and dark. We want there to be a right thing, an ultimate happiness, a sort of destination where we've escaped all the crappy things in life. Like passing a test. But that's not living. We can't outrun crappy, awful, horrible stuff. So the job of our lives is to let it exist alongside the good stuff, making the good stuff so much sweeter. Does that make sense?'

Still looking out over the gardens he nodded. 'It does,' he admitted.

The jet of the jacuzzi gurgled like a feeding baby.

'Being a widower isn't fun,' he said. 'And the person I want to tell me how to deal with all this is the one person who can't. I wish I could have her permission.'

'Her permission?'

Softly, he said, 'You know what I mean.'

And I didn't until right when he said it.

'Us?' I asked.

He nodded again.

'It's there, isn't it?' he said. 'It's not just . . .'

'Yeah,' I replied, looking at him. 'I think it is. But I don't want you to feel bad about it.'

'I feel bad that I *don't* feel bad.'

That caught me by surprise. 'I don't know what to say to that.'

'Me neither.'

Annie, take a chance, my inner voice gently said. *It's okay to want this.*

'Hey,' I said. 'Shall we robe up and explore these gardens? I promise this isn't an elaborate ruse to get you in the naked sauna. But it could be nice?'

'That does sound nice,' he agreed, downing his glass and moving to help me out of the tub. 'After you,' he said, and he followed me, catching my hand as I walked away.

He spun me around.

'Annie,' he said, and tipped my chin up towards him. His lips met mine and softly, so tenderly it was almost imperceptible, he opened his mouth and his tongue moved against my own. He drew me in greedily. I reached my arms up around him and tugged straight back.

'Hmmm,' he said, smiling. 'God, you're hot.'

We strolled around the gardens holding hands and, after that last kiss in particular, clasping my hand around his was as intimate as anything we could have done naked. That kiss was like a key to a door where we could touch more freely than ever, and so through the gardens Patrick's arm slung over my

227

shoulder, and on the walk home his hand was in my back pocket. We passed a supermarket and popped in for some chocolate. We broke apart for a moment, getting the delicious rush of his fingertips brushing against mine in the queue to pay, searching for me so we could touch again.

Back at the suite we took turns showering and getting ready for bed, and I was lying in my hotel gown and slippers when Patrick appeared in the doorway.

'Hey,' I said, and I knew what was going to happen.

He came to me in his towel, and the only small gesture that betrayed his otherwise poised demeanour was the way he swallowed, as if he was nervous but still determined. I sat upright as he joined me on the bed and solemnly, he reached for my hand and kissed my palm.

'Annie,' he said, almost moaning my name it was so soft.

I tipped my head and said, 'Yes?'

With all the gentleness he had in him, he took a breath, and still holding my hand to his lips turned to fully face me and deeply, with gravel in his throat, he said, 'I wondered if I could see those magnificent boobs again.'

30

If I thought he was nervous as he'd walked into my room, it took less than ten seconds to ascertain that in fact he was hard, and horny, and our bodies moved up against each other very, very well.

He looked me dead in the eye as I unlaced my robe, then he buried himself in my chest, kissing my breasts and taking it in turns to put each one of my nipples in his mouth. I ran my fingers through his hair and revelled in the conviction of his touch. He wasn't being gentle with me. I don't know what I'd expected but he wasn't shy about desiring me, about wanting me – and about telling me what to do.

He moved his mouth down over my stomach, issuing kisses as he went.

'Open your legs for me,' he commanded, and everything after that was a bit of a blur.

Afterwards we lay in bed eating the chocolate Tim Tams we'd bought earlier, my head on his chest so he could tickle my back.

'Did you think this was going to happen?' I asked.

'You and me? No. Yes. I don't know.'

'Same. I can't figure it out.'

'I mean. Where do you stand on . . . it all?' He gestured to his own naked form and then my own. 'Now?'

'We're two people who know what the other one tastes like,' I sniggered.

'You're a poet,' he replied, amused.

'And,' I said, trying to find the words that wouldn't scare either of us, 'we can just . . . see . . . where it goes?'

'Cool as a cucumber,' he noted.

'I could ask you to drink my blood under a full moon and commit to me until the second coming of Jesus, but I don't think either of us is in the market for that, are we?'

'Those are the options?'

I shrugged. The sex had been incredible. Amazing. I hoped we could do it again, and again.

'Alexander couldn't make me come,' I said. 'I don't know why I want you to know that, but . . .'

'Wait, really? Or are you messing with me?'

I pulled a face that I hoped conveyed that I was serious as serious can be.

'Really?' he continued. 'Did he know that?'

'I'm not proud to admit that I faked it once or twice, just to . . . I don't know. Keep him happy? But yeah, I think he knew. And I don't think he cared. It was all very . . . needs must.'

'What just happened when my head was between your legs – was that faked?' He looked so upset when he asked it was impossible not to let out a giggle. It made his face fall even further.

'Wow,' he said, and immediately I had to counter with,

'Patrick! I'm laughing because that was absolutely not faked. You had me writhing around . . .'

'You do writhe,' he said. 'I wanted to hold a hand over your stomach and pin you down.'

I wriggled out from under his arm and lifted a leg to straddle him.

'Nobody can fake writhing like that,' I said, lowering my voice and leaning in to kiss him. 'That was my point. You are . . .' I kissed him again '. . . a very gifted . . .' another kiss '. . . lover.'

'Is that so?' he asked, relaxing into my offering.

'Uh-huh.'

I could feel him growing harder. He suddenly lifted me up and flipped me over onto my back, holding my hands above my head.

'Let's see if we can't go in for orgasm number two . . .' he growled, and I squealed in glee.

31

'Good morning,' his voice softly echoed as he nuzzled into my neck from behind.

I rolled over, pressing my naked body against him. Mindful of my morning breath I situated my head towards his shoulder and kissed the spot between his neck and collarbone lightly.

'Good morning, Patrick,' I said, not even opening my eyes.

We lay, his hand dancing across the small of my back and down between my legs. When I let out a little giggle he took it as an invitation to stay there, and before I knew it . . .

'Orgasm number three,' he said, as I rolled off of him sweaty and satisfied.

'Do you remember those mugs printed with World's Greatest Dad?' I said.

'Uh-oh,' he replied. 'Is this about to descend into some Daddy Issues stuff?'

'Gross,' I said. 'No.'

'Sorry. Please continue.'

I rolled my eyes. 'I was going to say I could get you one of those mugs with "World's Greatest Fingers" printed on it, but you've ruined it now.'

'No!' he said. 'Don't say that! I really want that mug!'

I reached out a hand and patted his stomach. 'I'm sure you'll redeem yourself.'

He rolled over to his front and extended himself for a kiss.

'I can't believe we only have one day left,' he said. 'How shall we spend it?'

'So far, so good . . .' I grinned.

'I'll say.'

'Let's shower and go to Our Place for breakfast. Take the maps, maybe see if the barista recommends anything?'

'You had me at "let's shower",' he said, rolling off the bed and holding out a hand for me. 'I'm all for getting clean so we can get dirty again.'

It took us two hours to finally leave the hotel. Breakfast had finished at the café, and they already had the lunch menus out.

'So you don't regret bringing me along with you?' Patrick asked, as we finished off our coffee and headed, hand in hand, for a meander along the water.

'Oh, of course I do,' I said, trying to keep a straight face. 'Worst decision ever. Can't wait to get home.'

'No,' he said, mock-shocked.

'Patrick,' I said. 'Shut up. Bringing you was the best drunk decision I ever made.'

'Out of how many drunk decisions, is the question,' he joked.

We got gelato from a little hole-in-the-wall (a cup for me, a cone for him), and followed our noses from one beauty spot to another. We held hands, we nuzzled into each other's necks, we stole kisses, and I let myself enjoy it. I didn't question it, or try to understand what it would all mean once we were home. Was I really going to come back from all this with ... not a boyfriend, but a ... *something*? Because honestly, if all of what Patrick and I were was contained solely in Australia, if what happened in Aus stayed in Aus, I could live with that too, I think. Being away did exactly what it was supposed to have done: I was free.

'You look thoughtful,' Patrick said, from where we sat on the grass beside a huge willow tree, our faces hidden from the sun and our legs sticking out of the shadows.

'Hmmmm,' I said.

'Hmmmm?' he replied, and I knew I couldn't get away with saying something about the view. We knew each other, now – knew what each other's contented sigh sounded like, and how that sigh was different from a confused sigh or an angry sigh. And he looked at me as if he really wanted to know.

'I just . . .' I began. 'I suppose I'm starting to think about home.'

'Yeah,' he said. 'Same.'

'Yeah?'

'Yeah. I think I've been a bit airy-fairy with some stuff and being here has made me realize: I could do with cultivating some more responsibility.'

'Ha! And here I am, having learned the exact opposite.'

He ran his thumb across my knuckles. 'I'm listening.'

'I'm going to stop being scared,' I said. 'I think . . . I've just spent a really long time waiting to be awarded a qualification for being a person. Does that make sense? I've had this sense that everyone else knows what they're doing more than me, and that somehow I'm this huge screw-up and everyone else knows how to take up space on the planet except me. But . . . I actually don't think that's true.'

Patrick smiled but didn't say anything.

'And I don't think it's that everyone else is as clueless as me. I think that doesn't give other people enough credit. You're so self-assured about your place in the world, after everything you've been through, and it's just really made me think that I could stand to be more self-assured too. I'm tired of seeking some sort of permission to just *be*.'

'That sounds outrageously healthy,' Patrick said. 'The healthiest.'

'I've not judged myself on this trip,' I said. 'Well. Much. I've just . . . been in the moment. And it's made me understand that I don't think I've ever just been in the moment since, to be honest, I got to be bloody Tallulah on stage when I was fourteen years old. I've policed myself and bullied myself ever since then, and going home . . . I'm not going to do it anymore. I'm not. I've been keeping some screwed-up scorecard that marks up all the times I'm a good person and all the times I make a mistake, and if the good tally doesn't outweigh the bad – which, let me tell ya, it very seldom does – I write myself off as an idiot who is twenty times worse than every single other person on the planet.'

'Annie,' Patrick said. 'I knew you were hard on yourself, but I didn't know it was that bad.'

I shrugged. 'I don't think I did either until now. And the sun, the sea, the conversations, just the time away, having fun – I've never been more myself. I've spent twenty years trying to become something I'm not, and in three weeks here I've been able to see the actual truth about who I am and what I want, and that's been so exciting.'

'Wow,' said Patrick. 'Annie Wiig, coming home and ready to rule.'

'Literally,' I said. 'Yeah. I'm so over being a problem to fix. I think I'm understanding that I'm not a problem, I'm just me. And me is pretty awesome.'

'I co-sign that declaration.' Patrick grinned. 'And for what it's worth – seeing you see in yourself what I see you in you is so, so hot.'

I tipped my head back and laughed. 'Oh really?' I said, and he reached up to my neck to pull me in for a kiss.

32

Our last night was a haze of five very fancy courses in a sky-high restaurant, an incredibly heated snog up against an alleyway wall where a group of young lads told us to get a room, and a somewhat misguided double vodka shot in a karaoke bar we found ourselves in. I then lost a round of *rock, paper, scissors* to Patrick and so had to get up and perform a rousing rendition of Barbra Streisand's 'Don't Rain On My Parade'.

'Incredible,' marvelled Patrick as I returned to our table. 'You can actually sing!'

'Don't sound so surprised!' I squealed. 'I don't have balls to drop and ruin my pitch, do I?'

'Evidently not.' He laughed, and we made out and did another shot and when the karaoke took a break and Diana Ross's 'I'm Coming Out' started to play on the jukebox I leapt up and started singing along before heading to the dance floor. And that's where I stayed for song after song until Patrick finally gave in and joined me, and we danced together – drunk, sweaty, happy – singing the lyrics at each other until it was 3 a.m. and the bar was closing. We made the sensible decision to find a shop to buy two big bottles of water to rehydrate on the way home.

It would have ended if we'd gone back to our hotel, and even though we had to leave for the airport at 10 a.m. the next day we wordlessly seemed to agree to keep the night going. I suppose by refusing to end the night, we were keeping the whole trip going. It was strange to know that after more than twenty-four hours of travel we'd be back home, and whilst thoughts of seeing Freddie were exciting, not much else was. The most exciting thing was here with me, so what did I have to go back home for?

We found a twenty-four-hour corner store and as well as the water bought what we always did: Tim Tams for him and a mini tub of Pringles for me. Then we settled on a bench set back from the breeze off the water, still with views of the harbour. I wanted to be exactly where I was. How many times could I have said that in my life?

'Can we talk about what happens at home?' Patrick asked, lightly.

I crunched down on my crisps and, licking the residue from my fingers, said, 'I don't know. Can we?'

'To some people, this could seem like a lot,' he suggested.

I grinned. 'Good job I've been taught by an incredibly handsome man that it doesn't matter what other people think.'

He searched my face as if looking for something I wasn't giving him. 'Yes,' he said. 'But also . . .'

'Do you want my last Pringle stack?' I asked, and it had exactly the reaction I had hoped it would: he laughed, and the tension of the moment was broken.

'You're an idiot,' he said.

'An idiot you fell for,' I retorted.

'You said you're obsessed with me in your text to Kezza, so I don't know who the bigger fool is.'

He reached across and swiped the can from me, gleefully relishing in my shock as he pawed at the last of the pack. I shook my head as if I couldn't believe him.

'I'm going to ask them to put you in economy on the way home,' I said. 'See how you like that.'

'I don't believe you.' He laughed, brushing his hands together to get rid of the Pringle debris. 'You couldn't go half an hour without coming to the back of the plane to find me.'

'I hate that that's true,' I said.

'I see through your crap,' he told me. 'I see through it all.'

I rolled my eyes. 'Okay, you, that's enough cockiness. You've reached your quota.'

He winked at me suggestively. 'There's a joke in that sentence somewhere . . .' he said. 'But we can't do it here.'

'Patrick Hummingbird, you're the horniest man I've ever known.'

'Oh, you haven't seen anything yet,' he said, standing up and pulling me with him.

The sun was already coming up when we got back to the suite.

'You pull this face,' Patrick told me as he lowered me down onto the sofa. 'And it makes it very difficult not to want to take your clothes off.'

There was something different about his energy. He was more feral, rawer than I'd ever experienced him.

'My face is just my face,' I whispered, trying to be adorable.

'No. You know what you're doing. You know exactly what you're doing.'

239

I giggled.

'See?' he said. 'You're seducing me.'

He tipped my chin up and we kissed again.

'And now I'm going to seduce you. Starting . . .' he said, as his fingers tiptoed down my chest and to the top of my dress. 'With this.' He unbuttoned the first button, and then the second.

'Is this okay?' he asked.

'Yes,' I said.

He unbuttoned two more, and he no longer looked at my face, but at my chest, taking in the lace of my bra, the curve of my boobs. I wanted him to see me. I didn't want to hide how he made me feel. He reached the last button and pushed the fabric off my shoulders so I lay in just my underwear.

'You're gorgeous,' he told me, and I could tell he meant it. 'There were so many times when I thought I was going to kiss you. I couldn't tell if you wanted me to or not. I didn't know what was happening.'

He was so present. So attentive. He was deliberate and purposeful, as if we had all the time in the world – not mere hours before it all ended and Cinderella turned into a pumpkin on a flight back home.

'I feel like I've won the lottery,' he said, nuzzling into my chest.

I smiled.

'Can I ask you something?' he continued.

My tummy dropped. When somebody says, 'Can I ask you something?' it means they're about to say something you don't want to hear – an observation expressed as a question so it's less forthright.

'I was wondering,' he said, 'if you would be my girlfriend.'

240

His girlfriend! He wanted me to be his girlfriend! My skin tingled with elation.

'I would very much like to be your girlfriend,' I replied, and I think I giggled a little bit as I said it. But I suppose that's how it felt to be with him – light and fun. If being his girlfriend meant holding on to this giddy, fun mood for even a second longer, of course I wanted that.

I'd never had sex like what we did then, on the sofa of our hotel and then eventually on the floor. I'd never had sex that was so completely like a sweaty, thrashing commitment to becoming one. It was different to the night before. It meant something more, and there was a lot of eye contact, a lot of face-touching and reassurance, like finally it was okay to fully give in to this desire.

When we lay beside each other afterwards, happy and exhausted, a blanket pulled off the edge of the sofa and a cushion under his head, everything was right in the world.

'My girlfriend,' he said, and I could hear the smile in his voice.

'Do you think our fourteen-year-old selves would believe it?' I asked.

'My fourteen-year-old self didn't even know to dream it.'

'Ahhh,' I said, lifting my head to reach for a kiss. 'That was a cute thing to say!'

'Your boyfriend is a cute kind of a man.' He beamed.

33

Leaving the Australian sun and returning to an England that was officially in mid-autumn plunged me into a perpetual state of mild discomfort. My toes were cold, even in boots, and I had to keep a scarf permanently clamped around my neck to ward off the chill. I had a tan, though, which made even a polo neck jumper look chicer, and it wasn't until I was out of my oversized linen summer dresses and back into proper trousers that I realized I really had gained a dress size, maybe even two – and looked all the prettier for it. I suited more fullness in my face; I looked content and healthy. And when I'd gone to pick up a pizza from the Italian place for tea the waiter had called me *bella*. I knew I was supposed to rage against unsolicited compliments and that I'm more than how I look, but I'd been getting takeaway there for two years and it was my first time being called beautiful by the flirty owner. It felt like a sign: I looked different, I felt different, and even Giuseppe at *L'Antica Pizzeria da Michele* could tell. It was all I could do not to launch into a rousing chorus of 'I'm Every Woman' on the walk home.

Life was wonderful. I'd left feeling like the biggest loser in London, but I'd come home a happy winner, renewed with a sense of purpose. New Annie was triumphant and it was plain for everyone to see.

What you doing? Patrick's text pinged once I'd eaten.

I would say I broke into a smile, but I hadn't *stopped* smiling. I'd told Adzo that I didn't think we'd flown home, I'd simply floated us. I'd had a body part physically attached to Patrick – my boyfriend! – the whole way; we'd held hands in the car to the airport, and stood enmeshed together at check-in and through customs, fingers outstretched and searching under the bar in the departure lounge. We'd talked about how we wouldn't let the real world change what we'd become in our little Aussie bubble, but we'd still been clingy, right up until we kissed goodbye when he dropped me off at home, lingering over each other's mouths until the Uber driver asked us if we were sure we didn't just want to get out together, since we seemed attached at the mouth anyway.

Unpacking, I typed back. *By which I mean making several piles on my bedroom floor because everything needs to be washed. How does sand get in the things that didn't even go to the beach??* Then I added: *What you doing?*

Dots on the screen signalled he was writing back. I flopped down on the floor, resting my back against the bed. I was exhausted after the carby pizza and chilly walk, and wouldn't last much longer before hitting the hay. I'd waited as long as I could to go to bed so that I could try and get back on UK time as soon as possible.

It feels strange that you're not in the room across the hall from me anymore, he sent back. *Or that we won't share a bed tonight . . .*

We'd made a decision before we landed that we needed

to be in our own homes for the first night back so we could do all the logical stuff getting back from a trip involved – laundry, food shopping, trying to sleep – but no sooner had he pulled away in the cab than I'd started to pine for him. The house was too quiet, and I'd got used to the way a place felt with somebody else in it. Knowing Patrick was within the same four walls of the hotel suite as me had become a comfort. I'd loved knowing he was around, reading in the next room or showering as I FaceTimed home. I wished he was in the house with me, even if he was on the couch as I did my chores upstairs.

'Falling for somebody on a three-week holiday is the real-life equivalent of *months* of dating if you measure it out in hours, surely,' Adzo had commented during a brief phone call to get all my gossip. 'Do the maths. Twenty-four hours a day for twenty-one days is . . .' She quickly added it up. 'One hundred and twenty-six four-hour dates. That's a lot of dates. It's practically a year of dates! You've spent more time with him than most couples rack up in their first months together.'

I can keep tradition and make coffee for two in the morning? I volleyed back to Patrick, smiling at the thought of making it one hundred and twenty-seven dates. Adzo was right: in terms of time spent together, we'd clocked up our time. No wonder I missed him.

I'll be there, he replied. *In fact, I can bring breakfast.*

Perfect. Sleep tight.

You too, he said. *Dream of me.*

I didn't need to dream, though. Real life was good enough.

Frustratingly, I lay staring at the ceiling with jet lag at 6 a.m. I'd slept like a log for seven hours, but suddenly was wide awake. I knew that after lunch I'd be desperate for a nap that would probably last all afternoon, but what can you do when your body clock is telling you it's 2 p.m.? I decided to make a start on the piles of washing and go for a walk around the block, picking up some groceries on my way.

As the sky got lighter I circled around the back streets and up through the park – my old running route. I couldn't wait to have Carol back from Mum and Dad's so I could walk with her again. She'd fill the house with more life, too. The cold made my breath visible in front of me and I blew shapes like I was a kid, and by the time I got near the high street one of the cafés was starting to show early signs of life, so to avoid going home I slipped in for a caffeine fix and a scroll of my phone, doing what I thought of as my 'correspondence': replying to all the texts I'd missed when I was away.

I ordered a pot of tea and messaged Freddie to tell her I'd see her at the weekend, when we came to pick up Carol. I asked if I could get some dog content in the meantime – photos and videos to keep me going. In the Core Four WhatsApp I scrolled through everything that had gone back and forth in my absence, filling myself in on Kezza's family-finding progress with her social worker, Brianna's husband's new boss and Jo's continued obsession with rewatching *Mork and Mindy* because, 'Nobody does it like Robin Williams. I miss him!' She was due any day now and desperate to fill up her time to take her mind off it. I let them know I was back and asked when the next Core Four summit would be, assuming it would be after the baby came. I didn't tell them that Patrick and I were girlfriend-and-boyfriend official. All I knew is that inevitably Kezza had let slip about the kiss, and I reiterated in the thread that any stories I had to tell would have to be done in person, adding in a winky emoji to whet their appetites.

I texted Fernanda to ask if I could stop by soon with some Aussie thank-you souvenirs, and I texted Dad and Mum separately to say I was home safe, and briefly logged on to Instagram but immediately logged off because within three seconds it made me feel icky. Freddie had said to me before: *Annie, everyone knows privacy is the new luxury. Only old people post about their lives anymore.* I didn't have the patience for the highlight reels of other people.

Instead of social media, I flicked through the few photos I'd taken, and the ones Patrick had airdropped me on the flight, stored in my private and unpublished archive, for my pleasure only. *If a memory isn't shared online, did it ever really happen at all?* I decided yes, and that it was even sweeter that way. I scrolled up my camera feed to start from the beginning, where the photos were mainly selfies and snaps of my passport next to a glass of champagne, and an image of the view out of the plane window. It was so interesting to see, though, because as the trip went on the photos became less of 'stuff' and more of Patrick, or me and Patrick. There he was in his robe at the villa, so much paler than when we finally headed home. Then, the first beach trip, our glasses clinking at the wine tasting, a video of him driving us to the music festival. There were a sequence of shots from the night we'd canoed out on the river – a series where I was caught unaware, then turned to see him, then laughed, and another where I was covering my face.

I paused on the next one: the final one he took before I'd demanded he stop. My hair was loose and windswept, and I had golden freckles across my nose. I was laughing again, forcing a double chin and revealing the crooked front tooth I've always said I'd one day get fixed, and gazing off camera, just above it, my pupils as wide as the rest of my eyes. I was looking at Patrick, and it was a look of . . . Not love, but definitely something close. How early had I fallen for him? He'd walked into my existence at such a crucial moment and made it feel – almost, just maybe – like everything else was worth it. I dreaded to think how sad I'd be without him brightening up my days and making me believe the bad days were over.

Maktub.

It is written.

Without overthinking it I made a photo of us on the last day of the trip my phone's background wallpaper so I'd see it every time I picked up my phone.

Let me know when you're up, I texted him. *I'm thinking about you.*

On the way out of the café I passed a hairdresser's. It wasn't my usual place across in Spitalfields, but there was a sign in the window advertising a free 9 a.m. slot. And it hit me: I wanted my hair cut. I'd always hidden behind my hair. I relied on it being long and in front of my face, and if my face was now going to have as much delight in it as I'd just been reminded of in those photos then I wanted to proudly show that off. I wanted to see this brave new world I was going to conquer. I didn't want to hide anymore.

'Hi,' I said tentatively, peering around the door to the only man in the shop – a squat bloke in a striped shirt with the sleeves rolled up and tattooed forearms. 'Can I have that appointment?' I pointed to the blackboard advertising it.

'Sure you can, love,' he replied. 'Come in. What are you after?'

When I left fifty-five minutes later my hair was cropped close to my head, shaved at the neck and longer on top, with a little fringe, inspired by Twiggy in the Sixties, but darker. And what's more? It looked fabulous.

'I love it,' Patrick said, unpacking croissants and Nutella from his tote. I smiled. That tote had been all the way around the world with us, and now all the way to my kitchen – which he was in for the first time. 'You look like Winona Ryder before she started to steal stuff.'

'Excellent cultural reference,' I quipped, instinctively reaching up to smooth a hand over my newly naked collar. He leaned in for a kiss, something we did every few minutes, a reminder to ourselves that that was a thing we could do in England as well as back in Aus. The novelty of it hadn't worn off. We were all over each other, and it took the length of half a pastry and a mouthful of orange juice before we had sex on the sofa. Twice.

He stayed all day, helping me batch cook some chilli for the week and hanging out my laundry upstairs, just to be helpful. I loved it. It felt like the right place for him to be. As I predicted though, I crashed by early afternoon and we both fell asleep in front of the *EastEnders* omnibus and didn't wake up until it was dark outside.

He came over every night after that. We were both jet-lagged with wonky body clocks adjusting to the northern hemisphere, so it was a takeaway or a bit of Netflix and chill that got cut off at 8.30 p.m. His place was exactly eleven minutes on foot from mine, so where I'd had friends tell horror stories about trying to keep relationships across the city alive when it was ninety minutes door to door via public transport, being neighbours was yet another thing we seemed to have going in our favour.

Unlike him, I wasn't due back at work for another few days, so used the time in between laundry cycles and naps to google things like *can I change my job at thirty-two?* and *how much should I have in savings to change careers?* I found some information evenings for counselling courses that I bookmarked and went back to look at periodically, each time feeling braver about signing up for one. *Maybe I really can find a job I love,* I dared to start imagining.

As the emptiness of the house whilst Patrick was at work echoed around me, I also started to think about where I'd live next. I made a spreadsheet of my savings, fixed outgoings, and looked over what I normally spent in a month. I'd have to axe most of my luxuries immediately – no more ten-class passes to bootcamp, or expensive lowlights, or even brunches and cocktails. It was embarrassing to see in black and white how much money I'd gotten used to throwing away on frivolities. That had to stop. I'd way overspent in Australia, too – I'd embraced the YOLO attitude a bit *too* much.

I signed into my pension provider but knew I'd be crazy to touch that cash. I needed to figure out a way to find an affordable flat as soon as possible, preferably not in Zone 7 and still near all the people I loved and who loved me, which also happened to be in one of the most expensive cities in the world. I supposed that in the absolute worst-case scenario I could move in with Mum and Dad south of the river for a while, but God the week they'd spent in the house after the wedding-that-wasn't had been maddening enough. That would have to be Plan B or, rather, Plan Z. Adzo and the Core Four were out of the question, since nobody had any space anyway.

I set up some alerts for any new listings going live, and tried to avoid even considering moving into a flat-share. I didn't want to put that out in the universe; it would feel like a step back after everything that had happened. There *had* to be another way. Everything I came up with, though, seemed to indicate that even if I did want to retrain in something, or take a career break, I basically couldn't afford it. Still. I didn't want to get greedy – like Patrick had said, plenty of people didn't *love* their work. I told myself that as long as I had my health, my friends and family – and Patrick himself – that was more than enough.

I still kept checking for information evenings, though. I couldn't help it. The thought had burrowed itself deep in my head.

'We'll figure something out,' Patrick assured me when I brought it up in bed. My boss, Chen, had texted asking to meet up for a coffee before I started back, and it had put the willies up me. Adzo said I had nothing to worry about, but suddenly I was worried I'd end up losing my job anyway, somehow. Chen had never asked me for a coffee before – I wondered if I was going to get a talking-to, because she could tell somehow that my heart wasn't in it anymore.

'I won't see you on the streets – put it that way,' Patrick continued. 'Worst-case scenario, you can bunk up with me for a bit, okay?'

'Crikey,' I said. 'I couldn't do that. You'd get so sick of me!'

He shrugged. 'It's cool,' he replied. 'We know we can spend twenty-four hours a day together. The option is there.'

Mum would have a fit if I moved in with Patrick, even if it was temporary. It was one thing coming home with a boyfriend, but living with him? No way.

'Are you *sure* you want to meet my family tomorrow?' I pressed, for the third time. 'They're bonkers. You really don't have to. I can pick up the dog alone and meet you after.'

He pulled me in close, my night-time nakedness pressed up against his.

'Are you ashamed of me?' he asked, jokingly.

'I'm nervous they'll spot your cargo shorts in the holiday snaps,' I quipped back. 'I've got my reputation to think about.'

'What's wrong with my cargo shorts?'

I sniggered. 'Nothing . . . if you're planning on joining an All Saints tribute band.'

'Rude!' He laughed.

I shrugged, as if the truth couldn't be denied.

'I *want* to meet them, anyway,' he declared. 'I promise you, parents love me. I'm very wholesome to mums. I'm like boyfriend catnip.'

'Hmmmm,' I said, my tummy lurching. 'Just . . . don't take it personally if she doesn't. It's me she doesn't like, remember.'

'I hate that she makes you feel that way, Annie. I really do.'

'You'll love Freddie, though.' I didn't want his pity. New Annie wasn't for pitying, if she could help it. 'You'll get on like a house on fire.'

'I look forward to it,' he said, and my heart beat in double time at what was to come. I couldn't hide Patrick away forever though, could I? And anyway. It was time I stood up to Mum, once and for all. Worrying about her was boring, at best, and downright debilitating at worst.

'Goodnight,' I said, switching off the light.

In the darkness his voice echoed again: 'I meant what I said. You really can stay with me if you want.'

I kissed him instead of verbalizing a reply.

34

I was right about Freddie and Patrick: they got on like Patrick had been part of the family for years. I'd spent a lifetime second-guessing my own judgement, but I'd never for a single moment doubted Freddie's. She was like a sniffer dog for good intentions. Hearing them talk so easily warmed my heart.

'And so now,' Freddie concluded, halfway through an anecdote about a pupil-teacher stand-off she'd spearheaded at school, playing Mum's hostess-in-training and carefully handing Patrick a beer, 'they said they're going to officially review school policy on it. Mum told me that I was making a big fuss out of nothing and not to make a name for myself as a troublemaker, but Dad came into my room and told me not to listen to her and to do what I thought was right. But I obviously *was* right because they're going to change it. So I hope Mum will say sorry.'

She hadn't taken a breath since we'd arrived, and Patrick indulged her friendliness fervently.

'Wow,' he said, genuinely impressed. 'That's . . . badass.' He swiftly turned and looked at me. 'Wait. Can I say badass?'

I nodded. 'If that's what it is,' I answered.

Freddie beamed at him, satisfied at his compliment, and the fact that he'd used a 'grown-up' word to articulate it.

'It really is badass,' I told her, Carol happily snuggled into my lap, thrilled to be reunited. 'You're so brave, Froogle. It's much easier to keep the status quo than to challenge things, especially in big institutions like schools.'

'What's status quo?'

'Oh, um, where people keep things as they've always been, because change can be scary.'

'Dad says the only constant is change.'

I smiled. 'He's not wrong.'

Patrick caught my eye. 'A lot of good stuff can come from change,' he noted, and Freddie looked between us as we looked at each other. It was almost painful to sit across the room from him – if I was around him, I wanted to have his hand on my leg or the lower part of my back. I wanted his physicality. Needed it, almost – but I knew it would only confuse things if we were too overt with our affections. I tore my gaze away from his and back to my little sister. She narrowed her eyes suspiciously. I ignored the curiosity in her face.

'Do you want to see the holiday photos?' I asked.

She realized I wasn't going to engage.

'Yeah,' she said. 'Go on then. Mum says Australia is too far to go for a family holiday, but Mia's big sister is in Australia on a gap year and Mia says that we should go when we graduate. She said her sister works in an almond factory and shares a house with eleven other people! She says it's so good, like one big party, all the time, and they hardly ever go to sleep or even eat a lot of vegetables because nobody tells them what to do.'

The thought of eleven people in a house-share reminded me of my own living situation. When Jo had first moved to London, she'd rented a room in a converted warehouse up near Seven Sisters, and lasted five days before she left for a three-bed with two teachers down the road, a place that she'd originally thought she was too cool for. Turned out the home-grown weed and constant queue for the bathroom weren't for her. They wouldn't be for me, either. My anxiety about where to live was increasing. I didn't want to feel like I was regressing in my life. Not when in so many other ways I'd leapt forwards.

'Scoot over then,' I said to Freddie, trying to focus on the moment instead of my impending problem.

Patrick leant over from his spot on the floor to ruffle Carol's ears, waking her so that she hopped down to accept a doggy tickle from him, instead. He chatted easily with Dad as I pulled out my phone for Freddie. I could hear him asking about winter-flowering heather and if he knew much about what could add some colour to his patio at this time of year. Dad found him easy company, too. I could tell.

I told Freddie: 'I won't show you all of the photos, Frou, because that's boring, but you can get the official highlight selection.'

''Kay. I'll let you know when I've zoned out.'

I laughed. 'Deal.'

We flicked through sunsets and kangaroos and the stuff with the stingray. I told her some of the better, more adventurous stories like the road trip and music festival and she asked lots of questions about what we ate, which I was happy to recall in almost shockingly clear detail. Then she said, as easily as she might enquire as to a new nail colour: 'So is Patrick your new boyfriend?'

Patrick looked up at the sound of his name, and Mum froze at the doorway where she was carrying a bowl of olives and toothpicks. She'd stayed out of the way under the guise of prepping lunch in the kitchen, but I knew she was put out by Patrick's presence. I also knew she'd spoken to Fernanda whilst I was away, and was mad Fernanda had known more than she did about my travel companion. I could have gone to see if she was okay, but I didn't want to. I didn't want to walk into her emotional trap of guilt-tripping me in hushed tones, out of the way of others. I didn't want to give her the chance to ruin my happiness.

Dad squinted at Mum, slyly slipping his eye across to me, knowing my response would shape the mood of our imminent dining experience – which didn't seem fair, really. If Mum had spent even five minutes with us in the lounge as we'd all chatted, she wouldn't feel so much like he was a stranger. I could have made her feel more comfortable, and established some more common ground. She *wanted* to have an attitude. But this wasn't about her.

I looked from Patrick, to Dad, to Mum, and then back to Freddie. 'Yes,' I said, deciding in an instant that overexplaining would have worse consequences than keeping it simple and direct. 'He is.'

Patrick shot me a pleased smile with a wink, and carried on with Carol's belly rub.

'And I'm very happy about it,' I added.

'Good,' Freddie stated, and she gave me a pleased smile too. She leaned in to whisper, 'I really like him, Annie-Doo. And Carol does. Look.'

It was true: the dog was putty in his hands.

Mum leaned across to the coffee table to put down the bowl she'd brought through, muttering something akin to,

'Oh. How nice,' in a way that meant exactly the opposite, but Dad lifted up his glass in my direction with a cheers motion, letting me know it was no skin off his nose. Sometimes I wondered how a man so relaxed and accepting could ever survive with a woman as haughty as my mum. It couldn't be easy for him. Mum left the room, and I went back to scrolling through the photos with Freddie.

It took ages for lunch to be ready, and as we sat at the table waiting to be served Freddie showed Patrick the petition she'd just won at school, proudly telling him about her plans to skip university because she didn't believe in the system that made spending thirty thousand pounds on a certificate so that she could get a job to pay off thirty thousand pounds of debt seem sensible.

'I'm going to be an entrepreneur,' she said, proudly.

'What kind of entrepreneur?' Patrick asked. 'Or is that TBD?'

She giggled at his use of an acronym she understood. 'Totes TBD,' she replied. 'But I want to give more of the profits away to charity than I keep for myself.'

'That sounds very admirable,' Patrick said, and Mum stared at me as if it was my fault her youngest daughter wasn't planning on becoming a surgeon. Dad opened another beer, but Patrick switched to water, which I thought was sweet. He was keeping his wits about him.

Dinner was roast chicken with all the trimmings, and I was ravenous. The weather and my cobbled-together dinners from the freezer since I'd been home meant a proper English roast was the ultimate treat, and I piled swede mash and Yorkshire puddings onto my plate eagerly, already wondering what was for pudding. I hoped it was a crumble. Mum really knew how to make a good crumble.

'Go steady,' she uttered under her breath as Dad fussed with pouring Patrick's gravy. 'Don't overindulge.' She nodded pointedly at my small mound of roasties and immediately I flushed in shame. Nobody else had heard. I quickly used my fork to deposit all but one back onto the serving platter. My hands shook as I took my first mouthful of broccoli and peas. I couldn't taste any of it. Why did she always have to make me feel like I'd done something wrong? Why wasn't I ever good enough for her?

We got all the way to dessert before Mum issued her first tut.

Dad laughed a little bit too long and a little bit too hard at one of Patrick's jokes, and she took particular umbrage at it. It was so rude and obvious that Dad immediately stopped laughing and we all turned to stare at her. My jaw slackened as she continued to dish up the Eve's Pudding wordlessly, and it dawned on me that she wasn't even going to try and disguise her bad manners. Patrick looked at me for guidance on how to handle it, and I knew it was now or never: if I didn't have it out with her straightaway, I never would.

'What?' I said.

She didn't respond, only handed Freddie her bowl and then sat down to pick up her spoon.

'I knew you weren't happy we'd had a good time,' I pressed. 'What's on your mind, Mum? Go on. You obviously want to say something.'

I'd never been so direct with her before, *ever*. I'd spent years biting my tongue, avoiding confrontation, assuming it was always me in the wrong, but it was making my temples ache that she couldn't be as excited and happy for me as Dad and Freddie. Didn't I deserve it? I wanted her to know that

I didn't care what she thought – it was my life. I'd finally had enough of her naysaying. She could like it or lump it.

'Honestly, Annie?' she said, as she blew on the steam coming off her custard. 'Taking the Mackenzies' money and then inviting another man to go away with you. It's crass! I'm honestly embarrassed for you. Sorry, Patrick. But I am.'

Patrick coughed lightly, and before I could register that it meant he was going to defend me he'd already started speaking.

'I thought it was pretty cool of her actually,' he said, simply. 'Making lemonade out of lemons.'

Mum gave a light hoot. 'Well, you got a holiday out of it so it's not surprising you'd say that.'

I couldn't believe Mum would be so openly offensive.

'Mum!' I cried, right as Dad said, 'Oh for God's sake, Judy.'

'No, Peter,' Mum asserted. 'Somebody has to say something. You come here with all your hair hacked off like you're having a midlife crisis, making eyes at a man from that terrible drama school as if you're trying to be fourteen again. You're a grown woman, Annie. You can't hide behind a new boyfriend. You're showing yourself up.'

'That's not fair, Judy,' Dad said.

'I only want what's best for you,' she directed at me. 'And what's best for your sister.'

Freddie squealed, 'What have I got to do with this?'

Mum looked at her. 'She's supposed to be an example to you, Frederica.'

'Freddie.'

'She's supposed to be an example to you, *Freddie*.'

'But she is,' Freddie said in a strong voice. There was a rod of steel in her spine as she said, 'Annie is the best example of a grown-up I know. She's kind and silly and clever and never makes me feel like I'm alone. She's always there for everyone she loves. And I like Patrick. You're the only one who doesn't.'

The table fell quiet.

'Thanks, sis,' I said, putting down my fork and reaching out to hold her hand.

Mum took a massive breath as she considered how to proceed. She settled on: 'Patrick, I'm sure you're a very nice man. But my daughter was engaged to somebody else little over a month ago, and hasn't had a moment to herself to grieve it all. I'm sure it's been a wonderful holiday, but I'd be silly to play along with all of this. Have you even thought about where you're going to live, Annie?'

'I've told her she's always welcome at mine until she figures it out,' Patrick offered, and I knew he was trying to be helpful, but I cringed as he said it.

'Well isn't that the icing on the cake,' Mum commented. I didn't know what to tell her.

We ate quietly after that. I issued a shake of the head to Patrick, letting him know not to push it. As we finished up finally I said, 'The trip was beautiful, anyway, Mum. And not that anyone has asked but it really helped to put fifteen thousand miles between me and what happened that day. I'm doing fine. I don't need your permission for moving on. It was naïve of me to think you'd be happy for me. For us.'

Mum stood up to clear the plates. It was remarkable how she could continue to conduct the normal steps of a family meal whilst being so unkind. 'Just have a little dignity, please,' she said.

'What's that supposed to mean?'

'It means, Annie, that you just got jilted and already you've got yourself a new boyfriend. What do you think people will say about that?'

'How about,' I levelled, my face flushing and voice rising, 'I don't care? How about I don't give two hoots what people will say about anything, because I've spent my whole life caring and it's made me miserable?' I warmed up to my theme, words tumbling out and crashing into each other. 'What if, actually, nobody is even talking about me anyway because everyone is so concerned with their own lives and their own mistakes? Their own worries? Fuck-ups? What if we all only get one precious life and if we spend it peering through the lace curtains at how everyone else lives we end up missing the chance to make the most of our own?'

Mum said quietly: 'I don't want to fight. All I'm asking is that you give this a bit more thought. Okay? Do you really want to leap out of one relationship and into another?'

I half expected Dad to tell her off but he didn't, he just stared at the table, shaking his head, refusing to get involved any further. Mum took the empty bowls to the kitchen, and Freddie grinned at me across the table, loving how I'd finally given Mum a piece of my mind.

'Told you you're the best grown-up I know,' she said.

'You're the best grown-up I know, too,' Patrick agreed, quietly, squeezing my knee.

Dad reached for the water jug. 'I'll talk to her,' he said.

We left not long after.

35

Patrick's voice roused me from a sleep so deep it was like coming around from a coma.

'Annie,' he muttered through the darkness of the room. 'Annie, can you hear that?'

Kezza had told me that jet lag can take weeks to leave your system, and apparently she was right. It was like being shouted at down the length of a blacked-out cave.

'*Annie.*'

I reluctantly rolled over so my face was towards his.

'I'm awake,' I said, groggily, reaching out to feel him. It was pitch-black, so must have been about 3 a.m., and wind blustered outside, making me feel cold even under the warmth of the padded duvet.

'Listen,' he replied.

I didn't hear anything. And then there was a loud bang from downstairs. It immediately made me two hundred per cent more alert.

'Burglar?' I asked, quietly. I reached out for my phone, but it wasn't upstairs with me. I hardly needed my iPhone in bed when I had Patrick. I could see it in my mind's eye, downstairs in the bag I'd dropped in the hallway when he'd pushed me up against the wall after we got home, slipping an icy hand underneath my jumper and pawing at my bra 'for warmth'. I loved how he wanted me, and how I wanted him. I adored closing the door on the world and being back in our own little bubble, where it was just us two.

The noise came again. If it was a burglar, it wasn't a very masterful one.

'I think it's somebody at the door,' Patrick said, and my instinct prickled, thinking it was Dad and there was something wrong with Freddie, or that it was Mum and there was something wrong with Dad.

'Urgh,' I grumbled, clambering out of bed into the cold, predawn, air. 'Stay here,' I insisted. 'If it's a burglar, I'll scream and that's your cue. No point both of us getting cold.'

I slid the dimmer switch of the lamp up so I could see just enough to let my eyes get used to being open. My slippers were by the door, and luckily so was my big fluffy dressing gown, which was a relief because I'd already got goose bumps. I headed downstairs, Carol at my heel, listening out for noises again. Then I heard it: somebody saying my name. A man, from the other side of the front door. Carol started to grumble, but she didn't bark. Whoever was out there, she knew them. She cooed like a newborn baby.

'Alexander?' I asked, opening the door as rain spat against the windows at a hostile, angry angle. 'What the hell?'

'Annie,' he replied, as if he was shocked to see me, like it wasn't my door he'd been banging on in the middle of the night.

I didn't say anything. He looked . . . bloated. His cheeks were rosy through his tanned cheeks and his usual razor-sharp jawline had been replaced with something softer. It was the man I used to love, but fuzzier around the edges. Carol launched herself at him and he picked her up so she could lick his face, fussing with zeal at his return. If she was at one end of the spectrum, I was at the other. My mind raced at a million miles, scrambling to find a way to feel.

Hug him, was my first reaction. *It's Alexander!*

And then: *No, don't bloody hug him. IT'S ALEXANDER.*

It's really cold, I reflected, rubbing my arms. *I'm glad I put my slippers on.*

I watched Carol lick his face, delighted. *He looks so sad,* I started to think, before realizing I shouldn't care. *WHO CARES IF HE LOOKS SAD?* I decided. *SHUT THE DOOR IN HIS FACE.*

Then: *Maybe he'll finally say sorry.*

And then: *Neither of us is saying anything, maybe I should say something.*

Finally: *No, don't speak first. Make him squirm.*

'Annie,' he repeated, and I interrupted, disbelieving: 'What are you doing here?'

He went to speak and thought better of it, as if he'd figured out getting this far he'd now run out of steam.

He put the dog down and she issued a stern bark, warning him that it was time to come inside, now.

'Can I get out of the rain?' he asked, taking her cue, and hand on heart it was probably the first time in ten years I've ever heard him sound even the smallest bit unsure. He genuinely didn't know how I was going to respond, and I could tell. It made me thaw just a little towards him. He seemed miserable.

'Why should I let you?' I replied, aware of how my arms had snaked around myself for protection.

'Annie, please. It's freezing.'

'It's also the middle of the night.'

I said it sternly but stepped aside right after, making it clear he could inch by me. He stepped inside and muttered a thank you, lingering as I closed the door like I needed to grant further permission for him to go through into the lounge.

'Where's your key, anyway?' I asked.

'I got drunk and threw it in the Singapore Strait.'

'I see.'

He followed me, Carol lurching ahead to pick up her favourite ball to play with him, and he took in the sight of the place. I switched on a lamp and walked behind the kitchen island to the mug tree. Why is it that when we don't know what else to do, we make a cup of tea?

'I've missed being home,' he uttered quietly, leaning on the countertop opposite me. I threw two teabags into mugs and squinted at the light cast out from the fridge when I got the milk.

The noise of the boiling tap served as a way to silence any rebuttal I might give. He missed being home? The bloody nerve of him! He stayed standing even after I handed him his drink, and I had to fight the urge to wander to the sofa to get comfortable, choosing to rest against the wall by the freezer. How much could there really be to say? Surely not so much that I'd need to settle in for it. We were going to get married and then didn't because he left. I didn't want a big chat about it. After everything I thought I might say when I finally saw him, I suddenly cared less than I ever had. I had nothing except vague pity for the bedraggled ghost in front of me.

'Alexander,' I sighed. 'Why are you here?'

He considered it. He settled on: 'To say sorry. To fix it.'

Carol settled in at his feet, put out at lying on the cold concrete floor instead of the snuggly sofa but happy he was there. I didn't know what to say.

Eventually I asked, 'Why did you do it? Why did you just leave that way? You abandoned me.'

My voice wavered enough to betray my steely expression. I'd had the moment so many times in my head – rehearsed what I'd say if I ever saw him again – but it was too painful to make it some big dramatic scene. I'd deliberately left my misery behind in Australia.

'I don't know,' he whispered. 'I wanted to get a reaction from you, I think.'

'A reaction,' I repeated. Blood pulsed in my ears.

Alexander bit down on his bottom lip as he decided how to explain what he meant. 'It was like being with a robot,' he settled on. 'You never screamed or shouted or got mad. I'm fairly certain you were faking most of your orgasms. There was no . . . passion. I love you, but sometimes I don't even know you.'

'How can you love me then?' I volleyed back. I was legitimately curious. Had I ever really known him? Could I even call what we'd fallen into love? Or had it just been convenient?

'I don't know,' he replied. 'I don't know how, or why, I love you, I just do. You're my person, Annie. I want us to try again. Life is too hard without you.'

'Alexander. You left me on our wedding day. This isn't a *Sex and the City* movie. You can't say sorry and be charming and buy me a pair of shoes to make it all better again. You left me at the *altar*. I think I almost believe you when you say you love me, but jeez – you absolutely do not respect me.'

'I do,' he protested. 'Of course I do. I just . . . I got confused. Marriage is such a big thing. It's so final.'

I held up a hand. I was shaking. It really had just hit me that out of everything, the reason what he did was so horrific is that you don't humiliate people you respect. I'd spent a decade with a man who didn't respect me. That was mortifying. How had I ever let myself accept so little? I could have wept at the thought, were it not for the fact that I refused to let Alexander see me cry over him.

'Stop,' I said. 'That's enough. No.'

He said my name again, pleading entering his voice. It made him sound like a whiny little boy, and I hated it. I didn't hate *him*. I hated how he behaved, and how he felt entitled to ask for another chance. He didn't want that. Not really. If I gave in and said yes, he'd leave again. I didn't know if that would be next week or next year, but he would. He'd only ever look out for himself, and only people who don't love themselves settle for being treated that way.

'We're over, Alexander. You texted the wedding planner before you thought to give me a heads up on the situation. I was already in the dress, already at the church. I went on our honeymoon *without you*. Do you know how screwed up that is? I don't know why you're here. These garbled half-truths aren't for me to hear; they're for a therapist – or your next girlfriend. You're not my problem anymore.'

'I'm screwing this up,' he said, actually crying now.

'Past tense,' I replied. 'There is no "this" anymore.' I closed my eyes and held the bridge of my nose. My head clouded with weight, the exertion of standing up for myself forcing my temples to throb.

And then the sound of water rushing through the upstairs pipes cut through the tension.

Patrick had obviously flushed the toilet, and the knowledge that there was somebody else in the house dawned on Alexander's face.

'Freddie?' he said, and too quickly I nodded. I panicked. I could have easily told him it was my boyfriend, but for some reason telling the truth didn't occur to me.

'Uh-huh.'

Alexander might not know me in so many ways, especially now, but he and I had spent enough time together that he knew immediately that I was lying.

'Who's here, Annie?'

I was torn between upholding the lie and telling the truth.

'It's a man, isn't it? Have you got a man here?' He spun around and for a second I thought he was going to sprint upstairs. 'Have you got a man in our bed?'

Carol stirred, agitated by the rise in his voice. I shook my head, trying to settle on a response.

'You've got a man in our bed? Annie. Come on. No . . .'

His crying gave way to great big gulping sobs. Carol started to yap, distressed at his distress.

'Annie . . .' he kept saying, his head down on the counter now. 'Annie . . .'

I walked around to him and reached out to rub his back, but he recoiled at my touch.

'No,' he said. 'Don't.'

He braced himself and slowed his breath.

Without looking up he stood upright again.

'This is unbelievable,' he said to the kitchen taps. He struck his palm against the island with such force I wasn't sure if his hand would break or the countertop. The outburst made me flinch, but he stormed back towards the front door before I could say anything.

I didn't follow him. I listened in case he hit anything else, but all I heard was the door open, and then slam behind him. He was gone.

'You okay . . .?'

Patrick lingered in the doorframe, backlit by the hallway light. His face was the kindest face I'd ever seen. He was a good man. A handsome, tanned, *sexy* good man.

'I think it's hit him that it's over,' I said. 'Isn't that odd? Only now does he get what he's done. He blows up my life, and six weeks later he's the one who is upset by it.'

Patrick wrapped his arms around me, and I inhaled the scent of sex on his body.

'Come back to bed,' he sighed into my neck, and I did.

Before we fell asleep, I asked him: 'Do you think it's bad that we're together when the dust has barely settled with Alexander?'

Sleepily, he replied: 'No. Don't let him get in your head.'

He spooned me tightly and breathed into my ear, which I normally loved. I loved that he was as close to me as a person could be and it still wasn't enough for him. He was asleep within minutes, but I still lay there turning over the thought. Alexander was kind of right to be upset, I supposed, but he didn't know the details as far as I knew – that I hadn't planned it, and hadn't meant to fall for somebody else. I wondered if Fernanda had told him I'd taken somebody else away with me. She still sounded pretty mad at him in her texts. She could love him and still hate the choice he'd made. I knew she was embarrassed, too. That was a strange thought – that his own mother's anger could be outlasting my own.

I hadn't meant to jump from one relationship to another. It had just happened.

But then, maybe that wasn't such a good thing.

In the harsh reality of home, I couldn't help but ask myself: I was supposed to be actively choosing how my life would look from here on, wasn't I? Not just letting life happen to me. Holidays could happen to a person. What happened on holiday could simply unfold. But now, back in real life, I had to be smart. Patrick mumbled in his sleep and rolled over to the other side of the bed. Had I chosen this? Or hadn't I changed at all? Was I still just going with the flow when what I needed to do was question everything and be deliberate about my choices?

I remembered what Mum had asked.

Do you really want to leap out of one relationship and into another?

Shit, I thought, as Patrick started to snore. *Shit, shit, shit.*

36

The next morning, on my way to see Jo, Alexander sent a text.

I'm selling the house. You've got a month to leave or buy me out before I get lawyers involved.

I'd barely slept, exactly like after it all happened and I'd had insomnia. Patrick had asked if everything was okay before he'd left for the day, and I'd lied and told him it was. I'd never lied to him before. Not since we'd been properly together. I don't know why I did that.

Fine by me, I texted Alexander back.

I didn't want to be in Alexander's stupid house. I wondered what my having paid rent meant legally – if I could get that money back. It had to be nearly twenty grand! I wanted to cut every single last tie I had to him as quickly as possible, so that I could move on as happily as I had been doing when we were away. I resented being dragged back into the feelings I thought I'd gotten rid of, and the more I thought about it the more outrageous it was to me that if Alexander had to show up, he'd done so at two o'clock in the morning in the rain. Typical Alexander – it was a time and place that suited *him*.

Don't text me again, I added. *I'd prefer the paper trail of email, if we're going to start talking about lawyers.*

'So that's that,' I said to Jo over homemade crumpets and jam in her living room. 'I'm officially on the countdown to find somewhere new to live. Which I am crapping myself about, now. I'd been looking for places, but not really, you know? I was burying my head in the sand a bit.'

'Well, it's not fair that you have to find the mental bandwidth for a new house on top of everything else, is it?' She knelt down on a pillow by her coffee table, using a little wooden spoon to smother her crumpet with her mother's fig jam before settling it down in its own little wooden spoon holder, shaped like a trough. 'And he'll be lucky to find a buyer within a month, if that's what he's assuming. He doesn't have to be such an arse about it. All things considered.'

I chuckled, helping myself to more jam too. 'It's helpful, I suppose. Speeds the job up. All aboard the Change Train.'

'In for a penny, in for a pound?' Jo said.

'Something like that, yeah,' I replied. 'Everything I thought I wanted has crumbled, so now I have to start from scratch. Although I suppose I'm trying to look at it more as an opportunity, rather than an obligation.'

Jo considered what I'd said as she licked crumbs from her fingers. 'You seem really well,' she noted. 'That trip really did you the world of good. I'm happy for you. And you know, I think a lot of people would secretly like to have a do-over.'

'Do you think?' I asked.

'Yeah. I'm not saying I'd start again, but the idea that after

271

a rough draft I could live life for real is quite seductive, to be honest.'

Relief flooded my body. I hadn't realized how much I'd been needing to hear somebody say that – to tell me it wasn't my fault, how everything had blown up.

'Thank you,' I said. 'I couldn't stand it if you told me to grow up.'

'Why would I say that?' she exclaimed.

I shifted to pour decaf from the cafetière, adding in some of the cream she'd whipped and a little sprinkle of sea salt.

'This is so bougie,' I acknowledged. 'But so tasty.'

'It's Kwame,' she said. 'Every time he gets back from an LA business trip there's something else to add to the household menu. I act like he's ridiculous but I actually really love it too.'

I stirred the cream and watched it go from solid to liquid in my cup. 'I suppose I thought we got to a certain age and it was all for keeps,' I carried on, picking up my trail of thought.

'That would be depressing,' she replied. 'We're only in our early thirties. Sixty years of this being it? Treading water? No thanks.'

I sighed. 'So why is everyone else so settled? So . . . on a path?'

'Are you kidding?' she gasped. 'I don't think any of us know what's coming next. I mean, Kwame talks about starting up his own consultancy all the time, and no way can I stop him from doing that just because it's scary. It's his life too; he gets to reach for his dreams. But it affects me, and Bertie, and this unborn fella who I'm going to start charging rent to if he doesn't come soon. And that's . . . not ideal.'

I reached out to touch her belly. She really was ready to drop.

'Or look at Bri – she talks about moving out of London, but I think she worries we'd all forget about her if she wasn't six stops away on the 141. Kezza is about to give up her single, zero-responsibility days for motherhood but that doesn't mean she won't break down in tears every so often and ask us what on earth she's done.'

'But they're all such grown-up problems . . .' I said.

'And what, yours aren't?'

I shrugged.

'You got left on your wedding day and are dating a man – a widower – your mother hates, *plus* your ex is selling your home so you need to find somewhere else to live asap.'

'Patrick has offered me to crash at his place, but . . .'

She didn't say anything, knowing full well I'd fill the conversational gap if she didn't. I wasn't ready to articulate my thoughts out loud yet, though.

'Anyway,' I said. 'You lot have all got mortgages and husbands and children . . .'

'How is that any more grown-up than what you're dealing with?'

'I don't know,' I said, genuinely unsure. 'I suppose going flat hunting and considering retraining – maybe as a counsellor, I was thinking? – is something a twenty-five-year-old does.'

'I think you'd be a great counsellor. And, Annie, for what it's worth: I think it's pretty cool that you're going to create a life instead of settling for the one you might otherwise have just fallen into.'

'Even if it makes me feel like a child?'

'We all feel like children. I signed for the mortgage on this house with the worst hangover of my life. Last week Kwame wore swimming trunks under his jeans because neither of us had done laundry.'

I laughed. 'Is that true?'

'No,' she replied, moving a pillow to behind her lower back. I could tell she was really uncomfortable. The doctors had said if the baby didn't come within the next few days they'd induce her. 'I was just trying to make you feel better. But he *could* do that, and it wouldn't make him any less of a good partner, or dad, or human.'

'That's a very Patrick Hummingbird line,' I said, approvingly. 'He's very much into imperfection as a lifestyle choice.'

'Honestly, I cannot wait to meet him.'

I bit my tongue again, but she could tell I was hiding something.

'Annie?'

I shook my head. 'No,' I said. 'It's nothing.'

She smiled. 'If it's nothing, there's no reason not to tell me then, is there?'

I swirled the dregs of my coffee around my mug. 'I really like him,' I said. 'I do. But Mum said something, and it's really lodged in my head.'

'Now there's a shocker,' Jo retorted, rubbing her belly. 'Your mum is always saying stuff, and she is nearly always wrong. We know this. This isn't news.'

'I know!' I said. 'But she pointed out that it's a bit rash, getting out of an engagement and then having a new boyfriend a month later.'

'It is quick,' Jo said, nonplussed. 'But that doesn't mean it's wrong.'

'I've just not had a minute to think. I was so sad, and then meeting him and going away together happened so fast, and Australia wasn't real life, it was . . .'

'A holiday *from* life,' she supplied.

274

'Yeah.'

'It's not too late to slow it down. If it was too fast, now you can take your time and enjoy it. And look – if it isn't right, you don't have to stay together for ten years. It can be right, but for a month. It can be right, but for a year. Nobody is saying this has to be for a lifetime – by the sounds of it, not even your mother.'

I used the last of my crumpet to scoop up the jam that had gone rogue on my plate.

'He just seems so sure. I think it took a lot for him to get here after his wife.'

'And I can understand that. But, babe, that's not your responsibility. That's what you've learned after all of this, isn't it? You're not really making him happy if you're sacrificing your own happiness. He's a big boy. Whatever you need, you have to tell him. His reaction is his business.'

'You're right,' I said. 'I know you are.' I pondered it some more. 'But first: somewhere to live. Then I can decide what I think about Patrick, and Mum, and everything else that's keeping me awake at night.'

'Why put off today what you can put off tomorrow?'

'Exactly,' I said, licking the last of the jam from my fingers.

I spent the rest of the day trawling through websites looking for a flat that wouldn't cost my whole monthly paycheque, texting Patrick to say I was seeing the Core Four when actually I wanted to be alone. I don't know why I didn't just say that to him – I don't think he'd have minded. The lie just slipped out.

I was getting increasingly frustrated at the cost of a studio in London. It was all very well talking about how I disliked my job and wanted to retrain, but no way would I be able to afford to do that *and* live on my own. I knew that was a privileged problem to have. It's not like I was risking true homelessness or in need of a food bank. My version of hardship was middle-class hardship. But it still felt unfair, having to choose. I refused to consider a flat-share though. It was fun when I was younger but being relegated to a shelf in a shared fridge, or having to queue for the bathroom in the morning . . . nope. No way. Grown-ups made choices, didn't they, and my choice was to live alone, even if that put the kibosh on other plans I'd hope to make.

'So stay at work longer than you thought you would,' Adzo encouraged me as we took a morning walk to view one of the places I'd found that was mercifully in my budget. 'Give less of yourself to work but still take the paycheque, and train in your spare time.'

'Yeah,' I said. 'I suppose I just had this idea in my head of quitting my job and doing something I love and decorating a cute flat and everything going my way.'

'Mate,' Adzo intimated. 'Everything is going your way! Keep your job, have the cute flat, and take the leap in a year, or eighteen months. You never know what else life might have in store for you. What's the rush?'

There wasn't one, to be fair. I think it was more a case of waking up from sleepwalking through my life, and so impatiently wanting to fix it all, right now this second, in case I risked falling back asleep. But I knew it didn't work that way. True control over my life would look like relinquishing control over some stuff so I didn't waste my energy on things that weren't mine to control. Not to sound like Patrick, or anything.

'No rush,' I said. 'You're right. And plus, I don't really

have a choice. I'm not doing a house-share so that means keeping this job to pay for a flat.'

She steered me by the elbow out of the way of an old woman with a shopping trolley. 'I know I'm a badass at work,' she offered. 'But I don't actually love it.'

I stopped walking. 'Wait what? You don't?' I was genuinely shocked. I thought Adzo adored what we did.

She blinked slowly. 'I mean, it's fine,' she said. 'And it's not as if I have to be down the mines every day, or that we don't get a good-sized transfer into our account every month. But yeah, of course I wish that sometimes I could be a nurse instead, or a novelist, or the founder of a start-up.'

'So why don't you?' I pressed.

'Can't be arsed,' she replied, as we picked up our pace. When we stopped again, she looked up at where I pointed. 'This can't be it,' she said. 'Is this the address?'

I opened my email to double check. 'Number thirteen? Yup. This is it.'

She surveyed the dark brick and ramshackle windows. 'Okay . . .' She exhaled, slowly.

'Hmmm,' I agreed. 'I mean, I know it's not exactly a palace . . .'

'And this is six-fifty a month?'

'Yup.'

'Jeez.'

In a feat of comic timing, a rat the size of a small rabbit appeared at the corner of the cracked wheelie bin just beside the gate. We both screamed, leaping back.

'What the hell!' Adzo cried.

'Gross, gross, gross,' I said, pulling on her arm so that we almost collided with a passing cyclist who screamed out, 'Fucking watch it, dickheads!' whilst issuing the finger.

We screamed again and this time it was Adzo tugging at my arm, leading me to the street corner where she asked me in a hushed voice, 'Do you actually want to go in there?'

I shook my head. 'No,' I said, as if it was obvious. 'But it's in the right area, –ish, and I can afford it.'

'I think we need to go and wash our hands,' she said. 'I don't think this is the place for you, okay?'

I nodded. 'Okay. I have another viewing somewhere else tomorrow, anyway, and one the day after.'

'Email the guy to say you're not coming,' she prompted.

I nodded agreement. 'At least I can be early for my meeting with Chen.'

'Go,' Adzo insisted. 'Save yourself. Pretend this never happened. Urgh!'

37

I was still shivering at the thought of the giant rat as I uttered my thanks to the top-hat-wearing doorman at the entryway to the hotel Chen had mysteriously asked to meet me at. I'd been due back at work that morning, but she'd told me to come for a mid-morning brunch and start back tomorrow, instead. I noted that the polished golden sign ahead of me said to make a left for the restaurant.

'This is all very cloak-and-dagger,' I said as she stood up to greet me. 'I don't think we've ever met outside the office, have we?'

'Surely that's not true,' she replied brushing her hand through the air to dismiss my observation. Her sleek black bob framed her petite features perfectly, but I knew that for as girly as she looked, Chen had more fire than any man *or* woman I'd worked with. 'We've met like this many times before.'

I mean, we honestly hadn't, but her curt delivery made me question my own sanity. I wondered what it was like to go through life as Chen, so certain that she could bend the reality of others to fit her own. It was admirable, if not a little intimidating.

'Tea?' she asked, as a gloved waiter appeared, a starched white cloth folded over his arm. I addressed my response to him.

'Tea please, yes,' I said, and then sat, waiting for the reason of our meeting to become apparent.

'Now, Annie,' Chen said. 'We need to talk about your situation.'

'Okay,' I said, my stomach burbling. 'Is everything okay? I've really appreciated the time off to get my head together . . .'

'I'm worried about you.'

'Oh,' I said, trying to keep my face neutral.

'It's apparent to me that you're not being challenged enough,' she continued.

The chap with gloves returned with our tea and Chen interrupted herself to say, 'Are you hungry? I'm afraid I can't do solids before noon, but please, by all means you go ahead.'

I was starving, but it seemed rude to go in for the eggs hollandaise like the woman on the table across from us, who'd had the good sense to get a side order of hash browns too. I stole a glance at her plate hungrily, but even New Annie couldn't engage the 'Sod It' muscle it took to dig in when her boss was only having tea – and black tea, at that. She didn't even add any milk.

'Maybe some toast?' I said, feebly, and the server nodded obligingly.

'As I was saying,' Chen continued. 'You're wasted at the moment. You could do your current tasks with your eyes closed, and quite frankly that isn't good enough. I've known this for a long time.'

Crap. Definitely fired.

'The Antwerp lab love you. I've been reviewing the work you did for them in the spring, and Adzo agrees: it's quite remarkable. There's a position for you there, managing the team. You should take it.'

'What?'

'You need something new, Annie, and I would be an incredibly bad boss if I did not give you up for this role.'

I was astonished. Antwerp?

'It's the diamond capital of the world, and very good for shopping. Brussels would maybe excite you more, but it's only forty minutes on the train and of course the Eurostar connects direct to London from there, so you'll never be far away from us. I can organize it so that you're needed here for a week every few months, if you'd like the excuse to come back. They're offering a very competitive salary, which is more than I can find in our budget for you, and I've been told by Jules – you met him a couple of times in some Zoom meetings, I think? – to say whatever it might take to get you to say yes. I shouldn't think it will take a lot, will it? But either way, I'm not to let you consider turning this down, I'm afraid.'

'Right then,' I said. 'So I'm not fired?'

'Fired?' Chen repeated. 'Why would you say that?'

'I thought I was in trouble,' I said, blushing.

'Quite the opposite,' Chen said. 'Your absence this month has made it clear that we want to do everything we can to keep you. You're an asset to the company, Annie, and you've been missed. We'll be sad to lose you here, of course, but Antwerp will be lucky to have you. Let's get you over there for a few nights, shall we? You can go and meet everyone in person.'

'Okay,' I replied, as I let what she'd said sink in. It was the strangest twelve minutes of my life.

38

'I know they offered you the Antwerp position,' Adzo said when I called her immediately after leaving Chen. I was freaking out. Was this what I had been looking for? Was all the talk of retraining and switching careers actually just the thing to wake me up to the fact I needed a change in general, and just like that . . . this could be it? I'd never been to Antwerp before, but I hadn't missed London when I'd been in Australia. Maybe that was the problem – it wasn't my job, it was the city. I just needed new streets to roam.

'Why didn't you warn me?' I squealed. 'I literally just saw you!'

'Chen consulted me about it, asked me if I thought you could take it, that's all. I wasn't sure how fast she would move though – if she was going to ask you today or just test the waters.'

'*Do* you think I can do it?'

Adzo sucked the air through her front teeth. 'Mate. Come on. You're amazing at what you do. Antwerp would be lucky to have you.'

'Thank you.' I flopped down onto a bench. 'Isn't Antwerp something *you'd* want?' I asked. 'Out of the two of us . . .' I stopped talking because the truth was suddenly obvious. 'Oh. You didn't want it,' I said. 'They offered it to you first and you said no.'

'No!' she shrieked. 'Antwerp specifically asked for you. But,' she continued, 'San Francisco have specifically asked for me.'

'No!' I cried.

'Yes!' she said.

'Oh my goodness, that is so incredible, Adzo. Congratulations! I'm so happy for you!'

'I feel sad, though,' she said. 'Because I think this is the beginning of the end for us, whatever happens.'

'Damn,' I said. 'Yeah.'

'Yeah.'

Ever since I'd arrived at the company Adzo and I had been thick as thieves. I think my 'good girl' tendencies amused her, and I was in awe of this woman of the world and all of her outrageous stories. We complemented each other personally and professionally, often finishing each other's sentences – or should I say, theories. We had a shorthand together at work, meaning calling ourselves the 'Dream Team' really wasn't hyperbole – where I lacked Adzo filled in the gaps, and where she was less able I was able to pick up the slack. Half the time the only reason I looked forward to work was because of my Work Wifey, which is a horrible, girly, reductionist turn of phrase that wholeheartedly encapsulated the role we played in each other's lives.

'Did you say yes, then? To San Francisco?'

'In theory,' she said. 'I'm going to do a recce mission out there next month to see if it fits, and I've got questions about the package they're offering me. But yeah. I mean, it's San Francisco!'

'You're such a good negotiator,' I said. 'Chen wants me to go out to Antwerp to see the lay of the land. I haven't said yes. But I didn't say no, either. She basically didn't give me a choice?'

'Oh my.' I could tell she was grinning. 'You're finally going to get to meet the handsome Jules face to face. When I was out there last year it was like walking around town with a model or something. He's *gorgeous*. I cannot fathom how anybody can look that good and be that smart? But—'

'But he *is* that good-looking and is that smart,' I said. 'The stuff he sends through? His thinking is really inspired.'

'It's really hot,' Adzo agreed.

'Obviously I'm with Patrick though,' I said, and it was the first time I'd considered his role in all of this. Patrick. *Ah.*

'Yes, yes, yes. Of course you are,' Adzo said. Then: 'We should go out and celebrate. But at a restaurant. Let's go somewhere really fancy and have proper cocktails to start and wine with dinner and have shots to finish and tell each over again and again how marvellous we think the other one is, until they ask us to leave because they're closing.'

'Deal,' I said, but I was already wondering how Patrick would react to my news, and a tiny bit resentful that I had to consider him in any of this at all. I didn't want permission from him, or anyone, to investigate. I knew I needed to talk to him, to face my doubts head on. He deserved that.

I said goodbye and pulled up my internet browser, typing in: *flats to rent, Antwerp.* Just to get an idea.

I mused it all over as I nipped out to the corner shop for some bits. Since coming back from Aus I'd been trying to use up what was in the freezer, and instead of getting a big grocery delivery I was buying stuff only when I needed it. The corner shop didn't have any tinned coconut milk and I was desperate to use up some frozen sliced butternut squash for a Sri Lankan curry, so I took a punt and went a couple of streets over to the bigger one. If they didn't have any, I'd get a pizza. Carol needed walking, anyway.

I rounded the corner, tying her up outside and patting her on the head, and dipped in through the shop's door. As I looked up, there was Patrick, testing a series of melons for ripeness. He must have felt my eyes on him because he looked up, and it was the strangest thing: I didn't feel happy to see him. He could obviously tell because before his smile could reach full capacity he dropped it, as if he'd misunderstood something and now appreciated something different. He put down the two melons he'd been weighing up and took his AirPods out of his ears. Somebody came in the door behind me and I stepped aside to let them past, grateful for the excuse to break eye contact. When I looked up again, Patrick hadn't moved. I walked towards him.

'Hello.'

'Hello,' he said back. 'What's a nice girl like you doing in a place like this?'

He leant forward to give me a kiss, but instead of going in for a sloppy Frenchie I kept my mouth in a chaste pucker, quickly touching his lips and then pulling away.

'Coconut milk,' I said.

'Top shelf just before the loo rolls,' he replied, pointing.

I followed his gaze and said, 'Thanks.'

We stood.

'So I have news,' I began.

'About your meeting?'

'Yup. Chen asked me to consider going to work at the Antwerp HQ.'

'Antwerp? As in, Belgium?'

'Antwerp as in Belgium, yes.'

'And what did you say?'

'I said I'd go and do a recce mission out there. She's flying me out at the end of the week. Just overnight.'

His face puzzled over what I'd said. 'You've already agreed to fly out there? That's cool that they're interested but . . . you agreed without talking to me about it?'

'It's just a research trip.' I shrugged. 'I haven't taken the job or anything.'

An old man tutted as he tried to move past us. To be fair, we were taking up the aisle.

'That's . . . wow. Well, congrats. But . . . I don't feel great that there's not even a conversation about all this. Go, and everything, but I'm your boyfriend, remember? I'm happy they recognize that you're amazing but this feels like the kind of thing that could affect my life, too. Have you been avoiding me? Why haven't you wanted to talk about this?'

That was a fair thing to ask. 'I'm sorry,' I said. 'I've been a bit in my head. I don't know. Mum said that thing when we had lunch there and it's just made me wonder—'

'Since when do you listen to your mother?'

'I don't! But when she said it's no good leaving one relationship and jumping into another I just think . . . I don't know. Not that she's right, but . . .'

'So now you don't want this?' he asked, his tone shocked. This wasn't going the way I wanted it to at all. Everything was coming out wrong. Having blown cold from hot with him for the past few days anyway, there was apparently a lot he wanted to get off his chest – which he was entitled to.

'Of course I want this,' I said. 'But I kind of see her point, that's all. I planned my whole life around Alexander. I haven't learned anything if I start to plan my life around you, now.'

'I see. I didn't realize that's how you felt.'

'I need to at least consider this opportunity, don't I? You would never ask me not to.'

'No,' he replied. 'I wouldn't. But also, if the shoe was on the other foot I wouldn't explore moving anywhere, let alone abroad, without talking to you first. Do you see the difference? I know this is new, Annie, but I thought it was pretty serious . . .'

I moved aside as a mother and her child reached across to get to the dried pasta.

'You and me,' he continued. 'It's been good, hasn't it? This could really be something. If you want to move to Antwerp for a job you love then okay, cool, let's talk about it. But ten minutes ago you were all for quitting the stupid job.'

A single tear spilled over and ran down my cheek before I brushed it away with the back of my hand. I didn't even know why I was crying. It just started happening and I was helpless about it.

'Don't call my job stupid.'

'I didn't. You did.'

'Don't use my words against me, then.'

He rolled his eyes. 'When is this "research trip"?' I could hear the inverted commas in the way he said it.

'I fly Thursday morning. Back Friday.'

'Let me know how you get on, then,' he said. We stared at each other.

'I'm upset, Annie,' he pressed. 'I can't figure out what's changed in the fifteen minutes we've been home, but I feel you pulling away from me. We said being back wouldn't change us. But I can't fight for somebody who wouldn't fight for me. I'm not a mug.'

'Nothing's changed,' I insisted, but as soon as the words left my mouth I knew it wasn't true. It sounded hollow.

'Like I say,' Patrick carried on. 'I'm upset. I can't do this here. I'm going to go home and calm down, okay? Then we can talk. I don't think I'm being unreasonable about any of this.'

I nodded gloomily, still crying and tears blurring my vision. He walked away, making the bell above the shop door tinkle as he left. I knew I should have gone after him, but I didn't want to. Maybe that's what the tears were for. I had guilt from being pulled in two directions. I'd meant what I said: I couldn't plan my life around him. I didn't want to have to 'ask' him if it was 'okay' for me to go to Antwerp to see what the office there was like. I didn't want 'permission', or to put problems in the way of a chance I wasn't even sure I wanted to take yet. I just wanted to do it. To be free and able to be the kind of woman who said, 'Antwerp? Sure – get me on a plane!' without second-guessing myself. I hadn't done anything wrong by giving Chen's assistant my passport details to book the flight. Had I?

Urgh. I felt horrible. I had not expected the day to unfold like this when I'd woken up: this was too fast. It was too much to figure out. I liked Patrick! What was I playing at? And yet . . . That night was the first night we'd spent apart where I didn't text him before bed. Patrick didn't text me either. After so many firsts – first drink, first kiss, first meet-the-parents – we were officially having another: first fight.

39

I was scheduled on a 7 a.m. flight from London City Airport that got into Antwerp at just after 7 a.m., given the one-hour time difference. The plan was twenty-four hours in the city, with a meet-and-greet with the team at the lab, a group lunch, and then an evening of playing tourist before hopping back on an 8 a.m. flight the next morning, ready to give Chen my verdict.

Let's talk when you get back, Patrick texted as I waited to take off, after I'd wished him a good morning.

Okay, I'd replied, not really knowing what else to say. Adzo had counselled me through sitting with my emotions instead of trying to fix everything, which had been helpful.

'Don't rush into smoothing it all over until you're sure of what you want,' she'd said. 'After so much intense time together, maybe a few days apart is just the medicine. He'll be here when you get back.'

'Yeah,' I'd agreed, but part of me missed him already. Being in an airport was less fun alone than with him, and obviously the last time I'd flown was with him and his buckets of enthusiasm. I kept thinking about him, and about everything that had happened when we were away. I hadn't seen him since the corner shop, three days ago. He said he needed to take this time to sort out his feelings. He didn't want to say something he might regret, he'd explained. I felt like I was being punished.

I don't like fighting, I texted back.

Same, he said, followed by a row of kisses that could either be read as earnest, or putting a full stop to the interaction. I sent a row of kisses back and turned off my phone for take-off.

'Annie!'

I waltzed through customs in the easiest disembarkation I'd ever had to be met by a tall, blue-eyed man waving through the small crowd. I recognized Jules immediately from our Zoom calls, but in real life and higher definition I could see what Adzo had meant about the movie-star good looks that translated better in real life. He was stunning.

He reached out a massive hand and I shook it.

'It's wonderful to meet you in person,' he said, and his English was perfect. He had a tiny accent that reminded me of Sean Connery's. 'How was your flight?'

He gallantly took my overnight bag, despite my protestations, and we walked into the multi-storey car park as I told him how easy it had been to get from my house to the airport, and how incredible it was to me that in just over an hour I was there, ready to be wowed.

'Do you know much about the city?' he enquired.

'Is it bad if I say no . . .?' I asked sheepishly.

He chuckled. 'Nobody does, really,' he admitted. 'Which means it's all the more fun to play tour guide. I can show you all the best places, and not just because we're desperate for you to join us here. I'm also very proud of where I'm from.'

'Born and bred Antwerp?' I asked, as he paused in front of a black Toyota hybrid, hitting his keys to open the boot and effortlessly slipping in my bag without breaking a sweat.

'There's not a square or street or food stall in this city I don't know about.' He smiled, hitting another button to automatically close the trunk and swiftly moving to open the passenger door for me. 'You'll see.'

Jules drove fast but confidently, tapping out the rhythm of the music singing out from the radio. He wasn't wearing a wedding ring, I noticed, but he did mention his two little boys in passing, Mathis and Victor.

'We'll go to the lab,' he explained, as we zipped through from the main roads to quieter back streets. 'And after lunch we can check you into the hotel.'

It wasn't a question, so I murmured my agreement and watched as we approached what was presumably the centre of town. Jules shot me a grin as the buildings started to change, satisfied that I'd noticed the beauty.

'They say Antwerp is a world city on a human scale,' he explained, turning the music down. 'There's always something to see and do and eat, but it's mostly walkable and has a friendlier, more village-like feel than somewhere like London.' He looked at me again, and I raised my eyebrows.

'Would you be offended if I said I'm born and raised London, and so to me *that's* the centre of the universe?' I countered. I didn't even know if I meant that, but I felt compelled to stick up for the place I was from.

He laughed. 'Noted!' he said. 'And for the record, I love London. But we've had a couple of people transfer over here, and everyone says how nice it is to slow down. That London is a bit treadmill-y – you just keep going and going and going.'

'Fair enough. I *have* been wanting to slow down lately,' I admitted. 'A change of scenery could be nice.' As we pulled up to the kerb in a small side street a man who looked like Patrick passed by, and my heart skipped a beat until I realized that of course it wasn't him. How could it be? Jules parked up and looked at his watch as I fingered my phone in my pocket, resisting the urge to see if Patrick had sent a text.

'Coffee?' Jules asked, executing the perfect parallel park.

'Please,' I replied, taking my hand out of my pocket like I'd been caught doing something I shouldn't have.

We walked, and I hadn't been prepared for what I saw when we turned a corner into one of the main parts of the city. In a big square were tall stone buildings all pressed up against each other, with narrow windows scoring the front – like the area around Fleet Street back home. It was majestic. Imposing.

'Whoa,' I said, gaping in admiration.

The sun was shining and the sky was clear, and the pale stone of the buildings contrasted with the bright flags outside the biggest one, the one that looked like some kind of town hall or central courthouse.

'The Grote Market,' Jules stated, and I noticed his designer sunglasses and his stubble and the white of his pressed shirt against the blue of his navy suit. His teeth lined up like perfect ivory gravestones, and his full lips glistened where his tongue had darted out to lick them, just briefly. I couldn't wait to report back to Adzo that he was as attractive as she'd suggested. She'd love that I'd noticed.

'This is thirteenth century,' Jules said. 'But we reached our prime in the fifteenth and sixteenth centuries. That's when Antwerp was the most important city in the Low Countries.'

He moved to stand behind me and lightly put a hand on my shoulder. Lowering his voice and looking out in the same direction as me, pointing just beyond my eyeline he said, 'Imagine a bustling centre with Flemish merchants doing business with traders from all over Europe. These are all the guild houses, and that's the Stadhuis – the town hall.'

'This is seriously impressive,' I said, turning to him and instantly blushing. I couldn't help it. I felt disloyal to Patrick, but there was something about being in such close proximity to somebody that handsome. Kezza had briefly dated an actor who'd been in *Killing Eve* and all the Core Four had agreed: some people really are just otherworldly hot, in a way that defies the physics of humanness. Jules was one of them. I took a step away from him, in case his beauty blinded me. 'Totally picturesque,' I added.

'And at Christmas, Annie,' he said, and using my name in a sentence like that was a claim on me, 'it's unmatched. With the winter market and ice rink . . .'

He kissed his fingertips, like a happy chef. It really was breath-taking, and I let being somewhere foreign wash over me. Mere hours ago I was waking up in an empty house in London, Carol already across the road with Lenny and Dash, in the middle of a fight with my boyfriend and my ex-fiancé and counting down the days until I moved, not to mention the money in my bank account barely enough to cover first and last month's rent on wherever I needed to move to. And now I was here, in Antwerp, with a handsome man who was almost offensively attractive for a colleague, and a sense of adventure pulsing through my veins. Was my 'maktub' moment the fact that, right on cue, I was potentially able to move countries, and move homes? It would be one hell of a fresh start. If I got a promotion here I'd be able to afford to live on my own, and Adzo had said I'd get a relocation package to help me get up and running, meaning it wouldn't even cost me anything to set up afresh. Old Annie would never have got on the plane and explored moving to another country. Being here proved I'd changed. Australia, and Patrick, had made sure of it.

Patrick.

I was so mad at him for expecting me to be adventurous, but only once I'd consulted him. Our terse texts were so unlike us, but both of our feelings had been hurt. I hated the confrontation, but somehow knew it was important. I'd never stood up for myself with Alexander. I had to with Patrick, otherwise what had it all been for?

'About that coffee,' Jules said, interrupting my reverie. I turned my attention back to him. 'This is the tourist haven. Let me show you my Antwerp . . .'

I trotted after him as he strode ahead, glancing back to get one last look at the square. *Patrick would love it here,* I couldn't help thinking.

'Now,' Jules said, slowing so that we could walk in step. 'We must look out for number sixteen.'

'Number sixteen?'

'Yes. This is Oude Koornmarkt, and at number sixteen we'll see a sign to the Vlaeykensgang. I think you'll love it.'

'You're doing pretty good as a tour guide,' I observed. 'This is all gorgeous. I am really, really impressed.' I looked up just in time to see a faded blue sign hanging from an elaborate wrought-iron pole. 'Oh!' I exclaimed. 'Sixteen!'

'Right this way, then,' Jules demurred, holding out an arm to let me go ahead.

We entered a maze of small alleys that alternated between cobbled streets and dramatic paved walkways. The buildings were painted white brick and smooth ivory stone, and up above an awning bridged the gap between buildings so that ivy could grow theatrically. The buildings had painted wooden shutters that matched the window boxes, stuffed to overflowing with bright, colourful flowers, even in the chilly air. Signs in front said what I assumed meant art gallery, and the windows of some had treasures of paintings and tables and knick-knacks. At the corner, where two alleyways met, was a small café with tables outside, and it was just about warm enough to take a seat directly in the sun. I wished I'd thought to bring my sunglasses. It was very bright, in a way that doesn't happen in London during the colder months, where everything can be fifty shades of grizzly grey.

'Here,' said Jules, gallantly. 'You sit with your back to the sun.'

He ordered us coffee and pastries and water, and it occurred to me that I must have looked awful considering I'd gotten up at five thirty that morning. I smoothed down my hair at the nape of my neck and pulled out some lip balm from my bag.

'So,' stated Jules. 'Chen said I'd have to charm you as if my life depended on it.'

'Did she now?' I said, rubbing my lips together to spread the Vaseline. Was I flirting as I said it? I felt light. Playful. That's exactly what Aus had done to me – made me sprightlier because it felt full of opportunity. Hope is a dangerous gateway drug.

Jules was amused. 'I'm not afraid to rise to the challenge.'

'That's very noble of you,' I said.

He grinned. 'Something tells me you won't be strong-armed,' he mused, and I shrugged. Antwerp certainly was cute. Maybe Patrick would come with me and find a job, or maybe we would do long-distance. He'd made it seem that seizing this opportunity would be so black and white, but there were so many different ways we could navigate it together. If I wanted to. If *he* wanted to. Or maybe this would be it, and we'd break up. I didn't know. I felt clammy at the thought of it. Being in charge of my own future was more uncomfortable than I'd thought it would be. That's the thing they don't tell you about having choices – saying yes to one thing normally means saying no to ten more.

The Antwerp office was miles ahead of the aesthetic of the London lab. Glass-fronted with a swish lobby and an elevator that Jules assured me wasn't out of order every other week like ours in London. It was sunnier there. Antwerp was a light jacket in spring instead of a damp overcoat in autumn which, if I was being unkind, London could often feel like. I'd got used to that, but maybe the cold months didn't have to be a constant state of damp.

'Luke!' I squealed when we got to the research centre.

'There she is!'

Luke used to work in London too, and had left about two years ago. We'd got on well, and I always enjoyed work events more if he was there.

'It's so good to see you,' he commented. 'How've you been? Surely your hunk of a fella must have put a ring on it by now? Adzo said last time she was here that you were wedding planning for the event of the century.'

'Oh, actually – that ended,' I replied, deliberately keeping my chin high. I felt Jules looking at me. 'Happily so,' I insisted. 'It was time. University sweethearts don't always have to end up together, I've learned.'

'Oh,' said Luke, screwing up his face in sympathy. 'I'm sorry to hear it, but also – does that mean he's on the market? I've never seen cheekbones so razor sharp outside of the movies!'

I rolled my eyes playfully and changed the subject to ask about the facilities and how he was finding the city. He told me he loved it – the culture, the work-life balance, and how easy it was to travel around the rest of mainland Europe.

'I get home every few months, but to be honest my brother prefers coming out here with his wife when they can, and even my parents have got used to having an ungrateful traitor of a son who lives abroad. I see family maybe six times a year? I don't think I saw them that much when we lived in the same country!'

I laughed, silently questioning what my parents would think if I told them I was moving out here before reminding myself that I didn't care. Freddie would be old enough soon to come out on the train by herself, too, if somebody put her on in London and I collected her at this end. I'd miss being able to just pop in and see her, but if I wanted it I really could make it work. It wouldn't necessarily be easy, but it could be done.

I got a tour of the site and was able to chat with various faces I'd seen online but most of whom I'd never met in person. We talked about the formula we'd been working on, and I shared some ideas Adzo and I had about where it could go next, which seemed to impress everyone around the conference table. I told them about her heading over to San Francisco, and I got some morsels of gossip that had travelled on the grapevine to feed back to her.

We broke for an informal lunch at about 1 p.m., filtering out as a group of ten to a nearby restaurant where Jules ordered for the table and I skipped the wine I was offered because I was sleepy after the adrenaline rush of the morning and my early start.

'You'll need a power nap before our afternoon activities,' Jules commanded. 'Unless you'd rather have the evening to yourself?' he added.

I considered it. 'No,' I decided. 'It would be great if you could show me more of the city. I really appreciate it. I'm waiting for the other shoe to drop, to be honest. I'm wondering what the catch is.'

'It's a date, then,' he said, and I tried not to read anything into his phraseology. English was his second language, after all.

Luke leaned in to my elbow once lunch had finished and the rest headed back to the office and I'd thanked them for such a comprehensive breakdown of how everything out in their HQ worked.

'You make friends fast,' he said.

'What do you mean?' I asked.

'James Bond over there.' We both looked in his direction. It made me laugh because yeah, I thought his accent was a bit Sean Connery, but I hadn't made the mental leap to how his whole demeanour really was like he was an international spy. The tailoring, the smile, the magnetism.

'I'm here on business,' I said. 'Don't insult me.'

Luke raised his hands in surrender. 'Didn't mean to offend,' he said. 'I'm probably just jealous.'

'I have a boyfriend,' I added hastily, Patrick's face coming to my mind.

'Don't we all?' Luke laughed. 'What's the saying? We're all mortal until the second glass of wine and the first kiss.'

'Shut up!' I said, something about his comment landing heavy in my stomach.

40

Jules drove me to my hotel after lunch, issuing instructions to nap, freshen up, and then to meet him in the lobby at 6 p.m. In my room I texted Freddie with some photos I'd taken. She didn't know I was travelling with a view to move, just that I was away for work. She texted back: *I can't wait until I get to go on business trips to fancy places! Cool!* I sent back a GIF of a woman in a powersuit doing a big thumbs up, and told her I loved her.

Can we do something fun this weekend? she sent, a few minutes later.

Of course we can, Frou. Anything in mind?

She sent back: *Bowling maybe? Or the trampoline place? Then burgers. I miss u!*

Hearing Freddie tell me she missed me was like a knife to the heart. She'd never really said that before. She always made it clear when she wanted to see me, but she'd never said *I miss you* until I was in Australia.

You don't have to miss me, I texted back. *I see you all the time.*

I wished you lived with us, she said. *Mia lived with her sister and said she was annoying but it was also really cool. And Sofie's big sister lives with her 2!!*

I didn't know where her outpouring had come from. I instantly listed all the ways I'd been a bad big sister lately in my mind. *Has something happened?* I asked, in case I'd missed something. I *had* been absent, I supposed, what with all my travel and the upheaval of everything. When she didn't reply right away I tried FaceTiming her, but she told me she was in double maths and texting under the table.

I just want to do more fun stuff, she said. *G2G!* She'd had to teach me months ago what that meant – got to go.

Okay, Froogle. We'll have fun this weekend! I promise! I used exclamation points but my senses felt dulled. I wasn't even doing a good job of seeing her often enough when we lived in the same city – would it really work out if I moved countries?

I looked around my hotel room despondently. It was small and compact, a world away from the luxurious suites of my last trip abroad. I didn't need fancy things, but I sure had loved the taste of extravagance we'd had in Australia. It had been extra special because of Patrick, though. There was no denying that.

It's pretty here, I texted him. *You'd love it.*

I saw it come up with 'read: 14:22', but I didn't get a response.

Hello from Antwerp, I sent to Adzo. *Turns out wherever you go, you're still who you are,* I said. *I'm currently experiencing one thousand different emotions.* She immediately called me.

'I didn't mean to sound the alarm,' I said, instead of 'hello'. 'I didn't need you to call – not if you're busy.'

She chuckled down the line. 'Talking voice to voice is

301

quicker than texting,' she replied. 'Chill. Where are you? At the office?'

I took off my clothes as I explained I was back at the hotel and that yes, Jules really was that gorgeous. As I grabbed some complimentary water from the fridge she giggled.

'Yeah,' she said. 'When I was last in New York they were even talking about him. His reputation precedes him.'

'Oh God,' I said. 'Is he a shagger?'

'Oh, two hundred per cent,' Adzo said. 'A divorcé who looks like that? He gets his end away with somebody different on every single trip.'

'What?' I gasped. 'Even—'

'Yeah,' she said. 'Fine. You caught me. We hooked up when I was there. Can you blame me?'

In my pants and vest top I crawled between the crisp hotel sheets. 'No,' I admitted. 'I can't. But I do feel silly now. I felt like he was flirting with me, a bit? Maybe?'

'Probably!'

'Hmmm,' I said, wondering if I should cancel the evening. The risk of spending time with a playboy didn't feel appealing. I wondered if I'd have more fun on my own.

'Jules aside, though, what are you thinking?' Adzo asked.

I stared at the ceiling. 'One minute I think it's the best place ever,' I said, 'and the next I think there's no way I'll leave London. It's going to suck without you there, but do I really want to be apart from Freddie? My uni girls?'

'Patrick?'

'I'm trying not to let him factor in. Even though he does, obviously. But my baby sister? Yeah. She definitely sways me. I love the feeling of being somewhere new, and the possibility of leaving everything behind to *be* someone new, but at the same time . . .'

'That's a lot,' she supplied.

'Yeah. Maybe I should just be who I am, where I'm from. I can't keep running away.'

'Interesting,' said Adzo, furtively. 'Very interesting.'

'What do you mean?'

My eyelids were getting heavy. I knew I'd nap like my life depended on it.

'Well,' she started. 'Let's just say, if you did stay in London, I might be able to help on the flat front. So don't let money play in to your decision, okay?'

'What do you mean?'

'I know about a place,' she said. 'It's in your budget, and it's nice. But don't let that sway you! Appreciate Antwerp for Antwerp.'

'How can I do that now you've told me you've found me a place?!'

'Don't listen to me,' she insisted. 'I shouldn't have mentioned it. Have a snooze, have a night out with Jules, and when you're back tomorrow call me and I'll take you on an adventure. Okay? Promise me you'll still think about Antwerp?'

'I promise,' I said. 'Okay.'

I was lying, of course.

I dozed right through until the hotel phone rang. Jules was in reception, wondering where I was.

'Oh, crap,' I said groggily. 'I lost track of time. Give me ten minutes, okay? No. Fifteen.'

He seemed quite mad by the time I got downstairs.

'I hate waiting,' he said. 'Even for colleagues as charming as you.'

'It's like I've disappointed my dad,' I muttered.

303

'We're late is all,' he replied. 'Anyway. Come on.'

He walked fast, which is how I could tell he was still pissed off, and it made me think of Patrick (again!), how every morning he'd say, *Ready, ready, chicken jelly?* And even when I wasn't ready he'd sit and read a leaflet or look at the trees until I was. Patrick never once stormed off ahead of me, treating me like a naughty tween. Even when we were fighting, like now, he wasn't emotionally withholding or nasty. Jules was kind of . . . mercurial.

'Hey,' I said. 'I can show myself around the city if you'd prefer. I'm sorry I was late.'

'Thank you for finally apologizing.' His words were clipped. And then, softening, he added, 'It's fine. Let's walk to the other side of the water to work up an appetite, and then we can have dinner. Okay?'

'Okay,' I said, but I could tell he was still shaking off his anger.

We walked in silence for a while, heading through the underpass to the other side of the river so that we could see where we'd come from light up as it got darker. The odd after-work jogger sprinted past, and parents with kids on an evening gelato run meandered by. I smiled at an older couple strolling arm in arm.

'It's a very romantic city,' I said as a pensioner grinned at me before turning his attentions back to the wife he was clinging to. 'People seem happy. Like they have the time to do as they please. Does that make sense?'

'Absolutely,' he agreed. 'I'm very proud of where I am from.'

'It reminds me of the harbour in Sydney. The water and the view. The people.'

'I've been to Australia only once,' he said, and I smiled as

I took a breath to seize on this commonality with him. 'It's beautiful there, but it's very far away.'

'Yes,' I said. 'I was there recently, actually. I loved it.'

'Not as much as here, surely?' He looked out to the water admiringly.

I took in his smart suit and unbuttoned collar and blue eyes and blond hair, set against the city and the way everything seemed hazy and blue as twilight fell. I didn't want to lie, but I couldn't find the words for the truth.

Dinner was a feast of moules-frites and fresh crusty bread, inside a tiny little restaurant where Jules seemed to know the owner. We drank wine and laughed as he tried to teach me some basic Flemish.

'No, the accent is wrong,' he said, as he corrected the way I said 'Hallo'.

'Hallo,' I tried again, and he nodded.

'Exactly,' he said. 'It has a hardness to it. Now let's try *goodbye*.'

I ate with my fingers, using one of the mussel shells as a little pincer to pull apart the other mussels and scooping up the salty fries to dip in the sauce.

'The worst thing you can do is call these French fries,' Jules told me after I exclaimed how good they were.

'Why?' I asked.

'It's an ongoing dispute,' he said, flashing me that smile. 'We Belgians have records of fries existing way before the French.'

'You learn something new every day,' I replied.

Pudding was some sort of pastry crust with a cheesecake filling, and coffee was served with actual Belgian chocolates. I made a mental note to pick up a huge stash for Freddie and the Core Four at the airport tomorrow morning.

'That was incredible,' I declared afterwards, as Jules paid the bill and we headed back to the hotel. 'You've been a wonderful tour guide. Thank you so much.'

Jules offered me his arm and I took it, strolling in step with him through the darkened cobbled streets.

'I was sorry to hear about your fiancé earlier today,' he said, the notes of a street musician floating up through an alleyway. 'Luke said he was surprised to hear you'd broken up.'

It wasn't lost on me that in order for Luke to have said that, Jules must have asked about it.

'Oh, don't be,' I said. 'It hurt and then it didn't. These things happen, don't they?'

'They do,' he agreed.

We found where the music was coming from and stood to listen. A young woman sang in Flemish as a man accompanied on an electric piano. It was haunting and beautiful at the same time. She sang with incredible sorrow and pain for such a young person.

'She is singing about a love that went away,' Jules explained to me, coming in close to my ear so I could feel his breath on my neck. 'She is saying, "I sent my love away, but I wanted him to come back. My love won't come back, so now I am alone."'

Tears welled up in my eyes. I felt like I'd been sucker-punched square in the gut.

'She's so good,' I whispered, quietly, and when they finished we applauded and Jules put a note in their collection box. We walked home in silence. I was thinking about Patrick. How could I fix things, but without apologizing? I didn't want to admit to having done anything wrong, because I didn't think I had. But I missed him. I did. Everything was better when I did it with him.

'Here we are,' Jules said, when we got to where I was staying. We both looked up at the building and he turned to me.

'Thank you again,' I said. 'For everything you've done today. It's been really . . .' I couldn't find a word that I felt enthusiastic about. I settled on *informative*.

Jules nodded, and stuck out a hand for me to shake. 'Your fiancé is an idiot for letting you go,' he said, bidding me goodnight so I could walk into the reception area alone. I wasn't thinking about Alexander letting me go, though. I was thinking about how I'd be a fool if I lost Patrick.

41

I took a cab straight from City airport after I landed, near to Newington Green. Adzo had given me instructions to meet her by the entrance to my local park, the one near the hairdresser's who'd given me my pixie cut. To say I was shocked that she'd made it all the way to this side of town would be an understatement, especially before work, because I'd never been sure she actually knew this side of town existed. Adzo is one of the most well-heeled, well-travelled women I've ever met, but I'd always assumed that in terms of London extending further east than Oxford Street, for her intents and purposes I essentially lived in Essex. But here she was.

'Hold on,' she said. 'Let me just get my bearings.' She held her iPhone out in front of her, set to maps.

'Is this about the flat? Just tell me! There's a mariachi band in my head from too much wine last night, this overnight bag is a hindrance, and it's cold.'

'It is cold,' she said. 'Why don't you pop in there and get us a tea? Leave your luggage. I just need a second.'

I did as instructed, crossing the road and ordering a couple of cups of chai, watching her talk animatedly on the phone to somebody through the window.

'Okay, you're actually annoying me,' I said, handing her a tea and fishing about in the paper bag I was carrying too, bearing gifts of cake.

'Ooooh, yes please,' she said, taking both. 'Right. All will be revealed in . . . three minutes. This way.'

We headed through the side of the park and off to some residential streets that looked vaguely familiar from my days of early morning runs. I hadn't been out once since we'd got home – I hadn't had the urge. I hadn't worked out at all, actually. Unless sex counted, but even that was becoming a distant memory now.

'I need to talk to Patrick,' I said, after explaining to her that we'd barely had five texts between us. 'I'm just trying to be responsible and make sure I'm making my choices for me, finally, but I think I pushed him away. I'm scared! Surely he gets that.'

'I mean, I have heard rumours of couples directly communicating to each other about their issues,' Adzo conceded. 'It's urban legend, but the notion has been floated.'

That made me laugh in spite of myself. 'Adzo!' I mock scolded. 'Take this seriously! I don't know how to fight! I'm not used to getting mad!' It was true: I used to do anything to avoid confrontation. It was really uncomfortable for me to have any ongoing issues with Patrick, but I knew it was a strange kind of progress for me.

Adzo came to a stop. I looked around. We were in the middle of a street of Victorian terraces – the grand, roomy ones with high ceilings that cost a fortune if you own a full one, but most of which had been carved up into flats.

'Listen,' she said. 'I can't help on the Patrick front.'

I blinked.

'But like I said . . . I can help,' she continued, 'on the house front.'

She marched through the powder green gate of the end terrace, down the short path littered with pots of green leaves that undoubtedly smelled amazing every spring. She tipped one of the pots closest to the bins up on its side, used her foot to slide out a key, and stood back up holding it aloft saying, 'Ta-da!'

'This is the one that's in my budget?' I said.

'Babe,' she replied. 'You're going to love it.'

'What?! This is too fancy!'

'Come on,' she trilled, the key already in the lock and a foot inside the communal hallway.

The walls were chalky white with the kind of paint that's expensive – I could tell by the way the light was absorbed instead of reflected. I happened to know a lot about paint because of Bri's kitchen remodel. The carpet was a woven hessian finish, cosy and inviting, and a small table with a mirror above it bore two small piles of post.

'That's Mrs Archway,' Adzo said, pointing to the first door we passed. 'In the ground-floor flat. She's about a hundred years old but did get told off for disturbing the peace a few weeks ago when she had some friends over and they got a bit rowdy on the old gin. She used to be a theatre actress, and has got stories that make even me blush.'

She pressed on up a flight of stairs. I smelled spices. Somebody was cooking something scrumptious.

'That's Brigitte. She's a food blogger, and likes to leave food parcels on everyone's doorsteps because she makes so much. You'll like her too – she just came out of a relationship with her long-term girlfriend three months ago, and is oddly well-adjusted about it, which is fascinating.'

We climbed another set of stairs.

'And this,' she said, putting a key in the door and turning it with ease, 'is for you. If you want it.'

I eyed her suspiciously and headed past her and into a hallway very similar to the one downstairs: same chalky paint and knotted hessian carpet. It led to an empty bedroom to the left, and a compact bathroom to the right with a black and white tiled floor and a frosted glass window, and a tiny alcove that could probably fit a single bed and not much else.

I walked into the main part of the flat, an open-plan kitchen and living room area. At one end of the living room was a huge bay window overlooking the street, and the space was about big enough for a sofa and coffee table, maybe a tiny dining table. The kitchen was narrow but because it was connected to the living room felt spacious, too, especially with the massive windows and the lightness of the carpet and walls.

'What is this place?' I marvelled. 'Why do you have a key?'

'I know a guy who knows a guy.' She shrugged, and I shot her a look as if to say: *You're going to have to do better than that.*

'Okay fine,' she elaborated. 'Remember the guy I dated who wanted to take me to the Dominican Republic over Christmas break two years ago? The one with the handlebar moustache and predilection for quoting lines from *The Godfather*?'

'Oh my gosh, I do! You really liked him, didn't you?'

She nodded.

'I can't even remember why you broke it off with him now.'

'One reason was that he was a landlord of like, fifteen apartments and houses,' she said, her eyes going wide. 'I thought it was politically repulsive to make a living from keeping somebody else in the rental market . . . but that was before I had a friend who needed a rental . . .'

'This is Moustache Man's place?'

'It is. And he's somewhat still in love with me, so you are officially the first viewing. It's not even with the letting agents yet.'

'How much?'

'Top end of your budget, but with all your bills included.'

'Nooooo,' I said, bursting out into a Cheshire cat smile.

'Yes,' Adzo insisted. 'I can totally see you here. It's small but it's cute, the neighbours are great, it's not too far from where you are now but far enough that you won't have to ever walk back down that road with the memories if you don't want to.'

I flung myself at her, screeching thanks and 'OMG!'s at her.

'So you like it?' she said, pulling away from me.

I nodded. 'I really want to live here,' I said, reaching out to touch the wall. 'This feels like home. In my very soul, I know I'd be happy here. Can I bring Carol?'

She put an arm around my shoulder. 'You can,' she said. 'I checked. And for what it's worth,' she added, 'the only thing this cost me was a happy hour. Turns out Moustache Man is still quite lovely.'

'So we're even? I get a flat and you get a boyfriend?'

'Girl, please. Don't hit me with your heteronormative relationship labels. I'm moving to America, remember? But also, yes. We're even.'

The flat forced me to make up my mind for definite: I wanted to stay in London, and I wanted to live in that flat. Antwerp wouldn't have been right for me – I just couldn't leave Freddie.

312

Accepting that was a relief. There was being adventurous, but there was also knowing what mattered more.

I snapped several images of the rooms, already planning how I'd furnish it. Because it was so light and airy, and because all the furniture from the house would be too big anyway, I decided on the spot to go minimalist and essential. What better time in my life to pare down all the rubbish I'd accumulated and only hold on to things that sparked joy?

I sent a photo to the Core Four and pulled up Patrick's name to show him what Adzo had found for me too, but decided it would probably be a better conversation in person. Adzo was on the phone with her Moustache Man – my new landlord – locking down details of signing a private contract so we didn't have to deal with an agent, hardballing him into making it happen sooner rather than later. I sent a text to Patrick and asked if we could meet.

Sure, he said, writing back straightaway. *Tuesday? The pizza place? 7?*

Tuesday? I texted back. That was days away.

I'm in Manchester. I came to hang out with my bro for a few days x

It hurt me that he'd left London for the weekend and hadn't told me, and immediately I wondered if that was how he'd felt when I made plans to go to Belgium without giving him a heads up. If it was, I understood his reaction even more. When you're a team, there's common courtesies that are just rude if you don't follow – like disappearing to a new location without an in-real-time update. Ah.

I told him it was a date. *Have fun with Conor! Tell him hi! xxxxx*

'Okay,' Adzo said, once she'd hung up. 'Monday afternoon Moustache Man is going to come by the office if you can meet us there? He'll bring the contracts for you, and then we're going to do dinner if I can duck out early.'

'I've never been so productive on a hangover,' I said. 'I honestly can't thank you enough. I thought I'd be banished to some damp bedsit in Zone 24 and never be happy again. But I'll be happy here. I can feel it.'

'Me too.' She grinned. 'Here's to new beginnings.'

She raised her empty chai cup into the air and I reached to the counter to pick mine up and mirror her.

'To new beginnings,' I said, accepting that my next step really could be this easy if I let it.

42

On the same day I officially signed for the lease on the flat, I went to an open evening about a counselling course – even if it was something I couldn't do now, it was information for later, I figured. It was in a big stone building tucked away off one of the extravagant gardened squares, and inside a woman stood behind a fold-out table handing out pre-printed name tags. There were about twenty-five of us, segregated into rows of five, and I chose a chair at the back, closest to the aisle.

We were a motley crew. I reckoned I was probably one of the younger ones there, giving the sense that I wasn't alone in being interested in a career change. I wasn't sure how that made me feel – sad that counselling wasn't our first choice, or reassured that maybe it was something you arrived at only with a bit of life experience. Surely that was a good thing in a counsellor. Nobody wants life advice from a spring chicken who hasn't ever had a bad thing happen to them.

'Good evening.'

A woman stood at the front with a PowerPoint presentation

loading on the giant white screen behind her. 'I'm Esther Essiedu, board member of the British Association for Counselling and Psychotherapy, and this is our informal informational event about training to become a counsellor or psychotherapist.'

I settled in to listen to how it all worked, taking notes as Esther explained that most employers and clients look for practitioners with professional qualifications and membership of professional bodies. When I'd googled counselling, the thing I hadn't been able to figure out is what exactly the base qualification was, and she explained that that's because there isn't one – her association, which is one of many, set their own standards, so it turned out there was no compulsory training courses or qualifications as such. She did explain, though, that if we wanted to be registered with BACP, it would take about three or four years.

'It's a combination of independent study, placements, supervisions and often your own personal therapy, too. As a first port of call we recommend taking an introductory course to make sure counselling is the right career for you. At a further education college or adult education centre, you can get an overview of what training involves within eight to twelve weeks.'

I picked up some leaflets about that afterwards, when there was tea and coffee on offer with some biscuits, and we were encouraged to hang about and chat.

'You look like you've got quite the collection of reading material there,' Esther said behind me as I tried to juggle my handbag, the plethora of research I'd collected, and a paper cup of tea with two shortbread fingers. She'd given me a shock and I almost spilled my tea, but she saved me by taking it out of my hand at the last minute.

'Thanks,' I said. 'I think I was a bit ambitious with my balancing skills.'

'We don't knock ambition here,' she said, compassionately. 'Has tonight been helpful for you . . .' she looked pointedly at my name tag '. . . Annie?'

'It has,' I replied. 'I think I got about ten pages of notes,' I joked, and she laughed.

'I saw you scribbling away. There's definitely an inner student trying to wrangle her way out, isn't there?'

'I've always been that way,' I said. 'I used to love learning at school.'

'And since then?'

'I went to university and now I work. But I've got to say, it's been a long time since I picked up a new skill or tried something just to see what it was like. I don't think I've done that since I was at junior school, actually.'

Esther considered this. 'My husband and I have just taken up swing dancing,' she said.

'Oh, lovely!' A tiny pit of envy swelled in my stomach at the mention of a happy relationship.

'Not really,' she said. 'The only thing I enjoy about it is being able to say "we take swing dancing lessons". The execution of it is quite painful.'

It was kind of her to say. She was telling me, sideways on, not to be so hard on myself – wasn't that just the story of my life?

'Anyway. We're so pleased you could be here. Is there a particular aspect of counselling that's drawn you to learning more?'

'I think I'm interested in child psychology, maybe, or something to do with helping teenagers.'

I hadn't realized I wanted that until I said it. It just slipped out, and then hung out there for us both to see. It was as much news to me as it was to her, and we both nodded at this new piece of information.

'My teenage years were very painful, and it's taken me until now to understand the impact they had on my life,' I said. 'I suppose it would be nice to help any other young 'uns out there who felt like I did.'

'That's wonderful,' she said. She reached out and touched my arm as she spoke, and I understood that was a small signal that she would mingle with some of the others now.

'Thank you so much for your insights,' I said. 'It's been really great.'

She told me I was welcome, and I spent the bus ride home googling where I could start a foundation course, and exactly how much it would cost me.

This is getting totes awks now, Patrick texted me before bed, and relief flooded through me.

It is! I said. *I just want it to be tomorrow night now. A week is too long without you.*

Agreed, he sent back, followed by a heart emoji.

43

I was summoned to another meeting with Chen the next morning, in the conference room on the floor above mine. She theatrically pushed an expensive-looking brown envelope across the table to me.

'What's this?' I said, picking it up.

'It's your offer,' she replied, her face impassive. I think she'd switched tack from outright enthusiasm and pushiness to something more sanguine, interpreting my own coolness about Antwerp as a bargaining tactic.

Inside was a three-page document stapled together, and a single loose cover letter. I read it as Chen made a show of checking emails on her phone, as if she couldn't care less.

Dear Ms Wiig, it said.

We were thrilled to meet with you last week at our Antwerp headquarters. Your reputation as a great mind and extraordinary thinker precedes you, and to hear your thoughts on the manipulations of coding to debug the quantum software, as well further insight into the abstract manipulations of London's current work in the system modelling and simulation of optical fibre lasers, was exciting and extremely promising.

We have no doubt about the ways your relocation to the Antwerp office would positively contribute to the intellectual life of the institution, and as such please find enclosed the terms of our offer of employment here, which we are confident you will find favourable.

If you have any questions please do not hesitate to reach out. Otherwise, we look forward to hearing from you at your earliest convenience.

I flicked through the terms of the offer, scanning sections about the relocation fee they'd pay to help me ship my stuff and get me settled, including covering six weeks in a central Airbnb while I found somewhere to live. They were offering me what was basically a thirty-five per cent wage increase, two return flights annually to get back home, and twenty-five vacation days.

'This is incredibly generous,' I said, once I'd finished reading everything.

'I'll be sorry to see you go,' Chen agreed, putting her phone back down on the table.

I shook my head. 'But I'm not saying yes.'

She blinked. 'Of course you are.'

'I don't want to live in Antwerp,' I said. 'It's beautiful, but it's not for me. I have too much here, in London.'

She blinked again. 'Aren't you at least going to use it as leverage to get a salary increase here?'

'I'd like you to match the terms in the letter for the position I have here, yes,' I said. Adzo had made me promise I'd bargain with her, giving me a pep talk about how to ask for what I needed.

'You want a promotion.'

It wasn't a question.

'No,' I said. 'I want my loyalty to this office taken into consideration when it comes to my yearly compensation review. I won't be leaving for Antwerp, but that doesn't mean I wouldn't look for something else here if I don't feel valued.'

I surprised myself with how confident I sounded – exactly as matter-of-fact as Adzo had instructed me to. It wasn't about me, it was just a contract. That's all.

'If there's no fiscal wiggle room,' I carried on, 'I'd consider the option of a nine-day fortnight. In fact . . .' I was warming to my theme. Asking for what I wanted was fun! 'That would be preferable. I'd prefer to stay at the London office, in the position I am in, and in lieu of a wage increase I'd have every other Friday off. I'm pursuing some extra study, you see.'

I couldn't be sure, because her face barely registered what I was saying, but I swear there was a flicker of amusement that pulled the corner of her mouth upwards, just a little.

'And you don't want to take some time to reflect on this? Once I email them your refusal, you won't be able to change your mind.'

'I won't change my mind,' I assured her, and as I said it I knew it was true. Antwerp would be amazing for somebody else, but not for me. My life was in London, with the Core Four and Freddie and the new flat and a day a week to do something else. That was enough. In fact, it was more than enough. It was way too much to give up.

I felt ten feet tall as I left to walk off what had just happened. The sun was shining, even though it was chilly, and London was bustling and metropolitan. I passed posters for theatre productions and women walking dogs and couples holding hands and a group of schoolkids jostling on the pavement, being raucous and silly. I smiled at their laughter, right as a man cleared his throat and said,

'For God's sake, could you take it down a decibel or twenty?'

One of the sixth-formers – identifiable by a polyester high street suit instead of a school-issued blazer with the crest sewn onto the breast pocket – heckled loudly, 'All right, Grandad, keep your teeth in.' It forced her schoolmates to howl at her comeback, saying variations of 'Burn!' and 'Ouch, Mr!' They jostled down the pavement and I had to step out of their way. In the space between where they'd been and where I stood was Alexander.

'Annie.'

He was sat opposite a young, twenty-something brunette I vaguely recognized but couldn't place, at a pavement café. He wore a denim shirt with slim-fit chinos that revealed bare ankles, which didn't seem to suit him. He looked mismatched with his subtly lined face sitting at odds with his white trainers, like the top half hadn't passed along the memo that the bottom half of him wasn't the same age as his companion. I thought about ignoring him, but he looked so hopeful as he said my name that I made a choice to stay where I was.

'Hello,' I said.

I realized that his outspread hand was clutching the fingers of the twenty-something, and as he saw me notice he pulled away. The woman looked hurt.

'Cameron,' she said, with a little wave. 'We met at the Christmas party last year.'

'Yes,' I said, placing her now. 'Alexander's new assistant. Not new anymore I suppose.'

'No,' she said. 'I suppose not.'

'We were just taking a break to talk about a project we're presenting tomorrow,' Alexander said.

'Uh-huh,' I replied. Part of me wondered if this might have been why he left me, but as quickly as the thought entered my mind, it left. I didn't care if it was. He wasn't my problem anymore. I could ask Cameron outright, here in the middle of the street, or I could say something caustic, asking her if she was aware what he was capable of, but it wasn't worth my energy. Maybe he'd treat her better than he treated me. The probability was low, but anything was possible.

'I suppose it's good I bumped into you,' I said. 'Saves me an email.'

'Right,' he said.

'I've transferred you your share of the furniture I sold, and I'll just leave the key under the plant pot for you on Saturday. My lawyer will be in touch with yours to sort out the contributions I made to the mortgage. I know you'll be fair.'

'Yes, right. Of course,' he said. Then he looked at Cameron, saying to her: 'I'll just be a minute, okay? I'll be right back.' He stood up and gestured for me to keep walking with him in tow. As we were out of earshot he said, 'Thank you for being civil.'

'No other way to be,' I replied.

'There is,' he insisted. 'So, thank you.'

'Did you leave me for her?'

He coloured up, vindication bubbling in me that at least he had the decency to look embarrassed. 'Nothing happened until after we broke up,' he said.

I nodded.

'My parents miss you,' he said. 'I heard you delivered quite the Australian thank you package.'

'They've been very good to me.'

'Better than I have,' he said. 'I'm sorry. For everything. I don't think I ever properly apologized.'

'You didn't.'

He stopped walking. 'Really?'

'Nope.'

'Oh. Well. I really am. I was awful to you, and you didn't deserve it.'

I pulled a face. 'You set me free,' I said. 'And I haven't given you another thought since.'

I leaned in and kissed his cheek. I could tell he didn't know what to say to me. I gave him a smile and walked away, stopping only when my phone pinged to a text from Kezza: *Jo has had the baby! She's here!!!!!!!!!*

44

Last time Jo had given birth, the Core Four had gathered at the hospital in excitement. It was over-the-top, but she'd been the first of us to have a baby, and we wanted her to know that we were there for her. It was a way of saying *hey, we love you*, without being in the room, even though Jo only found out after the fact that we'd hung out there. It's just what friends do. So there was no question that we'd do the same now little Estelle Grace had been born. It was basically tradition.

The thing was, is that I was supposed to be meeting Patrick.

Can I call you? I texted him from the waiting room as I waited for everyone else to arrive.

Yes, he said. *Are you running late?*

I took a sharp intake of breath and hit his name on screen.

'Don't be mad at me,' I said when he answered. 'But Jo just gave birth, so I'm at the hospital waiting to see her instead of on my way to you for pizza.'

'Oh!' he exclaimed. 'She did? Well that's amazing! Tell her hi from me!'

Relief coursed through me. I'd worried he'd be furious, but he was the exact opposite. He was . . . kind, and lovely.

'You're not mad?' I asked.

'I'm not mad that your best friend had her baby, no.'

'I really wanted to see you.'

'I really wanted to see you too.'

I couldn't believe how wonderful he was. If I'd have stood Alexander up he'd have yelled, or made me feel small, or not understood why, on that occasion, Jo was more important than he was. But Patrick got it.

'I'm not going to Antwerp,' I blurted out. I couldn't wait to tell him. 'I thought you'd like to know that.'

I could hear his smile. 'Annie, you don't need to stay for me, you know.'

'I know,' I said. 'I'm not.'

'Charming.'

'I just don't want to put that on your shoulders. I'm staying for me. For Freddie. You're a bonus.'

He didn't say anything.

'I found a flat,' I continued. 'Adzo found it for me. Third floor, small but I can afford it. Just down the road from you, actually. Dad is going to help me move at the weekend.'

'Sorry,' he said. 'Can we just . . . did you say you're *not* staying for me?'

'I didn't mean—'

'What *did* you mean? Because it feels like you're always trying to make it clear that I'm not anywhere near the top of your list, but you still say you want this. You can imagine how confusing that is, surely? It doesn't feel very nice.'

God, he was so clear with his emotions. It was disarming.

I was still getting used to acknowledging my feelings, let alone saying them out loud.

'Look, let's just wait until we can have that pizza,' I begged. 'Tomorrow?'

'Next week,' he replied, and I couldn't pinpoint exactly where I'd screwed up the conversation, but I had. 'Once you've finished packing, and you've moved. It's fine. Maybe we did rush all this, Annie. I don't know. I can't do this if you're not all in. Doubts are normal, but . . .'

Heat rushed to my face. 'No,' I said. 'I'm staying. This can work. I did have doubts, but not anymore.'

He took a beat to reply. 'I hope we can work,' he said. 'But if we were only ever supposed to work in Australia, at least I helped you move on, you helped me move on . . .'

I couldn't believe what he was saying. How had we got here?

'Do you mean that?' I asked, praying he didn't. I hoped I'd misunderstood. I wanted to claw what we had back. I didn't mean to make him feel like I didn't prioritize him.

'I don't know,' he said. 'Your mother was right – it has all been so fast. I'm scared too, you know. But at least I'm gracious about it.' He tutted, stopping himself from saying anything that could hurt me any further. 'Go and see the baby. Move house. If we're going to do this I need you to be sure, and until you're sure . . . well. It's not my shit to shovel, is it?'

'I'm trying,' I said. 'I promise.'

He sighed. 'I know,' he said, eventually. 'It's okay. I'm not going anywhere. Not yet.'

'Okay,' I said.

'Okay,' he replied.

I hung up feeling exposed and sad, but I didn't want to

take that into Jo's private hospital room with me. As I held tiny Estelle Grace – named after Jo's grandmother – in my arms, I told Jo she was perfect.

And then I cried, wondering how it was fair that life could be so beautiful and feel so hard, exactly like my grandmother had warned, all at the same time.

45

The night before moving day I'd walked around the house slowly – in a way, I suppose, saying goodbye. I stood in the kitchen and thought about all the meals cooked and passive-aggressive arguments seethed, and stared at myself in the bathroom mirror for a long time, finally deciding I liked how I looked. The next morning I piled everything I was leaving into one corner and threw a bedsheet over it so that there wouldn't be any confusion when Dad and Freddie came to help, and sealed up the last two boxes of stuff that would be coming with me. I tried not to think about Patrick, because every time I did I wanted to call him, but when I rehearsed what to say every time a different version came out.

Let's be friends.
I want to be with you.
Don't break up with me.
Marry me.
You made me whole.
You ruined me.

I don't know what I want – you choose!

The doorbell rang.

'It's us!' Freddie said through the letterbox. 'We've got a van!'

I opened the door to them, shocked to see that Mum was with them too.

'You're all here!' I said, more than a little uneasy.

'As instructed,' Mum replied. 'We couldn't leave you to do this alone, could we?'

It turned out they'd hired a van so we could do everything in one trip instead of the several back-and-forths I thought we'd do in Dad's Ford Focus, but now I could see the size of it I knew I'd been naïve in thinking we could do without.

'Whoa,' said Freddie, wandering down the hall. 'It's so different in here.' She looked around the mostly unfurnished house curiously. 'HELLO!' she said, and her voice echoed in the hall. The only thing that remained untouched, as he'd requested, was Alexander's flat-screen TV.

'Come here, you,' I said to her. 'I haven't seen you in ages!'

'You've not invited me to stay with you in ages,' she said, matter-of-fact.

It hit me right in the heart. 'Things have been crazy, Freddie-Frou,' I said. 'I'm sorry.'

'Crazy with your new *boyfriend*,' she teased. She must have seen something flicker across my face. 'What?' she said. 'Why do you look like that?'

'Like what? I don't look like anything.'

'He broke up with you, didn't he?' Mum offered. I hadn't seen her at the other end of the kitchen. Dad looked at me sadly.

'No,' I said, an edge to my voice. 'Maybe. I don't know. We're in the process of breaking up with each other, I think,' I said. And then for Mum's benefit I added: 'Not that it was ever serious.'

Freddie said, 'But I thought you said you were falling for him?'

I blushed crimson and said, hurriedly, 'Yes, I was. And then I wasn't. And anyway, I've got a lot on. There's the moving, and the counselling course, which I can pay for if Alexander gives me back some money I gave him. So. End of story.'

'I'm shocked,' Mum said, meaning exactly the opposite. 'The redeeming factor in you taking Patrick away on your honeymoon was that at the very least you were serious about each other. But oh no, another one bites the dust, is it? Poor man. He probably never even saw it coming, did he? The hurricane that is my eldest daughter.'

I don't know what expression my face made at that comment but Freddie looked from Mum to me, to Dad, back to me. Old Annie would have let that fly, but I wasn't even expecting Mum to be here today, let alone for her to potentially ruin what was otherwise a super important day. I wasn't taking her bullshit into my new home.

'Mum, did you come today just to make me feel bad?' I said. 'Because I won't let you. Moving today is supposed to be a joyful, happy thing. This is a fresh start for me. So don't come and piss in my punch to spoil it, okay?'

'Oh don't be so melodramatic,' she replied. 'Honestly.'

Dad tried to calm things down by suggesting he'd start loading the van.

'Thanks, Dad,' I said. 'It's all through there, and I've labelled everything so we know where it needs to go when we get there. Freddie, would you get the two suitcases from my bedroom?'

She nodded but went reluctantly, knowing she was about to miss the action.

Mum went to follow Dad through to the kitchen, but I held out an arm and stopped her.

'I'm not being melodramatic, Mum,' I said. 'Don't dismiss my feelings that way. You can either be nice today, or go for a walk and come back when we're finished, okay? It's your call.'

'Annie,' she said. 'I'm your mother. Don't talk to me that way.'

I lowered my voice, because if I didn't consciously do that I would shout. 'No, Mum. Don't *you* talk to *me* that way. I'm sick of it. I am a grown woman and I am proud of who I am, especially after everything I've been through. You can either respect that or . . . I don't know what the alternative is. But at least for today can you just be supportive please? I don't have the energy to fight.'

'Yes,' she said in a small voice. 'Oh, Annie. I don't know why it's so hard for us to get along.'

'Because,' I replied, my teeth gritted, 'it's as if you don't even like me.'

'Of course I *like* you, darling!' she replied. 'Of course I do! You just . . . confuse me, most of the time. It's so frustrating to watch somebody as clever and talented as you hide under a bushel.'

Mum thought I was talented?

'That's not the way I hear it,' I said. 'You constantly nag at me. You pick at me. You belittle me!'

'It's not nagging, Annie. That's me caring. I think you're a remarkable young woman. I just wish you'd . . . I don't know. You can be very wet, a lot of the time. Find your backbone! I know it comes out clumsily, but that's all I mean . . .'

'Coming through!' Dad said, barrelling towards the front door with a big box in his hands. 'Watch yourselves!'

'Me too!' said Freddie. 'Suitcases on wheels coming through!'

'Whoa!' I squealed. 'The front door isn't even open. Hold on!'

I opened the door and took Dad's keys from his back pocket so I could open the van. Mum came outside and said to me: 'I love you, Annie. I'll do better, okay? I know we don't always see eye-to-eye. But I want to. I do love you, you know. I'm going to change. Let's make today nice for you.' I was so taken aback I just nodded, accepting her hug. I couldn't remember the last time she'd hugged me. My whole life we'd had friction, and now I'd stood up for myself she'd explained why? Wow. I'd just made more progress with her in three minutes than I thought I could in a lifetime.

I wish I could debrief with Patrick like this, I thought.

I hated that I'd probably lost him. I'd still not seen him. I was convinced we were doing a slow fizzle out. I was convinced we weren't in the process of breaking up so much as already broken up, and I just hadn't caught up to the fact.

'Annie?' Mum prompted, and I moved to help her with another box.

It took us forty-five minutes to pack up the house, and the three of them waited outside as I did one last check of the place to make sure I hadn't forgotten anything. My phone buzzed and Adzo told me she was thinking of me. I texted her back to say thank you, along with an invitation for pizza and bubbles later that night. I walked through all the rooms one last time and decided everything was fine, and then closed the front door.

It didn't take us long to unload the van at the other end, by which time it was lunch and Mum and Dad went off in search of food, taking the dog with them. Freddie and I said we'd be good with sandwiches, Mum said she needed something with a higher nutritional value, and Dad said he was really in the market for a Sprite, but only the one with no added sugar, so Freddie stayed with me as I tried to find the box with the plates and cutlery and Mum and Dad said they'd be back soon.

'Froogle, can you open that box over there?' I said. 'The white one, not the big brown one.'

'Uh-huh,' she replied.

I busied myself sorting through the boxes Dad had piled in the living room despite the fact they very clearly said 'bedroom' or 'bathroom' on them, and when I came back, Freddie was sat with my memory box.

'Sorry,' she said. 'It fell open and now I can't stop looking at all these photos.'

On the very top were some of the snaps I'd printed of Australia – just my favourites of me and Patrick. Freddie took a breath and instantly I knew she was about to say something I wouldn't like. I could tell by how quiet she'd grown that she was building up to it.

'Hey,' I said. 'I really am sorry I've not been a very good big sister. But now I'm moved in here, you can come and stay whenever you want. Literally, that alcove there should have a 'Freddie's Room' sign hanging down.'

'Yeah,' she said. 'Okay.'

'Freddie-Bug?'

'I feel sad that you and Patrick are breaking up. I liked him. He looked at you like you were the most important person in the world. I don't think you should.'

'Oh,' I said. I took the photos from her hand and looked at them myself. There was no denying the size of my smile in most of them. 'It was time for me to be an independent woman, Frou. A single gal.'

'But why would you break up with somebody who loves you?'

'I don't think he loved me, piggy-poo. We both had fun together, that's all.'

'But why did the fun end? Why wouldn't you want the fun to just keep going?'

I didn't have an answer to that.

'If somebody loved me, I wouldn't dump them.'

'We never said *I love you*, Fred.'

She sighed. 'But would you have done? Eventually?'

I thought about the question and shuffled through the photos in my hand. 'I don't know.'

'Did you love him?'

My head and my heart were saying different things. 'I'm scared to,' I admitted.

'What does that mean?'

'It means . . .' The realization dawned on me. 'It means that yeah. I think I do.'

'So what happened?'

'Freddie Wiig, you are thirteen years old. What's with the Spanish Inquisition? I didn't think it was cool for your generation to pin all their hopes on a partner, anyway. I thought being sassy and single and carefree was cool! Come on!'

She shrugged me off. 'Annie. I know I am younger than you, but I'm not an idiot.'

I nodded sagely. 'No,' I agreed. 'You're not.'

'I think you're making a mistake. I think you should be brave and tell him you love him before it's too late.'

I don't know what it was – the fact that it came from my baby sister, maybe – but suddenly my eyes welled with tears and my voice shook as I said, 'I don't think he wants me anymore. I pushed him away.'

She said, 'Can't you say sorry? I think being scared and being brave is what it's all about, isn't it?'

'Woah.' I laughed. 'You did *not* just say that. How did you get so wise?'

'My big sister taught me everything I know,' she grinned. 'You said that's what you liked about Bri getting married. She'd let love outweigh being afraid.'

'Shut up.' I laughed again but she knew I was only teasing. I *had* said that about Bri. It's funny the stuff a sibling can remember.

'Doesn't he live around here?' Freddie pressed, and I nodded.

'Around the corner,' I said. 'About ten minutes away.'

She smirked. 'What are you waiting for? Fix it!'

I stared at her, and she wiggled her eyebrows as if to say, *Huh? HUH?*

'I . . . don't know,' I said.

'Go!' she squealed. 'Go on!'

I was shaking as I picked up my phone and keys, absent-mindedly looking in the mirror but not even really seeing myself. She was right. It was self-sabotage. I was so utterly petrified that I was deliberately, unconsciously, pushing Patrick away when facts were facts: we were perfect together. I loved him. Mum had asked when we got back from honeymoon if I really wanted to jump into a new relationship after my engagement had ended like there was only one answer to it. But there wasn't. I *did* want to jump into this new relationship, because it was good and healthy and full of kindness and love. It was the best possible relationship to jump into, because it was everything my engagement wasn't. And so who cared about anything else?

I loved him!

I. LOVED. HIM!

'Are you staying, or coming with?' I asked Freddie, my hands trembling but my nerve steady. She was right. She was absolutely, totally right.

'Oh, I'm definitely coming with,' she replied, smiling. 'I want to see this!'

46

We started out in the direction of Patrick's, picking up pace with every street sign we passed.

'I've never been inside his house, you know,' I told her, counting up the street numbers as we passed each house.

'Who hasn't been to their boyfriend's house?' said Freddie, pushing into a light jog.

Her jog made me run faster, so that we started in a trot and then broke out into a canter so fast that we actually went past number 34b, where he lived, and had to backtrack by half a dozen houses when I realized.

'Okay,' I said, outside of the gate to the entrance of his basement flat. 'How do I look?'

'Urm, sort of sweaty,' Freddie said, pushing hair from my face.

'Urgh. How's my breath? I always get bad breath after I've been emotional.'

'I can help with that,' she said, holding up a hand as if to signify that I should hold that thought, and she rifled through the pockets of the hoodie tied around her waist.

She gave me a breath mint and I said, 'So, are you following me to his door, or . . .?'

'Just go!' she said, and before I knew it I was ringing his bell, resisting the urge to peer through his front bay window in case we locked eyes through the glass and then he decided not to let me in.

It opened.

'Patrick,' I said, and then I didn't say anything because between Freddie's call to arms in my kitchen and being stood there in front of him maybe ten minutes had passed, and in that ten minutes I hadn't really thought beyond getting to his place.

'Hi,' he said, looking around me and noticing Freddie up on the pavement. 'Hey, Freddie,' he said, confusion leaking from his voice.

'I messed up,' I said. 'And I have come to say sorry. And also, depending on how that apology goes, I've also come to say . . . I got scared. But. Basically. Well. The thing is . . .'

'Say it!' cried Freddie.

'I love you,' I said. 'I love you! There. God, that feels really good. Patrick, I love you, and I am sorry that I pushed you away. You are not my past. You're YOU! And I love you for it!'

I was breathing heavily, but couldn't tell if it was from the run or the rush of emotion.

Suddenly, my eyes adjusted and I could see cardboard boxes just over his shoulder. I realized he was holding packing tape in his hands. He looked down at his hands too, understanding that I was piecing things together, and looked embarrassed.

'Are you . . . moving?' I said.

He shook his head.

'Not exactly.' He stepped back so I could see into his hallway, and added, 'Do you want to come in?'

I nodded. I was *very* aware that I'd declared my undying love, and he hadn't said it back. He hadn't really said anything.

'Freddie,' he called to her. 'Do you want to come in?'

Freddie skipped down the steps to join us. She looked from me, to him, to the boxes, and knew better than to ask any questions.

Patrick fussed about getting us all a glass of water, which we gulped down like we were wise men wandering a desert and hadn't seen H_2O in days.

'Can I go and look at your books?' Freddie said, once she was done, and I wanted to squeeze her until her head popped off for her emotional insight, knowing it was time to give Patrick and me a minute alone.

'So, the boxes . . .?' I asked, and he pulled up a chair to sit opposite me.

'This is your first time here,' he said, as way of reply.

'Yeah,' I said. 'I said to Freddie I'd never actually been in here. I never thought anything of it until today.'

'Your place is so much bigger.'

'Was,' I countered. 'Today is moving day.'

'I know!' he said. 'I had to give myself a talking-to not to come and help with the boxes. I didn't think you'd want me there.'

'I wanted you there,' I said. 'Please forgive me. It's you and me!' I waited for him to say something, to explain the boxes, knowing that if I spoke again we'd go off on another tangent and end up discussing the weather, or the conflict in Syria, or sandwich fillings.

'I think I knew pretty quickly that this was different,' he said, gesturing between us. 'That's why I didn't want us to

340

sleep together right away – I just . . . oh God, this is going to sound so preposterous, but . . . I don't know. I worried it might be my last ever first time with somebody. And the last person I felt like that about . . .' Tears welled up in his eyes. 'She died. And it was the worst thing I have ever, ever gone through. I used to wish I had died instead of her, but then I wouldn't wish the pain of losing someone on anyone.'

'I can't even imagine how hard it was,' I said. And then, after a beat: 'I thought you didn't want to sleep with me right away because I was your first since you became a widower.'

Patrick shook his head. 'I have been with a ton of women these past few years.'

'Oh,' I said. 'Well. Good for you! That's nice.'

'I'm not showing off. It was always temporary and fleeting and a bit like putting a plaster on a gaping bullet wound. And then you and I got talking, and I flew to the other side of the bloody world with you . . .'

'Yeah,' I said, laughing.

'And I felt things. I knew I still missed Mala from the bottom of my heart, but being with you made it seem as if there was something to be hopeful for. I knew if we slept together it wouldn't be like the others. And I didn't know if I was just going to be a rebound for you . . .'

'I guess I thought you might be,' I admitted. 'I don't know.'

Now it was his turn to laugh. 'I never invited you here because I still had all our things exactly as they were when she was alive. Everyone said I needed to take some of the pictures down, and empty her side of the wardrobe, but I didn't want to. That's what the packing tape and boxes are for. That's what I've been doing since I visited my brother. He told me it was time, and this time I listened. I needed him to help me find the courage to move on, because . . .'

I clutched at his hands, the hands of this tender, kind, insightful, bruised, hopeful man.

'. . . Because if I didn't,' he continued, 'I knew I'd risk letting the next woman I fell in love with slip through my fingers, too.'

A voice came from the doorway. 'I told you he was in love with you!' Freddie said. 'I knew it! I could tell that day you came for Sunday lunch!'

Patrick let out a howl of a laugh. 'Yup,' he said, nodding at her, and then he turned and said to me, 'I knew I'd fallen in love with you that day at the naked spa. I just laughed so much, and you were so hot – sorry, Freddie – and . . .'

'Say it,' I told him.

'I love you,' he said.

'I love you too,' I replied, and he leaned in to kiss me and Freddie said, 'Ewww, okay, I'm going back in the other room now! I'm too young to see this!'

We broke apart but stayed nose to nose.

'I am so sorry for everything you've been through,' I said. 'And I promise I will never expect you to forget Mala, okay? I love you, and I know that you will always love her, too, even if you love me.'

'And I do love you,' he said, pulling me back in for another kiss. 'Did I mention that?'

'You did,' I said, into his mouth. 'But I don't mind if you want to tell me again and again and again.'

Epilogue

Early morning light cast shadows on the chalky walls of the flat. The double-height windows meant everything was so much more obviously seasonal, because there was so much more of the sky to see. It was impossible to ignore the rain when it lashed against the top-floor glass, but with the right lamps and candles and salted whipped cream with my coffee it was atmospheric and cosy. And, with the days getting longer and brighter, it was just as impossible to notice the shift in the clouds that drifted by slowly, deliberately, no rush to be anywhere and no desire to reach their destination. On mornings like this it made everything seem possible, and as I made the bed and ran a hand over the smooth linen of the sheets, arranging my throw pillows haphazardly at one end and artfully dishevelling a woven blanket at the other, I sighed contentedly at how everything I could see was by my own design. My home might have been shabbily chic and rented instead of owned, but it was a fair price and a room to call my own.

I walked into the lounge to grab the last of my coffee, my

eyes lingering on the framed notebook page that took pride of place above my mantel. It said:

From this day forward, I will stop trying to be perfect.

For better, for worse, I will throw caution to the wind.

For richer, for poorer, I will say yes to every opportunity that comes my way.

To have and to hold, from this day forth, I commit to my own happiness.

This is my solemn vow.

Forever and ever, Amen.

Everything had been leading to this.

I wandered over to the desk I'd set up in the bay window at the far end of the living room, casting an eye over my to-do list. I had an assignment due on Monday that was mostly finished but needed proofreading, and had a couple of Post-its with phone numbers of university students who were willing to pay a reduced fee in order to have appointments with people who were still training.

A text pinged on my phone.

I'm downstairs!

I looked out of the window to where Patrick sat in a hire car, pulled in against the kerb but the engine still running. It reminded me of that day back in Australia when he organized to drive us to the music festival. Had I dared imagine back then just what would unfold in the weeks and months after? It was hard not to smile at the thought of Past Annie. She was so scared to believe she deserved good things.

Two mins! I texted Patrick back.

I believed I deserved good things now.

On the way, we stopped to see Jo and baby Estelle, who slept soundly as we cooed over her in her crib. Kezza called in with Lacey, her newly adopted little girl, who played with Carol and Patrick in the garden.

'He's going to make one hell of a dad.' Bri grinned, as she caught me staring at him through the kitchen window.

I shrugged. 'We don't know if we want kids,' I said. 'We haven't decided. We're going with the flow. Happily so.'

She asked me about Adzo, and I told her how she was loving San Francisco – so much so that it was hard to stay in touch. Things hadn't worked out with her Moustache Man, who'd chosen to stay behind in England instead of heading out there with her, but from what I could gather she was having a whale of a time.

'I envy her,' Jo volunteered. 'I've got it pretty good here, but crikey. It will be a long time before Kwame and I will ever be that free again.'

'You know what Patrick would say, don't you?' I asked. 'That freedom isn't out there.' I gestured to the outside world dramatically, and assumed a hippie voice. 'But in here.' I tapped my chest with closed eyes, indicating to my heart.

'I hear my name?' he said, appearing at the back door with Lacey in his arms.

'Mummy, can we get a dog?' she said to Kezza, who looked at me as if to say: *Thanks for planting that idea, Annie.*

'Maybe,' she replied. 'Or maybe we can just dog-sit Carol sometimes.'

Bri laughed. 'This just worked out for everyone!' She giggled.

I looked at Patrick. 'Sometimes stuff just does work out,' I said, and everyone made a good-natured gagging sound before we headed out.

He drove us east, out of London until we hit the coast. We played the music we'd come to think of as 'ours' – all the songs that had a memory or reminded us of being fourteen, or travelling together, or what had played on the radio this past few months as we cooked eggs and ate them in my new bed, commenting, like we did, on what the sky was doing that particular day.

'I think I'll be able to take the leap soon,' I told him, as the traffic eased and the roads got quieter and the playlist we'd compiled finished playing. 'I think I really am going to do it.'

He reached out a hand to my thigh. It wasn't my knee, like a friend, but high up, a place only he was able to touch.

'I think that's a great plan,' he replied. 'And one day, you'll have your own practice, and a plaque on the door, and everything.'

I laughed. 'One step at a time,' I insisted. 'I don't plan that far in advance anymore, remember?'

He nodded, as if to say he wasn't going to argue, but also that he was going to order that plaque – just in case.

He said, 'I nearly didn't say hello that morning at boot-camp. Did I ever tell you that?'

We pulled up into an almost deserted car park, and Carol started whimpering in the back, instinctively understanding that we'd arrived, and the glorious freedom of a beach would soon be hers. We let her out and followed her towards the shore.

'Really?' I asked. 'Because I just can't conceive of a world where that's true.'

'Ha! Is that so?'

I shrugged coquettishly, pleased that we could still flirt this way. He didn't have my hand, but his arm, carrying our bag with a beach mat and supplies, was no more than six inches from me.

'I'm glad I did.'

I sneaked a glance at him and couldn't resist following up by giving him a kiss.

'What was that for?'

We lingered, nose to nose, satisfied and full.

'Just because,' I said, and what I meant was, *because I love you.*

Once we walked the length of the coastline enough for Carol to relish paddling in the water, roll over in the sand, and slowly start to calm down, we settled in a spot to eat the lunch he'd packed.

'I've got news too,' he said, halfway through a sausage roll.

'Oh?' I replied.

'I've put myself forward for a promotion.'

'That's amazing!' I gasped. 'I didn't even know you were thinking of doing that!'

'What can I say? You inspire me.'

'Look at us.' I grinned. 'I'm giving up some responsibility; you're leading the charge in taking up more . . .'

'We're rubbing off on each other.'

'Yeah,' I said. 'We are. You make me better, Patrick Hummingbird.'

'Don't get soft on me.' He winked, and it made me laugh. I was always laughing with him. My phone trilled, lighting up with a text message from Mum.

Agatha Mill's son has his own mental health centre and has asked if he can get your number, it said. *Is it okay to pass it on? I think he's hiring and I might have talked you up a bit . . .*

'Mum's got a lead on a job,' I said. 'Can you believe that? I think she's honestly being supportive?'

'Judy Wiig throwing in a third act curveball,' he commented. 'Who says a leopard can't change its spots?'

I stood up and shook off the crumbs from lunch, and then peeled off my T-shirt and unbuttoned my jeans.

'What are you doing?' Patrick asked, his eyes panicked and jaw slackened. 'You're not going in, surely?'

'Did you pack a towel?'

'Yes, but only in case Carol got wet.'

I continued to undress, my socks coming off with my trousers until I stood in front of him in my underwear.

'YOLO, right?' I said, beginning the descent down to the oceanfront.

'Aren't you scared it'll be freezing?' he yelled.

I shouted over my shoulder to him, 'Being scared is no reason to miss out. Didn't you teach me that?'

Carol started to bark, thrilled by the prospect of more sanctioned time in the water, and Patrick was right: it was freezing. For a moment I lingered, letting the waves tickle my toes as the sea pulled out and then crashed back in. I looked at the horizon and luxuriated in the sun on my skin and let the breeze tickle my neck as I photographed the moment in my mind, committing it to memory. This was what life's about – idle Saturdays at a beach with the man I love, a vague hope for the future but here and now being absolutely enough. I couldn't control anything except my own happiness, and I'd done it – I'd grasped for it with both hands greedily and unashamedly. I didn't have to know what would happen next year, or in ten years, or the trajectory of the rest of my life so long as Saturdays by the water existed.

Patrick appeared by my side in his boxers.

'If you're doing it, so will I.'

I accepted what he said with a kiss. We grinned at each other and time held still, just for a second, before I bent down so my fingertips reached the waves, scooping water up in my cupped hand and flicking it at him.

'Go on then,' I said, wetting him, and he lunged after me with a gleeful shout, following me into the cold, deep water, both of us relishing the heart-stopping surrender of diving in, simply because we could.

Acknowledgements

I dedicated this book to Katie, because as my editor her work ethic, kindness, and making-a-book-even-better *nous* floors me every day. Between her, Sabah Khan and Ella Kahn, the three women I have most contact with during the writing and publishing process, I feel truly held and supported, and that means I can do my job better. So. Thank you, all.

I wrote this book during the height of a global pandemic, where my only role in keeping my community safe was to stay home and work in my pants from the sofa. To the people who did the real work of protection, I am just so humbled. It seems silly to put that in a book in a lot of ways, but I don't know where else to say it. On paper and in ink seems as good a home as any in which to shout: fucking hell. Key workers, we owe you everything.

And to the readers, bookshop workers and bookstagrammers who tell me they've enjoyed my work and encourage others to read it too: I am humbled. I hope you found this to be my most joyful and escapist yet. I think about you with every word, on every page. I do it to make you smile. I hope *The Lucky Escape* was mission accomplished ☺

Publishing Credits

It takes a village to birth a book (and a career!), and this is everyone in *The Lucky Escape*'s village to whom I am enormously grateful:

Team Avon:
Becci Mansell – Press Officer
El Slater – Marcomms Executive
Elisha Lundin – Editorial Assistant
Ellie Pilcher – Marketing Manager
Hannah Avery – Key Account Manager, International Sales
Hannah O'Brien – Marketing Director
Helen Huthwaite – Publishing Director
Katie Loughnane – Senior Commissioning Editor
Molly Walker-Sharp – Editor
Oli Malcolm – Executive Publisher
Rachel Faulkner-Willcocks – Senior Commissioning Editor
Sabah Khan – Head of Publicity
Sammy Luton – Key Account Manager

HarperCollins:
Alice Gomer – Head of International Sales
Ammara Isa – Marketing Manager
Anna Derkacz – Group Sales Director
Anne Rieley – Proofreader
Ben Hurd – Trade Marketing Director
Ben Wright – International Sales Director
Caroline Bovey – Key Account Manager
Caroline Young – Designer
Catriona Beamish – Production Controller
Charlotte Brown – Assistant Audio Editor
Charlotte Cross – Key Account Manager, International Sales
Georgina Ugen – Digital Sales Manager
Helena Newton – Copyeditor
Melissa Okusanya – Publishing Operations Director
Mia Jupp – Film & TV Team
Tom Dunstan – UK Sales Director

Rights and international:
Zoe Shine, Emily Yolland, Iona Teixeira Stevens and the
  HCUK Rights Team
Michael White and the HarperCollins Australia Team
Peter Borcsok and the HarperCollins Canada Team
Emily Gerbner, Jean Marie Kelly and the Harper360 Team

For naming Bianca and writing her back story via my
Instagram: @tjj2287, also known as Tiff, from North Wales.

And for being my first and most encouraging reader: Calum
McSwiggan. We've come a long way, baby.

Nose in armpit.

Elbow in back.

Not every romance starts with flowers . . .

Don't miss the international sensation *Our Stop* – a not-quite-romance of near-misses, true love, and the power of the written word.

Available in paperback, ebook and audiobook now.

Penny has to choose between three.
But are any of them The One?

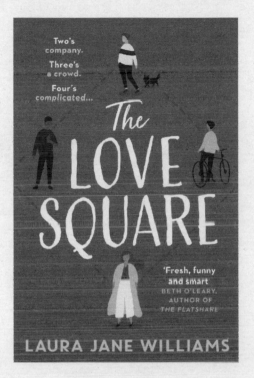

Laura Jane Williams will have you laughing, crying
and cheering Penny on in this funny and feel-good
exploration of hope, romance and the trust it
takes to finally fall in love.

Available in paperback, ebook and audiobook now.